Secret Agendas

by

Debbie G. Brownfield

ii

SECRET AGENDAS

Printing history: 1st edition, 1st printing/ March 2013

ISBN-13: 978-0615772844 (Debbie G.\Brownfield)
ISBN-10: 0615772846

Published by   CreateSpace
               7290 Investment Drive, Suite B
               North Charleston, SC 29418

PRINTED IN THE UNITED STATES OF AMERICA

Acknowledgments

Dedicated to my children who have patiently allowed me space to pursue my dreams.

The following people are real people who have graciously given their consent for use of their names and businesses in my book:

The Mustard Seed, Summerville, SC;
Devon who serves at The Mustard Seed;
Single Smile Cafe, Summerville, SC;
Dawn, the owner of Single Smile Cafe;
Ed, the manager of Single Smile Cafe;
Keith Miller, musician;
Kirby Easler, musician;
Joshua Jarman, musician;
David Metts, musician;
Flowertown Bed & Breakfast;
Veronique, proprietress of Flowertown B&B

A special thank you to the Mallery family for allowing me to use their lovely home as the model for both the back cover and for Gram and Gramps Merrill's farm house.

I am also very grateful to Chip Googe for his awesome photography and work on the covers and to the support personnel at SmartDraw for their help with the family trees.

iv

In *Secrets of the Enemy & Secret Agendas*

The Peters-Templeton Family

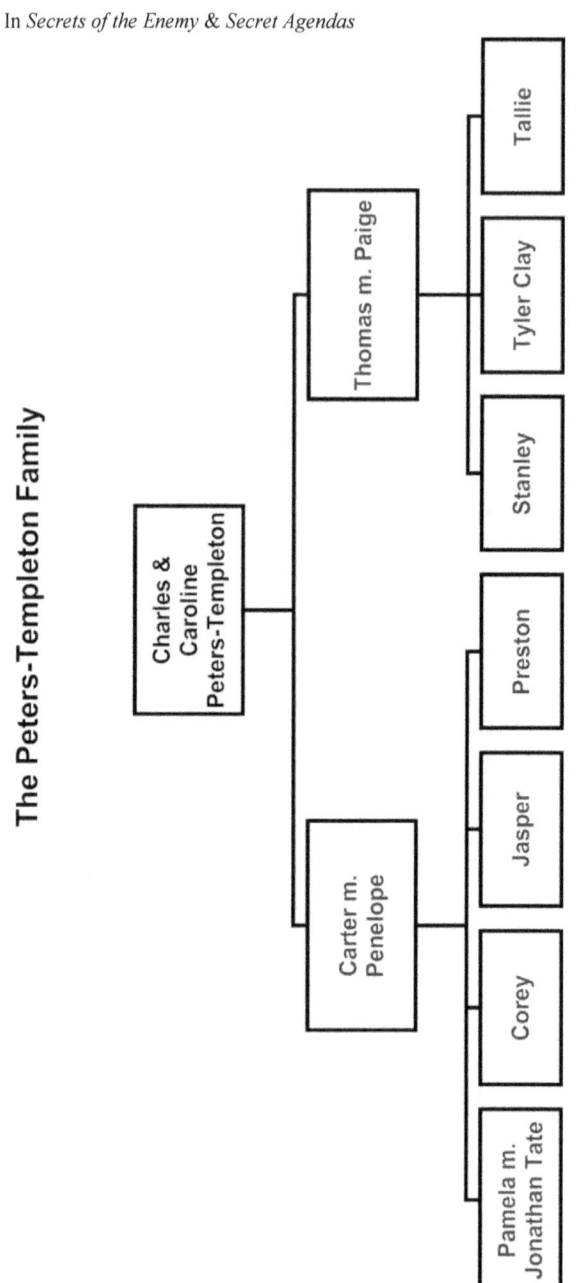

Charles & Caroline Peters-Templeton

Carter m. Penelope

Thomas m. Paige

Pamela m. Jonathan Tate

Corey

Jasper

Preston

Stanley

Tyler Clay

Tallie

In *Secrets of Two Sisters, Secrets of the Enemy, Secret Agendas, & A Secret Place*

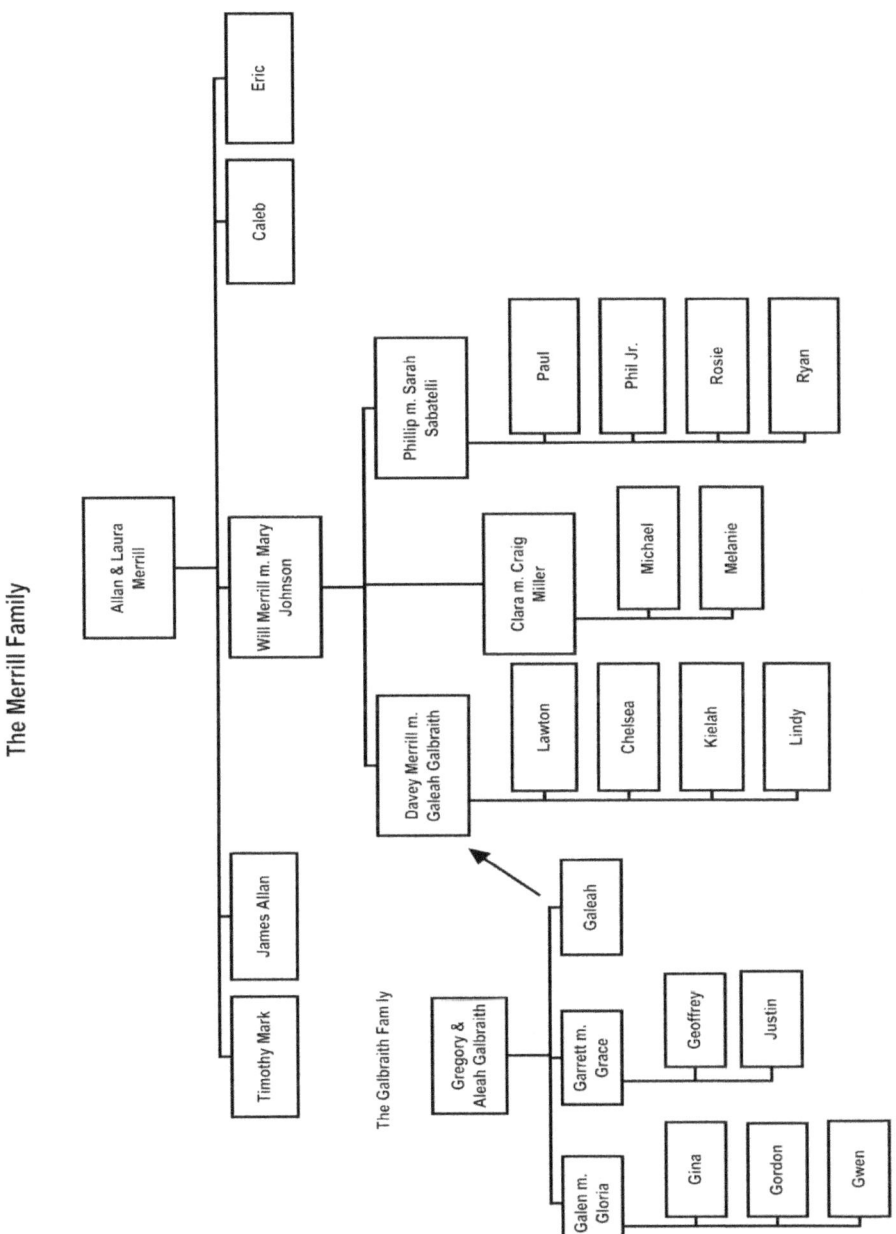

In *Secrets of Two Sisters* & *Secrets of the Enemy*

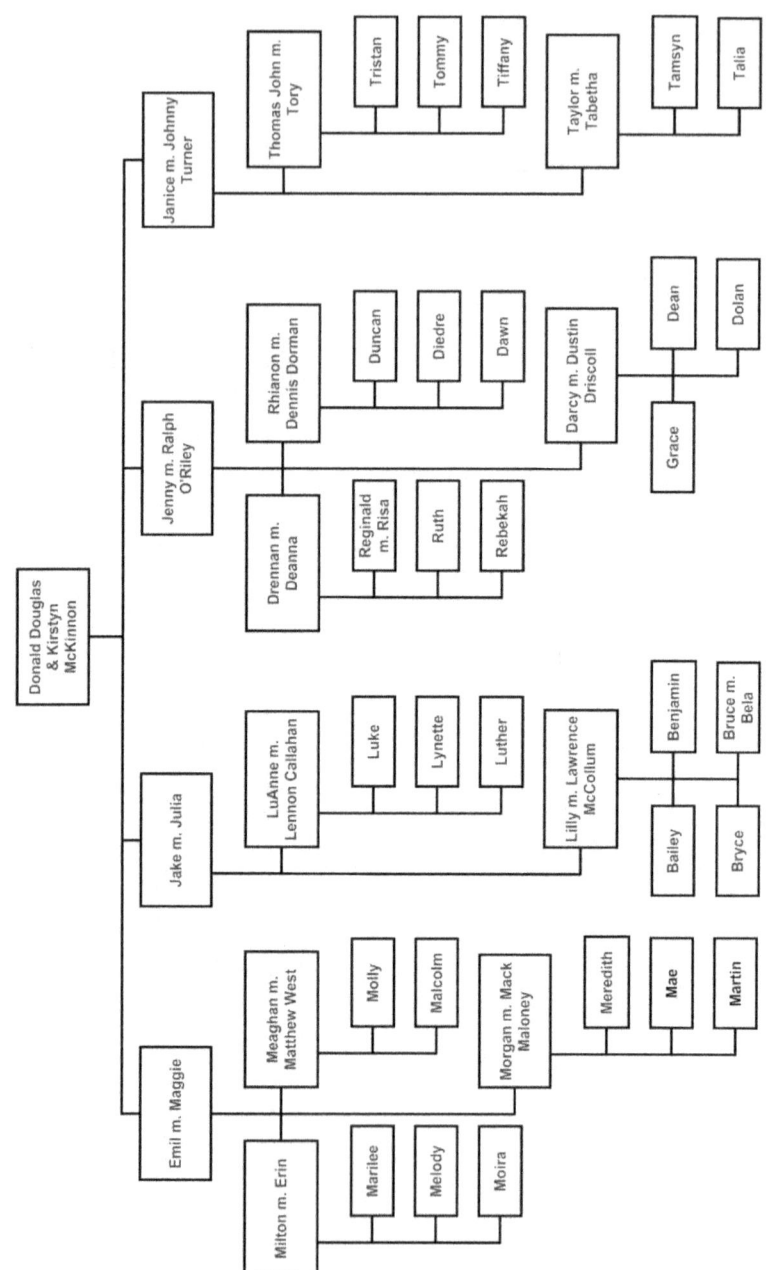

The McKinnon Family, Part 1

The McKinnon Family, Part 2

Donald Douglas & Kirstyn McKinnon

- **Joey m. Jonette**
  - Joel
  - Joanie
- **Donnie m. Deborah**
  - **Douglas m. Desiree**
    - Darla
    - Amy
    - Donnell
  - **Delcey m. Damien Donnelly**
    - Derek (dating Danielle)
    - David
    - Dustin (dating Sheridan)
    - Dorie
  - **Daniel m. Danette**
    - Katie
    - Kyle
    - Kevin
- **Shannon m. Marc Montaigne**
  - (Davey Merrill) m. Galeah Galbraith (see Merrill family tree)
  - **Melinda m. Marshall McCormick**
    - Morgan
    - Marissa
    - Maeve
    - **Michael m. Mia**
      - Emmett
      - Emil
      - Marleigh
- **Denton m. Alice O'Leary**
  - **Arland m. Ellie**
    - Enya
    - Estelle
    - Eaton
    - **Andrew m. Avery**
      - Audrey
      - Alexander
  - **Amos m. Annie**
    - Austin
    - Andrea
    - Apryll
    - Alden

In *Secrets of the Enemy*

The Dumotte Family

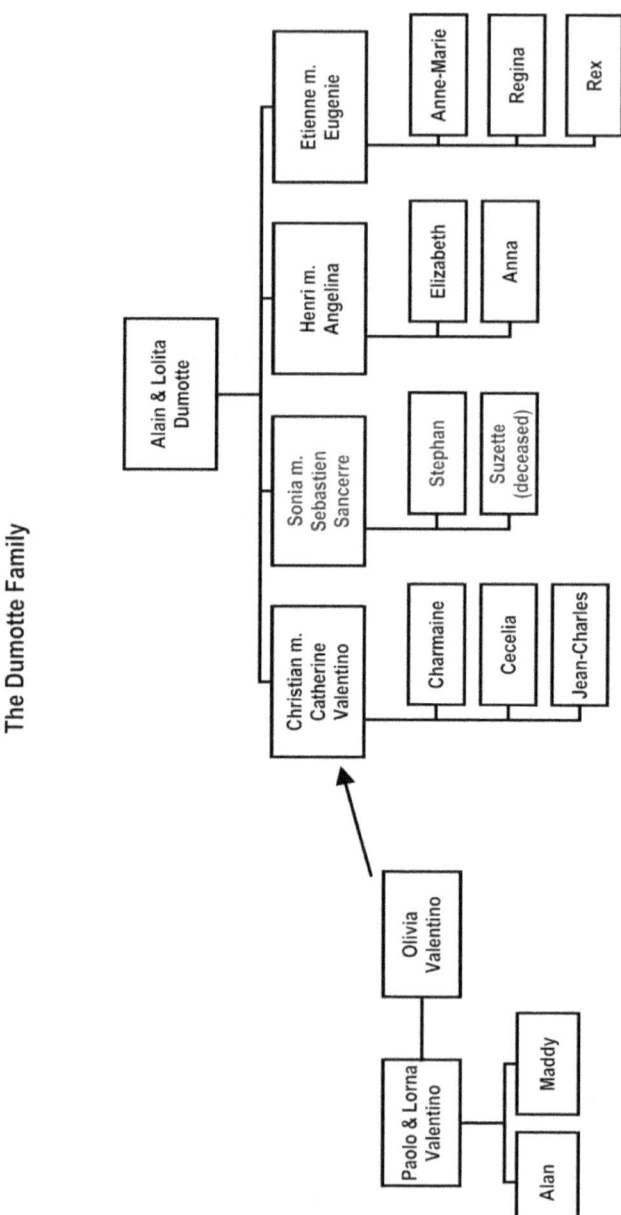

In *Secrets of Two Sisters* & *Secrets of the Enemy*

The Montaigne Family

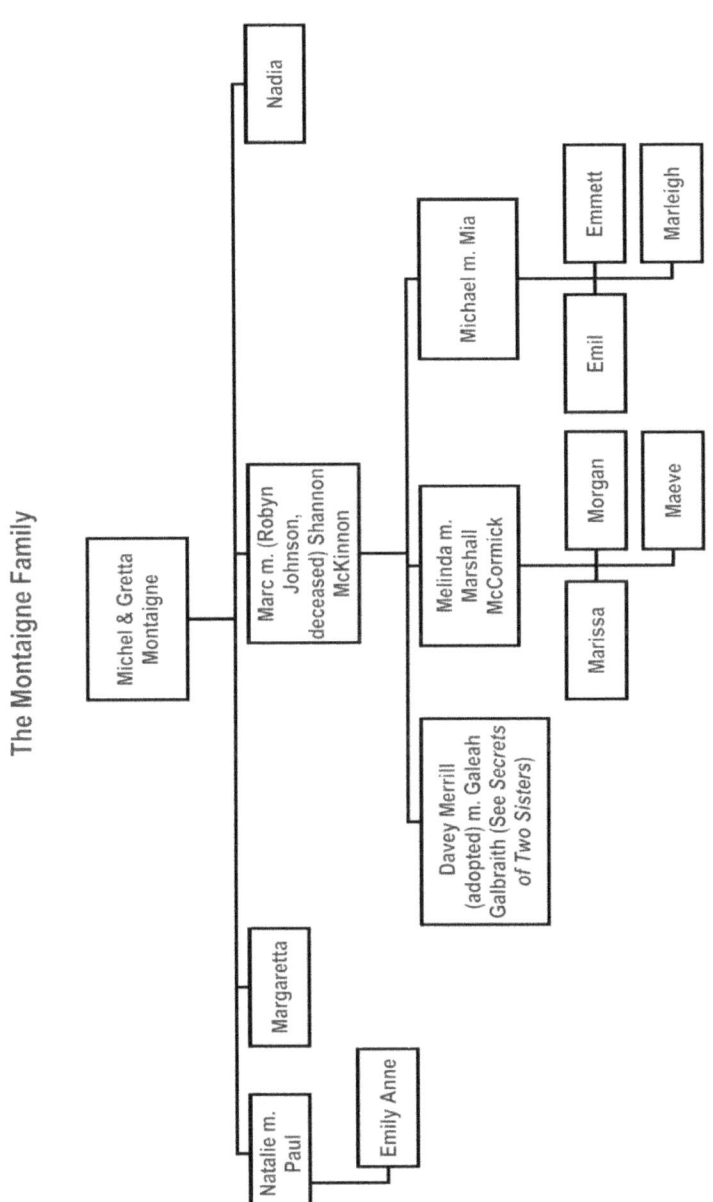

Michel & Gretta Montaigne

Nadia

Marc m. (Robyn Johnson, deceased) Shannon McKinnon

Michael m. Mia

Emmett

Marleigh

Emil

Melinda m. Marshall McCormick

Morgan

Maeve

Marissa

Davey Merrill (adopted) m. Galeah Galbraith (See *Secrets of Two Sisters*)

Margaretta

Natalie m. Paul

Emily Anne

x

Characters to Remember
(all others are superfluous!)

Gina Galbraith, single mom to Caden, teacher
     Renee Fleming, Gina's assistant in 3rd grade

Corey Peters-Templeton, real estate investor
     Jonathan Tate, real estate lawyer for the P-T family

Blake Lobel, bounty hunter
     Ricardo, Blake's best friend in Mexico;
     Jose, another friend in Mexico;
     Juan, another friend in Mexico;
     Pietro, another friend in Mexico

Tallie Peters-Templeton, human rights activist & Corey's cousin

Families from Mexico:
**Frank & Amelia Flores and their children, Francesca, Emilio, Eduardo, and April
**Stephan & Simone Garcia and their children, Susanna, Horacio, Hector, Gustavo, and Cissy
**Miguel & Molly Maderas and their children, Macy, Carlos, and Marianna
**Roberto & Rosa Rodriguez and their children, Catalina and Tristena
**Brothers, Eduardo & Phillippe Lopez and two of their girls, Esperanza and Selena

Bob Worthington, attorney for the Merrills, his wife, Belinda, and their children, Brian, Brant, and Brianna

(See family charts for other characters who are family members of the four main characters.)

Chapter One

As soon as she saw the dark blue car drive slowly by the house, she knew. Was it just pure luck that she happened to be standing by the baby grand piano in the front room, gazing through the sheer curtains at the street, but really at nothing at all?

She had been remembering something. Yes, she had seen a picture on the stand beside the piano, one of her and Bob when they had first met in college. They had been madly in love, were still, in fact.

And for that reason, when his attorney practice had grown and he had started to try bigger and bigger cases, they had put together a safety plan.

She walked purposefully toward the kitchen and the small alcove where she kept her pocketbook, emergency fanny pack, and cell phone, sweeping them all into her arms just as she had practiced so many times.

Flipping open the cell phone, she speed dialed a message to Brian's and Brant's teachers at the small private school they attended. She did the same for Brianna's pre-school. She sent Bob a coded message as well.

He was in court this morning giving opening statements for the Merrill property rights case. Was this situation connected to the case? Bob and his team had been researching, preparing for this day for slightly more than five months now.

The opposition was very powerful with the backing of many members of the United Nations. As his fame grew as a Constitutional attorney, so did the danger for his family. The sound of a car door opening sent her scurrying up the stairs.

In less than two minutes she was in the small hiding place Bob had created in the third floor attic. Finishing the large room, they had bought furniture and empty trunks to "store" there; their truly private belongings were safely stored in another state.

But Bob had built a three-foot walkway that ran along the front and sides of the house up there in the attic. Carpeting had made it a quiet place to walk, and a fake wall made of taut and painted fabric at the back of the closet leading to this walkway would fool anyone who gave it a casual glance.

She heard the motor of their car idling. It sounded like it was on the other side of the street. Good. The two men she had seen would either have to bring their car closer, or they would have to get out.

Closing her eyes since she couldn't see them anyway, she willed her ears to hear every detail of their movements. The other car door opened.

Now they were ringing the doorbell, once, twice. Shouldering the door didn't work. Of course it wouldn't. Bob had done everything possible to keep his family safe, including a specialized door and frame. Pop, pop, pop. They were using a gun.

She heard their steps as they moved through the house. The kitchen, dining room, living room, den, screened porch. Please don't hurt their beautiful Siamese kittens, Bianca and Butterball, she thought.

They were coming up the stairs to the second floor and the bedrooms now. Four bedrooms, three baths, five closet doors opened and closed.

Now they were on the stairs leading to the attic.

She barely breathed as she heard the door to the "closet" where she was hiding open and then shut.

"…not here," she heard one man say to the other.

The attic door shut. A creak sounded on the stair landing. Would they finally leave? Now they were on the first floor again.

The door to the garage opened and shut. Her car was safely parked there, a dead giveaway that she was not far away.

Silence for three long minutes—she knew, for she was counting the seconds. What were they doing? A faint metallic sound. Then she heard footsteps striding confidently down the front porch steps and across the street.

Two car doors shut. The motor revved, and the car moved down the road.

She counted to sixty and then left her hiding place. She ran to the bedroom. Nothing had been touched.

Picking up a packed backpack from the back of the closet, a small case with her jewelry, and a manila envelope with all their important papers, she headed down the stairs toward the kitchen and nearly opened the garage door when she caught the barest whiff of gas and a faint ticking sound.

Oh no. She was certain the house was going to explode any minute.

Now she raced through the screen porch, kicking the jamb to keep it open. Hopefully the kittens would think it was a game and follow her, but she had no time to check.

Out the back door, down the hillside, and through the woods in back of their lot she ran. Heading to the right, she crossed a creek and up the next hill.

When the explosion hit, she didn't look back even though like Lot's wife she wanted to do so. A wave of nausea hit her, but she clamped her mouth closed. She would not give in to it.

She cut across Mrs. Crosby's backyard while fishing in the fanny pack for another set of keys. She had them.

She unlocked Bob's old car that Mrs. Crosby allowed them to park in her drive and drove as sedately as possible to the parking lot where she was to meet the children. Would they be there?

They were. She thanked the teachers from each school, and then they were off. The children were, mercifully, quiet. She had practiced this with them several times in the past year; she could see in the rearview mirror that Brian, thirteen and the oldest, had questions. But he would wait quietly. Poor boy. He was most aware of the danger that they faced.

Brant, at ten was more exuberant, but he idolized his older brother and would do exactly as Brian did sans the concern and worry Brian kept to himself.

Brianna wanted her blanket. Brian retrieved it for her, and she settled down in her booster seat with her thumb in her mouth.

All at once, Belinda Worthington began to shake all over. The stress of the last fifteen minutes was catching up with her. She just couldn't fall apart now. She had to put some distance between her children and those who wanted to hurt them.

Chapter Two

Corey Peters-Templeton was the most pompous, arrogant man Gina Galbraith had ever met. But she couldn't stop thinking about him. He had piloted the plane that her cousin, Chelsea, had sent to pick up her and her sister, Gwen; her cousins, Kielah and Lindy; her mom; and Aunt Galeah for a gala weekend in Virginia to plan the wedding.

He had audaciously and impudently kissed her before she had disembarked from the plane. He had gently, but insistently poked fun at her cautious, carefully constructed plan for life which was so opposite his gung-ho, no-holds-allowed, caution-to-the-winds approach to life.

He had splashed water in her face when they were standing by the fountain on the waterfront in downtown Charleston, he had listened to her seriously when she was describing the multitude of problems she was encountering in the teaching profession, and he had captured her heart with his sensitivity to Caden, the little son she was raising on her own.

Chelsea and Jasper's wedding was six days away, and since the Virginia trip five months ago, as the maid of honor, not only had she been thrown into his company on many more occasions, but she found herself thinking of him when she should be concentrating on the circle of children listening to the next chapter in the Magic Tree

House book she was reading aloud in class or on what the principal was saying during the teachers' meeting.

Now, Harry Morrison, her fiancé, would be arriving tomorrow for the wedding. What was she going to do?

Her cousin, Chelsea Merrill, had announced her engagement in June to Secret Service agent, Jasper Peters-Templeton. Gina had been glad to be part of the events that led to their engagement, but she had finally finished her teacher's training at Charleston Southern University, and she was in the middle of her first year of teaching. She wanted to concentrate on her own life goals and dreams for a while, thank you very much.

Myers Elementary School had granted her a position teaching third grade, and she was thrilled that she finally had the financial means to care for four-year-old Caden the way she wanted.

The phone rang. It would be her mother calling to check on her and Caden. Her mother, Gloria Galbraith, had just taken a new job as a nurse at Tri-County Hospital, third floor coronary unit. Mom would just be going on duty to care for her heart surgery patients.

Gina smiled to herself, remembering how her mother had cared for her dolls' "heart ailments" with a stethoscope and Band-Aids. If only life were that simple now.

"Miss me, Honey?" asked a male voice, startling Gina out of the fond memory.

"N-n-no," she stuttered, caught totally off guard. Darn. Corey's calls, infrequent as they were, always seemed to come when she was thinking of him, making her aware of her jittery response. Had he guessed her reaction and enjoyed teasing her, or was this just his way of talking to girls?

"Here I am, pining away for a kind word from you, and you can't even lie and say you've missed me," he said teasingly.

"I've been hectically busy," retorted Gina. "The wedding is Saturday, but I'm still teaching until Thursday. Where are you, anyway? Shouldn't you be here already to support your brother, Jasper, as he marries?"

"Who says I'm not here?"

Gina's heart skipped a beat, and she looked around her tiny apartment, expecting to see him pop from behind the loveseat or the sofa. Silly, she chided herself. Still, she moved to the window and peered out cautiously.

"You just checked out your front window to see, didn't you?"

Gina drew her hand from the curtains guiltily. She straightened and threw her shoulders back. She would not let him disturb her.

"Where are you, Corey?" she asked in her best 'teacher' voice.

"Right now I'm standing at the window of one of the bedrooms of Flowertown Bed and Breakfast looking at the seminary across the street."

"Really?" She couldn't quite squelch the eagerness in her voice.

"Really. I just flew down with Jasper. Since he's going to be mooning around Chelsea all night at the Merrill's, I though maybe you and I could go out to eat, catch a movie, walk around town or the park or whatever you'd like."

Gina's spirits lifted then sank. She had so much to do to prepare for the substitute teacher coming in for her on Friday. And could she possibly get one of her cousins or her sister to babysit on such short notice?

And she really should consider the fact that people were beginning to pair them together when she was still engaged to Harry. But she so wanted to go.

Corey sensed her hesitation. "We don't have to stay out all night if you have some things to do for school.

Maybe I can help you," he suggested using all his persuasive powers.

"I still need to get a babysitter, and Harry's coming home tomorrow," she began, weakening.

"Harry isn't my brother's best man, I am. Isn't entertaining me part of your job description as maid of honor?" he said in a wheedling tone. "How about if I call you back in thirty minutes?"

"Okay. That will give me enough time to make some calls."

"Just don't think your way out of it," Corey advised before he hung up. "I need a relaxing evening. I've been flying all day, and now I need to unwind. You really are relaxing to be around, Gina." Then he hung up.

Gina stared at the phone. As usual, it was all about him with a backhanded compliment so she couldn't really get mad at him. His arrogance was still very annoying even though she knew he took his flying seriously.

What had she let herself in for now? Well, she had to talk to Corey sometime. Harry would be arriving tomorrow, and while Corey knew about her fiancé, Harry, Harry knew very little about the way she and Corey had been thrown together time after time since July.

He had even flown down more than a few times in the past months on his own, taking time to visit Grandpa and Grandma Merrill on the farm. Poor dears. They needed all the encouragement they could get right now with the county trying to take away their property rights.

They brightened every time they saw him. He was brilliant, really, and often argued the case back and forth with their attorney. He should have become an attorney himself. But he had told her he couldn't stand the pressure of a trial. He'd rather throw his dad's money around, wheeling and dealing in real estate.

It was all about property. She sighed, but then she chided herself for wool-gathering. She needed to make some phone calls and procure a babysitter.

Ten minutes later, her sister, Gwen, had agreed to come to her small apartment off of Main Street. Gina knew that in another ten minutes all the cousins would know she was going out with Corey that evening.

She couldn't, wouldn't consider it a date. How could she when she was engaged to another man? It was her duty, she decided, as maid of honor. Oh, how Corey would hate being considered a duty!

She ran the water for a bath while she waited for Corey's call. She ducked her head and looked into Caden's room. He was in his bedroom watching *Cars*. In his small hands he held replicas of the main characters. He would be absorbed until his little stomach grumbled for his dinner.

Just as she turned off the water, Corey called. "Hi, Beautiful. Did you get the babysitter lined up?"

"Yes. Gwen said she'd be here about five thirty."

"Super. I'll be there about five minutes after she arrives."

Great. That gave her an hour and a half to bathe, get dinner for Caden, and, hopefully, finish entering all the grades. Maybe she could stay up late and finish creating the handouts for Friday.

As she sank into the bubbles, leaving the door ajar so she could listen for Caden, she sighed. She had hoped her life would smooth itself out once she began teaching, and it had, financially.

She loved her little two-bedroom apartment. It was a bit shabby, but she had haunted the dollar stores, yard sales, and flea markets to get items that allowed her both comfort and beauty. She had thought she could live without either for the chance to prove, at least to herself, that she could survive on her own without her parents' assistance.

But she'd found that after a long day working, she needed comfort. And beauty was no less necessary. Her black and white kitchen was cheerfully accented with red, and a large oval green braided rug covered the worst spots of the bland beige carpeting in the living room.

And her bedroom. Here she had splurged on a wonderful antique four-tester bed of carved walnut. She had slept on the floor for two months before she thought she could afford the mattress set that would take the tired out of her bones each evening. The pale blues and dark wood tones created an ambience of rest.

Caden's room was crazy with colors, and smiling jungle animals adorned the walls. She wanted to provide him with all the stimulation babies and toddlers needed to thrive.

But while she was happy with her personal life, the place where she had envisioned herself confidently imbuing children with happiness and knowledge had been turning into a quagmire of petty jealousies, not-quite-blatant hostility, and festering resentment. She wanted no part of school politics, but as a rookie teacher, she found herself embroiled without even realizing it.

She was determined to put all of it aside for the sake of the children. They deserved a happy send off to Thanksgiving vacation.

Her confidence, however, had been eroded. She was so thankful for the support of her mom and dad. They had stood by her when she'd found herself, at eighteen, pregnant and deserted by her boyfriend who, instead of stepping up to the plate, had offered to pay for an abortion instead. When she had refused, he had spread malicious gossip about her all over the school.

Her mother had held her close as she had sobbed out her heartache. Her father, bless his heart, had wanted to kill Jack. Instead, he had called Uncle Craig who worked in homeland security, and they had gone to the Humphrey home to confront Jack and his father.

Mr. Humphrey had not wanted to believe them, but one look at his son's face confirmed the truth that he was guilty of the vicious rumors.

Jack still refused to acknowledge Caden as his son. But the miracle of Caden's birth had assuaged the heartache, giving her joy and shaping her goal of getting her teaching degree.

She had thought she would never date again. Who would want someone who was already saddled with another's child? But then she had met Harry. He was easy-going and generous, accepting Caden along with her into his life and his heart. He was gone frequently, working with the paramilitary support team that scavenged for underwater mines.

But he was returning tomorrow, having been granted special permission to take time off for Chelsea and Jasper's wedding.

And that led to her new problem. Spending time with Corey had made her question her attachment to Harry. Did she love him enough to marry him? Was she falling for Corey?

She hoped not. She didn't want to care for him. He was unpredictable, arrogant, and impervious many times to the feelings of others whereas Harry was comfortable, undemanding, kind, and generous.

Yet Corey made her feel acutely alive, and she was certain she had caught glimpses of a vulnerability that seemed foreign in someone so self-assured. Life was such a muddle sometimes.

The water was cooling, and she needed to quit dawdling. She had no time these days to over-think her problems. Once the wedding was over, she would use the rest of her vacation time to think through everything she promised herself. Right now, she needed to get ready and fix dinner for Caden. *Cars* was nearly over, and her sweet little boy would be hungry.

Chapter Three

At five thirty-five sharp, Corey knocked on her door. Gwen was in the bathroom watching Caden splash in the water. He loved his bath.

When Gina opened the door, instead of seeing Corey's face, she saw the largest bouquet of pink roses she had ever seen. Her breath caught in her throat. Oh my! She counted at least thirty. Three dozen roses all for her!

From behind his back, Corey produced a smaller bouquet of white roses. "These are for Gwen," he said in an exaggerated whisper. "Where should I put them?"

"Here on the table. She will see them, especially since her name is on them."

"Let me go see my man, Caden," he said, neatly stepping over the cars and trucks her son had left on the floor in the hallway. Gina went to get a vase from the cabinet for her roses. She could hear his deep voice contrasted with Caden's high, excited one.

Gwen came into the kitchen area, looking around expectantly. When she saw her flowers, she held them up and with closed eyes, sniffed appreciatively.

"How come he's taking just you?" she asked.

"Wedding stuff," Gina answered feeling somewhat guilty. When did the line get so blurred between "wedding stuff" and "friendship?" she wondered. Of course, he couldn't be more than that, and she was still rather shocked to find that she really did consider him a friend.

But when he returned from his visit with Caden, she noticed he looked especially fine in dark wool slacks with a soft cashmere sweater of forest green over a white-collared shirt. The ensemble seemed to pull the reddish highlights out of his dark hair. While she was arranging the pink roses in a vase, she feasted her eyes then caught herself.

But he wasn't looking at her. His gaze was riveted on the TV. He turned up the volume without asking and watched the newscast with intense interest.

A house had exploded in the Belton Woods subdivision, a subdivision known for its 1-acre lots. The neighbors had seen nothing, heard nothing until the explosion.

The home had been the residence of Bob and Belinda Worthington and their three children. Mrs. Worthington was believed to have been home at the time of the explosion, but Mr. Worthington could not be reached to confirm this.

Bob Worthington was the famous attorney representing the Merrill family near Walterboro and their property rights case for which opening arguments had begun just last week. The fire department was investigating, and it was too early to determine the cause of the explosion.

Corey looked at Gina grimly. "This changes our plans. I need to call Bob right away. If this explosion is in any way connected with the court case, he may need my help."

"We still need to eat," said Gina. "In times like these we all need sustenance. Maybe Bob can join us for dinner."

"I wonder if he's back from downtown Charleston yet. I'll call him in the car."

He helped her with her coat, and they walked out to the vehicle Corey had rented.

Gina raised an eyebrow when Corey unlocked the door of a black SUV with tinted windows.

"What?" Corey asked, catching the look.

"I expected a sports car for you!"

"I'm here to help with the wedding, and I thought transportation might be helpful. Besides, wait 'til you see the inside."

She should have known, Gina thought. From flowers to cars, Corey never did anything by halves. The inside was outfitted much like the one Chelsea had described Jasper driving, one with all the bells and whistles.

"Where did you find this?" she asked incredulously.

"I have connections all over the world, Honey. I just made a phone call and, voila, here we are."

He pressed a button and asked the computer to call Bob. In half a minute Bob's voice was heard over the speaker.

Corey asked his location, and Bob said he had just examined the crater where his home had once stood. He sounded extremely weary.

"Come get dinner with me and Gina, Man," said Corey. "Do you have a place to stay tonight? No? I've got it all set up. You can have some privacy, and your family can join you."

"We'll talk about it at the restaurant," said Bob noncommittally. "Where are we meeting?"

A few minutes later, they pulled into The Mustard Seed, a quaint little restaurant in downtown Summerville. Gina watched in amazement as Corey talked to the manager, pulling out a few large denomination bills and asking that the tables around them not be filled.

"I want to be able to talk without being overheard," he explained to Gina.

Corey ordered an appetizer and drinks, which arrived at the same time Bob did. He stood, and they exchanged back slaps and half hugs. Corey signaled for the waitress, Devon, to stay while they placed their orders.

"So what gives?" asked Corey.

"My wife and children are at a secure location. We knew something like this might happen because of the work I do, so we set up a safety plan two years ago."

"So you think this is related to the case?" asked Corey, leaning forward with interest.

"I'm sure of it."

How could he be so sure? Gina wondered.

"Belinda and I have secured phones and code words just in case. She saw the men who planted the bomb and spread the gasoline. And she had the presence of mind to note the model and make of the vehicle they drove as well as part of the license plate." He shook his head in wonderment and admiration.

"I gave all the information to Police Chief Blackburn this late afternoon when I arrived back in town. He has opened an investigation. But we are not talking to the media. The Chief wants to be sure this is connected to the court case."

"That's wise," said Corey. "Is that why the media doesn't know if your wife is safe or not?"

"Precisely. I can't compromise her whereabouts, so it's better to say nothing at all."

"You are up against some very powerful people," said Corey soberly.

"I know it," said Bob, rubbing his hand wearily over his face.

"But I want you to know that I know some very powerful people, too."

Bob looked at him enquiringly.

"My mom and dad," said Corey with a sheepish air. "But don't underestimate that connection. They truly do know all the right people to fight against corruption in high places. They were trained as part of an elite group that protects the interests of America, and, more importantly, a group that upholds the principles set forth in the Constitution."

"That's good to know. I've hired a private investigator myself as well as some security guards." He nodded to a gentleman dining with a lady seated several tables over. "There's another one out by the cars."

"Really? Good job. Now about tonight. When I booked a place for the wedding, I decided to book the whole facility. Why don't you make it your headquarters while you're here in town. That way, you'll be out of harm's way at your office. Do you have security on the premises there?"

Their dinners arrived. Gina hadn't had a chance to say much, but she listened in awe to their conversation. She didn't really like being 'involved' in this cloak and dagger stuff. It was like the danger Chelsea and Jasper had been in all over again.

It was just as well that she was engaged to Harry. She would never fit into a family like Corey's. Yet she would do anything to help her grandparents, and God help anyone who tried to harm Caden.

Perhaps people engaged in dangerous living, not because they were daredevils, but because they cared for their loved ones. Of course, Corey was the exception. He was, obviously, a daredevil.

When Gina rejoined the conversation, they were discussing in even lower voices the whereabouts of Bob's family.

"...in a relatively rural part of Virginia from my wife's mother's side of the family, so it would be difficult to trace."

"You know my family is from the Chantilly area in Virginia," stated Corey. "My mom is the consummate hostess, and if you ever need a backup, send your family there. My parents often joke that their place has more security than the White House. Here, let me give you their number."

While they put their cell phones side by side to exchange phone numbers, Gina was reminded of the first time she had visited Corey's home in Virginia.

Right after the announcement of her engagement to Jasper Peters-Templeton, her cousin, Chelsea, had called asking Gina to be her maid of honor. Gina had gladly agreed. They had been playing together and sharing secrets since diaper days, literally.

Although Chelsea was a year older, their moms were very close, so the two had played together from the very beginning at either the Merrill home or at the Galbraith home.

When she called, Chelsea had already returned to the D.C. area to complete the last seven months of her service with the President as one of his aides.

Jasper was on assignment with the Secret Service who knew where, but his mom wanted Chelsea's family to stay at her place during their visit, so Corey had been requisitioned to pick them up in the small, Gulfstream IV jet that the Peters-Templetons used for business.

Gina's first impression of Corey was hazy until that kiss. She had never been separated from Caden for more than six hours, and to leave him with Aunt Clara for three days had made her a nervous wreck.

She had triple-checked what she packed for him, giving scant attention to her own suitcase. She barely noticed Corey as he took her suitcase, for she was calming her fluttering nerves and swallowing back her tears.

But once she had taken her seat and the jet had taken off from the small airfield near the Charleston International Airport, her nerves and tears finally began to take backseat to the novelty of the experience.

Gwen, Kielah, and Lindy were having a lively discussion of the agenda Chelsea had sent them. Once they arrived, they would be driven to Rosemont, and then they would all meet for lunch at a restaurant near the capitol followed by an afternoon of pampering at a spa to which Chelsea's future mother-in-law, Nell, had introduced her.

Chelsea had a surprise lined up for dinner and afterwards, but the next day would more than make up for their first day of leisure. They would be shopping the entire day for Chelsea's dress and the bridesmaid's dresses.

Just then, the door to the cockpit was opened and Gina got her first real look at Corey. He took a seat in one of the vacant passenger seats, turning to face them.

"How are you ladies today?" he asked. "I'm Corey, Jasper's brother, and you must be Chelsea's mother," he said to Gina's Aunt Galeah. He stood and held out his hand to her. Instead of shaking it, he pressed his lips to the back of her hand with practiced ease.

"Yes, I'm the mother of the bride," answered Galeah. She looked at him quizzically.

His presence in the cabin instead of the cockpit totally derailed all conversation among the girls.

Kielah and Lindy looked at each other. Cheerleaders aren't shy, and as school habits die hard, they both raised their hands.

Corey looked at them. "Yes?"

"Who's flying the plane?" they blurted out together as they sometimes did.

"Oh, that's right. You never saw Jonathan. He's acting as co-pilot today."

All the women visibly relaxed.

Gina was too polite to say so, but she wondered if he had done that on purpose just to make them feel nervous, awkward, and gauche. His attitude seemed a bit supercilious to her.

"You two must be Kielah and Lindy, Chelsea's sisters, right?"

They both nodded.

He turned to Gloria. "Chelsea's Aunt Gloria?" He repeated the same gesture with her.

Turning to Gina and Gwen, he said, "You must be Chelsea's cousins although I don't believe I know your names."

Gina really didn't want to reply. She wouldn't be seeing much of him once they arrived, would she? Her unsettled emotions combined with his very suave, very cosmopolitan attitude grated on her nerves.

Gwen saved her from replying. "I'm Gwen, and this is my sister Gina." She held out her hand. Corey kissed her hand as well, but turning quickly he saw the slight frown on Gina's face that she did her best to turn to a yawn.

Corey held her glance for a long moment. He must have read the disdain in her eyes because he suddenly leaned down and brushed her cheek with his lips.

"Well, I've got to get back to the controls," he announced as he straightened, unconcerned with her consternation. "We'll be landing in less than an hour."

He left a cabin of women with varying degrees of amusement, awe, and interest. Kielah and Lindy immediately exclaimed over his tall, dark looks and his hand kissing.

"That's just being polite in Europe where he does a lot of business for his father," said Galeah firmly, trying to quell the coming crushes the girls would have on him.

"I can't believe he actually kissed Gina," Lindy exclaimed.

Gloria looked at her two daughters. Gwen would take the attention philosophically and chalk it up to experience as she usually did. But if she didn't miss her guess, Gina was not very happy with the young man.

"He's just being polite," she said. "Oh look at that lake down there. Isn't that Lake Wylie?" Distracted, the others had to look.

Thanks, Mom, thought Gina. Her composure was trying to desert her. Normally she would have laughed at such attention. But she already missed Caden terribly, and all she wanted to do was cry.

Chapter Four

Gina thought they would not see Corey once they had disembarked from the plane, but she was wrong.

Corey drove them from the airport to Rosemont. His brother-in-law, Jonathan Tate, acted as tour guide, giving them a history of the area and, incidentally, of Jasper and Corey's family as well.

The scenery was beautiful. Rolling pastures and wooded areas passed. And then they were entering the gates of Rosemont.

A black iron fence decorated with spear heads and fleur de lis surrounded the property, meeting at the gated entrance. Corey drove up the gracefully winding drive that ended in a circle.

The double set of steps, on the north and south sides of the front porch that soared two stories, joined at a circular, pineapple-shaped fountain.

Why was it called Rosemont? Gina wondered. But then she saw that the brick of the house was a rosy hue, and, in addition, the rose garden to the left of the house showed the origins of the name, Rosemont.

As Corey rolled the car to a stop beside the steps at the south side of the house, Chelsea and a tall, blonde, strikingly beautiful woman emerged.

"There you are," the beautiful woman said. She was beaming, clasping her hands together, and radiating excitement. "My name is Nell, Jasper and Corey's mom.

I'm so excited to meet you all! Please come in while the boys bring in your bags."

Two other young men assisted Corey and Jonathan in carrying the bags up the outside stairs. The use of an elevator beside the inside stairs leading to the second floor made short work of luggage distribution, and then Gina heard the two young men tell Corey they were returning to their work in the stables.

Meanwhile, Nell was leading them into her kitchen and morning room and offering drinks to everyone. Chelsea vouched that the peach-infused iced tea was excellent, so everyone had to try some.

It was delicious, and Gina had a second glass as they sat around the table in the sunny breakfast nook that was really an extension of the kitchen. Corey's mom was a southern hostess who knew how to make sweet tea! If her lovely home had not won their admiration, her sweet tea certainly did.

Once everyone was served, including Corey and Jonathan, Chelsea began introducing her guests.

"Nell, I want you to meet my mom, Galeah Merrill."

"I'm so glad to meet you, Galeah," Nell said warmly. "I'm so looking forward to spending some time down in Charleston with you all as the wedding draws closer. I'm just sorry Carter and I weren't able to be there for their engagement announcement."

"You were otherwise engaged," said Chelsea dryly with a laugh.

They all remembered that terrorists had attacked the ball Nell was hostessing at the same time that Chelsea and Jasper had been under attack down in Charleston.

"These are my sisters, Kielah, who is eighteen and Lindy, who is sixteen. Kielah will be attending Clemson University in the fall."

"Congratulations, Kielah. I'm sure you'll enjoy college."

Turning to Lindy, she said, "Don't be too eager to join your sister. You're young only once."

Everyone laughed at that.

Chelsea continued the introductions. "This is my aunt, Gloria Galbraith. She is a nurse in the coronary care unit at Tri-County Hospital."

"I'm so happy you could come," said Nell.

"And this is my cousin, Gina. She's my maid of honor," said Chelsea.

"A pleasure," said Nell. She linked her arm in Gina's.

Apparently Nell made instant friends, Gina thought somewhat wryly.

"Corey is the best man, so I'm glad you two can meet right away. You two will be helping the bride and groom with the details of the nuptials."

Corey shook her hand albeit with a twinkle in his eye.

Oh great, thought Gina. Now I'll have to be nice to him.

"And this is Gina's sister, Gwen who is also sixteen."

"Sixteen is such a great age," observed Nell as she gave Gwen a hug. "Now I want to show you my house," she continued. "That is if we have time?" She looked questioningly at Chelsea who nodded yes.

The large, airy kitchen where they were congregated, some sitting and some standing, was done in bright yellow with accents of royal blue. The café curtains were pulled back, letting in the sunshine from the east and giving them a view of a huge flower garden below and a large vegetable garden beyond that.

In the distance, they could see the barn which housed the stables from which one of the stable hands was leading a beautiful, black mare. Three black labs cavorted around the horse, but she seemed to pay them no mind.

Nell explained that the horses loved having the dogs around. "Their names are Mo, Bert, and Liz, short for Mozart, Schubert, and Liszt."

Kielah, Lindy, and Gwen were enchanted with the names of the dogs and wanted to go outside and play with them, but Chelsea said they'd have to leave soon for lunch.

Chelsea linked her arm in her mother's. "I'm so glad you finally made it up here," she said. "Nell is going to be an awesome mother-in-law, and Carter, her husband, is great, too. But I've missed you all, especially after all that happened."

Gina, overhearing, knew she was talking about a few weeks ago when those terrorists had threatened to blow up the North Charleston Coliseum during the concert by their new friend, pop rock star, Charm Dumotte.

Nell was already in the next room talking. "This is our family room. It's an ark of a house, but we've tried to make it homey rather than ostentatious. However, we are required to entertain frequently, so we have to have room to accommodate all of our guests."

The family room had dark bench rail paneling with vivid royal blue accents. But the comfortable sofa in rich cocoa and golden paisley swirls and the dark walnut and cherry furniture gave the room a masculine feel. Above the fireplace, the mounted, piked marlin added its own blue accent.

Out in the hall, Gina was struck with the immensity of the house now that she saw on the left hand side the grand entry way with its double curved staircases that led from the magnificent double doors up to the level where she stood. These stairs were done in marble and highly polished golden oak. Over all this grandeur hung an immense crystal chandelier.

To her right was a huge meeting room with about fifteen groupings of chairs, loveseats and tables. The entire eastern wall consisted of windows that, again, overlooked the flower garden below. In the far corner was a baby grand piano that actually looked dwarfed in contrast to the windows.

Further down the hall and also on the right was the library paneled in golden oak. Green velvet drapes lined in gold hung at the immensely tall windows that faced the backyard, and a desk sat in front of them. An inviting brown leather couch was positioned on the plush Aubusson carpet that covered all but a foot of the hardwood floor around the perimeter of the room.

All three remaining walls were covered with bookcases containing hundreds of books with the exception of the south wall where the fireplace was. Here, tall bookcases flanked the mantel from the floor to the fourteen-foot ceilings.

"And this is our bedroom," Nell was saying when Gina caught up with her. She was amazed to find that the color scheme was the same she had for her bedroom: restful blue and white, accented with dark wood pieces. Spacious closets and a shower and Jacuzzi tub done in marble added to the luxury of the suite.

They took a small service stairway to the second level of the house.

"All the children's bedrooms and most of the guest bedrooms are up here," said Nell. "Corey's room is here on the right facing the front of the house, and Jasper's room is opposite on the left. Preston's room is here beside Corey's. The rest are guest bedrooms until we get to the end of the hall."

They had glimpses inside various guest bedrooms on the left. On the right was a sitting area with several bookcases. A railing six to eight feet from the front of the house opened to the foyer below.

As they came to this end of the hallway, they noticed their bags had been placed inside various rooms. Chelsea said, "This is Pammy's old bedroom, and this is where I stay when I'm here."

Nell added, "You can change rooms if you want. Just make yourselves at home. Do we have time for the lower level before lunch?" she asked looking at Chelsea.

Chelsea shook her head no.

"Well, the lower level has an indoor pool; several more guest bedrooms; a family room with all the latest techno gadgets, you know, TV, blue tooth, Wii games; a kitchenette; and a squash court, but you can see it all later if you want."

Gina was awed by the grandeur of the house. No wonder Corey acted rather arrogant sometimes. Their families had some very nice homes in Charleston, but nothing like this mansion.

Still, she had heard from Chelsea of the large-scale entertaining Nell and Carter did. Sometimes they had more than two hundred people in their home for an event.

Once again they piled into the car, and once again Corey drove with Jonathan acting as co-pilot. But now Nell and Chelsea took over as tour guide.

Chelsea wanted to show them where her apartment was before they drove to the restaurant for lunch. They finally pulled up in front of a small Lebanese restaurant in Silver Spring.

Chelsea caught the dubious looks of her sisters. "Trust me; they have some awesome food here. This is where Jasper brought me on our first date on his sister's recommendation. We've been coming here ever since."

They were seated immediately at a table with snow-white linens and gleaming silver. Dark wood paneling and muted sconce lighting created a warm, intimate ambience.

Gina found herself seated across from Nell between her mother and Corey. She really didn't want to sit beside him, but she couldn't very well change her seat without looking rude.

After drinks and appetizers were ordered they all looked at their menus.

"I can recommend the pecan-crusted chicken with raspberry soy sauce or the pistachio encrusted Tilapia with dill," said Chelsea.

"Their Thai chicken with chestnuts, mushrooms, bean sprouts, cilantro and lime over saffron rice is great if you want a rice dish," Nell added. The waiter brought their drinks and then poised his pen above his pad, ready to take their orders.

Corey ordered the pistachio-encrusted Tilapia. Gina preferred the Thai chicken with a small salad. She suddenly found herself ravenous from lack of sleep and nerves about leaving Caden.

Nell wanted to know all about their lives in South Carolina.

"Galeah, you're a librarian?" she questioned.

"Yes. I work at a small middle school in the heart of Summerville, mostly in acquisitions and accession, but I also do checkout when the other girls are busy helping the students find what they need."

"That sounds like so much fun!" said Nell. "Have you read *The 39 Clues* series? I have to confess, I've read all of the first eleven."

"Those books fly off the shelves," Galeah affirmed. "Everyone likes that series. Another series the students all like is the *Conspiracy 365* books. They're all action-packed."

"And tell me more about the nursing industry, Gloria," said Nell.

While Gina's mother answered, Corey, like a gentleman, passed the curry puffs and crab roll appetizers to Kielah, Lindy, and Gwen to his right. When they had made their selections, he asked Gina what she wanted to sample.

"I'll try the curry puffs," she decided.

"And what do you do down in Charleston," he asked as he deftly served her.

"I just finished college this past spring, and I've signed the dotted line to teach third graders this next year. It's my first real job, and I'm really looking forward to it. How about you?"

"Oh, I handle the details of real estate deals for my dad, and fly his planes, sail his boats, and kiss pretty girls," he said with a mischievous grin.

Wanting to give him a set down, Gina said, "Nothing serious then, I guess."

"I take the girls I kiss very seriously," he responded, refusing her jab.

Not wanting to get personal, Gina just said, "Hm."

But Corey wasn't finished. "I see you're engaged," he said, looking at her ring. "Found Mr. Right?"

"Yes, thank you very much."

"Oh? Who is he? Some Steady Eddie CPA type?"

"Actually, Harry dives with a military crew retrieving lost bombs and military equipment."

"Wow! I'm impressed!"

Just with what he was impressed, Gina didn't discover, for Nell overheard the last part of their conversation and was instantly fascinated with such an interesting job. She had all sorts of questions to ask Gina.

Their dinners arrived, and Gina was glad to concentrate on her food instead of on the oaf sitting beside her.

Chapter Five

When they had finished their lunch, Corey drove them to the spa. He muttered something to Nell about too must estrogen, kissed her briefly on the cheek, and left, promising to pick them up later when they were all done.

Gina had never been to a spa for the whole works before. The enzymatic/herbal mud bath to remove toxins was interesting, but the body massage afterward released the rest of the tension she had been feeling about leaving Caden.

Their scalps were massaged before a shampoo, cut and curl; makeup was applied, and the finishing event was having their finger and toe nails painted.

They all agreed they felt like new women. While their nails were drying, Chelsea asked for their attention.

"And now for our evening surprise," she announced.

Gina, watching Nell's face, knew she was in on the details.

"My boss, President Bell, and his wife have invited us to dinner at the White House!"

The girls and their mothers looked at each other in awe.

"But what do we wear?" asked Aunt Galeah.

"President Bell and his wife insisted that we not overdress for the occasion as this is a private dinner. But we will return to Rosemont before we go to the White House."

"I wanted to show you all where I work," Chelsea continued, "but with security concerns, it was going to be awkward, so this was the ingenious way Mrs. Bell decided to handle it."

"That's very kind of her," said Aunt Galeah.

"She is very kind," said Nell. "But don't forget that your daughter and her friends solved the puzzle of the terrorist hit sites, and the President is extremely grateful."

Just then Corey appeared in the doorway of the small reception area. "Your carriage awaits, ladies," he announced.

Gina wondered if he would be attending dinner with them, too.

Her question was answered when Nell asked if Jonathan was with him or if he had gone home to get ready for dinner.

"He and Pammy are already at home getting ready," said Corey. "And we need to get home, too, if we are to be ready when the limousines come for us."

Gina was so relaxed that she nearly fell asleep on the way back to Rosemont.

But Chelsea wanted to discuss the wedding. "It's going to be at Summerville Baptist Church, and I've always wanted to get married at Christmas or in the spring, but we don't want to wait until the spring, and Jasper's schedule isn't very clear for December, so we decided on the Saturday before Thanksgiving."

"What are your colors?" Lindy wanted to know. "Because if you make us wear orange or forest green, I'm out."

"Why in the world would I make my sisters wear orange or forest green? You might look okay in orange, but you'd look terrible in forest green, Lindy."

"I know: brown!" said Kielah dramatically.

"The groomsmen are going to wear a dark brown," said Chelsea. "And the bridesmaids will be in a very pale pink with brown velvet ribbons."

"Pink is good," said Lindy. "All of us girls will look good in pink."

"That's what I thought, too," said Chelsea. "I've been looking around, and at first I was thinking of red for the bridesmaids since it's more of a fall color, but I think pink will look much better on everyone."

"I know Gina is your maid of honor, but who have you asked to be bridesmaids?" asked Galeah.

Kielah and Lindy, of course, but also Lanie and Gwenie, here," said Chelsea. "I think four is a good number, don't you? I asked Pammy, Jasper's sister, but she declined."

"She did?" asked Nell. She had been talking to Corey about what to wear that evening, but now her head whipped around, and her eyes narrowed.

"Yes," responded Chelsea, but she did not elaborate except to say that Pammy would be helping her with the planning instead.

When they arrived at Rosemont, Chelsea led them upstairs, explaining that the closets were stocked with clothes that Nell had bought on sale. She loved to shop off-season and get great clothing at ridiculously low prices. They were free to wear anything they found that they liked.

Aunt Galeah and Gloria opted to wear the summer suits they had brought with them. Galeah's mint skirt and jacket looked awesome with her dark hair and delicate coloring while Gina thought her mom looked beautiful in the pale lavender that highlighted her dark, upswept hair.

Kielah, Lindy, and Gwenie went crazy over the closets, running back and forth between rooms until they found dresses that they really liked.

Gwenie had inherited the dark hair and high, Native American cheekbones from her father's side of the family. She chose a royal purple dress with a beautiful lace collar.

Kielah and Lindy, both blondes like their grandpa, Will Merrill, chose pink and pale apricot sheath dresses in silk.

Gina couldn't decide what to wear. She had a perfectly good white sundress with tiny sprigs of blue flowers in the flowing skirt. It was somewhat simple, but with the strappy silver sandals, she thought it would be good enough. She'd rather be comfortable, and the events of the day had already been rather surreal.

When Gina was finished dressing, bored with the girlish chatter of the younger girls, she and Chelsea, who was also ready, headed down the central stairs to the foyer.

Carter and his three sons, all dressed in suits, were waiting below. Chelsea caught Gina's wrist to hold her back a few seconds.

"Aren't they a handsome group of men?" she whispered.

"All men look great in suits," responded Gina noncommittally, but she privately agreed.

Jasper had obviously inherited Nell's blonde hair though in a darker shade than hers. Corey had a rich mahogany tone to his hair with hints of curls.

Their younger brother had the same fine, dark hair that their father had although the older Peters-Templeton had a frosting of silver at his temples.

They were all tall, and even the youngest son she later discovered was Preston, stood a good ten inches over five feet. Kielah and Lindy would flirt the entire evening she was sure.

Carter crossed to his wife and gave her a quick kiss. Corey was looking at his watch and frowning while Jasper had caught their movement down the stairs and was hurrying forward to embrace Chelsea. The President had contacted Jasper's boss so he could be present at dinner. Preston stood rocking back on his heels, watching the tableau.

When Gina saw the look on Corey's face as he caught sight of her, she couldn't help but be glad that she had chosen to dress rather simply. She still didn't like him much, but it's always nice to receive that unspoken affirmation for how a girl looks she thought.

Just as Kielah, Lindy, Gwen, and their mothers were descending the staircase, the two limousines from the White House were announced over the intercom.

When Kielah and Lindy saw Preston, they looked at each other. The White House and a cute guy? How delicious could life get? Gina and Chelsea both caught their looks. They couldn't help but smile as they interpreted the unspoken exchange correctly.

Nell and Carter rode in the limousine with their youngest son, Preston. Aunt Galeah, who wanted to keep tabs on her younger daughters, also rode with them.

That left Chelsea, Jasper, Corey, Gina, Gloria, and Gwen in the second limo. Once again, Corey sat by Gina, his thigh pressed firmly against hers. It seemed almost too intimate to her, but she could hardly move without drawing attention to her discomfort.

Instead, she concentrated on watching Chelsea and Jasper opposite her squeezing hands and exchanging unspoken love messages. Okay, that wasn't going to work either.

Corey must have had the same thought because he asked her more about college and graduation in May.

"Truthfully? I enjoyed college, but with a job, a toddler to care for, and all the work to do, I was exhausted and barely had time for myself."

"A toddler? You have a child?" he asked in shocked surprise.

"Yes, a son, Caden. He's the light of my life," she said in a challenging tone. She wanted to say more, but she wasn't going to bare her soul to this virtual stranger, especially with her mother sitting right there.

"I'm sorry if I seemed... shocked." He was obviously at a loss for words. "You just seem so, so pure," and aware he was seriously putting his foot in his mouth, he added quickly, "And that's a compliment, believe me."

"I'll take it as such, then." She said rather stonily. To deflect the attention off herself, she added, 'How about you? Where did you go to college?" although she really didn't care.

"I went to Harvard in Boston the first two years. I took two years of law school, and then I switched to a business major. I also did the last two years online as much as possible."

"Why is that?" asked Gina

"Dad had to have heart surgery several years ago, and he was in the middle of some large real estate transactions overseas. I used to go straight to his office after classes and ride home with him on weekends. Sometimes we didn't get out until very late, and I started paying attention to what he was doing. It was just natural, I guess, for me to help him."

"That was right around the time that Jonathan came on board with the legal firm we used for all our transactions," he continued. "We were able to keep things going for Dad even when he was really sick."

He didn't mention that he'd had to drop out of classes for six months to be able to run his dad's office, including firing a junior clerk who clearly thought it the perfect opportunity to try to embezzle a large amount of money from his family.

Jonathan had stuck with him, helping him through the really tough times when he couldn't ask his dad what to do or add any more worry to his mother's overburdened shoulders.

After a late night discussion with Pammy in which the tears had been perilously close, she had volunteered to help in the office even though it was definitely not her forte, and that's how she and Jonathan had met.

He didn't think his mother knew even now the full extent of the burden he'd carried, but his dad had found out from a business associate, and it had forged a strong and unbreakable bond between them; with Jonathan and Pammy, too.

He was lost in thought for a moment about it all. Gina sat patiently beside him, realizing there was more to the story than he was sharing.

He glanced down at her quiet, composed face, noting for the first time the strength of purpose and resolve in her quiet blue eyes. Her mother next to her was busy talking to Chelsea and Jasper, so he decided to tell her more of the story.

She listened without interrupting. Then she impulsively squeezed his arm.

"Thanks for telling me," she said. "I'll tell you about Caden's father sometime, just not here and now."

"Counting on it, Babe," he said. He watched as anger sparked green flecks in her eyes. She sure didn't like familiar endearments.

Gina pointedly said something to Chelsea, and the conversation grew more general.

They drew up to the South Portico. Jasper obviously knew the Head Usher at the door. He let them in, and another usher led them to the blue room where President and Mrs. Bell were waiting for them.

Gina had seen these rooms many times in pictures, but seeing them in person she realized the grandeur and the size of the rooms, the grand staircase and the opulence of the furnishings.

And the smells. All older homes had different smells. And this one was no different. Candles were definitely burning somewhere, and overlaying that was the smell of the masses of roses and other flowers in various bowls and vases around the room.

After introductions were made, they were escorted personally by the President and his wife on a tour of the west wing where Chelsea did most of her work.

They meandered through the rose garden on the way back to the residence. Mrs. Bell gave them a personal tour of the East Room, the Green and Red Rooms, and the kitchen where their dinner was being prepared.

Then they went upstairs where the first family actually lives to the dining room where a fabulous dinner was served around a large table with service for the eighteen of them, including the President's two teenage sons, Ryan and Wilson.

Nell and Aunt Galeah were seated on either side of Mrs. Bell. Kielah was seated on the same side of the table next to Ryan. Grace and Gina were seated directly across from Mrs. Bell.

Lindy and Gwen were seated together further down the table close to Wilson and Preston and near Chelsea and Jasper. The President and Carter sat at the other end of the table. Corey made sure he sat by Gina.

After grace, Mrs. Bell said, "Tonight I am not the President's wife and that is not the President." She pointed to her husband. "We are all just friends and family eating together and celebrating the engagement of two wonderful young people, Chelsea and Jasper."

Everyone applauded. "If you all would just call me Anne and my husband Henry," she said, "except for those two young men." She pointed at her sons. Everyone laughed.

The first course was served, and Nell immediately began talking recipes with Mrs. Bell. Soon all of the women were chatting like old friends, sharing recipes, favorite summer foods, and gardening tips.

Meanwhile, Gina noticed that Chelsea, Jasper, and Corey, all good conversationalists, engaged Kielah and Ryan, Lindy, Gwen, Preston, and Wilson in discussions about school, music, and other activities.

Gwen, Preston, and Wilson all discovered that they shared a passion for books. This generated a discussion that even included Carter and the President although the two men soon left the conversation to talk about real estate markets around the world and the economic standings of various countries.

"And what is your favorite book right now, Gina?" asked Corey.

With a very serious face she replied, "*Goodnight, Moon.* I read it to Caden every night."

The other girls and even Jasper had to laugh at the expression on Corey's face.

"Gotcha!" said Gina, laughing until Corey very deliberately slid his hand down her arm and said silkily, "Maybe you can read it to me tonight."

The only reply she would give was an indignant stare, which caused the green in her eyes to spark dangerously.

40

Chapter Six

Esperanza woke suddenly to the sound of a creaking door. Rough hands hauled her to her feet, removed the gag from her mouth, and untied the cords that bound her hands in back of her.

"Not a sound from any of you," the coarse, gravelly voice of the captain demanded or..." he made a slicing motion across his throat.

Esperanza didn't doubt him. Her little cousin, Maria, had been shot when she complained of needing to use cuarto de bano, to pee. The shock of seeing the little girl lying so still on the floor in a pool of blood had kept them quiet for the duration of this trip by ship from her home town of Tampico.

The food for all ten of them had been left on a tray on the floor. She wanted no food. She was sick with worry over what was happening to her and her best friend, Selena.

One minute they had been at the market flirting with the clerk. The next minute after saying adios, they had fled from the path of a careening, white van.

The driver had shouted curses at them, and then a side door had opened, two men jumped out and had hauled them into the hot, windowless interior.

The men must have drugged them, for she only vaguely remembered stumbling up the gangplank in the dark onto what must have been a huge ship.

Now they were trapped in a small room with seven other girls. Maria would have been the tenth.

"...too small anyway," she had heard the gunman mutter to someone outside the door as they had dragged Maria's lifeless body out of the room. "Don't know why they think we can use ninas pequenas as prostitutas."

"Prostitutas!" She had heard of girls being kidnapped but had never thought it would happen to her. Even at fourteen, she was not muy bonita, but her cousin, Selena, already at twelve, had the body of a sixteen-year-old teenager.

Selena had heard, too. She looked at Esperanza with large, frightened eyes.

"Some would pay for such a little one. I could have made some fat gringo pay for her."

Esperanza closed her eyes. She wanted to weep wildly, but fear kept her from doing so. Instead, hot tears scalded against her closed eyelids, and she prayed fervently to Dios she would be rescued.

*****

The weather was hot, even for summer in the South. While several of his nieces enjoyed the cooler climes of Virginia and dinner at the White House, Craig Miller was reading a memo on his work email.

All officers in Homeland Security must go through training on implementing the new law on human trafficking. That was fine by him. He was a little weary of the more mundane aspects of his job right now. What was that quote? "The same old sins done in brand new ways," or something to that effect.

The next email was a news bulletin. The body of a girl had washed up on the Texan coast. She looked like she was about eight years old, Mexican, and had a single gunshot wound to her head, point blank range.

He shook his head. He could remember Melanie at eight years, a brown-haired, blued-eyed little girl with a smile that would melt the heart of the biggest grouch.

This was the thirteenth body to wash up on southern American shores in the last two months. Most were girls, aged six to eighteen, but two had been little boys.

Something awful was happening to the children of Mexico, and he and his team needed to discover just what. The fact that they were washing up on American soil made the United States complicit in what was happening.

Perhaps it was part of a human trafficking ring. Children and women and even men were nothing more than property to be sold to the highest bidder for God only knew what purposes.

The "lucky" ones were not used for lewd and deviant sexual acts, but those who were placed into forced labor were no less slaves.

Slavery is alive and well in the United States, he thought wearily. Welcome to reality.

Just then his supervisor, Scotch Dorello, called to him on the walkie-talkie. "Time to hit the docks with the dogs," he announced.

Maybe fresh air would do him some good, he thought. Just a routine check of a few big boats, a quick search for drugs. With a million ways to smuggle drugs into the country, a bust would not staunch the flow. But God help him, it would be fewer drugs for his son, Michael, his daughter, Melanie, his nieces and nephews and all their friends to face.

The dogs were ready. Mulkey and Frenchy, named after two downed fire fighters from the Charleston area, pranced happily beside him, their full tales wagging back and forth over their backs.

He knew the captain of the first ship. John Smith, a descendant of the Captain John Smith who had helped settle early America. While Scotch talked to the captain, he let the dogs sniff around the upper decks and then each of the lower decks. Each inspection took about an hour.

After the third boat, he was ready to take a lunch break, but Scotch wanted to inspect one more ship. It was named The Cortez and the manifest said it was from Brazil.

As soon as the dogs hit the top deck, Mulkey went crazy. She picked up a scent mid-deck and, nose down, followed the scent to the railing of the vessel.

Scotch, who had been talking to the captain, began watching the dogs.

Craig was puzzled. If drugs had been thrown overboard, why would only Mulkey react? Frenchy should be reacting, too.

But he didn't have time to think about it. When he turned to mention it to Scotch, he saw in horror that the captain of the ship had pulled a gun on his boss. Scotch, still watching the dogs, didn't have a clue.

Without even thinking, Craig grabbed his gun and, pulling the trigger, shot the captain in the head, killing him. The first mate pulled his own illegal weapon, but training took over and Craig whipped his Glock to the right and shot the first mate as well.

It was over in a matter of seconds. The rest of the crew had no weapons, or if they did, they weren't about to show them. Those few who had been watching, lost no time in busying themselves somewhere else.

Scotch recovered quickly and called for backup. In less than four minutes, Craig knew, the dock would be swarming with agents, police officers, and security.

"Hey, Scotch," he called. Scotch moved his direction, thanks on his lips, but Craig cut him off.

"Mulkey worked with the police force for a while. I think she's onto something besides drugs. Try to hold off the questioning for a few minutes while I see where she goes."

Mulkey had been whining and trying to nudge Craig up some stairs by the captain's quarters. Frenchy watched his companion with an inquisitive look on his face and his head cocked to one side.

"Okay, girl. We don't have much time." He followed the impatient dog up the stairs toward the quarters of the radio man was Craig's guess.

The door was locked. He put his shoulder to the door, not wanting to shoot it open without knowing what was on the other side. He wouldn't want to cause an explosion.

Fortunately, the door gave on the second try and he stared into the faces of nine Mexican girls cowering back into the corners. They had the terrified looks of trapped animals on their faces.

"Scotch, now," Craig said into his radio. He slowly, very slowly and deliberately put his gun back in its holster and crouched low so he was not towering over the girls, intimidating them even more.

"Are you alright?" he asked in Spanish.

One girl nodded slowly.

As Scotch approached, without turning, Craig waved for him to slow down.

"Madre de Dios," Scotch muttered. "Let me get Lucy here. She'll know what to say, what questions to ask."

He called on his radio for agent Lucy Buenuevo. "Craig, they've got two dead bodies to process and a crew to round up, and they're calling for you. I'll post a guard here until Lucy arrives."

Craig looked at the terrified girls. Somehow he had to comfort them with his very limited Spanish. "Es bueno, es bueno," he said and hoped they understood.

He stood and moved with resignation to where the bodies were located. He hated this part of his job. Already agents had painted around the bodies and bagged their hands. He noticed the guns the men had held had been bagged as well.

The next thirty minutes he patiently answered the questions asked of him, the two dogs sitting quietly beside him. He saw Lucy arrive, her dark hair down and dressed in some kind of Hawaiian outfit. Obviously, it had been her day off.

Scotch finally rescued him by telling the coroner he was needed with the girls.

"What do they need? Isn't Lucy getting the information from them?" he asked rather testily. His patience was wearing thin.

"Actually, I thought you needed the break," said Scotch, clapping a large hand on his shoulder.

"Thanks, man," said Craig, a weary grin stretching across his face. He squatted beside Lucy and just listened as she talked to the girls.

One girl seemed to be the spokeswoman for the group. Craig discovered her name was Esperanza. He picked up enough to understand that they had been kidnapped. Slowly, Lucy wormed out of them what they had overheard about being sold as prostitutas.

Selena, the one most obviously endowed began sobbing quietly. When she broke down, the dam of reserve broke, and the other girls began sobbing, too.

Through their tears, both Craig and Lucy finally picked up the name they kept repeating: Maria. At first Craig thought they were calling on the Holy Mother Mary, but slowly Esperanza told of Maria's cold-blooded murder.

"I'll bet that's the body washed up in Texas," he muttered.

Another half hour passed before the girls quieted.

"So where do we take them?" he asked. "The detention center?"

Lucy rounded on him. "Absolutely not. They are not criminals. They need food and baths and decent beds to sleep in tonight, and I know someone who might be able to help," she said hotly.

"But we need to keep tabs on them," protested Scotch.

"That's true, but I'm not going to have them terrorized any more than they've already been. We don't need a repeat of last year when that Mexican girl they found in a daze wandering the streets committed suicide. They locked her up as if she had committed a crime."

Lucy stopped to take a breath and glared at Craig. She punched a few buttons on her phone.

"Hi, Bonnie. Lucy here. I have nine girls from Mexico who need hot baths, cool sheets, and a kind touch. Can you accommodate them? Okay. Got it. No I can't repeat the directions. I've got an audience. But I'll be there in about an hour."

Looking at Craig, she added, "They just finished preparing this home for such a situation. We are so lucky today. "

Esperanza, who had been following her words closely, shook her head. "No luck. Es Dio."

Lucy lapsed back into Spanish, explaining to the girls that she was going to personally take them to a private home where they would be cared for. Then she looked at Craig.

"We need to discuss prosecution. With the perpetrators dead, I'm going to guess the rest of the crew knows nothing. In that case, we will have nothing to prosecute, so these girls will need to be reunited with their families. Can you make sure I'm kept up to date on this?"

Craig agreed to do so. He knew why sometimes victims had to be kept in prison until their testimony in a court of law could be heard by a judge.

But he sure didn't have to agree with it. He hoped more people like Bonnie would be willing to offer their homes and services to help children like these ones.

So much for being tired of his job. He was willing to have a few more boring days now. He walked to where the dogs sat patiently. Mulkey and Frenchy would go home with him tonight where they would get plenty of treats, love, and attention from little Caden.

Chapter Seven

"Earth to Gina." With a start, Gina realized she wasn't in Virginia meeting the Peters-Templeton family or going to the White House for dinner. And it certainly wasn't summer.

"You must be really tired, Babe," said Corey. Four months ago she would have taken umbrage at the endearment, but it barely registered now.

"Yes, I am," admitted Gina.

"I was wondering if you would like to go out to the farm in Walterboro with us to visit your grandparents."

"Oh, yes. I'll take any chance I get to visit them. Besides, Gram might be able to use some help in the kitchen for Thanksgiving."

"It's settled, then," said Corey, turning to Bob. "Let's drop your things off at the bed and breakfast, and then you can ride with us."

When they arrived at Flowertown Bed & Breakfast, Veronique, the proprietress was only too happy to accommodate Bob. While Corey explained the extra security, Gina admired Veronique's decorating flair, especially the black and white toile wallpaper in Bob's room and the fine French pieces of furniture that had once belonged to Veronique's grandmere.

"The extra security will make us feel very safe around here," Veronique joked.

Before they left, Bob made one more trip to his vehicle. He returned carrying something wrapped in a towel.

"Do you think your grandparents would take care of this for me?" he asked Gina, carefully lifting a corner of the towel and revealing a beautiful, white Siamese kitten.

"Oh, how sweet!" she exclaimed. "Of course they will. Let me hold her. What's her name?"

"Her name is Bianca. She has a brother named Butterball, but I couldn't find him. I hope he somehow escaped the explosion, but it's not likely."

Gina insisted that Bob sit in front with Corey on their way to the farm while she cuddled in the back with Bianca. She had so much to consider before Harry arrived tomorrow.

She realized she didn't want to think about it, really. It was stressing her. Instead, she thought about Gram and Gramps Merrill.

They weren't really her grandparents. They were Chelsea's. But her grandparents on her mother's side had passed away when she was too young to remember them.

Grandma and Grandpa Galbraith were great friends with the Merrills, so whenever the Merrill clan got together, the Galbraiths were always invited.

It happened so frequently that over the years, she and Gwen, her brother, Gordon, and her cousins, Geoffrey and Justin had come to think of them as their grandparents, too. In fact, Chelsea's aunts and uncles on her father's side were considered Gina's aunts and uncles, as well.

The farm had belonged to Grandpa Will's parents, Allan and Laura Merrill. Now, Great-Grandma Laura lived there with Grandpa Will and Grandma Mary.

When they pulled up to the farmhouse, Gina was reminded of a Thomas Kinkade painting. Light poured out of nearly every window, glowing softly against the early night of winter, highlighting the white of the four, two-story columns that graced the front of the house.

Gram was at the kitchen door at the side of the house to welcome them, in spite of the chill in the air, giving them all hugs, even their attorney, Bob. She was wearing a cheerful red apron with a Thanksgiving cornucopia cross-stitched on the bib.

She had a spatula in one hand which meant she had just pulled a batch of cookies from the oven. Gina sniffed. She could smell the cinnamon already. Yep. They were oatmeal raisin cookies, her favorite.

Gina quickly showed Gram the tiny white kitten. Gram, used to such lost souls, retrieved a basket for Bianca, and soon the kitten left the comfort of the basket to sniff at the bowls of food and water. She began eating ravenously.

"She'll be fine," said Gram. "Let's get some cookies."

With a last look at Bianca, Gina crossed to the cabinet and pulled out small plates and glasses. As Gram removed the rest of the cookies from the cookie sheet, she poured milk into the glasses.

Each of them placed a few cookies on their plates and moved to the den where Gramps was watching a show on the Discovery channel. He turned it off quickly and stood to his full six-foot, four-inch height. Gina was reminded once again that he had been a star basketball player in both high school and college.

Gramps reached for Bob's hand as if to shake it, and Gram grabbed the other one. "Your wife?" he asked simply.

Gina realized all at once that her grandparents were even more afraid to hear that Bob's wife had perished in the explosion—they must have seen the news on TV—than they were of losing the farm.

"She's fine."

"God be praised," said Gramps. He had tears in his eyes as did Gram.

"We put together a safety plan several years ago. It was enacted today. However, I must warn you that the media does not know, and I'd prefer if you didn't say a word."

"The media gets their facts wrong all the time," sputtered Gramps. "They kept representing our case wrong until I set them straight," he said, satisfaction in his voice.

"Now, dear," said Gram. She tugged on his arm until he reseated himself in his chair. She sat, too, next to Gina on the sofa.

"We suspected you might not know the true state of affairs. That's why Corey wanted to bring me out here tonight. It is a shock to lose most of our immediate belongings. But Belinda had already stored suitcases of clothes and essentials in the trunk of our spare car. She and the children are in a safe place."

"Is the cleanup here on the farm finished?" asked Corey. He had been there when the first letter had arrived and the first inspection of their property had occurred.

Once again, Gina's mind spun back to their first trip to Virginia. Corey had flown them back home. Uncle Davey, Chelsea's father, had met them at the small airport in the old, green family van. He brought it out of retirement when it was more practical to use than taking two cars.

Gina was shocked to hear Corey ask if he might tag along as his father wanted him to look at some real estate in Summerville and Charleston.

"Just give me a few minutes to get my plane into a hangar. I won't be long."

By the time her father had stowed the luggage in the back, Corey had returned.

Once again, Corey sat by Gina in the seat directly behind Uncle Davey and Aunt Galeah. The girls behind her were already chattering animatedly. Gina, however, could immediately sense the worry in Uncle Davey and so did Aunt Galeah.

Taking the direct approach, Aunt Galeah asked, "What's wrong?"

"Something to do with the farm," said Uncle Davey. He turned to include Gloria as well as Gina and Corey in the conversation.

"Dad showed up at our house with a letter, and Mom was with him. Both of them were very upset, and Mom was near to tears."

"And they wouldn't tell you anything?"

"Not a word. They're waiting at the house for us now. He wants everyone present, so all the siblings are on their way right now."

"Oh, dear. That sounds serious."

"I think it is," said Uncle Davey. "Not much upsets mom. If she's shaken, something bad is headed our way, I'm afraid."

Shaking off the gloomy mood, he asked, "So how was the trip?"

"Chelsea dragged us all over town yesterday, but she's decided on both her dress and the bridesmaids' dresses, so I think she feels less anxious about pulling off a wedding in five months."

"If I know our Chelsea girl, she'll have the entire affair organized within a month," Uncle Davey said chuckling.

Gina thought about her upcoming wedding guiltily. She and Harry hadn't really set a date yet although they had discussed an April wedding. She had wanted to finish school and get into teaching before she contemplated the next big step in her life.

Corey's mind must have been traveling along the same lines, for he turned to her and asked quietly when she and Harry were planning to marry.

"We've set a tentative date for April," Gina answered rather haughtily.

"Oh? Why the wait?"

"I wanted to finish school and begin teaching first," she began to explain, but his raised eyebrow stopped her.

"Why are you looking at me like that?" she asked.

"I always thought when you met the love of your life you'd want to get married as soon as possible or at least move in together."

"How do you know Harry doesn't live with me?" Gina asked, stung by his reply.

"Gina!" her mother said, shocked.

"I'm just giving an example," Gina said trying to defend herself. She looked at Uncle Davey and Aunt Galeah. They seemed absorbed in their own conversation.

"That's okay," said Corey. "It just gives me more time."

"More time for what?" asked Gina.

"More time to find the most extravagant wedding gift I can," he said.

Well, that would be just like him, thought Gina. Dating and discarding girls, and then when they finally found someone and married, sending an impossibly wasteful and elaborate gift.

Fortunately, she was already engaged, so her heart would never be his to discard.

They pulled into the Merrill's driveway in downtown Summerville. Gina found her father's car amongst those also parked in the circular driveway in front of the garage and bunkhouse. Uncle Garret and Aunt Grace, Uncle Craig and Aunt Clara, and Uncle Phillip and Aunt Sarah must be here too, she thought when she saw the rest of the cars.

Several of her cousins, Michael, Paul, Phil Jr., Geoffrey and Justin, were kicking around a soccer ball on the front lawn. As soon as they saw the car, they stowed the ball and came to help with the luggage.

The luggage placed in various cars and bedrooms, everyone assembled in the living room. Normally, they met on the spacious screened porch for family gatherings, but the summer humidity was already creating a stifling heat outside.

The living room was a long room with one entire end devoted to a television, stereo system and other electronic systems hidden in two large, matching, antique armoires.

A baby grand piano stood at the other end with several open music books on the rack and a pair of pink flip flops on the floor by the pedals attesting to its regular use.

The golds and reds of the Queen Anne styled wingback chairs and sofa were caught again in the beautiful area rug that graced the space in the center of this seating arrangement.

A bouquet of yellow tulips sat in the middle of a small coffee table. Various other chairs as well as the piano stool had been requisitioned to seat all the family members; the youngest sat on emerald, ruby, and sapphire jewel-toned cushions on the floor.

Corey pulled Uncle Davey aside and said quietly, "If you'll give me a recommendation for a rental car, I'll just leave quietly. I didn't know your family would be meeting today."

"Nonsense," said Uncle Davey. "Your brother is marrying my daughter, so you are already part of this family. Besides, we may need your expertise in real estate matters if this is about the farm. Please stay."

"If you're sure," said Corey politely.

"Of course," said Uncle Davey clapping him on the shoulder.

As soon as she entered the house, Gina had run upstairs to the playroom to scoop up Caden and hold him close. She buried her face against the little golden curls on his head, realizing that she had missed her small son immensely.

"Mommy!" Caden squealed. His arms wrapped around her holding her tightly, squeezing her heart as well.

She came down the stairs with him in time to hear Corey's conversation with Uncle Davey.

Gina thought that if she hadn't heard this exchange, she would have been angry at Corey for barging in where he wasn't wanted.

Fair is fair, she thought to herself. Even though she was upset with him for his insensitivity about her wedding date, she couldn't fault his courtesy now.

Corey sat across the room from Gina in the corner beside the piano. He had a view of all the occupants in the room; he had found that sitting back and watching people's faces in a meeting gave him an edge in understanding them better both in business and in interpersonal relationships.

"Grandpa Will is going to pray now," he heard Gina say quietly to Caden. He appreciated the tableau they made with the lamp shining down on them, Gina with the sweet look of a Madonna on her face as they both closed their eyes.

Grandpa Will, as was his usual habit, opened their family meeting with prayer. Mercifully, he was brief since everyone was on tenterhooks to know what was happening.

"This all began Friday when I was in town meeting my friends for breakfast as I do every Friday morning. Some men from the County came out to the farm and nearly scared Gram here to death. Tell us what they did, dear," he said looking at Gram.

"How many men were there?" asked Uncle Craig to get her started when she hesitated.

"Three. One was the spokesperson. That was Jeremy Saxon. Some of you know him, I think. He had two really big men with him, dressed all in black and carrying guns. I thought they were going to haul me off to jail right then and there. They had a kind of mean look in their eyes."

"What did they say?" asked Uncle Garret who was on the police force for North Charleston. Aunt Grace was in forensics.

"They wanted to know if I was the owner of the property. Of course I said yes right away since Grandma Laura had it put in our names last year," she said, looking at her husband.

"They showed me some papers, saying they had come to inspect the property. I didn't know what to do and your Grandpa wasn't there, so I let them."

"Egregious oafs," muttered Gina's father, Galen, the professor in the group. "They knew Gramps wasn't there. I'll bet a two-dollar bill on that."

"Did you walk around with them?" asked Uncle Craig. "What were they looking for?"

"I couldn't keep up with them, they walked so fast. I gave up and went back to the house."

"How long did they stay?" asked Uncle Garret.

"Only about fifteen minutes. They walked so fast, it seemed as if they knew what they had come to see."

"Does anyone know what they wanted? Maybe they were looking for some escaped convict or something," said Uncle Davey.

"No. I have the letter right here," said Gramps with a great sense of timing. He waved a letter in the air over his head.

"What letter is that?" asked Uncle Davey.

"It's the follow up letter and bill for inspecting our property."

"A bill? For doing an inspection that you didn't request? That's crazy!" stated Uncle Phil. "Furthermore, it smacks to me of a violation of your Fourth Amendment rights under the Constitution." He taught history when he wasn't helping to coach the Summerville High School football team.

"That's right!" "You tell them, Uncle Phil!" "Well-said, brother!" came the various murmurs of agreement from the group.

Gramps held up his hand for peace. "Let me read it to you," he said.

When he was finished, the group sat in stunned silence. Then the questions and comments ran wild.

Chapter Eight

"Let me read that once again," said Uncle Davey, grabbing the letter from his father's hand.

The top of the page said Colleton County, Municipal Services Agency, Department of Neighborhood Services, Code Enforcement Division.

"Services," my foot, thought Uncle Davey.

Under these words and the county logo were the words "NOTICE OF VIOLATION," in all caps.

By this time, Uncle Craig and Uncle Garrett had crowded around Uncle Davey so they, too, could read the letter with their own eyes.

"Since when does Colleton County have a 'Department of Neighborhood Services?'" asked Uncle Craig.

Under the NOTICE OF VIOLATION were the names of the owners, Will and Mary Merrill, and their address as well as a Case Number and the date.

Uncle Craig and Uncle Davey read aloud together: "The following violation(s) of Hampton County Rebeautification Ordinance were observed at the above-referenced property, creating a public nuisance. The owner(s) has two weeks to address and correct the violation(s), at which time another inspection will be performed."

"This action has resulted in cost for the county. The property owner will be held responsible for all inspection fees and costs incurred by the county. It is to your advantage to correct the violation. You will receive your billing notice(s) with the specific amount of cost incurred in a separate mailing."

"How can they fine us for a violation when we weren't even aware of any codes or laws or whatever?" exploded Lawton, Grandpa Will's oldest grandson and Chelsea's brother.

"That's a very good question, Son," answered Uncle Davey. "We need to find out why we haven't heard of any such codes or bylaws before."

"So what are the violations again?" asked Uncle Phil.

"Abandoned structure with collapsing roof and structural instability, piles of...."

"They must mean the old cow shed that Grandpa Allan built when he actually had cows," said Uncle Garrett, interrupting.

"That was over twelve years ago," said Uncle Craig. "All of us used that cow's milk for our kids. I remember going out to the farm every Saturday to help Dad and Mom, but also to pick up several gallons of milk and whatever produce was available."

"That sure helped out with our food budgets," said Uncle Davey, agreeing. He and Uncle Craig each had four children, all present with the exception of Chelsea who was still in the D.C. area.

"It's not structurally unsound," protested Uncle Phil. "I helped build it myself."

"We'll have to talk to Jeremy and find out what he means by that. It does need a new roof though. Some shingles came off last summer during all those afternoon thunderstorms we had," said Uncle Davey.

He held up his hand for quiet and began reading again: "Piles of rubbish, including but not limited to, tires and yard debris..."

"Don't they know town folk will use those tires as containers for growing vegetables? Everything is recyclable and reusable," commented Aunt Grace. "I've even used a few from the farm for the squash in my backyard."

"Yard debris?" sputtered Uncle Davey. Of all the siblings, he went out to the farm to work most often, saying it was a good break for him from all the computer programming he did.

"Yard debris?" he said again. "We break up all the branches and dead wood from the trees and burn them in the fireplaces and the stove during the winter. Saves a bundle on your electric bill in the winter, doesn't it, Dad?"

"Sure does, Son," responded Grandpa Will.

"Anything else on that list?" asked Uncle Garret.

"Just non-functioning vehicles and farm equipment," read Uncle Davey.

"When was the last time we cranked up Grandpa Allen's old tractor? Hasn't it been at least ten years? By now it should be considered an antique," commented Uncle Phil.

"I was the last one to crank up that old tractor," said Uncle Davey. I plowed the cornfield with it, and just as I was driving back to the barn, it died."

"Dad and I left it where it was," piped up Lawton, "but we worked on it all summer trying to get it working again. We had to borrow Gouvenor North's tractor to plow the other fields and his tiller in the fall."

Lawton had been in his early teens then and very interested in engines and how they worked.

"The tractor, the hay rake, and the tiller should all be considered antiques," said Aunt Clara thoughtfully. "Surely exceptions can be made for those."

"What about the other vehicles?" asked Uncle Galen. "Grandpa Allan has five old Nashes from the fifties parked on the 'back forty' as he used to call it."

"We could probably sell them to collectors and use the money to pay for the fees," said Uncle Garret.

"We are not paying the fees," said Grandpa Will stubbornly. "They came on the property, scaring my wife half to death in direct violation of our Constitutional rights," he said, pulling a small booklet from his front pocket.

"Here. Read this," he said to Uncle Davey.

"This is a copy of the Constitution," said Uncle Davey, looking at the front cover, "and this is the Fourth Amendment: 'The right of the people to be secure in their persons, houses, papers, and effects, against unreasonable searches and seizures, shall not be violated, and no Warrants shall issue, but upon probable cause, supported by Oath or affirmation, and particularly describing the place to be searched, and the persons or things to be seized.'"

"Did they have a warrant, Mom?" asked Clara.

"I don't know. They were holding papers, but they didn't give me a chance to really look at them," said Gram.

"So what are we going to do about all of this? Do we hire an attorney or do it ourselves? We have a lot of work to do." He ran his fingers through his hair in frustration.

"I think we need to take two approaches to this," said Uncle Galen thoughtfully. "First, I think we do need to clean up the property better, not because the County is after us, but because it's a trust, a heritage left to us by Grandpa Allan and Grandpa Will here can't do it all himself."

"I'm with you," said Uncle Phil. "But I think it needs to be all of us, including the grandkids." He looked around on the group.

A chorus of agreement met his remark. All the grandkids loved the farm. It had been an integral part of their childhoods.

Gina could remember the aunts canning the fruits and vegetables several times each summer that Gramps with the help of the uncles had grown. She had been Gramps shadow, tending to the orchards, the fields, the animals.

She looked around at the group and knew that each one of them had special memories of the farm and, more importantly, of the relationships built with each other as they worked together there.

"What's the second part of your plan, Galen?" asked Garret.

"We need to do some investigation of this Department of Neighborhood Services. Something doesn't sit right with me about this whole thing. I mean, why did they wait until Dad was in town with his buddies, why did Jeremy Saxon bring two armed men with him, and what gives them the right to come on the property unannounced like that?"

"Great points, every one of them," said Uncle Garret. "We should probably set up an appointment with Jeremy right away. Can everyone take off, say next Wednesday or Thursday? I'll call Monday and set up an appointment with him, but I think all of us need to hear what he has to say."

"Jeremy Saxon knows we have three police officers in our family," said Uncle Galen, looking at Uncle Craig who was in Homeland Security and Garret and Grace, who both worked for North Charleston Police Department, Garret on the force and Grace in forensics, "so he wouldn't do what he did unless he felt he could."

"That's a good point, Galen," said Grace. "I never did like Jeremy Saxon when we were growing up. He was mean to younger kids and had a chip on his shoulder. But he's not a fool. Who's backing him? That's what I'd like to know."

"What day is everyone available?" asked Uncle Garret again.

"Before we decide that, maybe we should consider taking off several days so we can get this job done faster. Many hands make light work," said Uncle Phil.

"So who's going to do some background investigation for us?" asked Uncle Galen.

Galeah, Lawton, Gordon, and Paul immediately volunteered.

"I don't have to return to work at the school until August, so I have time," said Galeah. "And Lawton, Gordon, and Paul are all awesome on digging up information on the computer. I think we'll make a great team!"

Everyone agreed.

"So now how about if we arrange some work days at the farm?" asked Galen. "This notice says we have two weeks. Can everyone go out to the farm tomorrow afternoon?"

"Let's all meet out there after church and bring our food with us," suggested Gloria.

"Wait. Time out," called Uncle Phil. "Before you women start discussing the food, shouldn't someone make a list of all the jobs that need to be done?"

"I'll do that," said Uncle Davey. "I've been out there more and know what needs to be done. Plus, we still have crops to help Dad harvest."

He turned to his dad. "You get around pretty well for an old man, Dad, but I still think you could use some help."

Gramps snorted. "I can always use help. Won't ever turn any away, that's for sure," he said. He had a gleam of satisfaction in his eyes.

Corey, watching, realized this meeting had gone exactly how he had wanted it to go.

Uncle Davey raised his hand for silence again. "Before we do anything else, I'd like to have Corey give us his opinion. He's Jasper's brother, as most of you know, and he and his dad are in real estate. What are your thoughts, Son?" asked Uncle Davey.

"I think to be on the safe side, you should hire an attorney. However, you should probably look for a Constitutional attorney, and if I remember correctly, those are few in number and extremely expensive."

"How expensive?" asked Uncle Phil.

"The retainer fee will probably be in the neighborhood of seven or eight thousand dollars, with a minimum of fifty thousand in expenses incurred."

"Whew!" said some while others whistled.

"It's a lot of money," admitted Corey. "But I'll talk to my dad. He'll know some good attorneys or at least be able to get recommendations. Maybe you could promise him some produce from the farm for the next ten years," he added to lighten the somber mood.

A few of them chuckled, but most of them were too angry and frustrated to see the humor in what he had said.

Aunt Galeah, Gloria, Aunt Grace, and Aunt Clara stepped out to the kitchen where Grace, Clara, and Grams had placed the food they had brought.

Clara had thoughtfully brought two coolers full of sweet tea since Galeah had been out of town.

Gram had brought seven dozen homemade chocolate chip and oatmeal raisin cookies while Grace had made a lime jello, Cool Whip cake.

Just then, Uncle Davey entered the kitchen. He kissed his wife hello, and then opened the refrigerator with a flourish. "I bought two peach pies and some vanilla ice cream this morning when Dad called this meeting. Aren't you proud of me for thinking ahead?"

"You're the best, Honey! That's why I married you!" She gave him a huge hug.

Gina had taken a sleeping, worn out Caden upstairs and put him on Chelsea's old bed. Entering the kitchen to help set out the cups and napkins, she was just in time to hear them, and she grinned.

She enjoyed watching the affection they displayed. Her parents were a little more reserved. She hoped she would develop that kind of unembarrassed playfulness in her relationship with Harry.

Oh heavens! She had totally forgotten about Harry. He was supposed to call tonight from somewhere overseas. He never would tell her where he was; he said he didn't want to worry her.

She had asked him once how she would ever find out about it if he was killed in his line of work. He had assured her that his boss would let her know, but that he didn't plan to die for at least fifty more years.

Idly, she wondered how news about the farm would affect him. He was a city boy and didn't seem to care much for it. Did he realize how much it meant to her?

She re-entered the living room and saw several of her uncles talking to Corey. In spite of the huge house in which he had grown up and his real estate deals all over the world for his father's business, she suspected he would be just as comfortable in Gram's kitchen or working in the field with her dad.

Chapter Nine

And he was. Following church the next day, the families reconvened at the farm. Gina was surprised to see Corey walking beside her Uncle Davey carrying two boxes of Krispy Krunch Chicken.

The day was warm, but the mugginess had been chased away by a breeze that danced in the tall trees along the curving drive and around the house.

Gram chose to set up everything except the drinks along the far end of the screened porch where the largest magnolia tree Corey had ever seen provided ample shade.

The table was laden with the fried chicken, mashed potatoes and gravy, and coleslaw from Krispy Krunch, but also with a new black-eyed pea salad Aunt Clara had wanted to try on everyone.

They all agreed that the cold black-eyed peas, tomato, green onion, cucumber, pasta, and dill tossed with a warm vinaigrette of olive oil, bacon bits, sugar and vinegar tasted awesome.

Gram had plenty of corn on the cob from the garden, and Aunt Grace brought two huge watermelons on ice. Aunt Sarah contributed two blackberry cobblers, and the Galbraiths brought vanilla bean ice cream to complement them. With the gallons of southern sweet tea that Aunt Galeah brought, the meal was complete.

Corey tried to find a spot to sit near Gina, but she was preoccupied, first with serving everyone their drinks and then with feeding Caden.

Following the meal, Uncle Davey quickly organized the family into teams to tackle the outside work.

Lawton, Paul and Gordon had brought their laptops, hoping to be able to look up information about this new Rebeautification Ordinance. Galeah, still recovering from the trip, was happy to stay inside in the cool. In fact, the migraine headache she developed became so bad that Gram finally persuaded her to lie down upstairs.

That left Geoffrey, Justin, Michael and PJ to climb on the roof of the old barn and begin removing shingles. Uncle Will was going to order the tar paper, shingles, roofing nails, and two nail guns the next day.

The girls were requisitioned to work on breaking up piles of branches and stacking them neatly in boxes. These would be stored in the spacious garage/workroom and used for kindling and firewood in the three fireplaces in the winter.

The uncles and Corey went toward the rear of the property to check on the old cars. They had been covered with tarps for the last ten or fifteen years but had been exposed to the elements before that, so they didn't know what they would find when they pulled back the tarps.

They found a lot of rust and a great deal of deterioration of seats and floor boards, but for having sat open to wind, rain, humidity and the occasional snow or ice storm, they were in good condition.

The tires, or what was left of them, were sunk into ground that had hardened around them.

"We'll have to soak the soil," said Uncle Garret, looking critically at the soil and kicking at a tire.

"The spickot is over there," said Uncle Davey, pointing in a southerly direction. "I'll have to get one of the boys to drag a hose out here."

They heard some whooping and hollering from the direction of the barn.

"We'd better go check on the lads and make sure they don't break any bones or their mothers will be putting us in dog houses for the next week," said Uncle Craig jokingly.

They found the boys having the time of their lives. Corey decided to join them. Seeing a bar positioned over the top of the door at the far end of the barn, he pulled himself up and then flipped his body up onto the roof.

"How'd you do that?" asked PJ in amazement.

"Leverage," explained Corey. "And upper body strength. You should be able to do it," he said, noticing that PJ was well-muscled from working out in the school weight room.

"Go ahead. Try it," he urged PJ.

Soon all of the cousins were practicing it instead of working on the shingles. Michael saw Uncle Garret and Uncle Galen come out of the house where they had gone to get some iced water.

"We'd better get back to work," he said, nudging Geoffrey and Justin and pointing toward the house.

They buckled down, and began working with enthusiasm, Corey throwing shingles over the edge of the roof with the rest of them. The work was hot and sweaty, and soon they had shed their shirts, not caring if they became sunburned.

Gina had chosen to stay inside, putting away the leftovers and washing up the dishes with Gram. She had put Caden down for his afternoon nap and wanted to keep an eye on him.

She and Gram smiled when they heard the boys shouting exuberantly.

"You should go take them some iced water," said Gram. "Go ahead. I'll listen for Caden."

They fixed a tray with glasses full of ice and water with a pitcher of more iced water, chilled from being in the refrigerator and a small bowl of sliced lemons and limes.

When Gina turned the corner and saw them on the roof, she had to stop and stare.

Corey truly was at home here, she thought in amazement. She remembered the magnificent home where he had grown up and dinner at the White House with all of the men in his family dressed to kill in dark suits.

Now she was seeing him with his shirt off, his tanned skin glistening in the sun, his muscles flexing and moving as he shoveled loose shingles and tossed them over the side of the barn.

She nearly admired those buff muscles, but then her thoughts screamed at her. No! He's just showing off.

He turned just then, catching her glance, and grinned at her in a mock-licentious manner.

"You're a sight for sore eyes," he said. "That water has my name on it."

He slid down the slanted roof on his feet as if he was skateboarding, grinning like a fool at her discomfiture. He jumped lightly to the ground in front of her and nonchalantly reached for a glass of water.

The rest of the boys came down a little more slowly and crowded around her, glad to be in the shade and enjoying the cool of the water.

Corey had clearly become their hero. They had been impressed with his brother, Jasper, when they discovered he was a Secret Service agent. But to Gina's disgust, they seemed to idolize Corey just as much.

She was about to take the empty glasses and pitcher back to the kitchen when Corey touched her arm.

"Go for a walk with me later when I get cleaned up?" he half-asked, half-commanded.

"Perhaps," said Gina. "I have a young son to care for, but if it works out, well, maybe," she said with a shrug.

Corey stared at her for a long moment. "Okay, Babe," he said. "Have it your way, for now."

Now what was that supposed to mean, Gina fumed as she headed for the kitchen. She didn't like this guy. Everything he said seemed to have a double meaning.

At times like this, she really wished Harry wasn't so much of an absentee fiancé. She could use his calm, reassuring presence. He was so… so uncomplicated compared to Corey.

By the time the afternoon waned and they were all ready for showers and more food, barely a dent had been made in the work.

Half of the barn roof had been de-shingled, and the girls had neatly stored ten boxes of kindling and wood in the garage for Gramps, but so much more needed to be done.

They took turns getting showers, but finally when most of them were assembled and munching on leftovers, this time in the family room, Corey was able to sit beside Gina on the floor as she helped Caden with his dinner.

He watched as she coxed Caden to eat some corn that she had sliced from the cob she was eating.

"Come on, Caden. You need to eat your corn," said Gina.

"I no want to," he responded.

He picked up each kernel with his fingers instead of using the small fork Gina had provided and squished the kernels between his fingers.

Corey had an idea. He picked up a kernel and put it on one of his teeth so he looked like he had a corn tooth. He did another and another, grinning widely at Caden with a corny smile and winking.

Caden clapped his hands together and laughed. Then he tried the same. Gina tried to look sternly at Corey, but he looked so funny with corn for teeth that she began smiling and then laughing, too.

When the rest of the family realized why Gina was laughing, they began laughing, as well.

Finally, Caden had eaten his fill. Gina was going to head upstairs with him for a bath, but Gwen stopped her.

"Let me. You know I love to play little games with him with all his bathtub toys."

Gina gladly acquiesced. She sat back with a sigh of relief.

The computer geeks went back to their computers. They seemed to be onto something they wanted to investigate. The men were content to sit and talk over what needed to still be done. They had helped harvest peaches after looking at the old cars.

The women began heading to the kitchen with miscellaneous plates, cups, and forks. Gina started to get up to help them, but Corey tugged on her wrist.

"Go for a walk with me?" he asked in a wheedling tone.

"Go ahead, Dear," said Gram. "You helped me all afternoon. Take a little break."

"Okay," said Gina.

Why not, she thought. She loved the farm, especially at dusk on summer evenings when the warm air was caressed by a cooling breeze, the birds were settling down for the night, chirping drowsily, and the scents of magnolias, tea trees, oak, and crepe myrtle blended with the aromas of the corn, okra, tomatoes and other fruits and vegetables growing there.

If she closed her eyes and concentrated, she could analyze and differentiate among all the smells, such as the roses and gardenias growing right beside the kitchen door on the west side of the house.

Beside her, Corey studied her face. She reminded him of his mother, tall with sun-beached blonde hair that she kept short since Caden's birth. When she opened her eyes, they were a very dark blue.

She had such beautiful eyes, he thought. Did she know it? Probably not. She seemed very unpretentious, but he was beginning to suspect that it resulted from a lack in self-confidence.

The driveway that wound gracefully among tall trees and circled back out to the road also continued on the west side of the house and past the back lawn, circled behind the house and to the east toward the barn.

Gram had a large vegetable garden to the west of this back drive. Past that was an orchard of peach, pear, and pecan trees with a few other varieties as well. To the left of the orchard was a quarter acre of corn.

Corey had seen the barn and the cars beyond it to the east. Now he wanted to see the garden and orchard. He started walking in that direction and Gina fell into step beside him.

"How long has this farm been in your family?" asked Corey.

"Grandpa Will's father bought it in the late 1950s. Someone in my family has farmed it ever since."

The peach trees were already laden with ripe fruit due to the extreme heat earlier in the summer. He had heard the aunts discussing when they were all coming out to the farm to can. Apparently, they canned enough for all five families plus the grandparents.

"Is this a good time to tell me about Caden's father? I don't want to spoil this perfect evening," said Corey.

The sun was setting before them, tingeing the clouds an apricot-rose color that faded to that magical soft lavender tint only seen in southern skies.

"Now is as good as any time," Gina said with a sigh. "It's a pretty typical story. It just hurt me because it's mine, my life. Jack and I began dating the end of our junior year. He said he loved me, would love me forever."

She hung her head. "We never thought a baby would result from our relationship. After all, Jack was always very careful to use protection."

Gina laughed bitterly. "I guess that was a blessing in disguise because I found out later that he had been a major player in his previous high school, but miraculously, I never caught any of his STDs even when Caden was conceived."

"He categorically refuses to claim Caden as his son which is fine with me. And he delighted in telling anyone who would listen about what a whore I was, always begging him for sex. He made my senior year a nightmare."

Corey grabbed her hand and tilted up her chin.

"He was your one and only wasn't he?"

Gina nodded. "I never slept with anyone else."

"He had a precious gift in that, a priceless pearl, and he threw it carelessly away, showing what a stupid, moronic prick he is."

Gina could only stare at his vehemence.

"Don't let his idiocy make you scurry for cover and cling to only what is safe in life. Dare to let go of the safety net, Gina," he said passionately.

Again, Gina could only stare. She didn't know what he was trying to say, but it sent shivers up her spine, shivers of excitement and fear.

Whoever he loved would never doubt it. He would tell her in a thousand ways both big and little. But she would have to be willing to follow him into danger, for he lived on the cutting edge of life.

Would he feel the same way when he had children? She didn't know, and she didn't want to stay around him long enough to discover the answer to that question.

Inside the house, Uncle Davey stepped into the front room to check on his wife and the computer gurus. Her headache had finally abated. They had turned the room with its antique furnishings into a command center. Lawton saw him and pulled his dad aside.

"We think we've found something on the Rebeautification Ordinance."

"What have you found, Son?"

"Do you know what Agenda 21 is?"

"No."

"Neither do I, but I think somehow it's tied to this Rebeautification Ordinance."

Chapter Ten

The weekend accelerated into a Monday. Aunt Galeah was still off from school library duties, and Uncle Galen wouldn't begin teaching until late August. Both Paul and Gordon, nineteen, had summer jobs until college began again in the fall.

Aunt Clara, too, was home. Uncle Craig made enough for her to be able to stay home. She had become the go-to aunt when anyone needed help during the day. She loved being in the middle of everything and was genuinely glad to help the others.

Corey flew back to Virginia early Monday morning. Gina didn't see him before he left. She still didn't understand what he'd meant when he'd said, 'Dare to let go of the safety net.' But she doubted she'd see him much, especially with school starting in about four weeks.

She had the morning off from the part time job she had at Wal-Mart, and she wanted desperately to sleep in, but Caden had other ideas.

"Breafust, breafust," he chanted in a sing-songy voice.

"Okay, Sweetie. Just wait while Momma mixes up the pancakes. It will only take a few minutes."

He loved "cake-cakes" right now and, strangely enough, bacon. Gina quickly poured some batter onto the steaming, hot surface of the griddle, and while that was cooking, she poured some apple juice into Caden's blue, Thomas the Train sippy cup.

They were finally in her new apartment—at least it was new to her. She had saved and saved and finally had enough for rent for two months. Mrs. Weathers had graciously waived the deposit since she had known Gina when she was in diapers.

Learning how to do everything on her own was scary sometimes, but she'd had only a few minor mishaps, like when she'd let the boiled eggs scorch while she was trying to find the toys for Caden's bath when they had first moved here.

She missed the comfort of her mother's kitchen with the smell of fine, gourmet coffee in the morning as well as her dad's presence and the occasional clearance of his throat as he perused the morning paper. This was a luxury he only had in the summer since he chose to teach all the early morning classes.

Her cell phone rang just as Gina was pouring the syrup on Caden's pancakes. In his eagerness to get to them, he nearly fell out of his high chair.

"Yes?" Gina asked breathlessly. She already knew it was Kielah.

"Mom and I still have a few things to buy at the mall before I leave for college, and I know you are still shopping for your apartment. Do you want to go with us?"

"What time are you leaving?" asked Gina, deftly refilling Caden's cup while she talked.

"Probably around ten. Lindy's still in bed."

"I don't know. I have to be at work at two this afternoon. And I have to have time to get Caden his lunch before I take him over to our house. Dad's going to watch him for me."

"Oh. That doesn't give us much time for shopping."

"Exactly. I'd better take a rain check, but thanks for asking, Kielah."

She knew from experience that between spending the time it took for her to unload Caden's stroller and keeping him from damaging any items in the stores they visited, she would have precious little time for actual shopping.

Other girls who didn't have kids had no clue. Besides, she couldn't really buy anything right now. She had to watch every dollar. But it was kind of Kielah to think of her.

If she hadn't allowed herself to be led astray by Jack, she would have been able to enjoy her college years. She stifled thoughts of envy over Kielah's excitement.

She had only felt trepidation when she had enrolled in college. With a small baby at home, even with the help of her family in caring for him, she'd had very little faith in herself that she could really get a degree.

And forget all the activities in which a student could engage. She rushed home after her final class each day, feeling guilty for having to rely on family to help her.

She sighed and finished making the pancakes. The leftovers would freeze well for tomorrow's breakfast. She had already learned that at least.

She wanted to look over the curriculum and lesson plans the outgoing teacher, Miss Kennedy, had given her. But the morning was cool enough to take Caden to the small park around the corner. She would do that instead.

Gina never noticed the two men in the car who watched her and her little boy with interest.

*****

Uncle Craig, meanwhile, was once again unhappy with his workplace. This time it wasn't due to boredom. Counseling? Really?

Yes, of course, he had killed two men, he told the sympathetic counselor who looked like she had just stepped off a college campus. It was clearly a case of kill or watch his supervisor get killed, minimum damage.

How did it make him feel? What was he supposed to say? Should he tell this young woman a story? She was probably gullible enough to believe him if he told her that he was miserable with grief over it and couldn't sleep at nights.

But the truth was, he felt like a hero. He felt as if he had made a difference in the lives of nine little girls from Mexico. And he really couldn't take much credit. Mulkey should get the most credit for his incredible nose.

Training had accomplished the rest. If he hadn't been trained to view everyone around him as a potential threat in a crisis situation, he would not have sensed the first mate's evil intent. The first mate's gun had been moving toward him. He had just pulled the trigger faster.

Should he feel guilty? He refused.

The next blow came when he returned to his office. Suspended with pay? Why? They had to investigate the shooting, make sure it was justified.

Just a matter of following protocol, Scotch said. Protocol be hanged. But then it occurred to him that now he would have ample time to work on the farm.

"I do have a job for you to do, unofficially of course," said Scotch with a twinkle in his eye. "You're going to like this one, I think."

"What is it?" asked Craig warily, not trusting the look on Scotch's face.

"I can't be sure, but I don't think we are going to have a case on the double shooting. And even if we did, we really would only need that oldest girl, what was her name?, to testify."

"Esperanza," said Craig automatically. Translated Faith. And she sure did have faith in el Dio that He would rescue her and the rest of the girls. He could see in her eyes her unwavering belief and awe that el Dio had actually heard her prayers. It was remarkable in her and personally challenging to him all at the same time.

"…they'll need to go back to Tampico," he tuned in to hear what Scotch was saying. "Lucy will be the official liaison, and a DSS (Department of Social Services) worker is flying with her. But I want you to fly with them just as back up for Lucy."

"Yeah. Lucy's going to be in her element around all those Spanish-speaking folk. She loves talking to people, and this is going to be right up her alley, you can bet," responded Craig. "So when do we leave?"

"Lucy wants it done as quickly as possible. A fund was set up to fly the girls home and to raise more funds for Bonnie's home thanks to the media."

"Hah! The media gets it right sometimes," said Craig although, truth to tell, they only had one station in their area that tended to sensationalize things.

"Lucy's thinking Wednesday, Thursday at the latest."

"Okay. I can do that."

"Now comes the hard part," said Scotch. "I have to take your gun and badge since you're not on active duty."

"You can't send me to Mexico without my gun," Craig said protesting vehemently. "Come on, Scotch."

"I told you this was going to be hard. I'm going to try to get them both back for you before you leave. That's why I'm holding out for Thursday. But in case I don't, you have guns at home, don't you? And if you ever tell anyone I asked you that question, I will deny it."

"Yes, of course," said Craig.

"Well, there you go. And I really am going to try to get them back, especially your badge. I want you to go officially, but if you can't go officially, I just want you there."

Craig nodded. Call it male chauvinism if you pleased, but he and Scotch were old-fashioned. They would never let two women go into that situation alone even if

Lucy was a crack shot and could take care of herself in most situations.

"We've only hit the tip of the iceberg with this situation," Scotch continued, "and I've got a feeling we're going to run into some big, bad hombres before this is all over," he said gravely.

"I'll take care of the girls. You just get me back my gun and my badge."

"I'll call Tuesday night," said Scotch.

They clapped each other on the back.

Craig packed anything he didn't want prying eyes to see and, after turning off his computer, he walked out of the office to his souped-up Ford Explorer.

Hey, on the bright side, he could surprise Clara and take her out for lunch. He would even go to Single Smile Café with her though he felt like the proverbial bull in a china shop whenever he went there.

*****

Lawton was on his lunch break. He felt guilty because he had promised Lanie, his fiancée, that he would actually remove himself from his computer and go eat lunch somewhere else, preferably outside.

She was right. He always felt better for taking a break from computer work.

But he was very curious about Agenda 21 and what it had to do with the Rebeautification Ordinance in his county. When he typed in the words, "Agenda 21," and began to read, he was dumbfounded.

Quickly he reached for his cell phone. It vibrated as soon as he picked it up. It was Paul. He felt another vibration even before he read Paul's text. It was Gordon.

He read their texts and called Paul first, then Gordon, setting up the three-way conversation.

"Can you believe what you're reading?" asked Gordon. "This is amazing."

"Wait until Aunt Galeah gets hold of this information," said Paul. "She's going to go crazy with it."

"Can you call your mom and ask her to call another meeting at your house tonight?" asked Gordon. "The uncles really need to see this."

"Yep. I'm afraid--what was Jasper's brother's name? Corey?"

"Yes," chorused Lawton and Gordon together.

"I'm afraid he's right. We're going to need a Constitutional attorney, one who is familiar with all of this."

"Gramps was right, too" added Lawton. "This stuff goes against the Fourth Amendment, especially the way it's being done, trying to intimidate ordinary Americans."

"They picked the wrong guy to start with if they think Gramps is going to be intimidated," said Gordon.

"You know, I wonder if they've served these 'Notices of Violation' to anyone else?" asked Paul thoughtfully. "We need to ask around, discover if anyone else is being harassed."

"Wow! I never thought of that," said Lawton. "Maybe we can get the girls, Kielah, Lindy, and Gwen, to go around to the neighbors and ask them."

"Geoffrey and Justin would probably like to help, too," said Gordon. "I don't think the aunts are going to let those girls go by themselves."

"You're right. Parts of Walterboro aren't very safe these days, and Mom would never let her two cheerleaders go talk to people they don't know very well by themselves," said Lawton. "I wasn't thinking about that. I was just thinking that since they are cheerleaders, they can get anyone to talk."

"That's for sure," said Paul, laughing. He had two younger sisters of his own.

"Okay, Guys. I'll call my mom. Meeting at my house tonight, probably around seven."

"We'll be there," Gordon and Paul said together.

Chapter Eleven

For a second night in three days, the entire Merrill and Galbraith clans were together in the Summerville Merrills' living room.

Once again, Grandpa Merrill opened the meeting with a prayer, but this time, Aunt Galeah directed their attention to the TV screen. Lawton, Paul, and Gordon had hooked up their computers to the screen so everyone could see the information they had uncovered.

Lawton was the first to speak.

"Yesterday, as we were digging in South Carolina State Legislature archives for information on the Rebeautification Ordinance, we kept seeing the words 'Agenda 21.' We corroborated our discoveries and finally realized that behind the Rebeautification Ordinance is Agenda 21. Gordon, tell them what we found."

"We didn't have time to look into Agenda 21 much yesterday, so today at noon during our lunch breaks, we all must have had the same idea to look up this phrase on the internet. And what we found is that the United Nations is behind Agenda 21. Then we found some information that will knock your socks off!"

Paul picked up the thread of the story. "We texted each other, and Lawton immediately set up a conference call about it."

With the click of a button, Lawton brought up the first screen. "Everyone goes to the 'most trusted source' of information, right?" he asked, using his fingers to highlight the sarcasm of the quoted words.

"Wikipedia," said Gordon, melodramatically.

"Right," said Lawton. "Here is what Wikipedia has to say about Agenda 21: 'Agenda 21 is a non-binding, voluntarily implemented action plan of the United Nations with regards to sustainable development.'"

"Actually," said Paul, "Wikipedia is a good starting point, but we wanted more detailed information. So we looked up the phrase 'sustainable development' to get a clearer definition of what all of this is about."

"The definition posted by World Bank Group, quoting the Brundtland Commission" he continued, flashing a website on the screen, "says that sustainable development is 'development that meets the needs of the present without compromising the ability of future generations to meet their own needs.'"

"And going back to our friend, Wikipedia," continued Gordon, "they define it as "'a pattern of economic growth in which resource use aims to meet human needs while preserving the environment so that these needs can be met not only in the present, but also for generations to come.'"

"Sounds okay, so far, right?" asked Aunt Galeah. "But what does this have to do with the farm? we asked ourselves. So then we did some more digging. I called the boys at about three o'clock today to find out if they were finding what I was finding."

"It sounds good," interjected Kielah. "I mean, they talk about sustainable development and recycling in our science classes at school. It can't be all that bad."

"It can't be good if they're giving Grandpa grief at the farm," protested Lindy. The twins, Ryan and Rosie nodded their heads vigorously in agreement.

Paul, the peacemaking moderate in the group of grandkids reached over to tweak Lindy's ponytail. "You're right, Pipsqueak. It's not good, but it's not all bad either. Recycling, land conservation, and working together and buying goods on a local level are all good things."

"So is empowerment of women and minority groups and helping out the poorest in our world," added Gordon. "One of their stated principles is that all people 'are entitled to a healthy and productive life in harmony with nature.'"

"I would think all of this depends on who's calling the shots," said Uncle Galen, the first of the uncles to speak.

"Yep. That's exactly what I was thinking," added Uncle Phillip.

"You're absolutely right, Uncle Galen and Uncle Phil," said Paul.

"Recycling is good, but not if the town of Walterboro is going to weigh everyone's trash and then impose a fine if they find too many recyclables in a person's garbage. They just shot down a measure for that in Summerville last year," said Lawton who kept up with such things.

"And land conservation is good, but if you follow through with what the United Nations wants to do, you discover that they want to eradicate private property ownership and move everyone to 'sustainable cities,' mostly in the coastal areas of the United States, leaving the interior open for whatever devious plans they have," said Gordon.

"Oh, so this boils down to private property ownership?" asked Grandpa Merrill.

"Not exactly in our case," said Paul. "What they are pursuing is a step-by-step process. As far as we can tell, the first step is control of private properties, telling people what they can or cannot do on their property."

"How can Walterboro County get away with that?" exploded the usually calm and thoughtful Uncle Galen.

"They can get away with it because South Carolina accepted government funds for the Rebeautification Ordinance, and those funds are made possible by our compliance both as a state and as a nation with Agenda 21's program," said Aunt Galeah.

"But it goes against our Fourth Amendment Constitutional rights," protested Grandpa Merrill.

"You're absolutely right. It does," said Aunt Galeah. "But I'm going to guess here that the United Nations feels their mandates and ordinances supersede those of any government."

"Oh, it gets worse," said Gordon. "Here's a quote directly from one of their conferences in Vancouver: 'Private land ownership is also a principal instrument of accumulation and concentration of wealth and therefore contributes to social injustice; if unchecked, it may become a major obstacle in the planning and implementation of development schemes.'"

"That's preposterous!" exclaimed Grandpa Merrill. "That's socialism!"

"That's what we're up against, Gramps," said Lawton, shaking his head.

"Let me show you this YouTube clip," said Gordon. When they had finished watching the video, a profound silence settled on the group.

"That's awful," said Aunt Clara.

"I can see how this has crept into our schools," said Aunt Galeah. "'Biodiversity,' 'socialism,' 'green growth': it's in all the textbooks."

"What's the name of that organization that has local chapters?" asked Aunt Clara.

"ICLEI. International Council of Local Environmental Initiatives," said Lawton.

"That's it," said Aunt Clara. "I think it's telling that George Soros has funded many of the local chapters of ICLEI."

"Well, I think it's interesting that Libertarians and Democrats are against Agenda 21, not just Republicans," said Uncle Davey.

"Personally, I'm encouraged that the governor of Alabama signed a bill to prohibit their state from participation in both ICLEI and Agenda 21," said Lawton. "I think South Carolina needs to do this, too."

"So what do we need to do about all of this, especially in relationship to the farm?" asked Aunt Sarah.

"I think when we question Jeremy Saxon we need to dig around a little and see if we can get him to admit this is part of Agenda 21. That would add some weight, some seriousness to our situation," said Uncle Davey to Uncle Garrett.

"I tried to call him today, but his secretary said he was 'unavailable,'" said Uncle Garrett.

"I have a bad feeling about this," said Uncle Davey slowly. "Can we ask for an extension on the cleanup, buy ourselves some more time while we decide exactly what we're going to do?"

"I'll call again tomorrow and find out, either from him or from his secretary," said Uncle Garret.

"Let's try to get a one-month extension. Then none of us will have to take off from work. I agree with you, Davey. This is not going to go away, even when we've 'complied' with all of their demands. We need to keep a few days off in reserve," said Uncle Craig.

This was the first time he had spoken. He needed to tell his brothers-in-law about his trip to Tampico. Just in case. Normally, he didn't talk about his job, but since his name had been smeared all over the news anyway, he would talk to them this time.

"What do you think about checking back with Corey about a Constitutional attorney, Dad?" asked Lawton.

"I think we have a distinct possibility of needing one," said Uncle Davey soberly.

"I'll call him. I got his phone number before he left," said Lawton.

"Would anyone like dessert?" asked Aunt Galeah. "All this brain work makes me hungry. I have some watermelon and some peach pie and vanilla ice cream. Can you girls come help me?" she asked her daughters.

Caden was already asleep upstairs, so Gina helped too, serving coffee and sweet iced tea to everyone while Kielah sliced the watermelon and Lindy helped Aunt Galeah dish up the pie and ice cream.

Kind Aunt Clara shooed the other aunts out of the kitchen, saying they had all worked a full day at their jobs already. She pulled out the plates, forks and glasses and helped in any way needed.

Gordon, Paul, and Lawton entertained everyone with funny videos from YouTube. But with a nod from Uncle Craig the uncles drifted one by one to the library.

When they were all assembled, Craig told them about his upcoming trip to Tampico.

"It's not an official trip yet, and if I don't get my badge and my Glock back, I'm going to need some serious hardware for backup."

"You think you're going to run into some trouble over there?" asked Uncle Garret.

"I think we've just uncovered the tip of the iceberg, and if we hit a nerve bringing back those girls, their parents won't be the only ones sending out a welcoming party."

"What you need is someone not associated with your group acting as a tail, seeing if you stir interest in other sources," said Uncle Garret.

"I wouldn't complain. You have any ideas?"

"Well, provided we can get an extension with Mr. Saxon, how about if Grace and I take a little time off to vacation as a couple in Tampico?"

"I can just see Grace in a little sundress, wearing those big sunglasses and posing as a tourist with a 'camera,'" said Uncle Davey with a chuckle.

Everyone laughed. Grace could certainly act any part she chose, but a helpless tourist in heels and a sundress was not her normal character.

"And if we can't get the time off, I've got a contact, Blake, who is a bounty hunter. He'd be an asset in any difficult situation. He's always calm, but he can be mean as a cornered copperhead in a fight with the bad guys."

"Give me this guy's number," said Uncle Craig. "I'd much rather have you at my back, but I don't want anyone else in this family endangered right now. I may need you later. "

Uncle Garrett hit a button on his phone and retrieved the number. He showed it to Uncle Craig who punched it into his phone.

I'll run it by Scotch and see if the department can afford him. Maybe we can use some of the money we've recovered from a drug bust."

"I'm sure they are doing this, but I have to ask," said Uncle Garrett. "Is your department checking out whoever the captain was supposed to deliver the girls to?"

"They are, but with so many avenues open for transportation—truck, boat, plane—we're rather stymied right now."

"True," said Uncle Garret.

"You need a break in this case, but I'd hate it to be at the expense of the physical and emotional well-being of some more children," said Uncle Galen.

"Wish I could use this as a wakeup call for some of the spoiled, rich kids I have to coach," observed Uncle Phil.

"Use whatever you read in the papers," said Uncle Craig. "Just don't repeat what you hear from me. I'm already in enough trouble." He grimaced wryly.

"No, I won't tell tales. But do you suppose that these bastards limit themselves to Mexican children? What about missing children from this area? I would think stealing children from this area, one here and one there, would be more cost effective than transporting them from Mexico."

"You've got a good point," Uncle Craig conceded. "However, I think the language barrier helps to ensure the silence of the kidnapped kids."

"And it depends on the demand as well," said Uncle Garret. "Kidnapping five or ten girls at one time from the streets of Charleston would raise an alarm. These people want to operate under the radar."

"Well, they're on our radar now. I hope we can bring them down before any more children get killed," said Uncle Craig grimly.

Chapter Twelve

Blake Lobel respected two things in life: guns and the power of greed. He owned quite a few of the former in his fight against the latter.

The worst kind of greed was the kind that abused and defiled women and children, using them for lascivious self-gratification.

He had agreed to meet Craig Miller at Azalea Park in Summerville for a morning jog. The loose-fitting sweat suit hid well-honed muscles as well as some hardware. "Don't leave home without 'em" was his motto about his guns.

Craig knew his man immediately although he had not been able to find even a whisper about him on the internet, let alone a picture.

He knew everyone who ran the park in the morning by sight if not by name as well. He varied his route but never his routine. It kept him fit and reasonably in shape.

Blake fell into step beside him, and they jogged together in silence, one lap and then two. At the end of the second lap, Craig slowed down to a walk, and after a long drink from a bottle of cool water, Blake finally spoke.

"Garrett said you needed backup on a trip down South."

"Yes."

"Does this involve those girls you found on the ship in the harbor?"

"Yes."

"And you think that when you return them, you'll be stirring the proverbial hornets' nest?"

"Yes."

"I'm to be on the lookout for any unwarranted attention you draw as well as your backup if the bad guys start a gunfight or try to harass the ladies?"

"That about sums it up. I see Garrett briefed you well."

Blake smiled and Craig realized the younger man could be persuasive with the ladies if needed because the smile transformed his serious, somewhat saturnine face into something his wife and daughter would probably term attractive in a dangerous sort of way.

Thankfully, his daughter was a little too young for Blake. Craig judged his age to be about twenty-six or so.

"Any questions?" asked Blake.

"I've got two questions: How much will you charge the department, and what kind of hardware will you be packing?"

"Perhaps I will go as a studious, do-gooder tourist, one who wants to see the sights but who also wants to see the, shall we say, less desirable sights. That way I can keep tabs on you all and take a lot of pictures without looking too suspicious although if the situation changes, my plans will change, too. Are you okay with that?"

Craig nodded.

Blake continued. "I've worked in Mexico before, so not only do I speak Spanish, but I have connections down there that might be useful to me should we need reinforcements."

What he didn't tell Craig was that he had lived in Tampico during his middle school years when his mom had remarried a man who had promised the moon, but who had failed to deliver.

Those years of having to watch his mother being abused by the sophisticated, worldly and very wealthy

Patterson Jones, had not only taught him how to be a shadow, always watching but seldom seen, but had also forged in him a hatred for the abuse of the innocent.

On her deathbed, literally, his mother had given him a key to a private, safety deposit box and had made him swear he would leave Patterson, never looking back.

He went straight to the bank after the doctor declared her dead.

The bank president deferentially left him in a secluded room to peruse the contents of the safety deposit box alone.

He pulled out a deposit book for the bank and found that his mother had been depositing money in his name for four years from her considerable "allowance" from Patterson. More papers told him that a small fortune had been left to him by his father's mother in property and funds.

A letter written by his mother and dated only a month earlier told him of the beautiful land he would be able to claim at the age of eighteen. He just had to disappear and stay alive for two more years.

Immediately, he began to plan. He was no longer a helpless teen. He had watched Patterson throw money around like used matches, and he knew that he could survive both by buying his way and by living invisibly.

In the last part of his mother's letter, she asked him the impossible: to forgive Patterson.

"After your father's death, I was so lonely. I wanted to count with someone. Patterson made me feel like I was valuable to him. Not until we moved to Mexico did I realize his gifts and his allowances had strings attached. I was not only his wife—I made sure of that—but I was also a highly paid consort for his rich friends. If I didn't cooperate, he would make sure I suffered. He knew how to leave bruises in inconspicuous places, but his emotional abuse, making me feel worthless, was even worse."

Blake could barely see the words for the awful memories crowding in front of his hot, dry eyes.

"The only thing that kept me going was you, Blake. You became my heart, my reason for living. I watched you become a shadow, and it hurt so badly that you were forced to give away your boyhood to help me survive. I vowed to leave you enough funds to live on following my death."

Blake swallowed and nearly groaned aloud. He would gladly have fled with his mother. He could have cared for her much better than Patterson had done. Her next written words seemed to read his thoughts.

"I was even making plans to escape with you, Blake, Sweetie, but the last blows I received from Patterson damaged my kidneys. I could feel it happening. So now you will have to go on your own. I regret my choices these past years, but at least I will die knowing you have the means to escape as I could not."

"And now comes the hardest request: please forgive me for getting you into this mess. But even more importantly, you must find forgiveness in your heart for Patterson. If you don't, you will never be free of him. Don't allow him to control your future, but become the honest, upright, courageous, thoughtful, and generous young man that your father and I trained you to be."

This could not be! How could he forgive the man who had so viciously treated his mother? Where would he even begin in this impossible task she requested of him?

"Go to your grandfather in North Carolina. He is an upright, God-fearing man who will do everything he can to help you in this final task I've asked of you. Tell him everything. He needs to know it all so he can help you."

Blake's heart rebelled, but he read the final paragraph.

"And now let me tell you once more how very much I love you, Blake, my sweet, wonderful boy. You have been the 'light of my days' as Telemachus was to

Eumaeus a very long time ago. Though these last four years have been difficult for you, I'm confident God will use it all to mold you into the man He wants you to be."

And that was all. But it was everything. It was more than enough to give him the guidance and direction he needed for the nearly insurmountable tasks he would be required to accomplish in the next few days.

He sat, his dark head bowed, remembering all the stories his mother had read with him both before Patterson ever came on the scene and after their move to Mexico.

Reading together was kept a secret activity between mother and son because of their intuitive knowledge that Blake must not appear to be anyone of importance. Patterson had a certain radar for using and corrupting good. If he had suspected their strong bond, he would have used Blake's well-being against his mother; perhaps he had tried to do so. Blake didn't know.

He sat a few more minutes, clearing his mind and compiling a list in his head as his mother had taught him to do. She had made a game of it, giving him a list of tasks to accomplish each day. The list kept him focused and allowed him to feel useful, but he suspected it also kept him away from the house when the most evil was occurring.

First, he would retrieve anything from his mother's room that was personal, a few mementos for remembrance. Then he would make sure his mother received a proper burial.

Next, after he had packed his meager belongings, including the contents of the safety deposit box, he would go to the small airport at the far end of town and fly one of Patterson's planes to Texas, rent a car, and make his way to North Carolina. It was a plan. He worked better with a plan of action.

He found several things in his mother's room that she would want him to have: a necklace given to her by his father long ago and buried in the back of her jewelry stand, a bottle of her favorite perfume, her favorite scarf, white silk shot through with the iridescent colors of the rainbow, the one he had given her for her birthday shortly after their arrival in Mexico during happier times.

He heard the news from a passing maid just before he entered his own room. In an ironic twist of fate, Patterson had been shot by his gambling partner the same hour his mother had passed.

His heart rebelled, but, stoically, he planned two funerals: a private, intensely personal one for his mother with only her personal maid and himself in attendance and a second very public one for the man who had caused his mother so much pain.

When it was over, he felt drained, but he was not free yet. In a visit from Patterson's attorney, he was told, rather coldly, that several former wives and mistresses and their offspring were contesting Patterson's will, and he would have to leave the premises immediately.

Blake could not bring himself to care. He had his own plans. Before the afternoon was over, he had filed a flight plan and was flying one of Patterson's planes over the Gulf toward Texas.

"What about the price tag for your presence?" he heard Craig ask as if from a great distance.

Blake snapped back to attendance. "I'll take that up with your boss, Scotch, if you will give me his number," said Blake.

"That will work," said Craig. He flipped open his phone and read the number to Blake.

He would charge. He had learned very quickly that his services were valued more if he charged a somewhat steep but reasonable price.

However, since he didn't really need the money, he would donate it to the newly opened House of Hope established to aid women and children caught in the mire of human and sex trafficking. It provided the girls physical as well as emotional support. He would do it in memory of his mother.

"You do know that in reuniting these girls with their families you run the risk of putting a price on every one of their heads, right?" he asked Craig.

"No. I hadn't thought of that."

"Sure. If the traffickers have any suspicion that they might be recognized by any of the girls, they'll make sure the girls won't talk. They'll probably murder them and their families as well."

"What do you propose we do?"

"I think you should offer the families asylum in Oklahoma, but advertise that you're offering them asylum in Texas."

"I'd better tell Scotch right away," said Craig with a worried frown. "That will need to be set up right away."

"Can I offer another piece of advice?" asked Blake.

Craig nodded.

"'Leak' some of this concern to the media, especially the states closest to Mexico, as well as to the news outlets in Tampico. It might buy the girls and their families a few extra days."

Chapter Thirteen

Gina sat on the floor in the living room with Miss Kennedy's lesson plans and curriculum for the year spread in a fan-shaped semi circle around her. Her father, bless his heart, had volunteered to look after Caden so she could begin lesson plans.

At first she had been overwhelmed by all the material she needed to cover with her third graders. But, gradually, after forcing herself to just read the long-term lesson plans for the entire year, she had begun to make sense of the layers Miss Kennedy had built into the plans.

She saw no point in recreating the wheel; she would simply resubmit Miss Kennedy's plans with her name at the top which is what Miss Kennedy had herself suggested.

In college, she had always worked ahead. She never knew when Caden would be sick or when she might have to work overtime. She had always taken as much overtime as possible to build her little nest egg.

She still worked extra hours if they were offered, but only if it didn't impose a burden on her parents. She supposed she was too self-conscious about that, but she couldn't stand free loaders, and she refused to be one. As long as she was able-bodied, she wouldn't sponge off of either the government or her parents.

The long-term lesson plans done, she turned to monthly lesson plans. She had finished August's, and was beginning on September's when the phone rang.

She was pleasantly surprised to see it was Chelsea calling. But on a Thursday afternoon?

"Hello? Chelsea?"

"Yes! I'm free for the weekend, so I thought I'd fly down. I've brought some company with me. It's one of Jasper's cousins. Her name is Tallie. Tallie Peters-Templeton!"

"She's more than welcome. Where will she stay?" Gina looked around at the mess on her living room floor and fervently hoped Chelsea wasn't in the mood for a girls' night out at her place.

"Oh, she's staying with us. But she's a human rights advocate in Washington, D.C., and since they're all following the story about Uncle Craig finding the girls, she wanted to come down here with me and talk to him before he leaves to take the girls back to Mexico."

"I heard Mom and Dad talking about it. He's leaving tomorrow morning with the girls."

"Good. She didn't miss him. You didn't miss him," she heard Chelsea say to someone else.

"We were wondering if you had to work tonight or if you could come over for dinner. Uncle Craig and Aunt Clara are coming with Melanie and Michael. But aside from all that, I want you two to meet. I think you'll like each other, and then we can talk about the wedding, too!"

Gina had suspected that wedding talk would somehow be a part of the conversation.

"Well alright, but only if Gwen is free to watch Caden. I don't want Mom and Dad to feel they have to watch him all day."

"Just bring Caden along. You know everyone will be keeping an eye on him," said Chelsea.

Gina had her own ideas about that. She preferred to have one person watching her son. And if they were paid to do it, they usually did a more conscientious job. But she stifled a sigh as she thought of the dent in her budget. It wouldn't be for too long, and she could use a break from her own cooking.

"Okay. What time?"

"In about an hour. That will give us time to freshen up from the trip."

The first person Gina saw when she arrived, was Corey. He and Lawton were in deep conversation in the front room, and Lawton had some of the information about Agenda 21 on his computer screen, so she guessed correctly that Lawton was giving Corey the details.

She tried to sneak by the door without being seen to take Caden up to the playroom, but Corey seemed to sense she was there.

"Gina!" he exclaimed, coming toward her with both hands outstretched and a smile on his face. "You're a sight for tired eyes!"

Gina doubted that, but she couldn't say anything without seeming ungracious. She automatically put out her hands to meet his, but instead of a quick, polite, neck-up hug, he pulled her into his arms and, giving her a bear hug, buried his face in her hair.

Startled, Gina tensed slightly; she couldn't help it. What in the world did he think he was doing? Surely sharing her background about Caden's conception didn't warrant such an overflow of emotion from him, did it?

Okay, so he wasn't quite the playboy every one thought he was, Gina thought, mentally reviewing and realizing that he had shared something of his past, too.

But that didn't mean he could just waltz in and out of her life, throwing her off-balance every time he came into town. And what was he doing in town anyway?

Gina pulled away slightly although he still held her in his arms. "What are you doing here?" she asked bluntly.

"Here me eyes have been pining for the sight of ye," began Corey in a rich brogue, "and she can only berate me," he said with a laugh, turning his head and addressing Lawton with the last words.

"Our Gina won't let her heart go very easily," said Lawton wisely, taking in the tableau and storing it away in his mind to tell Lanie later.

Corey finally released her and said, "Your cousin, Chelsea, wanted to fly home. My cousin, Tallie, wanted to fly down here and talk to your Uncle Craig. My plane was available, so voila, here I am."

"You can't..." Gina began, but she didn't know how to continue.

Corey's eyes grew dangerously intense. "I can't what?" he asked quietly.

Gina bit her lip nervously. "Never mind," she said breathlessly. She didn't trust that look in his eyes one bit. "Where are Chelsea and Tallie?"

"Chicken," Corey said softly so only Gina could hear. "They're upstairs," he said in a louder voice, "along with your son."

Gina fled before he could make her feel more of a blithering idiot. She couldn't believe she had forgotten all about Caden in the exchange with Corey.

By dinner time Gina had calmed herself. That was not difficult to do as Chelsea tended to pull people into whatever she was doing at the moment, although she did it in a very nice way.

Caden was busy with a train track set featuring Gordon, Henry, James, Percy, and, of course, Thomas in the play room.

Chelsea, meanwhile, wanted to introduce Tallie, Corey and Jasper's cousin, who was a human rights activist and lobbyist in Washington, D.C. She was very concerned about what would happen to the girls Uncle Craig had found after they were returned to their families in Mexico.

Gina listened, somewhat awed by what Tallie had already accomplished in such a short lifetime and the places she had traveled. She told of helping Sudanese children in Africa, of narrowly escaping with her life while trying to get information on the brutalities against "foreigners," by the Gbago regime, a Hitler-type ruler in the Ivory Coast, and of her observation of atrocities committed in Israel and Lebanon.

Now she was being re-assigned to Mexico and Central America as her bosses considered these areas less dangerous.

Chelsea wanted to know how she had hidden her coppery red hair while on assignment.

"Madame Clairol is one of my best friends," replied Tallie with a laugh. "And I frequent the tanning salons then stain my skin with tannic acid to make my skin even darker before I go. Sometimes I even dress like a man. It all depends on what my assignment entails."

"I don't think Mexico is any less dangerous than where you've been," said Gina after mulling over Tallie's new assignment. "People will do just about anything to protect their drug trade, and I suppose they will do the same to protect their investment in 'slaves.'"

"I think you're absolutely right," said Tallie. "But try convincing my bosses of that."

The conversation turned to the coming wedding.

"I've asked Tallie to be my fifth bridesmaid," Chelsea said to Gina. Turning to Tallie she said, "I'm so glad you're home and stopped by Rosemont to visit Nell and Carter so I could get to know you."

"Me, too," said Tallie. "We live only a few miles down the road, but everyone is gone on summer vacation. Mom and Dad are in Japan and China, Stanley is studying in Europe, and Tyler is working at a camp in the Adirondacks. The house was just too empty when I came home, so I went to Aunt Nell's. She and Pammy are always working on some scheme or another, and I thought I could help in between assignments."

The girls had been so absorbed in their conversation, they were unaware of family arriving until thirteen-year-old Melanie, Uncle Craig's daughter, appeared in the doorway and told them dinner was about to begin.

Because the group was small, only fifteen for a change, they all sat at the dining room table. The younger girls, Melanie and Lindy, sat at Aunt Galeah's end of the table along with Aunt Clara and helped serve the food since the door to the kitchen was closest to them.

Since Tallie wanted to talk to Uncle Craig, Lawton thoughtfully sat beside his father at the other end of the table. Tallie and Chelsea were seated across from them.

Gina was surprised to see her brother, Gordon, enter, but then she saw Paul and rightly guessed that they had been doing more research on their computers. She was also surprised to see that Uncle Craig had brought a surprise guest who sat on his right.

The young man was tall with dark hair and an angular face that looked rather sad. She noticed that he checked all the windows and the exits before he was seated. Law enforcement, she guessed. Then he saw Tallie, and for a fraction of a second he seemed entranced.

Seeing a chance to play matchmaking, Gina steered Tallie to sit directly across from the young man. She sat on Tallie's left, and Chelsea sat on Tallie's right.

Corey was appreciating the old greens and golds and the pineapple of hospitality displayed prominently in the window treatments, in the long oak table with the green silk table runner and placemats, in the tall, golden candelabras with crystal droplets hanging from the arms as well as from the two chandeliers above the table.

Normally, he wouldn't notice such things, but his mother always asked for such details, and to notice them had become a game. He missed his opportunity to sit by Gina, so he opted to sit across from her by the newcomer.

After Uncle Davey asked the blessing on the food, Uncle Craig introduced his young friend as Blake, his backup for the trip to Mexico. Chelsea introduced Tallie as her fiance's cousin.

"Her name rhymes with Callie, but with a 'T,'" she told the group. Then she introduced everyone to Tallie. Laughter erupted as Tallie attempted to say everyone's names. She only missed two, mixing up Paul and Gordon. Everyone clapped.

"Whew! I'm glad I'm not in school."

"School doesn't begin until August twentieth; you're safe," Gina assured her.

"When do you leave for Mexico, Craig?" asked Uncle Davey. "I thought you were leaving this morning."

"A small hiccup in plans, and I'm glad. I've got my badge and gun back," said Uncle Craig with satisfaction. "We leave tomorrow bright and early."

"What was the 'hiccup' or can you tell us?" asked Uncle Davey.

"I believe it will hit the eleven o'clock news, at least part of it, so I'll tell you, but please don't discuss it in public." He leaned forward and spoke softly but intensely.

"We found through some of our seedier sources that the little girl, Esperanza, who has become the spokesperson for the group, was supposed to be assassinated as she checked into the airport for her flight."

"Really? I thought security had been upgraded," said Aunt Galeah.

"It has, but we aren't taking any chances. So we've arranged a private plane for transport to Tampico. It will be arriving in Tampico at the same time as the commercial flight. That may foil a few plans."

He didn't tell them, but Blake would be flying the commercial flight, watching for suspicious characters and for any tails they might acquire once they landed.

"So what are your plans once the girls are reunited with their families?" spoke Tallie for the first time.

"What do you mean?"

"Once the girls are reunited with their families, what then? Are you going to just leave?" she asked.

"Why do you ask?"

"Because once you leave, don't you suppose the girls will all be killed? The kidnappers/human traffickers can't chance that they might be recognized. I would even guess that the girls and their entire families will be murdered."

Chapter Fourteen

Blake sat back and watched with admiration this beautiful woman with the cloud of silky, red hair take on American law enforcement.

"I'm sorry," said Tallie to Uncle Craig. "I don't mean to put you on the spot. And I should probably tell you what I do. I act as a liaison between the human rights advocates' office where I work and with people who are directly impacted by violations of human rights."

Blake decided he could get Craig out of the hot seat. "We have thought about your point," he said. "But do you think the families will be willing to relocate?"

"That's what my job is," said Tallie. Her warm brown eyes sparkled with her passion for what she did. "I can help them relocate immediately. My office has nine spots open in various parts of the United States. Three spots are here in South Carolina, some are in Georgia, and some are in Alabama."

Blake leaned forward. "I would think that persuading them to move would be the hardest part."

"It is, but if I can come with you," she directed a glance toward Uncle Craig, "I can help persuade them."

"Do you know any Spanish?" asked Blake skeptically.

"Si. Yo sé mucho Espanol, gracias," affirmed Tallie. She didn't add that she was fluent in five languages, seven if you counted the dialects she had picked up in the Middle East.

But Corey couldn't be silent. "Tallie knows five languages fluently, and I'll bet she learned a few more on her last stint in Israel and Lebanon, or was it Jordan?" he asked Tallie.

"It was Lebanon, a very beautiful country," said Tallie. "Languages seem to come naturally to me," she said half apologetically.

Blake was still skeptical. He didn't doubt her enthusiasm, but she was so young, and he wondered if she could really pull it off. A botched job would end with victims and he didn't want cold corpses on his watch.

"If you do convince them to move, they will need to be moved within three days or even less. The traffickers will have eyes and ears everywhere, and they will not hesitate to kill all of us."

"I'm aware of that," said Tallie soberly. "My office has planes already in place at the airport ready to leave at a moment's notice. The pilots and their mechanics are all agents who regularly fly into Tampico, so they won't raise any suspicions."

Blake was finally convinced. A girl who was beautiful as well as smart? Amazing. But he still wanted proof that she had a good dose of common sense. So many things could go wrong.

"What about ground transportation to the airport?" he asked.

"That's where I need help. I wanted to talk to Mr. Miller here before he left. When Chelsea discovered that her Uncle Craig and 'Mr. Miller' were the same person, she made sure I could talk to you. My bosses just talked to Scotch about," she looked at her watch, "two hours ago."

"I'm sorry to barge in on your dinner," she continued, looking at the entire group, "but time is of the essence." She directed her attention back to Blake. "I didn't know you were part of this party. But I'm not above begging for help when I need it."

A slow smile transformed his somber face into a breathtakingly handsome member of the male species. Even Aunt Galeah and Aunt Clara commented on it later.

"I have a few connections in Tampico. I once lived there."

Now he had Uncle Craig's attention who would bet even Garrett didn't know this little piece of information. "I didn't know that," he said.

"Not many people do," said Blake smoothly. The second time he had lived there was when he was nineteen. His grandfather had just passed, but he had acceded to his grandfather's wishes for him to go back to Mexico and clean up the mess Patterson had left.

Patterson's attorney, the same one who had asked him to leave, had been obsequious in attention now that Blake had proved beyond doubt to be Patterson's only heir. His mother's wedding certificate had been the clincher.

Blake had, without a second thought, put Patterson's estate on the market. At the low price Blake asked, it sold within two weeks. But while he was there, his mother's room, left untouched, had been both his bedroom and his office. Once again, he had felt her calm presence, her practical, pragmatic outlook on life, and it helped him as he made many difficult decisions.

In the one month he'd spent there, he had once again renewed his friendships with those who had helped him stay invisible: taxicab drivers, shop keepers, dock workers, a small and very poor family on the outskirts of town, a cabana boy, really a man, who had let him stay in the pool house, and the owner of a neighboring estate.

And it was the taxicab drivers he thought of now. Some had mentioned a chop shop. If he could line up some vehicles that would immediately be taken to the chop shop and some drivers with facial prosthetics to alter their appearance, he could move the families without implicating or endangering anyone else.

Everyone was watching him, a new experience and one he didn't particularly like after all his efforts at invisibility. "Let me make a phone call tonight," he said. "I'll have the transportation for you tomorrow night."

"Tomorrow night? What if we need more time?" asked Tallie.

"You probably won't, but if you can't convince a family to leave, remember, it's their choice."

Tallie slowly nodded her understanding. "Let's discuss more of the details after dinner."

"We'll meet in the library," affirmed Uncle Craig.

The talk became general. Kielah was still getting ready for college. Paul and Gordon groaned and said they didn't want to talk about college. Kielah retorted that it was different for girls. They had to plan.

Lawton wanted to talk more about Agenda 21 with Corcy, but he didn't want to talk over his uncle and Blake. Fortunately, his father brought up the subject.

"Corey," he began, "has Lawton told you about the discoveries he and his cousins have made about Agenda 21?"

"Yes, sir, and I think you all are onto something. I talked to Dad and also to Jonathan, Pammy's husband."

He leaned forward so Uncle Davey could hear him clearly. "Jonathan had several questions. He definitely thinks you should discover if this is, indeed, linked to Agenda 21. Two or more of you need to talk to Jeremy Saxon and see if you can 'trick' him so to speak into revealing what he knows."

"That's a good idea. I don't think Garrett has reached him yet, but we're all going to be spending the next three days at the farm, with the exception of Craig here, and we can find out what Garrett knows of Mr. Saxon's whereabouts."

"It seems as if Mr. Saxon is avoiding him," said Lawton.

"Well, of course he is! But Garrett won't let Mr. Saxon or his secretary give him the run around for too long. Garrett likes to cut straight to the chase," Uncle Davey said, smiling over some remembrances of Garrett's forthrightness.

"I have some names of attorneys, as well. Jonathan seems to think you'll need a Constitutional attorney, just as Grandpa Merrill has said."

"Oh good. I'd like to start finding an attorney as soon as possible," said Uncle Davey.

"Jonathan warned me that Constitutional attorneys are very selective of the cases they take. And not very many of them are in practice, so finding one that will take your case may take some time."

Uncle Davey and Uncle Craig looked at each other with concern.

"Another thing Jonathan said to tell you is that nationwide, very few attorneys will tackle a Fourth Amendment or property rights case. The chances of winning are not high, especially in areas of the country where Agenda 21 has made a headway."

Everyone was listening by now, and they all sat back with gloomy faces. Finally, Lawton spoke.

"We're Merrills and Galbraiths. We fight for our rights all the way to the finish."

"That's right," and "You tell them, Lawton," was heard around the table.

"I'm glad you all have that positive, fighting attitude," said Corey. "Because the last thing he told me is that here in the South you have a better chance of winning such a case."

"We believe in courtesy and manners here in the South," said Aunt Galeah. "But we also are strongly in favor of defending our rights, especially state rights and property rights. Historically, we always have."

"Our guests don't know your family's story, Honey," said Uncle Davey. "Perhaps the girls can serve dessert, and you can tell them."

Kielah and Lindy immediately agreed and jumped up to bring the dessert cups filled with creamy chocolate mousse, topped with real whipped cream to the table.

"My maiden name is Galeah Galbraith. My grandfather was of Scottish/Welsh descent and my grandmother was a descendant of the Cherokee Indian tribe that once lived in the Carolinas."

Lawton's fiancée, Lanie, entered, and they all scooted down and made room for her.

Galeah continued. "My great- great-grandfather married the granddaughter of Tsali, Cherokee hero. Her mother, Ancih, named her Little Nancy after Tsali's wife. Tsali has come to represent all that is best in both Cherokee Indians and Southerners: respect for the land and property rights, loyalty to family, and willingness to die for the protection of both."

"I know some of that story," said Blake. "I was fortunate enough to live with my grandfather in North Carolina for three years following the death of my mother. Other than my childhood, those three years were the best of my life."

Tallie wondered if he was in any way related to Tsali. His next words made her realize how small the world really is.

"My grandfather often talked about Jake, one of Tsali's sons. He was one of my ancestors, so I can only conclude that I'm related to some of you." Blake looked around the table.

Gina and Chelsea looked at each other. "That makes you a cousin of ours in some way," said Gina, somewhat uncertain of how to word the connection.

"Welcome to the family," said Galeah, and they all laughed and raised their glasses. They would sort out the exact relationship later. But clearly, he was related to the Galbraiths which included Galeah and her children.

Blake was taken back. Just like that, he was accepted into their family. After the loneliness of his childhood, that immediate connection was both heady and frightening at the same time.

Watching him, Tallie sensed the confusion in his mind, the tangle of emotions as he tried to sort his feelings. She had seen this before: people who had felt so alone and alienated, some separated by war or by poverty or by natural disasters, struggling to adjust when they discovered they were no longer alone in the world.

Those who had learned to exist alone often put up walls to keep the hurt at bay. But those walls also kept out joy as well as sorrow. Dismantling those walls sometimes took only seconds, but Tallie guessed that in someone who was as intense as Blake was, the tearing down would take more time.

And now they were going into a very dangerous situation together. She had seen television interviews with the police officer, Lucy, who had first talked to the girls and with Bonnie, the owner of the home, so she understood their personalities somewhat.

Tonight was her first meeting with Uncle Craig and now Blake. She liked knowing the people with whom she'd be working so closely because soon she'd have to transfer all of her attention to the girls and their families.

Dessert finished, the group split up. Uncle Davey wanted to meet with all of the Merrills and the Galbraiths who would be spending the weekend at the farm the next three days. He had created a sign-up sheet for the various jobs.

In addition, the rest of the peaches needed to be harvested so the aunts could begin their canning. And Gram had asked if about two hundred ears of corn could be picked so she could boil and freeze it in portion-sized plastic bags.

Meanwhile Uncle Craig, Blake, and Tallie headed for the library to discuss a more in-depth plan of action. Surprises were certain to occur, but discussing various scenarios would make all of their respective jobs easier.

Corey lingered in the dining room. He was listening to Uncle Davey, but he had his eyes on Gina as she hurried from the room, probably to check on her son who was upstairs with Lindy's friend, Gabby.

If she was avoiding him, she would find he was very patient. They would at least hold a decent conversation before the evening was over.

Chapter Fifteen

Gina snuggled with Caden on the bed in Chelsea's room. Caden had eaten his meal without complaint and then spent a happy half hour playing with his toys in the bathtub upstairs. By the time he was out of the tub, Gina had arrived to hear his bedtime prayers and to give him a kiss goodnight.

She had half expected that Corey would try to sit by her at dinner. Instead, he had sat across from her, and she found herself way too conscious of his smile and his intent gaze on her at awkward times during the evening.

Resolutely, Gina put Corey from her mind and thought, instead, of Harry. In their last phone conversation, he had spoken of possibly coming home in early September.

"You'll be teaching by then, so do you think we can set a date for our wedding?" he had asked.

Although they had been engaged since the previous Christmas, Gina had wanted to wait until after her graduation from college and starting a job before setting a date for their wedding.

Perhaps she'd wanted to prove to herself that she could do life on her own before she allowed anyone else other than her parents to assume any type of responsibility for her.

She had met Harry her sophomore year in college, the brother of Kelly, the one friend she had managed to keep with her busy schedule as a single mom, college student, and cashier at Wal-Mart.

Harry had just begun his civilian job in bomb dismantling and removal after four years in the Navy. An unexpected holiday had brought him home for three days. Gina and Kelly had met him at the coffee shop on campus.

Harry was pleasant and even funny with a dry sense of humor that kept Gina laughing, a too-rare occurrence since the birth of Caden.

His blue eyes twinkled when he gave a particularly funny punch line, and his tanned face was lined from sun exposure in warm climes. His blonde hair, kept in the perpetual military crew cut, gave his otherwise youthful personality an air of command and authority.

The next afternoon, Gina stopped by Kelly's house where once again she met Harry. He invited her to sit on the porch with him for a few minutes and sip a glass of iced tea. Reluctantly, Gina agreed. She didn't want to be late for work, but she was actually running early.

Harry was fun and entertaining. Moreover, he watched the time for her, so she wouldn't be late.

"That's enough tea, young lady," he said. "We can't have you late for your job."

That evening on her way home, her phone rang. She thought she would hear Kelly's voice, but instead she heard Harry's baritone voice.

"I'm only here for another two days, but I was wondering if you would go out to dinner with me tomorrow evening?" he asked.

Gina's breath caught in her throat. She had not expected to date anyone for a while. Who would want "damaged goods," especially after all the lies Jack had spread about her?

"Well, yes," she stammered. Her thoughts somewhat scattered, she was glad to remember she had the next evening free.

Tiny wings of hope lifted her heart. She was going to go out on a date like other girls!

She was nervous and excited the next evening, but she kept a calm attitude that fooled everyone except her mother. Harry was polite enough to come in and meet her father who mostly hid behind his newspaper, her sister who thought it high time she dated, and her mother who hugged her impulsively as she left.

They ate at a new steakhouse by Tanger Mall, and then drove down to the Battery on Charleston Harbor for a walk. Harry held her hand and even put his hand on her back to steer her around some tipsy tourists.

Most of their conversation was lighthearted tomfoolery although Gina discovered he had attended Wando High School before his parents had moved to the Summerville area.

"Did you ever go to any of the football games against Summerville High?" Gina asked curiously. He would have been a junior when she was a freshman.

"Every one of them!" Harry said, laughter in his voice. "I was on the football team although I was a scrawny little thing."

"Oh."

"You wouldn't have noticed me anyway with those shoulder pads and a football helmet on my head. Besides, I wore my hair long back then," he said, tweaking a strand of her hair.

"You're probably right. And I was just a silly, little girl back then." She thought of the quick growing up she'd had to do and wondered if she should say anything about Jack and Caden.

But the vessels in the harbor caught Harry's attention, especially a lovely little yacht with a fine set of sails.

He wanted to go over to the yacht club by California Dreaming, but Gina told him she needed to get home. She had to work the next day as well as write a paper for class on Monday.

He gave her a quick, shy kiss at her door, just a peck, really.

Gina was jarred from her thoughts about Harry when Chelsea entered the room.

"Sorry," Chelsea whispered.

But Caden was sound asleep. Gina no longer had an excuse to stay upstairs. Cautiously, she tiptoed downstairs, but didn't see Corey anywhere.

She decided on some coffee to help her stay awake. And nearly bumped into Corey who was just exiting the kitchen with three cups in his hands.

"Oh, excuse me," said Gina.

Corey just looked at her, his attention quickly turning to the cups he was trying to balance.

"For goodness' sake. Let me help," said Gina.

"Thanks."

"Who are these for?"

"Me, Uncle Davey, and Lawton."

"Tell you what: let me pour myself a cup, and then I'll help you carry these to the living room."

"Okay," said Corey. "In that case, I think your brother would like a cup, too. Do you know how he takes his coffee?"

"Gordon likes his coffee black with one teaspoon of cream," said Gina.

"Same as me!" said Corey.

"You and my father, too," said Gina. She finished fixing her coffee—she liked lots of cream and nearly as much sugar—and they made their way to the living room.

Lawton and Gordon were showing Aunt Galeah some more information about Agenda 21 on their computers.

Gabby was flirting with Michael, Uncle Craig's son, while Lindy and Kielah talked to Melanie.

Gabby's mom had given her permission to spend the entire weekend with Lindy, so the girls had decided to break up wood for fireplace kindling together. That way they could talk about boys, including Lindy's male cousins who were just "so cute!" according to Gabby.

"You haven't signed up for a job yet, have you Gina?" asked Uncle Davey.

"No Uncle Davey. I just want to stay close to Caden, probably a job that's near the house."

"Actually, I do need a gopher. If you can run messages as well as drinks and snacks, that would be very helpful," said Uncle Davey.

"I'd be glad to," said Gina. She wanted to do her fair share and not be seen as a slacker.

"I'd be glad to take Caden with me for awhile," said Uncle Davey.

Gina knew she was being overprotective, but Caden was her responsibility, and she couldn't bear to think of her son lost in the cornfield or some other place on the farm if Uncle Davey's attention lapsed.

"Okay," she began to say when Uncle Davey's phone rang.

"Hello. Oh, hi, Garrett. Really? Really!"

By now several of them, including Lawton, Corey, Gordon, Gina, and Aunt Galeah were shamelessly listening to the conversation.

"So tomorrow morning at eight? Craig will be sore that he's missing it."

Gina put her hands together, her face alight with anticipation. Had they finally obtained a meeting with Jeremy Saxon?

"That's true. I'll see what they have to say about it. Where do we meet? Okay, we'll all be there."

Uncle Davey closed his phone with a snap. "We've got a meeting with Jeremy Saxon tomorrow morning at eight," he said triumphantly.

"Can I come too?" asked Galeah.

"Of course, Dear. You don't have to say anything. I just want you to watch the expressions on Jeremy's face. I think his supervisor will be there, too, so watch his expressions, as well. You can listen for nuances in what they say, and we'll all compare notes afterward. Where's Craig? He'll want to hear about this."

"Wait," said Lawton. "Can I come as representative for the cousins? We're all involved in this, too."

Uncle Davey looked at him consideringly. "Sure. Corey, can you come? You will be a new face for Jeremy to consider. We'll call you our legal advisor!" he added jovially.

"As your 'legal advisor,' I don't think it's wise for me to come," said Corey.

"Why not?"

"If someone new is there, he'll be on his guard. You want to get him to tell you whether this has anything to do with Agenda 21 or not, and he's going to say as little as possible with me in the room."

"What room?" asked Uncle Craig. He, Blake and Tallie had decided to take a break for some coffee. They wanted to discuss some more ideas but were getting sleepy.

Uncle Davey explained the meeting with Jeremy Saxon and his supervisor, Walt Spencer, set for eight the next morning. "I sure wish you could be there."

"Of course I'll be there. The commercial flight doesn't leave until 9:54. If I'm packed and ready to go, I'll have just enough time to drive from Walterboro to the Charleston airport."

"That's cutting it too close," protested Blake.

"Doesn't Walterboro have an airport?" asked Corey.

"Yes."

"Well then, why don't I fly you all to Walterboro and back. It will save time, and if your meeting goes longer than expected, you won't have to worry about it."

It was a great plan. Uncle Davey called Uncle Garrett to tell him of the new developments. Uncle Garrett promised to call the rest of the families.

An expectant group met at the small airport next door to the Charleston International Airport the next morning. The clear sky and muggy breeze predicted a scorching hot day, but it was beautiful flying weather.

None of the other aunts were able to come. Aunt Sarah and Aunt Gloria both had to work at their respective hospitals, and a four a.m. shooting in North Charleston in front of a Waffle House had Aunt Grace swamped with two body bags, bullet trajectories, and gun powder residue to process. At least she had access to plenty of coffee.

Paul had asked to come. He was often an antidote to his father's fiery temper, so Uncle Davey agreed. In fact, his even temperament was often noted. Aunt Sarah had the fine Italian spirit of her ancestors and Uncle Phil had an even more volatile nature. How Paul missed the "blessing of such passions" Grandpa Merrill often wanted to know.

Corey had thoughtfully arranged transportation from the Walterboro airport to the building by the courthouse where Mr. Saxon's office was located.

The nine men and lone woman filed into the conference room followed by Corey who knew the value of scoping out locations for future reference.

Like civilized beings, they shook hands and made introductions. Corey, still in the room, escaped having his name introduced. He stood with Lawton and Paul, and he guessed correctly that Mr. Saxon and Mr. Spencer assumed he was one of the cousins.

"Have a seat," said Mr. Spencer, amiably enough.

They all sat in the upholstered chairs around the long wooden conference table.

"You have some questions?" prompted Mr. Spencer.

Uncle Davey, flanked by Grandpa Merrill on one side and Grandpa Galbraith on the other side acted as the spokesman for the group. He carefully drew the Notification of Violation from the black, leather day timer he carried.

"Dad received this from your office after an unannounced visit from Mr. Saxon, here," he began, waving a hand toward Jeremy Saxon.

"Unannounced? We sent a letter stating we would be inspecting the property."

Uncle Davey turned to Grandpa Merrill. "Did you receive a letter from them, Dad?"

"I don't open the mail, Mary does, but she would have shown me such a letter immediately," he said positively.

"Obviously, we didn't receive such a letter, gentlemen," said Uncle Davey. "Can you get a copy for us?"

Jeremy looked at Mr. Spencer who nodded. "Excuse me a moment," he said.

He stood and walked to the door. Corey stood also, and, exiting with him, asked the way to the men's room, loud enough for the occupants of the room to hear.

What in the world? wondered Paul and several other members of the Merrill family. Corey was obviously onto something the rest of them had not yet caught.

Chapter Sixteen

Corey followed Jeremy Saxon to the small cubicles at the back of the building that housed the offices and personnel for the Office of Neighborhood Services.

He heard Mr. Saxon ask one of the secretaries to find a file for him.

"No, not the office file. We already have that in the conference room," said Jeremy impatiently. "The file on this case that contains all my notes."

Corey let the door to the restroom close softly. He flushed the toilet and then ran water in the sink. He emerged wiping his hands on a paper towel in time to see the secretary return from the partitioned back room with the file in her hands.

Mr. Saxon hustled down the hall to the conference room with Corey following close behind. He would chat up the secretary later. Secretaries were usually a wealth of information if you treated them with respect and courtesy, something Jeremy clearly did not do.

As Mr. Saxon entered the room, he pulled a piece of paper from the folder in his hands and handed it to Uncle Davey.

"Here's the letter we sent. It's dated July 6, as you can see."

"Did you send it certified mail?"

"We did not. I didn't see the need for that," said Mr. Saxon.

"So when you came on the property, you did not see the need to ask for permission first, before walking around and inspecting the property?"

"We sent a letter."

"But you came on private property. If I'm not mistaken, you cannot walk on someone's private property, especially to inspect it, without a warrant from a court of law unless, of course, someone's life is in danger, or unless you have their consent. Isn't that correct?" Uncle Davey asked Uncle Garrett and Uncle Craig, the lawmen in the family.

They nodded their heads in agreement.

"So let me ask you again, what gave you the authority to come on our property?"

Mr. Spencer leaned forward. "Davey," he said placatingly. "Let's not pick a fight. My assistant here was only following orders. Officers from the State Rebeautification Board asked us to make sure every property along I-95 was up to code, so, of course, we have to inspect every property in Colleton County that borders I-95."

"State Rebeautification Board? We have a state Rebeautification Board? How did this happen?"

"When the law was passed in the State Senate, they authorized a Board to be formed to help establish and enforce the Rebeautification codes."

Paul, Lawton, and Aunt Galeah were furiously taking notes. They had wanted to take a tape recorder, but Corey had advised them against it.

"So where can I find a list of the codes this Board has established?"

"I'm sure they're online," answered Mr. Spencer. "But Jeremy can get you a copy of them on your way out today."

Grandpa Will couldn't contain his exasperation any longer. "But what about my rights as an American citizen?

The Fourth Amendment of the Constitution guarantees my rights as a citizen for safety and security on my property. When you come on my property as a government official, I don't feel very secure."

"This is not about rights," said Mr. Spencer. "It's about whether or not you're in compliance with the codes."

Grandpa Will was still fuming. "Whatever I have on my property is also my property whether it's yard debris to be broken into kindling or livestock or a shed that needs to be re-roofed. You don't have a right to tell me what to do with or on my property as long as I'm not doing anything illegal."

"Not according to the codes," answered Mr. Spencer with a slightly superior air.

Uncle Davey laid a restraining hand on Grandpa Will's arm.

"So what if we agree to clean up the property as specified by this 'Notice of Violation'? Can you give us an extension? That's an awful lot of work to accomplish in two short weeks."

Jeremy Saxon looked at Mr. Spencer. "That would be Mr. Spencer's call, but I'm sure we can give you an additional two weeks. Surely that should be enough time."

Mr. Spencer nodded his head in agreement.

Watching closely, Corey noticed that Jeremy Saxon had relaxed when Uncle Davey requested an extension. He had obviously expected more of a fight. In addition, they still had not discovered anything about Agenda 21, yet it had to be revealed in an innocuous manner. He slid a note under the edge of the table to Lawton.

"What about the fines?" asked Lawton suddenly.

"What about them?" asked Jeremy Saxon, bristling once again.

"I would think you could dismiss them if we are going to comply with this Notice of Violation," said Lawton evenly.

Jeremy turned to Mr. Spencer.

"I'm sure you understand that we need a pay check every week just like you do," he said urbanely.

"Doesn't the Rebeautification Board give you a paycheck each week? It shouldn't come from the fines you levy against the citizens of this state," asserted Lawton.

"You're right," answered Mr. Spencer hastily. "I'm sure we can dismiss the fine if you voluntarily agree to comply with the Notice and allow us to re-inspect your property.

Grandpa Will looked down and shook his head, but he didn't say anything.

Lawton looked at Corey who was carefully analyzing Mr. Spencer's response.

Corey shook his head slightly. They would have to do some more legwork in determining just where the Rebeautification Board was obtaining its funding. He would bet not much was coming from the State of South Carolina.

Mr. Spencer stood and looked at his watch. "I'm sorry, gentlemen, and Mrs. Merrill," he said with a smile in Aunt Galeah's direction. "I have another appointment in a few minutes. Did you have any other questions?"

By habit, most of the uncles stood as well.

Corey realized that Mr. Spencer had just made a tactical move. He had given all of the concessions he was willing to give. Furthermore, Uncle Davey had asked his question with a condition: "If they complied." He had not said they would.

But by standing and ending the meeting at this critical juncture, Mr. Spencer had obliquely roped them into compliance. Good move, Mr. Spencer, Corey mentally applauded him. He hoped that at least one note taker had recorded Uncle Davey's question exactly.

"Can I have in writing that we have an extension?" asked Uncle Davey.

"Sure," responded Mr. Spencer. We'll have one of the secretaries type and mail it to you this afternoon."

Corey pushed himself toward the door. "I'll go get the list of codes," he said to Uncle Davey but making sure that Jeremy Saxon heard him.

He exited before anyone could respond. Time to chat up the secretaries.

He made his way down the hall once more.

Paul appeared beside him. "You're up to something, I can tell," he said to Corey.

"Watch and take notes, pal," said Corey with a laugh.

He stood casually at the counter that separated the office from the hall with the doors to the bathrooms and the small, back lobby area, noting the back door entrance. Outside was the back parking lot, probably where the secretaries, Mr. Spencer, and Jeremy Saxon parked their vehicles.

"Stephanie, is it?" he asked pleasantly of the petite, ash blonde secretary who sat at the desk behind the counter.

"Yes." She was all smiles for these two handsome young men.

"Mr. Saxon said we could get a list of the codes for the Rebeautification Ordinance from you."

"Oh, yes. Right here," Stephanie said, pulling a sheet from one of the file folders in the organizer at the side of her desk.

"Have you worked here long?" asked Corey, leaning casually against the counter and giving her another smile.

"About a year. I was just happy to find a job, you know, here in Walterboro." She waved her hand toward the back door. "Walterboro's not a very big town, you know."

Several uncles came down the hall to use the men's room before the trip back to the airport. Mr. Spencer quickly made his way out the back door. Corey hoped someone was delaying Jeremy Saxon.

"Do they have any good eating spots?" he asked Stephanie.

"A few. Especially down by the freeway. There's a good steak house over that way, you know."

"That's good. We might need to be here around lunchtime in the future."

He widened his eyes as if the thought had just occurred to him. "Maybe I can take you out to lunch there. What are you doing tomorrow for lunch?"

"I'm free for lunch tomorrow," said Stephanie breathlessly.

Corey looked at his watch. "I'll just barely make it here after my morning appointments. Can I meet you at the restaurant?" he asked.

"Oh sure. It's called The Roadhouse. Right off I-95. You can't miss it, you know."

Corey held out his hand. When Stephanie held hers out in response, he took it and placed a quick kiss on the back. "Until tomorrow," he said with a wink and turning, strode rapidly down the hall to the front entrance with Paul behind him.

When they got to the car, Paul couldn't control his laughter any longer.

"Will you be able to handle 'you know'?!

"Of course," said Corey, arching an eyebrow.

Lawton wanted to know what had happened. Paul gave him the details of Corey's conversation with the secretary.

Lawton grinned and laughed. "She may be an airhead 'you know,' but don't lead her on too much, especially if you're going to pursue our Gina," he warned.

Corey sobered instantly. "I won't," he said. "Dating and courting are two different things."

The doors of the rented van opened, and the uncles and Aunt Galeah entered, effectively ending the boys' conversation.

When they were all seated and underway, Uncle Davey asked, "So feedback? How do you think that went?"

"I thought we were going to stand up for our Constitutional rights," said Grandpa Will, very disappointed with the outcome of the meeting.

"It wasn't the time or the place," replied Uncle Davey. If his father's disapproval bothered him, he didn't show it.

"You're right," said Uncle Galen. "We needed to get information, not just stand up for our rights."

"If we're going to stand up for our rights, I'd like to do it with the Rebeautification Board and more than several state senators present," said Lawton. "It seems they're the policymakers, not Mr. Spencer and Jeremy Saxon."

"How do they get away with making those kinds of decisions for us without us, the citizens, having a say in it?" asked Uncle Phil in an angry voice.

"Good question," said Lawton. He'd like to know the answer to that question, too. For that matter, he'd like to know just how this government business worked and exactly how much policymakers like senators can decide for taxpayers without their direct input. It didn't seem fair to make decisions for people like that.

"Should we look at hiring an attorney at this point?" asked Uncle Davey.

"I don't think so," said Uncle Craig. "If we clean up the property, and they inspect it and don't charge us any fees, well then, no harm, no foul."

"But it's our property and our rights as citizens that are under attack here," protested Uncle Garrett.

"I agree," said Uncle Phil and Grandpa Will together.

"But we don't have the money for an expensive attorney," said Aunt Galeah.

"Well I think we need to do more research about where they're getting their money. If it is from the United Nations, we need to tread very carefully," said Uncle Galen.

"What do you think, Corey?" asked Uncle Davey.

"Well, first, I think you played right into Mr. Spencer's hands. He was just waiting for you to ask what you did about complying. Then he agreed to a few concessions to pacify you all and left before you could ask any more questions and before you could reiterate that your compliance was theoretical."

"With that being said," he continued over Uncle Davey's sputter and Grandpa Will's "I told you so," "I agree that you need to do more research and then wait and see if they do what they say they're going to do. If they don't, then I'd hire an attorney and make it a huge issue."

"We still have work to do at the farm this weekend," said Uncle Davey.

"That's right," and "We'll be there," answered the majority of the uncles although most were not in a very happy mood. Everyone was taking off Friday from their jobs to work on the farm with the exception of Uncle Craig.

"And I have to avoid getting myself shot, rescue nine girls and their families, and keep three women safe this weekend," said Uncle Craig.

He looked pretty grim about the next forty-eight hours. That ended the discussion about the property for the moment. One of their own was going into a life and death situation, and none of them liked it one bit.

Chapter Seventeen

So far so good, thought Uncle Craig with satisfaction. Most of the girls had been terrified of flying in a plane at first. But with Esperanza's cajoling and Lucy's calm, matter-of-fact explanations, they had ascended the steps to the plane.

Uncle Craig had been a little nervous himself but for a different reason. He knew that with Blake catching a commercial flight, they didn't have the protection they really needed for the walk to the plane.

Scotch had asked for backup, and Garrett had actually been on duty, guarding them while they were in the small, commercial airport and during embarkation on the plane.

The media had helped by advertising conflicting departure times form the large, international airport just around the corner.

Uncle Craig was always afraid of a rogue cameraman and reporter determining the truth. But none had appeared, and they had hurtled down the runway and into the air without a hitch.

Lucy had distracted them from their fears by drawing a crude map of Tampico and discovering where they all lived.

Apparently, they all lived within a four-mile radius of each other and had been kidnapped within a few hours on that one, fateful morning.

Lucy looked wordlessly at Craig. They had so few clues to go on here. Was this the work of an organized gang that hit a neighborhood and then left, or was this the work of a local gang who knew these girls and their habits?

Their job wasn't to get involved with those who had kidnapped the girls. Their only job was to ensure the safety of the girls and their families.

Tallie watched this unspoken communication and asked, "Should I talk to the girls now before we disembark?"

Craig and Lucy both nodded yes. It was their best chance to answer the inevitable questions before meeting with the families.

Bonnie, who had replaced the flu-stricken social worker at the last minute, gathered the youngest girl, nine-year old Francesca Flores, on her lap.

Tallie gathered the girls around her, telling them she had "informacion importante." As Tallie talked, Craig watched their eyes and saw the same terror in them he had seen when he had first rescued them.

However, Esperanza immediately saw the sense of what Tallie was saying and nodded her head in the affirmative. Seeing Esperanza nod, her friend, Selena, nodded as well. Several others were hanging back and shaking their heads no.

Quietly, Esperanza said "Maria," and a stricken look came into every face, even hers.

Tallie waited for a moment and then spoke again, explaining that she would personally help each one of them relocate with their families to the United States. Her job for the next year would be to help them with the adjustments to such a move.

She pulled out her notebook and began writing down the names of each girl and their family members. She then went around the circle again, asking what the parents did for a living, if any owned shops, if any had relatives, such as grandparents, who would need to be moved, if their parents had talked of moving to America, if they had any relatives already living there.

Craig was impressed with her organization. But now their flight was nearing its end, and they had to move the girls as quickly as possible out of harm's way.

Using Lucy as interpreter, he told the girls that first, they were to answer no questions from news reporters. Secondly, until Tallie, Lucy and Craig had talked to their parents about relocating and even after, it was to be a secret. All of their lives depended on it. He asked each girl individually to promise to speak of moving to no one.

His phone rang, and he held up his hand for quiet. It was Blake whose plane had just landed. Theirs was circling, awaiting Craig's orders.

"You have a mob of people here at the Aeropuerto de Tampico to welcome the girls home." They had discussed alternate landing sites until the wee hours of the morning.

"Do you think we should implement Plan B?" asked Uncle Craig.

"No. I talked to my friends here, and they said the runway of the old Javier Mina airport is overgrown. They only use it to land helicopters now."

"So backup to Plan A then." The backup was to secure a room for the families and have them meet the girls there.

"Yes. We've already obtained a room, and two of my friends are circulating among the crowd, moving the families to that room."

"Okay. We'll land the plane. East or west side of the building?"

"East. Just flashed my badge. I'll meet you on the tarmac and help get everyone in safely."

Uncle Craig gave directions to the pilot and relaxed slightly. He was certainly glad to have Blake doing all the ground work. He had one more question to ask Blake.

"Good job. Did you have any other interesting-looking fellow passengers?"

"You bet. Three actually. I took the liberty of contacting two other friends in Tampico I've worked with before. They've already tipped off police they trust, and let's just say these three are getting a warm reception from law enforcement. They'll be taken in for questioning."

"I just hope you didn't miss anyone," said Craig soberly in spite of Blake's attempt at humor.

"My friends will tail anyone else they suspect. Sentiment against the kidnappers is high due to the media coverage, so they have a few friends helping them."

"Just don't let our names out."

"Of course not. Undercover has its uses! Your plane is taxiing toward me now."

The plane landed and taxied to the building with only enough clearance for the stairs. With Tallie, Lucy, and Bonnie acting as human shields, the girls were shepherded in the door and down the hall to the room.

Inside the room, stifling with the heat of the day and the smell of overpowering perfume and "tight-packed, humanity," parents searched anxiously the faces of the girls.

Cries of relief and pent-up feeling erupted as mothers once again embraced daughters. Aunts and grandmas joined the mothers, fathers embraced or shook hands, their faces wreathed with relief, and sisters and brothers attached themselves to whatever finger, arm or leg they could find.

One last family was ushered in by Blake's friends. A man, a member of the press, was ushered firmly out.

Blake's two friends and their three compadres stood at the back of the room. Blake and Craig stood side by side at the front of the room on a small platform.

Maria's family had already been given their bad news several days before. They entered with bowed heads, dressed all in black, and instantly a cold hand of silence in the presence of death quieted the most loquacious mouths.

Craig cleared his throat in the silence and all eyes swung to the front of the room. He motioned, as had been prearranged, for Blake to talk.

Blake introduced himself, using only his first name, and then told of the rescue by Craig. Heartfelt cries of "Gracias," "Gracias, Senor," echoed around the room.

When they had quieted again, Blake continued talking, introducing Lucy and Bonnie. Again, thank yous echoed around the room.

Then all eyes turned questioningly to Tallie. Blake told the families that they now faced the most difficult decision of their lives.

He explained that although the girls had been drugged, the kidnappers, afraid of being recognized, would probably try to murder each of the girls and possibly even their families. Tallie was here to arrange their move to America, but it had to occur within twenty-four hours or even sooner if possible.

They would give each family the opportunity to discuss such a move, but Tallie would speak first.

Tallie again acknowledged what a difficult decision they must make, especially with extended family and businesses to think of. But she also, with mounting enthusiasm, described the educational opportunities for the children, the houses they would occupy, the help to obtain employment they would have. She reminded them that from the most difficult of circumstances often arose the most excellent opportunities.

Neither Craig nor Bonnie could understand what Tallie was saying. But they certainly understood the power of her words, the pictures of hope she gave which were reflected on the faces of those in front of them.

She concluded by saying that she would stand up front and make arrangements for their travel and relocation as they made their decisions.

Blake then spoke again, telling them that absolutamente, under no circumstances, was anyone to discuss their move with anyone else.

"You and your family may get out of town alive. But think about the last family to leave. Do you want to be responsible for their deaths because you couldn't be quiet?"

He then told them that once they had talked to Tallie, they would be escorted by armed police to their homes.

Craig marveled at how Blake had arranged all of this in the short five hours they had for sleep following their discussion that had ended in the wee hours of this morning. He could only hope each person present would take Blake seriously.

Esperanza's and Selena's families, the Lopezes, were the first to approach Tallie. The Lopez brothers, Eduardo and Phillippe, had already begun packing two days before, recognizing right away the danger they faced.

Catalina and Tristena, two sisters from the Rodriguez family were the next to come forward with their family. They begged to be allowed to bring their aging grandparents from both sides with them. Tallie believed this would be possible if they were willing to live together. With tearful laughter, they assured her they could all live in one house if necessary.

The Tomás family was next. They refused to move in spite of their daughter's pleas. Rachel Tomás was a talk show host, and her husband was a well-known car salesman who knew most of the politicians in town. They didn't think the perpetrators would dare to kill them or any of their family. Tallie sincerely hoped they were right, especially as she saw two sweet-faced twin boys peeping out from behind their mother's skirt.

Three more families agreed to leave--the Garcia, the Madera, and the Flores families, but the Monterreys also refused. And Maria's family, offered the same opportunity, also refused to leave, bitterly denouncing America despite the fact that the kidnappers had been Latino.

Blake had his own list. He had coordinated his list of taxicab drivers with Tallie's list of pilots. He had also contacted the pilots at first light of morning. He was already on the phone with the pilots, giving them the coordinates of where to pick up the two Lopez families and the Rodriguez family. He talked to Eduardo and Phillippe Lopez and Frank Rodriguez telling them exactly who their drivers were and where to meet the pilots.

Blake was in his element. He trusted no one, and so he had chosen places where planes could land on nearly deserted roads on the outskirts of town. In addition, he had planted decoy planes and taxicabs at the airport and all over town.

After consultation with the Flores family, they said they would be ready before midnight. The Madera family would be all set by eight the next morning, and the Garcia family would be the last to leave at twelve noon the next day.

It sounded like everything was all planned, but both Blake and Craig knew that with so many things that could go wrong, they had best be prepared for any contingency.

The Maderas and the Garcias would be the most vulnerable families.

Each of the six families would be followed by one of Blake's contacts as they left the airport.

Everyone had left except for the Maderas and Garcias when Francesca ran back through the door, pulling her father by the hand. The rest of her family followed. She ran straight to Blake and hurled herself at him.

When he caught her, he could feel her body trembling. She was gulping air and trying not to cry.

"What's the matter, Pequena? he asked. She leaned close to his ear and with trembling lips said, "I saw him."

"Saw who?" asked Blake as Lucy and Bonnie headed in his direction.

"The hombre who kidnapped me," Francesca replied.

Chapter Eighteen

"Are you sure?" asked Blake.

Francesca nodded an affirmative.

"Did you see him?" he asked Senor Flores, fervently hoping he had. He did not want the little girl to leave the room again until all danger was past.

"She waited until we were behind a pillar, and then she pointed him out to us. I don't think he saw us. But he's dressed as an airport official."

"Is he close to the door to this room, or is he in the airport proper?" asked Blake, pulling his gun.

"In the airport proper."

Bonnie persuaded Francesca to come with her. Her mother, very shy, would hardly look at Blake, let alone take her child from his arms. But when Bonnie handed Francesca to her mother, Senora Flores' arms hugged her daughter hungrily.

"Come with us," Blake said to Senor Flores. "We'll approach from a different direction so you can identify him without him seeing you. Then I want you to come straight back to this room. Lucy and I will take care of him."

Lucy was already pulling her gun to check it. "Wait," she called.

The men, who had turned to leave, looked back at her questioningly.

"Draw us a map of the airport and show us where he was standing," she said snagging a piece of paper from

Tallie. "I'm not familiar with this airport like you are," she said to Blake. "I don't like being so disadvantaged."

Mr. Flores quickly drew a map, noting the location of the kidnapper.

"Let me approach him first," said Lucy, "without my gun showing, of course. I'll ask directions. You can approach him from the other side, and put handcuffs on him before he even knows what's happening."

"Okay, sounds like a good plan," said Blake. "Let's split up here," he pointed to a spot on the map, "So there's no chance of him seeing us together."

"That works. Let's go," Lucy said.

Blake glanced back at Tallie. She was hugging Senora Madera and her daughter, Macy, but she was looking at him. A current seemed to arc between them, but perhaps it was only his imagination. Her next words were not.

"Be safe," she mouthed, knowing that he couldn't possibly hear her voice across the room with the quiet sobbing of the women and the chatter of several younger children who didn't quite understand what was happening.

On a whim, Blake tried the door of another room on the hall and found what he wanted—a door to the outside. When they re-entered the small airport lobby from the back, the kidnapper was standing in nearly the same spot, his eyes on the hallway to the meeting room, his ear glued to a cell phone.

"Ready?" Blake asked Lucy.

She nodded and began walking toward the suspect while Blake walked toward the main doors of the lobby. As he reached them, he turned. He saw the man smile contemptuously at Lucy and pull his gun.

At the same time, Blake sensed movement behind him. He stepped aside to allow someone to enter only to be put in a choke hold.

"Tell the lady to come here, Senor," said a low, menacing voice in his ear. "Wait, my partner will help convince her, no?" chuckled the voice.

Blake watched with horror as the "airport security guard" walked Lucy toward him with a gun at her back, her hands held out in front of her.

He had only just met her, but he didn't think she'd go down without a fight. Ready for anything, Blake waited for what seemed an eon but was mere seconds.

At the same time he saw Lucy feint toward the left, he both heard and felt a bullet whistle past his right ear. As the man behind him slumped to the ground, Blake ducked and rolled to his left, coming up with his gun in hand.

He saw Lucy in a crouching position, gun pointed at the suspect, but he also had his gun trained on Lucy.

Blake fired. Again Lucy ducked and rolled, avoiding a hail of bullets. The suspect jumped forward, his back arched, and then jerked to the right as two bullets slammed into his body, his gun flying into the air.

Craig ran forward and picked it up before anyone else could grab it.

Not content to let his agents have all the fun, he had followed them and watched them walk right into the ambush.

He looked ruefully down at the gun in his left hand. Damn! In the space of one week, he had killed four people. He sighed, resigned to the questions and the paperwork with the Mexican government. Hopefully it would be briefer than the paperwork he had to do in the United States.

He heard a click and froze, but it was only a camera. The media? Already? Had this been planned? Really!

He and Blake made their way to Lucy who was bruised and sore but fighting mad for walking into a planned attack.

"What made you follow us?" asked Blake. "I thought we had it all under control," he added ruefully.

"Intuition," said Craig briefly. "And caution, I suppose. We're on enemy territory here, we don't know the lay of the land, and I just thought backup is always good."

Slowly the airport lobby came back to life. People emerged from behind poles and bushes where they had hidden. Travel agents rose from behind the desks where they had crouched. Two children began wailing with fright now that the danger was past.

A light was hanging by a tenuous thread of wire from the ceiling where a stray bullet had nicked the cord. The front doors opened forcefully, and the Mexican police arrived, guns drawn.

Craig automatically put his hands up and stepped forward, flipping open his light jacket before he did and revealing his badge before they could fire a shot at him.

Thirty minutes later they had reconvened in the meeting room.

Some discussion had occurred about Francesca identifying the dead body of the second kidnapper, the one who had held Blake in a choke hold.

But after questioning, they discovered she had only seen the one kidnapper before a bag had been put over her head.

And the women would never have allowed it. Tallie and Bonnie were horrified that anyone would even think of subjecting a nine-year-old child to such a horrific sight.

"What I would like to know," said Tallie, "is how many kidnappers are we dealing with here?"

"We tried to piece that together, but the highest number we could determine was four. Esperanza and Selena were the only ones to see four at one time. The rest of the girls only saw one, and their descriptions don't match, so we may have up to seven kidnappers or someone who used facial prosthetics really well," said Lucy.

"And don't forget," added Craig, "not one of the kidnappers is probably the mastermind behind all of this. It's probably some very rich tycoon who has paid these criminals to do his dirty work so his name is never linked to the more sordid aspects of this case."

"So what do we do next?" asked Bonnie. "I could use a good meal."

"Good point," said Craig. He looked enquiringly at Blake. "You're the closest we have to a native. Where do we eat?"

Blake held up a finger and hit a number on his phone. "Si. Ready for pickup." Turning to them, he said with that smile that transformed his face, "It may be a squeeze, but I suggest we stick together at least until we are fortified with food."

They gathered their few belongings and headed for the lobby. The Mexican police were just finishing processing the recent scene of carnage, and business was back to normal, or so they judged by the sheer number of bodies in the terminal.

The taxicab driver jumped out of his car and gave Blake a huge hug before talking so fast in his native language that even Tallie and Lucy had trouble following. But they deciphered enough to know that they were about to enjoy an enormous feast of authentic Mexican food.

And they did. After a hair-raising ride to shake any tails that might be following them, Ricardo, Blake's friend, took them, not to a restaurant, but to his madre's house. The modest, stucco-like concrete façade, painted a vivid yellow and guarded by black, grilled iron-work, hid a pleasant courtyard flanked on three sides by the house.

Two trees gave plenty of shade over the outside oven and firepit. A small table held the cooking utensils for the outside oven and a plate with a stack of tortillas. Another larger table, covered with a yellow, gingham-checked tablecloth, contained various dishes with serving spoons.

Ricardo's mother was one of the tiniest women Blake had ever seen, but she had a huge, sunny smile and a very firm grip as he observed when he shook her hand. Her curly, black hair was tied back with a bright blue ribbon to match her blue and green floral shift.

She welcomed each of them, using her limited English and much Spanish. But they were left in no doubt that she was happy to serve them.

Tallie and Lucy immediately began chatting with her and helping her prepare the rest of the meal. Lucy had helped prepare such meals before. She was soon flipping tortillas expertly and chatting animatedly with Ricardo's mom.

Delicious enchiladas, smothered with cheese and topped with paprika and sour cream; tortillas filled with beef, beans, cheese, onions, and a spicy sauce; and tacos filled with their choice of beef or chicken, beans, shredded lettuce, tomatoes, cheese, and onions soon disappeared.

Once everyone had eaten his or her fill, Craig called them to circle up with the chairs. He asked Ricardo to join them as he had the most accurate information about the city.

"In about three hours we begin airlifting six families to the United States," he began. "We, as Americanos, are a magnet for the kidnappers. Wherever we appear, they will think something is about to go down. I'm sure my face as well as Lucy's and Bonnie's have been pictured on the news, so I have some suggestions, but I need your input so we don't have any glaring omissions."

"First," he continued, "I think we need to get a message to the media that tomorrow at noon several of the families will be flying to safety, leaving from Aeropuerto Tampico."

Lucy interrupted, excited about her idea. "Why don't you and I go to the airport and make a big scene about purchasing tickets, say for the Rodriguez family right about the time they are leaving?! Do you have a credit card for such things?" she asked, belatedly realizing that might be a problem.

"That's a good idea, Lucy. Yes, I have a card. I think you and I should keep a high profile at the airport while Bonnie, Tallie, Blake, and Ricardo keep the families moving in the right direction."

"We need to keep in constant communication," added Blake. "I've given Ricardo a secure phone." The rest of the group found and held up theirs.

"To keep it simple, why don't we focus on each family in the order they are leaving. And I think we should all check in with Craig every thirty minutes. Things can go bad really fast, and I don't think I need to remind you that we are in hostile territory."

Ricardo held up his hand. When Craig nodded at him, he began talking in a torrent of Spanish. Blake began interpreting.

"Ricardo thinks that the families are vulnerable right now. Without our presence and help, they may change their minds or even be attacked. The kidnappers surely know something is happening, and it won't be long before they discover what it is. He thinks the Lopezes and the Rodriguez family will be okay, but we should check on the Flores family, the Garcias, and the Maderas and trouble shoot any problems they may be having."

"Okay. I agree. Can Ricardo take Tallie with him and you, Blake, take Bonnie? After Lucy and I make our appearance at the airport, we will head to whatever location you think we're needed most. Is that agreeable to everyone?"

Blake had hoped to spend more time with Tallie, but since Bonnie didn't know Spanish, she would not be able to accompany Ricardo. Besides, Blake trusted Ricardo nearly as much as he trusted himself, maybe even more after the fiasco at the airport this morning, he thought wryly.

Ricardo made a call on his phone, and three taxicab drivers arrived at the front gate.

Just before they left for their respective destinations, Blake's phone rang.

He held up his hand for silence. His face remained impassive, but from his extreme stillness, everyone immediately knew something was wrong.

When he hung up his phone, he said, "Ricardo was right. The families are in more danger than ever. The Rodriquez's house was just bombed, and their taxi driver has disappeared."

Chapter Nineteen

The computer geeks had bravely set up shop again in Gram's living room. The rest of the cousins were gloomily playing card games in the den. The work on the farm had come to a standstill when thunderstorms rolled into the area.

The uncles had escaped to the barn following lunch, ostensibly to check for leaks in the roof, but really to escape the ennui of the cousins and the unanswerable questions of the aunts.

Gina was in the kitchen, helping Gram and the aunts bake cookies and boil the fifty or so ears of corn that had been picked and husked before the rains began. They didn't really need her help, so she was listening with only half an ear to their gossip.

Really, she was wondering if Corey was going to make an appearance. Then she reprimanded herself. Why was she thinking of Corey when she should be planning her wedding to Harry?

When should they get married? Not February, especially around the fourteenth. That was so cliché-ish. Maybe in April. She wanted a very simple wedding, nothing like the lavish affair Chelsea was planning.

But after the wedding, then what? Where would they live? Was Harry expecting to move into her apartment? Would he continue in his job? If he did, he would be absent more than he would be home as her husband.

They really needed to talk. She was always afraid of saying too much, of saying something that would alienate him, of saying something that would distract him from his job and get him killed. Instead, they talked lightly of pleasant things, nothing too in-depth or emotional.

She sighed. She enjoyed talking to him, but her life really went on the same before and after his phone calls.

She was startled out of her reverie by a loud knocking sound at the side door. Aunt Sarah opened the door for the dripping figure of Corey. He shed a water-laden overcoat and carefully placed the wet umbrella outside the door.

His larger than life personality instantly energized the occupants of the room. Gina could only watch with amazement and sigh, again.

"Hi, ladies," Corey said with an exuberant smile as he combed his fingers through his damp mahogany hair.

Hearing the commotion and hoping to snag a few cookies, Lawton, Gordon, and Paul appeared in the other doorway.

"Hey, Man! Did you survive 'you know'"? asked Paul cryptically.

The four laughed.

"Did you discover any new information?" asked Lawton eagerly.

"Yes, and yes," answered Corey, turning to each one as he answered.

"Have some cookies, boys," said Gram, bustling about the kitchen, pulling out some small, blue and red paper plates left over from their Fourth of July celebration on which she placed the large, palm-sized chocolate chip cookies.

More cousins appeared in the doorway. They had heard Corey's voice and smelled the heavenly scent of the cookies. They clamored for cookies as well.

Gina pulled out Styrofoam cups and poured milk and iced tea as some preferred tea with cookies over the milk, especially in the summer.

"So?" asked Lawton impatiently. "What did you learn from your lunch date?"

"'You know,'" said Paul, flipping his head from side to side with a grin.

Gina's head swiveled sharply from Lawton to Corey. Corey had been on a date? He sure worked fast, she thought sourly.

Corey's eyes met hers warily.

"Hey," said Kielah and Lindy together. "Don't diss cheerleaders, "finished Lindy in an oft-repeated mantra.

"I'm not dissing YOU this time, Pipsqueak," said Paul, pulling on her ponytail. "I'm talking about Corey's lunch date, the 'you know' Miss Stephanie."

Gina finally made the connection between the repetition of "you know" and the Stephanie who had been Corey's companion.

"Quiet, everyone," said Lawton loudly, clearly exasperated at not getting the information he wanted. "Let the man tell us what he learned."

But just then, the uncles walked in on the commotion.

Paul took one look at Lawton's frustrated expression and began laughing. Soon everyone had joined him.

The uncles were puzzled until Paul explained.

"Corey just returned from a date with Jeremy Saxon's secretary, and Lawton has been trying to find out for the last ten minutes what he discovered. Something juicy, we expect."

"Well then, let the man speak," said Uncle Davey.

All eyes turned to Corey.

"She was totally unconcerned that I might repeat to you all what I discovered," began Corey, purposely stringing out his story.

"And she was really happy that I am not related to any of you, especially after she found out that I flew my plane to the Walterboro airport."

"I finally asked her why the properties had to be inspected, just to see how much she knew."

"'Why, it's the new law, you know,'" she told me.

"So I asked her if they had inspected many other properties," he continued. "And guess what?"

"What?" everyone chorused.

"Your property was the first. They have a top five list of properties to inspect, but eventually all the properties along I-95 will be inspected."

"Just along I-95?" asked Grandpa Merrill with a snort of disbelief.

"Actually, I discovered some more information. Mr. Saxon was avoiding you because he and Mr. Spencer were waiting for a visit from the government."

"Who? The Lieutenant Governor of South Carolina?"

"No. Two men from the United Nations," said Corey.

The entire room was quiet for a full beat, then two and three while they pondered the implications of what Corey had just said.

"Really?!" said Lawton breathlessly.

"Oh yes. Stephanie was very impressed with their limousine. She had to tell me all about it. And even more important is the main result of their visit."

"Which was?" asked Uncle Galen.

"She told me that she will have her job for a very long time because once all the properties along I-95 are inspected, they plan to do more inspections, branch out, so to speak, until all the properties in South Carolina have been inspected for compliance with their rules and ordinances."

"The United Nations has no right to do that!" exploded Uncle Phil.

"Oh, they think they do," said Lawton. "They believe their laws, covenants and ordinances are higher than the Constitution. I've been digging deeper into the information about them."

"Tell us more, Son" said Uncle Davey. "We might as well know the worst."

"The ultimate goal of the United Nations is to move everyone into 'sustainable' cities, mostly in coastal areas so we don't leave such an impact on nature. If people live in such communities, it will eliminate the need for vehicles, further reducing mankind's footprint on the planet."

"Their goal is very admirable," said Uncle Galen.

Everyone was aghast that he should take their side, but he held up his hand and continued.

"However, I see two flaws in their thinking. First, the second law of thermodynamics has to do with entropy or degeneration. Even if humans don't leave so much as a print or a cigarette butt, nature is still in a state of degeneration as well as rebirth."

"I don't think they would necessarily argue with that although they might put a spin on it," said Uncle Davey thoughtfully. "What's the second flaw?"

"I know some people will disagree, but I believe they are putting creation above the Creator. In the natural order of things, even in evolutionary thinking, man is higher than nature, not the other way around."

"So what do we do next?" asked Aunt Clara.

Uncle Davey looked over at Corey. "I think it's time to look for an attorney. Where is that list of lawyers, Son?"

"It's outside in my briefcase. As soon as the rain lets up a bit, I'll go get it, and even though it's Friday afternoon, we can at least leave a message, asking them to contact us."

Lawton and Gina both noticed Corey's use of "we," Lawton with satisfaction and Gina with confusion. What did it really matter to him?

"I don't suppose anyone has noticed, but the sun is trying to shine out there," said Gordon dryly.

"Oh goody," said Lindy. "A rainbow. Let's go find a rainbow." She grabbed Gabby and Melanie, and the trio exited.

Lawton, Paul, and Gordon were more interested in digging up more information on their computers, and most of the uncles followed them to the living room.

Gina had planned to make her escape and check on Caden who still took a very short afternoon nap.

But Caden, awakened by all the voices, was tugging on Michael's gym shorts. Michael hoisted him onto his shoulders. "Let's go catch a rainbow, Buddy," he said.

Caden nodded his head emphatically yes. "See a rainbow, see a rainbow," he chanted.

Gina, seeing a glint in Corey's eyes as he looked at her, tried to think of some other chore upstairs, but her hesitation cost her.

"Let's go find a rainbow, Gina," said Corey, smiling down at her and tugging at her hand.

She couldn't refuse without seeming churlish, and besides, she wanted to see Caden's reaction.

They found a double rainbow. The colors shimmered vividly in the raindrop-laden air. One of the rainbows seemed to end right in Grandpa Merrill's cornfield, the other in the orchard where they had walked the weekend before.

"Have you ever tried to find the end of a rainbow?" asked Corey.

Gina smiled whimsically in remembrance. "A long time ago when I was a little girl," she said as they watched Michael with Caden still on his shoulders, running slowly around the yard so Caden could "catch" some of the few raindrops that still fell.

"Why don't we try to find the end of the one in the orchard?"

Lindy and Melanie heard him.

"Let's find the end of the rainbow in the orchard," they called to the rest of the cousins who had come outside, and they started toward the orchard.

Most of the aunts were standing by the door, absorbing the delicate beauty of the scene before them.

Gina stood still for a few more moments, enjoying the streams of sunlight bursting through the clouds, the dancing colors of the rainbows, the scent of the rain-drenched earth and fields, the calls of birds and cousins in the orchard.

Then she turned and followed Michael and her son. Michael had placed him on the ground again so a stray branch wouldn't hit little Caden's face. Michael held his hand firmly. Corey caught up to them and grabbed Caden's other hand.

Michael wanted to join the girls. Gina suspected the crush Gabby had on him was mutual.

Corey obligingly placed Caden between himself and Gina.

Darn. This made them seem too much like a little family unit. Fortunately, Caden's childish chatter covered Gina's awkwardness as the thought crossed her mind.

She stole a glance at Corey. He was listening to Caden and patiently answering his questions about rainbows.

They caught up with Melanie, Gabby, and the rest of the cousins who had come outside. The girls were dancing at what they were sure was the end of the rainbow.

Frankly, Gina couldn't see it. But she still enjoyed the little breeze on her face that cut through the humidity and watching her son, his face wreathed in smiles, his laughter a silvery sound as he ran in and out of the girls, his arms stretched high and his face tilted up to the sun and the lovely colors.

It was a beautiful, golden moment that blew away the tensions of the day. But it only lasted a moment.

A cloud slid over the sun, and the raindrops started coming down in earnest. The cousins began running back toward the house, laughing. Corey scooped up Caden and dashed to the house, Gina right behind him.

He deposited Caden on the step and made sure he and Gina were inside before he dashed to his vehicle to retrieve his briefcase with the list of lawyers.

Chapter Twenty

As Ricardo and Tallie approached the home of the Garcias, Ricardo asked the driver to drive past the house before circling back so he could get a sense of their situation and see if anyone was lurking in the area.

Their house was mint green. It had no porch; the front door simply opened onto the street. But next door was a crepe myrtle tree in bloom. The tiny, crimson flowers added beauty to an otherwise drab street Tallie thought.

Across the street was a small cemetery with numerous gothic crosses and tombstones. Most were painted white, but some were simply made of concrete, and one was made of rosy granite. Tufts of dried out grass and weeds grew amongst the tributes to the dead. A lone figure sat on one of the tombstones underneath a tree.

The pavement ended about a hundred feet past the cemetery and the house. Behind the house was a field with a fence made of old posts but brand new, taut barbed wire.

Ricardo wanted to keep an eye on the figure in the cemetery, but he urged Tallie to knock on the door and enter. His gift was street smarts. Hers was helping people.

The door was opened immediately by Senora Garcia. She ushered in Tallie immediately, closing the door quickly behind her.

Tallie saw a small living room with an old television sitting on a coffee table at one end. Directly opposite the front door was a large doorway to the kitchen. A tiny table sat under an equally tiny window with starched white curtains opened to show the back field with a lone tree. The back door opened onto a very small patio area.

To her left she saw Susanna standing in the hall to the bedrooms with her three little brothers and a sister peering at Tallie from behind her. Then she saw the worry in Simone Garcia's eyes. "What is wrong?" she asked gently.

"My husband left on his bicycle to talk to his brother about taking our goats two hours ago." She motioned to the back window, and now Tallie saw that a small shed pieced together with a patchwork of shapes and types of wood had been added to the back of the house. Unmindful of the August heat, three goats were eating placidly in the field.

"He has not returned, Senorita Tallie. I am worried."

"I will let Ricardo know. Perhaps he can help find your husband."

Tallie heard the taxicab drive past the house. She expected Ricardo to knock on the front door but instead saw him in the back of the house. Senora Garcia opened the back door. Tallie explained the situation to him, and he promised he would look for Stephan Garcia.

"Do you know who is sitting in the cemetery?" he asked Senora Garcia.

Simone Garcia crossed the two rooms and looked out the front window. "I thought it was old Timoteo mourning his wife, but now I'm not so sure."

"I'll meander over there and have a look. I don't think whoever it is saw me exit the taxi. I had the driver let me out another block over by a tree. He'll be back in an hour."

Ricardo looked around the impoverished living quarters. "Can you help them pack? Maybe they can leave as early as tonight. I'm sure Blake can make the arrangements with the pilot."

"We have no suitcases, just backpacks and bags," said Senora Garcia apologetically.

"I brought some suitcases with me. Did you get them out of the taxi before he left?" she asked Ricardo.

"Si. They are down the street behind the tree. I will get them after I discover who is in the cemetery. I won't be long," he said with a cheerful grin at the children before he quietly left out the back door.

Tallie assessed the situation. Each child had several sets of clothing and a few toys. They were piled in the middle of the two rooms used by the children. Susanna had been helping her mother pack their belongings in their room. The kitchen had been untouched.

"Can I pack some kitchen items for you? Do you have any treasures that you want me to pack carefully?"

Senora Garcia took down from the highest shelf an intricately carved wooden bowl. "Mi abuleo made this for my wedding day," she said caressing it gently.

"It's beautiful," said Tallie. She heard a soft thud outside the back door. Looking through the window, she saw Ricardo hold up the set of suitcases. They were packed in each other, five pieces in all. Ricardo had disappeared even before she opened the door to retrieve them.

"We should be able to pack everything and get you out tonight," said Tallie.

But a look of hesitation crossed Senora Garcia's face. "My husband wants to work tonight so he gets his pay check. He has worked so hard for it. And he doesn't know how he can explain to his boss his leaving. He can't pick up his pay check until tomorrow at eight."

"Where does he work?"

"On the docks."

"Well, let's pack everything, and when Ricardo returns, he can talk to Blake. I don't think staying here tonight will be safe for any of you. I'll see if you and the children can stay at a hotel tonight. That might be the best thing."

Tallie went to the immaculately clean kitchen where she packed the kitchen items quickly and efficiently. Then she helped the children zip their suitcases, making a game of it with the three little boys and causing them to go into a fit of giggles.

Senora Garcia and her two girls were nearly finished in the parents' bedroom when Ricardo appeared at the front door. He was talking quietly on his phone.

"Si. I give him a nice nighty-night knock and take his phone. I'll make sure the policia get it," he said to the person on the other end.

Tallie looked out the front window but could see no one in the cemetery.

She looked at Ricardo in wonder, but he just winked and dropped a second cell phone into his pocket.

"Is that Blake?" she asked.

"Si."

"May I talk to him? You need to hear this, too," she said, motioning for him to stay when he looked like he was going to go into the hall.

Quickly Tallie explained the situation with Senor Garcia's job and asked if she could take the rest of the Garcia's to a hotel. They would be finished packing in about fifteen minutes.

Blake gave her the name of a hotel that he considered safe.

"It's a little pricey. Do you have money or a card?"

"Oh, yes. The agency makes sure I have a fully loaded card when I travel. They know I won't be using it on shoes!"

Blake laughed. Shoes were the last thing on both their minds.

"Bonnie and I are with the Maderas. If we can get them packed, I'm going to try to get them out of here by six in the morning. The children want to bring their cats and dogs. Do you think the pilots would mind?"

"No, not at all. They're used to strange and unusual cargo. Trust me. I once arranged passage for a camel. I'll have to tell you about that one sometime."

"Okay. Can't wait to hear that story. The kids will be glad to bring their pets with them to America. Hope they have crates. If not, I'll have to improvise. I don't want to have to buy some at a store here. It might create too much talk."

"The pilots should have some crates. And maybe one of your taxicab drivers might be able to find some."

"That's a good suggestion."

"Gotta go. Mr. Garcia just came home."

"Later."

All of the suitcases, bags, and backpacks were lined up by the front door. Ricardo was keeping an eye on the street, waiting for the taxicab driver.

Stephano Garcia was being hugged by his wife. She quietly told him about the plans to leave earlier and stay in a hotel. Tallie watched Senor Garcia's face sag with relief. What a strain these people carried. She was so glad she could help even a little.

"Everyone ready?" asked Ricardo. He could see the taxicab two blocks away. The children crowded by the door until their mother told them sharply to help with the bags and backpacks, saving their lives.

The taxicab was going awfully fast. Ricardo's street smarts went on high alert.

"Everyone down," he yelled, diving into the room and slamming the door shut with his foot.

They heard the taxicab rocket by, and then the unmistakable sounds of machine guns and motorcycles filled the air. The youngest boy was held firmly down by his mother's arm flung over him.

Ricardo watched the spray of bullets. He figured the only thing that saved them all was the curb which was about a foot higher than the floor of the house.

The hail of bullets ceased, and the sounds of the motorcycles faded. Ricardo warned them to stay down. They waited, faces down for three minutes, four. It seemed like an eternity.

Pulling his phone from his pocket, he called his friend, the taxicab driver.

Si, the motorcyclists were gone. He had seen them at the store eight blocks up the road, and he could tell they were up to no good. Then he heard one of them say the name Garcia, and he thought that if he drove by really fast, it would give Ricardo the warning he needed.

"Muchas gracias, hombre!"

"De nada." Then he explained that a friend of his had an old work truck. Wouldn't it be better to transport the family in that? All of them would fit comfortably in the back, and it would arouse little suspicion.

In less than five minutes, an old rent-a-truck was idling its motor outside their door. In spite of a leg grazed by a bullet, Senora Garcia bravely shut her mind to the pain, and in three minutes everyone was in the back except for Ricardo who elected to stay in the front with his phone handy.

The Garcias were on their way to the hotel.

Meanwhile, Blake and Bonnie had their hands full with the lively Madera household.

Their house, similar to Ricardo's mother's, had a central courtyard. Several older boys were gathered at one end of the cul-de-sac street, practicing their skateboarding techniques on an improvised ramp of wood and cement blocks.

After depositing Blake and Bonnie in front of the Madera's house, the taxicab driver drove down to the boys and had a spirited conversation with them. Then he executed a slow turn and, missing the ramp and blocks, drove back to where Blake and Bonnie stood watching.

"El ninos will watch the street for you," he said with a grin. "I know their fathers. I will return in an hour as we agreed, but I think you will need more time with this family."

Blake nodded. He was sure his friend was right.

Inside, Mollie Madera was a dynamo of cheerful energy. She was trying to leave everything spotlessly clean as she left. But the four cats, two dogs, and three children impeded her efforts.

Bonnie observed the situation, and then clapped her hands and whistled loudly.

Blake regarded her with admiration. Who could have known that such a quiet, petite woman could possess such a piercing whistle?

Everyone and everything instantly stilled and quieted, their attention riveted to her.

Bonnie looked at Blake and ordered him to translate.

"You don't have time for this," she said sternly. "The Rodriguez's house was blown up this morning, and the Garcia's home was just shot through with bullets." She had heard Blake's conversation with Tallie.

"You," she addressed the oldest boy. "What is you name?"

"Mi llamo, Carlos," he said meekly, needing no translation.

"Do you have crates for the dogs?"

"Si."

"You need to get them in their crates. Make sure you pack some food and water for them. Have you finished packing your clothes and anything else you want to bring with you?"

"Si."

"Bueno." Bonnie had picked up a few Spanish words. "When you finish with the dogs, you are to find the cats and do the same thing."

Turning to Macy, Bonnie asked if she had finished packing.

"Si," said Macy with a pert grin.

"Has your madre finished packing your little brother's things?"

Macy looked uncertainly at her mother who shook her head no.

"Then you need to help her and if your little brother cries or fusses, you need to keep him happy."

She turned to Mollie who knew a fair amount of English already.

"Have you packed everything for you and your husband?"

"Almost," replied Mollie.

"You must finish within the hour," said Bonnie, ruthlessly ignoring Mollie's gasp. "You don't have time to clean anything. Now show me first what you want me to pack in the kitchen. Everything else must be left. You can call your brother or sister when you are on the way and either give whatever is left to them or have them store the rest of your belongings for you."

Everyone stared at Bonnie. "Well, let's go!" she said impatiently, and everyone silently moved to do as she had asked.

Blake nearly laughed aloud. Who would have known? He busied himself helping Carlos and then moving luggage and bags near the front door.

His mind, however, was on the missing Rodriguez family and the Flores family. Craig was supposed help the Floreses, but what had happened to the Rodriguez family and their taxicab driver?

Chapter Twenty-One

Two hours later, the Garcia and Madera families, except for the fathers/husbands, were ensconced in an undisclosed hotel with Bonnie. Blake had rented the entire third floor of the hotel and posted guards, men he knew he could trust, at each of the three entrances to the third floor.

The Lopez families were at their designated rendezvous point awaiting two planes, and the taxicab driver for the extended Rodriguez family, Jose, had finally checked in with Blake.

When Jose had arrived to pick up the family, it had become apparent that they would need another taxicab or a small truck for the luggage.

But Jose was a good friend of Blake's who was just as streetwise, and he felt jumpy; he had a sense that they needed to get out of there right away. So he'd loaded as much of the luggage as he could into his trunk.

Several choice pieces of furniture that had been handed down in the family to the grandparents had already been placed in a shed that stood behind their house fifty or sixty yards.

Jose kept insisting that they needed to leave immediately, but then he had gotten a flat tire. A pal of his just happened to be in the neighborhood, so they had reloaded everything into his pal's car.

Jose, left behind, had moved his vehicle to a shady spot under a tree just down the road. If he had to change a tire, he wanted to be out of the blazing sun.

He had stepped into the shade of the tree when he noticed another vehicle driving slowly by the Rodriguez's house. Three men jumped from the car. Hiding behind the tree, Jose had watched as they kicked open the front door, and threw a gas can inside with a Molotov cocktail after it.

The house erupted in flames. The three men stopped to exult in their evil handiwork, but the driver impatiently tapped his horn, so the three jumped in, and the car sped away.

Jose pulled his cell phone and called a friend on the police force with the make, model, and plate of the car. Then he called another friend to bring him a tire.

He was about ready to leave his hiding place behind the tree when a sixth sense told him to stay. In disbelief he watched the same car with the same men come around the far corner again.

Again they stopped at the house and, jumping out, threw more flares at the house, this time smashing the windows of the bedrooms.

As they drove past his car, they threw the last one in his open window. No! They couldn't destroy his car. No!

But the flames licked greedily at the upholstery, and in mere minutes, the entire car was an inferno ready to explode.

Jose had just enough sense left to leave the protection of the tree and sprint down the street.

The explosion made him stagger, but he made it to the end of the street where he collapsed onto the sidewalk, dazed with grief.

"So where are you now?" asked Blake.

"Waiting for the plane at the meeting point," said Jose gloomily. "My friend gave me a lift here. I wanted to make sure the family made it into the aeroplane all right. These banditos, they play for keeps."

"Don't worry about your car," Blake began to say, but he was cut off by Jose.

"Here is the plane now. We catch up later, man."

That meant the Lopezes should be leaving, too. Blake waited tensely by his phone. Jose and his other amigo, Juan, should be texting him soon that the families were safe.

Juan's text came first. Both Lopez families were safely on their way. Jose's followed. Three families safely on their way, three to go!

Blake quickly texted Juan, asking him to tail Senor Garcia as he left for work and make sure no harm came to him.

He gave Bonnie, who was tending Senora Garcia's leg wound, the thumbs up sign and headed to the door. He would make sure the Flores family was safe, and then he would also shadow Senor Garcia at work tonight to make sure he stayed safe.

Craig and Lucy had played to the crowd at the airport, but instead of sending them to work with the Floreses, Blake had sent them to retrieve Miguel Maderas. They would make sure he was reunited with his family at the hotel.

Blake punched Ricardo's number even though he really wanted to talk to Tallie.

"Blake," came Ricardo's urgent whisper. "Don't call Tallie. "She and the Flores family have been kidnapped. I'm tailing them."

"Give me your location," said Blake tersely.

"Doesn't matter," said Ricardo. "I overheard them. They're taking them to Laguna del Carpintero and feeding them to the crocs. I heard them talk about the salon. That's on the southern tip of the Laguna. How soon can you be there?"

"Five minutes. What does their car look like?"

"You won't like this. It looks like one of the taxicabs you hired."

"Just don't lose them. I'll find them. Call when they pull over."

The Laguna del Carpintero or Carpenter Lake was a fifty hectare lake in the middle of the city. The city had improved it in many ways, building walkways, parks, picnic areas, and even a convention center along its perimeter. But it was infested by crocodiles.

He couldn't imagine Tallie bound and thrown into the Laguna for the crocodiles to munch. He had just met her, yet no girl had stirred him like she did. He couldn't lose her when he had just met her.

Meanwhile, Tallie was holding Francesca on her lap so her mother could hold six-month-old April. Her little brothers, Emilio and Eduardo, were being comforted quietly by their father. They were all crammed in the back of a taxicab.

Tallie had heard enough of their plans to be terrified. Her one hope was that Ricardo was on their tail. He had disappeared when the door had burst open and men with guns had quickly subdued and rounded them up.

Grimly she thought of her mother's reaction. A thrill of vindictiveness stiffened her spine. Her mother, the fiery Paige Marshall Peters-Templeton, would never rest until her daughter's death was avenged.

She would not die. Not here and not now. But she had to think quickly and find a way to rescue all of them. The kidnappers in the front had slowed down and were arguing about where to turn the car.

Good. She had an idea that sooner or later the kidnappers would bind them, so she quietly whispered in Francesca's ear, telling her how to hold her wrists if she were tied to give her more flexibility to get out of her bonds.

"Now pretend you want to snuggle with your papa, and tell him. Trade places with Emilio, and I'll tell him."

It was all she could think of to do. But she had often seen that when people felt empowered, they were able to conquer their fears and persevere in the face of the most difficult odds.

Just as she finished talking to Emilio, the car ground to a halt. About an hour of light was left. That certainly was an advantage, too, since she didn't know the area well.

They were herded out of the car at gunpoint. Looking around the nearly deserted area, Tallie saw a rounded building across the Laguna and a smaller rounded one to her right. Then she saw the tail lights of a car wink out just behind a bank of trees some thirty feet away. Was that Ricardo?

Ricardo and Pietro, the driver, jumped out of their vehicle. Ricardo, already on the phone with him, had the presence of mind to flag down Blake's car.

Jumping out, the three drew their guns and slid from tree to tree in the gathering dusk. They saw Tallie submitting to the bandito's demands to put her hands behind her back and begin tying them with rope.

Only two kidnappers. This would be almost too easy. Blake saw Ricardo nod to the right, indicating he would take out the kidnapper on the right. Blake slid to the tree where Pietro was hiding.

"When we move in, grab two of the children and run with them to the taxicab. Tell them to stay down. We'll be right behind you with the others."

He and Ricardo had worked together before. They moved as close as they dared, some twenty feet away. He saw Ricardo's arm come up and begin the count, three, two, one.

Ricardo's gun felled the one kidnapper. The other was already grabbing one of the boys and holding a gun to his head, but bless her, Tallie sent a glance of desperation to the mother and then bowled into the kidnapper as hard as she could.

The gun fired harmlessly over Ricardo's head. The mother rolled her baby across the grass and bravely tried to wrestle the gun away from the kidnapper. When they turned sideways, Blake finally had a clear shot. He squeezed the trigger.

And it was over. Pietro already had Francesca and Eduardo and was heading up the small hill toward the taxicab. Blood pumping, Blake pulled his knife and cut the bonds on Tallie while Ricardo did the same for Frank Flores.

Frank went directly to his wife, Amelia, who was cuddling the crying baby. Ricardo gently helped Emilio to his feet, telling him over and over what a brave boy he had been.

Frank turned his attention to his small son. He picked him up and held him close in his arms. Emilio buried his face in his father's shoulder and sobbed.

Blake crushed Tallie close. She could hear and feel his heart pounding in his chest. Then he released her abruptly and began herding everyone toward the cars.

After a quick discussion at the cars, Pietro and Ricardo put Francesca and Eduardo in Blake's car and headed back to the Flores's home to finish packing the car with their luggage.

Blake drove the family to the hotel. He was supremely conscious of Tallie sitting behind him, holding Francesca and comforting her. But he needed to focus on work. He called his friend at the desk, and they were allowed to use a small service elevator in the back to get to the third floor.

The family was shown to a room where they collapsed wearily onto the beds. Blake left them to Tallie's tender ministrations.

Meanwhile, Craig and Lucy had just arrived in the next room with Senor Madera. They had stopped and ordered food for everyone after a phone conversation with Bonnie.

Blake was anxious to get them on a plane before midnight. But they all needed a break from the tensions of the afternoon. So he sat in silence, planning the next few hours in his head while watching the Madera children eat and then feed their menagerie of animals.

He was so deep in thought that he jumped when Bonnie put a hand on his shoulder.

"The Maderas want to know when they can leave," she said gently.

"Right away. However, I'm going to use a utility van like we did for the Garcias. Let me make a phone call and get Jose working on getting us one."

He pulled out his phone. Minutes later it was all arranged. A van would be at the back door in about thirty minutes.

Jose's mood changed when Blake assured him his taxicab would be replaced. Si, he would find a van for them.

He then called the pilot, making sure he knew where his pickup would be.

Pietro and Ricardo arrived with the Flores's luggage, their pets, and most of their household goods. Blake wondered how they would get all these things plus the Floreses into Pietro's taxicab, but Pietro had solved the problem by asking for the help of a friend that both he and Ricardo knew.

Blake considered waiting until morning to fly the Floreses out of Tampico, but Frank and Amelia both insisted that going now would be fine. The children would sleep most of the way, making things easier for Amelia, especially in caring for little April.

Pietro and Ricardo headed to the meeting point with the Floreses while Craig and Lucy escorted the Madera family. With one last check on the Garcia family and

Tallie, Blake headed to the docks to help Juan guard Senor Garcia. He sure hoped the night would be uneventful. He'd had enough excitement to last him the rest of the year.

Chapter Twenty-Two

Uncle Craig, Lucy, Bonnie, Blake, and Tallie arrived back from Mexico early Saturday morning. Uncle Craig slept for two days straight with breaks only to eat and debrief with Scotch.

The last three families had embarked on their flights without incident. All six families had flown into Charleston, South Carolina.

Blake was tempted to sleep as well, but he had unfinished business to do. Sunday morning he once again took a commercial flight to Tampico.

His first stop was at the Lopezes' hardware store. He talked to Christopher, their nephew who had been left in charge, and discovered he really did know the hardware business. He would do well even though he had only just graduated from high school. His mother, Lupe, was available to help him.

What Christopher did not seem to know much about was why his uncles had left.

"They will have a great opportunity to start a new hardware store in the United States. Maybe they will start a chain of stores and invite me to America, too."

Blake could see the dreams in his eyes. He determined to help this young man in the future. Christopher said nothing about the kidnapping of his cousins, and Blake didn't ask. He didn't want to reveal too much. Instead he suggested surveillance cameras be installed as soon as possible, considering the area in which the store was located.

Christopher agreed, mentioning a few other modifications he intended to pursue. Blake could not fault his perception of the market nor his enthusiasm.

When he left the store, he called Jose. Jose was very gloomy. He had lost his car, and he had no hopes of getting much more than a clunker any time soon.

"Donde esta?" I'll come pick you up, and we'll go car shopping."

"Really?" Jose brightened considerably. He wanted to chose a Dodge Charger, but Blake directed him to the SUVs, particularly the ones with tinted, shatterproof glass and armored panels.

Jose ran his hands over the smooth leather interior. He whistled appreciatively but shook his head.

"Come. I have a new job for you."

When Jose got into the back seat, Blake took out his checkbook and wrote a check for the amount the salesman asked.

They continued to drool over the GPS system and all the other extra gadgets that had been installed.

The salesman returned, his face wreathed in smiles. He bowed to them as if they were royalty and handed Blake the keys. Blake made arrangements for his rental car to be returned, and then he drove to the Lopezes' hardware store.

"See this store? Your new job is to guard it. Come back tonight, and chat up the new owner, Christopher. He's a young hombre, and he's going to need a new friend like you. Take him for a ride in your car. Let the banditos know they are not to mess with him."

"Got it. You my new boss?"

"Si. I put money in your account twice a month if you do this and run other little errands for me from time to time. "

"Okay, boss!" responded Jose enthusiastically.

Blake pulled into an Oxxo parking lot and switched places with Jose.

"Now let's find Juan, Pietro, and Ricardo. I have another plan."

Juan lived not too far from Ricardo's madre. He agreed to meet them there. Pietro was harder to find, but he gave them careful directions, and soon, the five were enjoying a great meal.

Blake had them list the people who had helped in rescuing the families of the kidnapped girls. Twelve others plus the chop shop owner. He wanted them paid for their time and their courage.

Then he told them of his plan. He wanted to send a message to the kidnappers and try to discover the head of the human trafficking ring.

Another vehicle like Jose's would be available for Ricardo to retrieve from the dealership in two day. He would have new tires, impenetrable to bullets, shipped to a small house on the outskirts of town that he had purchased after the sale of his step-father's mansion. He outlined a few more ideas, but he soon realized their attention was straying to the vehicle parked outside.

What the heck. It was time to ride.

Tallie, poor girl, didn't get much time to sleep. She wanted the families temporarily housed in a secure place. And she had two families, the Garcias and the Floreses who had gone through terrible ordeals.

Her cousin, Corey, still in town, had met them each of the families at the airport. Instead of taking them to a hotel as instructed, he had rented the Flowertown Bed and Breakfast so they could have more privacy.

The families enjoyed the calm and peaceful ambience of the bed and breakfast and especially the wonderful meals Veronique, the proprietress, provided. She made a special effort to fix foods they would enjoy and even invited them into her kitchen to show her some of their Mexican specialties with a shopping trip for provisions first.

Tallie knew she had to arrange who would stay there in Summerville and who would go on to Georgia, but she thought she would let the families enjoy a bit of Summerville and acclimate to the United States for a few days first.

She was especially concerned with the trauma the Garcias and Floreses had endured, but their tight family structures coupled with the relief of having their girls returned, as well as the holiday mood this little vacation provided was enough to elicit smiles from even the shyest.

A philanthropic group in Georgia wanted to adopt the Rodriguez family. One of the women in the group owned a small hotel chain, and as she opened a new one, she wanted to coach Roberto Rodriguez into the role of manager.

The grandparents would be able to live in the hotel with the family, and with plenty of security cameras, they would be safe.

Miguel Madera, already a professor, would be put in a university close to the hotel. Molly Madera had promised to visit the grandparents at least once a week. Tallie was satisfied.

A businessman in the same group wanted to help the Lopez families. He was in construction and had done well. Now he was looking to open a lumber and supply company. It was similar to hardware, and he would be able to use the Lopez brothers' business expertise in running a store.

Blake returned late Monday evening. Knowing Tallie would be staying with Chelsea, he decided to visit the Merrills.

During the entire trip home, he had thought of the beautiful, intelligent Tallie who could hold her own in confronting top law enforcement, who could console and cuddle a crying baby, who could organize the travel of six families, who could give children courage in a life-threatening situation by calmly showing them how to position their hands.

He hadn't wanted to think of her. His was a job best done alone with no emotional ties to another.

But her combination of delicate skin and spine of steel combined with that cloud of glorious red hair was so potent, it stirred his senses as nothing had in, well, forever.

Dared he believe she might return his interest? She had mouthed those words, "be safe." And she had definitely clung to him when he had hugged her close after her near-death in the crocodile pits. But were those merely exaggerated affections due to the extreme danger they had faced together?

And how would their lives fit together? He couldn't ask her to give up her work as a human rights liaison. Her passion for her work was clearly discernable to anyone inclined to see.

Perhaps he was presuming too much. He had only one way to find out. So after dropping his bag in the middle of his bedroom floor, cleaning his guns, and sleeping in his own bed once again, here he was Tuesday morning with his hat in his hand so to speak, hoping he might get her to go to lunch with him.

He knew enough not to go to the front door. Instead, he let himself in the black, iron gate and knocked at the back door.

Galeah opened the door and welcomed him warmly. "You're just in time for breakfast. We're eating al fresco in the sunroom today. Can you take this bowl of fruit out there for me?" The girls just took the eggs, ham, and utensils out."

Mr. Merrill was seated at one of the tables, coffee cup steaming and newspaper folded open in one hand. Chelsea in white jeans and blue shirt and Tallie in khaki pants and crisp white top had their backs to him as they set their platters down on the table.

Galeah stuck her head around the corner. "How do you take your coffee, Blake?"

Both girls turned quickly to regard him.

"Black," he said automatically to Galeah. But his attention was on Tallie. Faint circles showed under her eyes, and she looked tired.

But her quick, somewhat shy smile welcomed him and dispelled some of the unease he was feeling.

Now why would she suddenly be shy? he wondered as he crossed to the laden table to serve himself.

"Good morning," said Chelsea. "We haven't seen you for several days."

So. His absence had been discussed. Dare he hope he had been missed?

"I flew back to Tampico to clean up some details," he said.

Tallie looked at him sharply. "What details?" she asked as she served herself from the buffet.

"I wanted to make sure the Lopezes' nephew would suffer no repercussions from his uncles' move to the United States. And I'm going to try to discover just who is the brains behind this kidnapping and human trafficking business," he said with a glint of steel in his eye. "How are the families doing?"

"They are doing just fine. My cousin, Corey, decided they needed to be at the Flowertown Bed & Breakfast instead of the hotel where I had arranged for them to stay. They are really enjoying it, and I'm going to enjoy handing the bill to Corey!"

"Have you smoothed out the details of where each family will be living?"

"I think so. A group of philanthropists in Georgia will be working with four of the families, the Lopezes, the two Rodriguez families, and the Maderas. I've located homes and sponsors for the Garcias and the Floreses right here in Summerville."

"Good. Once the families are settled, I want to have what they placed in storage shipped to their homes."

"That's a kind thing to do, Blake," said Tallie.

"But of course," he said, sketching a bow before he sat at the table where she had sat to eat.

"No. Really. I think you are going above and beyond the call of duty."

"Don't let it get out," said Blake. "I'm still billing the Department of Homeland Security for our expenses while we were down in Tampico. And that includes the drivers who helped us."

Chelsea joined them, and Galeah, after giving Blake his coffee, served herself and joined her husband at the next table.

"Do you think the nephew is in danger?" asked Chelsea, picking up the last conversational thread she had heard.

"Possibly," answered Blake. "But I have some men keeping an eye on him." He didn't go into details.

Lawton appeared in the doorway. For once he was dressed neatly in khakis and a collared shirt and ready for the day. Normally, he made an appearance at the breakfast table dishabille in a garish red and purple silk robe.

"Good morning everyone," he said cheerfully.

"Who are you, and what have you done with my brother?" asked Chelsea in mock fear.

"Lanie has a new job at Single Smile Café, so I went and had coffee with her first thing this morning," Lawton said rather smugly.

"Coffee always works wonders on your disposition, and Lanie, does the rest," said Chelsea. Lawton had finally given Lanie a ring. They had been high school and college sweethearts, and Lanie was an integral part of the family already.

"Don't forget the 'fiesta' we are having Thursday night at the bed and breakfast as a send-off for the four families that will be moving on to Georgia on Friday," reminded Tallie.

"Wouldn't miss it," said Lawton. "I love Mexican food!"

"I'll be there," said Blake with a glance at Tallie.

"Good. I was hoping you'd come," she said simply.

Just then Blake's phone rang.

"Hola."

The others guessed he was talking to someone in Tampico.

"No, I haven't seen the news yet."

Blake suddenly went still. "All of them? Even the children?" he asked.

"Si. We'll keep in touch." He shut his phone and stared down at his plate, his jaw working.

"What's the matter?" asked Tallie gently, putting a comforting hand on his arm.

"The Tomas home was bombed just a few hours ago. Jose doesn't think anyone survived. Excuse me."

He stood abruptly and left the room.

Tears came to Tallie's eyes as she remembered the twins peeking from behind Rachel Tomases' skirt and their twelve-year old daughter, Christe.

Galeah and her husband joined them at the table. Chelsea squeezed Tallie's hand, and Galeah put her arm around her shoulders as Tallie began to tell them about Senora Tomas, her family, and her absolute belief that she and her family would be safe.

Blake, meanwhile, was furious with himself. Why hadn't he thought of the Thomases? He had just been there. How could he have ignored them? Yes, it had been their decision to stay, but he had the manpower to protect them, and he had failed, failed them miserably.

And were the Monterreys and Maria's family safe? He opened his phone and savagely punched redial.

182

Chapter Twenty-Three

The weather cooperated for Thursday's fiesta. After the sweltering heat of an August day in the South, a morning thunderstorm with the accompanying pyrotechnics cut the humidity and gave way to a beautiful rainbow and a balmy breeze by evening.

Veronique decorated the eight foot deep piazza and the trees in the garden with colorful piñatas, enough for each child to take one with him or her. Hanging in garlands from the eaves were white mini lights.

The garden, with hundreds more mini lights became a fairy wonderland when the twilight deepened. But while the sun shone, the garden was still a sensual feast for the eyes, ears and nose with layers of texture and color, scents and sounds.

Blake had enjoyed the reds and oranges of zinnias and poppies contrasted with the green foliage and the silvery gray of the Spanish moss that hung from an old, well-spread oak as well as several crepe myrtle trees.

He knew all about the lights as he had helped Greg, Veronique's husband, string them in the trees and bushes along with aid from Carlos, Esperanza, and Macy.

And he was acutely aware of Tallie, slim and regal, even in the white shorts and pink top she had chosen to wear during the hottest part of the day. She was in and out of the house and the guest house in back, tasting the cooking and baking or organizing games for the children or helping with the decorations.

When he was ready to hang the piñatas, she came outside to help with that as well. As he stood on a ladder to hang eight of the piñatas from the porch eaves, he looked down at her, and he would swear awareness once again arced between them, especially as she handed him the piñatas.

He didn't want any awkwardness between them, so he asked her to tell him about her family. She already knew some of his story, and he wasn't quite ready to tell her the parts she didn't know.

"Where is your family from?" he asked to get her started.

"Both of my parents are from Virginia. My father, Thomas Peters-Templeton married a Marshall, a descendant of John Marshall, the Supreme Court Justice. When his daughter married a Harvie, we lost the Marshall name, but one of my ancestors handily married back into the Marshall family, so Mom has benefited from it ever since."

"Wow! Your family goes back a long way."

"So does yours. I can't claim to have any famous American Indian ancestors as famous as Tsali."

"My grandfather traced his ancestors back to the early settling of North Carolina, but I haven't taken the time to really analyze his papers about it," confessed Blake.

"That should give you something to do on a cold, winter day," said Tallie as she blew her hair away from her face which was pink and damp from the mugginess.

"You would love a cool, winter day right now, wouldn't you," asked Blake. "When we finish hanging the piñatas, let's go get a frappe."

"That sounds good," said Tallie, "especially since we didn't get a chance to get lunch the other day."

Blake hadn't minded. He had been able to chauffeur Tallie around town as she had run errands and to watch her perform magic in procuring housing and household necessities for the two families staying behind in Summerville.

Then Veronique and the Spanish women had wanted them to sample the foods they had been baking all morning, so they had eaten at the bed and breakfast.

"So my family, huh?" Tallie interrupted his thoughts. "My father is Thomas Peters-Templeton, banker. He owns six or seven banks in Virginia and has no desire to own more. He actually enjoys helping my mother. She inherited two hotels in the Richmond area, and she pours much of her efforts into making them one of a kind."

"What about your brothers? You have two, right?"

"Yes and no sisters, so I'm really excited that Jasper is marrying Chelsea. Stanley is twenty-six. He just finished his graduate program at William and Mary in communications. He's doing an internship with some bigwig company in Europe this summer and fall. He'll finish just in time for the wedding."

"Is he older or younger than you?" asked Blake as he moved the ladder to hang the next piñata.

"He's older. I'm only twenty-three. Tyler Clay is older, too. He beat me by two years. But since I'm the baby and a girl, I naturally get more attention, so I think that makes up for it," she said rather smugly.

"What does Tyler Clay do?"

"He helps Mom at the hotels, majored in hospitality so he can bring 'fresh, new ideas' to the place. Mom just about had a fit when he said that to her. She was afraid he'd want to modernize the décor with abstract paintings and art."

"What taste does your mother have?"

"She likes her traditional styles but with all the plush comforts one can have. I had to calm her down and point out that Tyler Clay has the same taste in styles as she does." Tallie laughed softly to herself at the memory.

They had finished with the piñatas. Blake wiped his forehead on the sleeve of his t-shirt. Then he held out his hand.

"Come. Let's go get those frappes. I need to get out of this heat."

"Me, too!" said Tallie. She slipped on the sandals she had discarded.

Holding hands, they walked around the back of the house to the graveled parking area where Blake's car was parked. It would be a cool oasis after the work of the mid-afternoon.

****

Gina was running late. Her supervisor at Wal-Mart had been expecting a visit from the corporate office, and she wanted every register area cleaned before a cashier went off duty.

Then the babysitter, a new girl, couldn't find Caden's favorite toy, a little stuffed elephant, so another ten minutes was wasted in looking for it.

She needed something summery to wear, and a new shipment of sundresses had arrived, unusual since it was really the end of the season, but fortunate for her. She chose one in baby blue with a sprinkling of silver on the bodice.

It was nice to have something new. She wouldn't think tonight about the dent it had put in her budget. Instead, she would enjoy her evening and hope no one noticed that she would be fifteen minutes late.

No one did except Corey, and he was wise enough not to mention it. He wanted to tell her how beautiful she looked, all cool and elegant in ice blue with the same strappy sandals—see, he'd noticed the shoes like his sister had advised him do—she had worn to dinner at the White

House. But something in her eyes warned him not to say a word about it.

Instead, he offered her his arm to escort her through the hall from the front entry with the beautiful chandelier and tongue-in-groove woodwork on the ceiling, past a priceless French armoire and an equally priceless desk with inlaid wood to the wide back door and onto the piazza.

How did he always do this, wondered Gina, making her feel like a queen? It wasn't just in his old-world courtesies but also in the looks he gave her, bolstering her courage.

When they walked onto the porch, Caden, who had been holding her right hand, clapped his hands and exclaimed with delight at the sight of the colorful piñatas and mini lights. A long buffet table was situated against the wall to Gina's right, and it was laden with food, both Southern and Mexican.

Seeing Caden, Gloria set down her plate and scooped him up in her arms.

"There's my sugar," she said. "Come give Grandma a hug." She gave him a quick kiss as he wiggled to get down. He was about to dash into the garden, but Gloria held him firmly.

"Let me see to Caden," she said to her daughter.

Corey led Gina to the buffet table.

"I already have a plate," he told her. "Let me get you something to drink. Would you like some Sangria or a white wine?"

"Actually, I'd rather just have a sweet tea," said Gina. She didn't want to sound stuffy, so she refrained from stating the obvious: I have a child for whom I'm responsible. Responsibility involves not drinking.

Not only had Aunt Clara fixed her famous fried chicken with real mashed potatoes, but Aunt Sarah had made a lasagna from an old Sabatelli family recipe. Aunt Grace brought the black-eyed pea salad Aunt Clara had introduced, and Galeah had made Chelsea's favorite macaroni salad with the garden-fresh cucumber, green and red peppers and the purple onion she liked.

Gina saw that Gram had already begun harvesting the peaches, for she had brought some freshly made peach salsa for the tortilla chips. Some was mixed with cream cheese, and some was plain although she didn't think Gram's peach salsa could ever be termed plain.

In addition, the families from Mexico contributed chicken enchiladas with a spicy guacamole spread and amply laden with cheese; Mexican corn casserole with black beans, corn, cream and cheddar cheeses, and herbs; bean and beef burritos with tomatoes, cheese and cilantro with plenty of sour cream on the side; and more.

Gina realized suddenly that she was ravenous. She decided to try all of the Mexican dishes. When would she have another opportunity to sample such authentic dishes again?

Corey returned with her iced tea. He watched her load her plate.

Wickedly he asked, "Would you like me to get another plate for you?!"

But Gina refused to get riled. "I haven't had anything to eat since breakfast, and I'm famished. Besides, this array of food is marvelous. And I'm sure I'll work it off at Wal-Mart tomorrow if not chasing Caden around the garden," she retorted, looking out at the white, linen-covered tables set up throughout the garden.

Corey led her to the table where he had placed his plate. Blake and Tallie were already seated there with Chelsea, Lawton, and Lanie.

For the first time in a week, Gina allowed herself to relax. The food was marvelous and the ambience sophisticatedly casual. Her son was being cared for by his grandma, and she was surrounded by friends and family.

She still didn't like Corey all that much, but he was attentive and …kind. Really? She hadn't thought of him as kind, but he really was being kind to her tonight. Perhaps they could just be friends. Even the thought was relaxing.

The conversation flowed brightly around the table. It was amazing, given the fact that they hadn't known each other that long that the seven of them had so much in common, could talk so freely.

Tallie didn't stay at the table long. She had to talk to the groups at each table, making sure everyone was happy and well-fed.

Blake watched her, unaware he was being watched, especially by Corey and Chelsea. While his face remained passive enough, his eyes told the tale of his growing affection for his red-haired siren.

When everyone had eaten their fill, Veronique and Greg let the children each pick a piñata to take home with him or her. An enormous piñata was strung on a wire, and each child had a chance to hit it, beginning with the youngest child and moving to the older ones.

Carlos was the hero of the day. He gave the bull-shaped piñata a mighty whack, and candy poured from every cavity.

As the twilight deepened, Veronique turned up the music, and the dancing started. It was a magical evening, dancing under stars and the fairy-like mini lights.

Mollie Madera taught Tallie, Chelsea, Lanie, Veronique, Kielah, Lindy, Gwen, Melanie, Rosie, Ryan, and the aunts some Latin steps and moves. The men joined them while the Rodriquez grandparents sat on the piazza and watched with fond memories of their own.

Tallie sensed Blake's eyes on her everywhere she went. She knew he still had issues from the part of his past she hadn't learned of yet. But he was watchful, not tortured, wounded, but not bitter. He understood her job, and she knew a lot more now about his.

She had seen him work under extremely stressful situations, yet he retained his cool and didn't lash out at people when things went wrong. Now she was seeing him relaxed and full of helpfulness. She liked this sensitive, intelligent, and battle-scarred man.

His arms around her as they danced made her feel secure and happy. This was the haven she had waited to find.

Chapter Twenty-Four

Gina's mind whirled after the first two in-service days at school. She was hot with excitement and cold with nervousness that she would do something wrong. And the students hadn't arrived yet.

Her aide, Renee Fleming, assured her she would do just fine.

"You love kids, right?"

"Yes."

"You're not a sex offender, right?"

"No. Of course not."

"Then you'll do," said Renee.

Gina had checked and rechecked each item her twenty-six students would need for the first day. Each desk had a child's name in Gina's own neat hand writing taped to it in the top left hand corner. Cubbies were marked, and twenty-six workbooks for each subject were labeled with twenty-six different names.

In addition, a bright, cheerful poster welcoming the students to her class was on the door, the alphabet in cursive writing marched above the white board, and a large bulletin board divided neatly in two sections displayed posters and pictures about science on the left side, and rules for the first math unit on the right side.

Two large picture windows overlooked the playground, but a large tree just outside reduced the glare. In one corner at the back of the room, a cheerful red, yellow, green, and blue rug was bordered on one side by low bookshelves filled with books that third graders would enjoy.

Gina was happy with the results. She hoped her students would be as excited about being in her classroom as she was about having them in her class.

At home, she laid out clothes for both herself and Caden for the big day and then packed her teacher bag and Caden's backpack. He would be attending the K-4 class down the hall from her for half a day. Grandpa would pick him up shortly after noon.

Gina was up early, ready for her new life to begin. She tried to remain calm as she made breakfast for Caden and herself, but with the butterflies in her stomach, that was nearly impossible.

She arrived fifteen minutes early and was greeted by both Roger, the janitor, and the principal, Mrs. Weston.

Caden's teacher, Miss Trask, was an older woman, a grandmotherly type who knew just how to make her small students feel comfortable in new surroundings. She greeted him warmly, and he was quickly lured into her room with interesting, "new" toys.

Gina, feeling comforted, moved along to her room.

Renee arrived, and then the students began trickling into the classroom. Helping each student find their cubby and their desk eliminated her nerves, and she was past the math and social studies lessons and into reading a book to her class when a knock sounded at the door.

The secretary, Deb Lawrence, held a huge bouquet of yellow roses in her arms.

"Special delivery," she announced.

Twenty-seven pairs of eyes scrutinized her response as she placed the vase on her desk and opened the card.

She had a feeling that the flowers were not from her parents. They didn't usually send roses. Her dad preferred daisies and carnations.

The card read, "Enjoy the first day. You've worked hard for this!" It was signed with a huge "C."

Corey. It had to be. He had left the day after the fiesta, and although he had flown down twice more to help her dad and uncles find an attorney, she had not seen him.

Just then, another knock sounded at the door. Another bouquet. Ah. Here were the carnations and daisies from her parents.

For some reason, the flowers made a huge impression on her students. At recess she heard one little girl tell another, "She must have a boyfriend who really likes her."

The other little girl responded with a sigh saying, "Yeah. It's sooo romantic. Let's tell the boys they'd better behave or Miss Galbraith's boyfriend might beat them up."

They ran over to the boys who were playing with a kickball before Gina could stop them.

Renee began to laugh. "Oh, that's a good one! Don't dispel that myth. They'll be your slaves forever."

"He's not my boyfriend. He's just an…" she started to say acquaintance, but she remembered Corey's passionate "Dare to let go of the safety net, Gina," and his protection of Caden as they had run to the house to escape the summer shower after looking in Gram's orchard for the end of the rainbow.

She tried again. "He's just a friend. I'm actually engaged to someone else named Harry. Corey is my cousin's fiancé's brother. We get thrown together a lot because of the wedding planning."

Renee just looked at her skeptically. Gina winced inside, thinking her explanation sounded lame even to her ears. Wisely, she shut her mouth. People would think what they wanted.

"If you say so, Honey. But a man who sends flowers your first day, and one who doesn't? You figure it out."

The rest of the day flowed even more smoothly than the first half. Gina, however, was exhausted as she headed home with an excited Caden. He loved Miss Trask. And he especially liked the toys in the classroom.

Gina wanted to sit for a few minutes, but she knew she would fall asleep if she did. So instead, she dropped her bag on the floor beside the sofa and started some water for some mac and cheese. Luckily, she had some hot dogs in the freezer. That would be dinner.

For all his excitement, Caden fell asleep after his dinner. Fortunately, Grandpa had given him a bath when he'd picked him up after his half day at school, saying that he must have had a great time on the playground. Gina didn't think she had the energy to do much more.

She wanted to spend some time working on reading group assignments, but as soon as she pulled out her grade book, she fell asleep sitting in her recliner.

She was awakened several hours later by her phone. It was Harry.

"How was your day?"

"It was fine." She waited for him to say something about the importance of this day for her, but he was silent. Had he really forgotten that this was her first day teaching?

"How was yours?"

"Very intense. We found a live bomb under an American ship in a harbor in Yemen. Nearly blew myself up, but we dismantled it correctly and saved the ship. Everyone had evacuated by the time we finished."

"Wow. Sounds like a difficult day."

"It was. But I had so much adrenalin pumping through my body that in a way it was a real high. Not that I want to do it again any time soon," he added hastily. "But all we were really looking for were duds on the bottom of the bay."

Gina made a noncommittal sound.

"I just wish you were here, Babe. It would be so much nicer to do a lot more than talk to you after a day like today."

Gina ignored the huskiness in his voice which usually made her insides melt. "So when we do get married, will I travel with you, Harry?"

"Well, not all of the time. But sure. Some of the time you could be with me. Think of what an education that would be for Caden. A world traveler at a young age."

All Gina could think of was trying to care for a young boy on her own for most of the day in countries not especially favorable to the United States and its interests.

"But what about my job teaching?" asked Gina.

"Oh. You'd have to be there for that. But you could fly to wherever I am on holidays. And then we'd have the whole summer together."

"My place or yours?" Gina asked somewhat sarcastically.

Her irony, however, was lost on Harry. "Wherever I am, I suppose. Or better yet, I have a lot of time off earned. We could spend the summers at your place in Summerville."

"What about a placed for us, Harry?"

"We could buy a house if that's what you want. I have plenty of money saved from all these dangerous missions."

"Have you ever thought about getting another job so you could be home at nights with me and Caden?" asked Gina.

Now she had his full attention. "Do you want me to get another job? He sounded worried. "I hadn't thought about it. Is that what you really want?"

"I'm just trying to find out what your plans are after we get married, Harry. That's all. Just think about it, okay?"

"Okay. I sure miss you, Babe. After a day like today, I need so much more than a phone call. I want you here on this bed beside me," and he proceeded to tell her some of his ideas of what they could do.

Hearing the hunger and the passion in his voice made Gina shiver all over. Who would not be flattered to be desired like that? A little voice in the back of her mind, however, reminded her that passion and desire were not love. She had been down this road before with Jack.

And, once again, the issues plaguing her peace of mind were being overruled by his passions and needs.

He finally slowed down in his murmured endearments and told her he missed her.

"I miss you, too, Harry."

Gina hung up several minutes later. She still hadn't had a chance to tell Harry about her first day at school as the teacher instead of as a student.

Of course he cared, she thought. He had just had a very difficult day.

But darn him. He was so phlegmatic, he wouldn't really think through what he wanted his life to be like and then go for it.

Or maybe this was what he wanted his life to be like: a girl waiting for him whenever he happened to come home from his great, important, life-endangering work.

No. She wouldn't think that. It was childish of her. Give him a chance to process their conversation and come down from the adrenalin high he seemed to have. Then maybe they could have a serious conversation about it all.

She sighed and switched her mind to her class. Thinking of her first day of school gave her a great deal of pleasure.

Gina worked for several hours on the reading groups until she had what she thought would be a good mix. She would watch the students interact the rest of the week and see if she should make any changes before she began reading groups next Monday.

At last she turned off the lamp beside her chair, leaving just a dim table lamp with low wattage burning on the little table at the beginning of the hall. She saw her face reflected in the mirror above the table and made a face at herself. She'd better get some rest and get rid of the circles under her eyes.

But first, she would pack a lunch for tomorrow and plan dinner. They couldn't eat macaroni and cheese the rest of the week for dinner.

198

Chapter Twenty-Five

The dog days of August melted into the golden days of September.

After the first week of school, Gina's extreme fatigue at the end of each day lessened. She was comforted when Caden's teacher, a veteran at the job, told her that all teachers felt the same weariness that first week. She advised Gina to take thirty minutes for herself each day after school, drinking tea, reading a book, or taking a walk.

It was good advice. Gina began walking around Azalea Park each day before heading to her parents' house to pick up Caden.

Just as she was adjusting to her now very different and very structured schedule, two events occurred at the end of September that interrupted the flow of her life.

At Corey's suggestion, the uncles had hired Constitutional attorney, Robert Worthington, to represent them.

At their first meeting with Mr. Worthington, he told them bluntly that they had only a fifty percent chance of winning the case, a statement that sent the uncles into a tizzy and elicited another round of family gatherings.

Gordon and Paul had returned to college, and Aunt Galeah was swamped with beginning of school meetings and work. Lawton alone continued to research Agenda 21 and the implications for South Carolinians.

He discovered that a number of "sustainable neighborhoods" were being developed. If they were operated and controlled by local governments, they could be beneficial to the people of South Carolina.

However, the more he dug, the more he found links to the United Nations and their plans for world control.

He found all of it very troubling, but he didn't want to laden his family with his findings; they already had enough with which to be concerned.

Jeremy Saxon posted a note on the side kitchen door of Grandpa and Grandma Merrill's house in the middle of September, stating the county would be inspecting the property in one week.

The uncles were gloomy about it. Rain showers the end of August had prevented them from doing much of the work that still needed to be done.

Then they'd had to race to finish harvesting the corn, the last of the peaches, and the cotton that Grandpa Merrill sold to a coop that negotiated with a much larger purchaser.

"That's how farming goes," said Uncle Davey philosophically. "Some years the weather cooperates, and each crop is harvested with no overlap. But other years…?" He spread his hands.

"We have to go with the flow, and Jeremy Saxon is just not on the same schedule as nature this year."

"You got that right," muttered Uncle Phil.

The uncles were all gathered on a Sunday afternoon on Gram and Gramps porch. Lawton was in the living showing Aunt Galeah his latest findings. The uncles were waiting for him before they began their discussion about the county.

The other cousins were busy on various parts of the farm, breaking up wood or cleaning up and organizing the barn which now boasted a new roof. They were working under the supervision of Grandpa Merrill and Grandpa Galbraith.

Gram and the rest of the aunts were just finishing boiling ears of corn, cutting the kernels from the cobs, packing the kernels in pre-labeled plastic bags, and stacking them flat in one of the freezers.

They had nearly three hundred packages of corn already frozen. These would be distributed among the five families and the two sets of grandparents at a later date.

"I'm so glad to see the last of the corn for another year," said Aunt Clara, wiping the perspiration beading her forehead with a paper towel after cutting the kernels from the last eight ears.

Gina re-entered the kitchen. She had just put the last batch in the freezer, laying each bag flat like Grams had taught her, ages ago, it seemed.

But she was in a hurry to get back to the kitchen. Corey had flown in the day before with his mother since Nell had been anxious to visit and establish good communication between the families, and Gina enjoyed listening to her talk.

At first the aunts had been subdued in her presence, but Nell soon put everyone at ease by casually putting on an apron and washing the dishes in the sink.

The conversation naturally revolved around cooking, and soon they were all sharing their favorite foods and preparation techniques, all while processing the last of the corn that Lindy, Melanie, Rosie, and Ryan had just husked.

"I think it's marvelous the way you all work together like this to provide for your families," said Nell.

"As your children marry and begin their families, you'll do more," said Grams, patting Nell on the shoulder.

"It has saved us so much on our grocery bill," said Aunt Galeah who along with Aunt Sarah had four children.

Aunt Sarah shook her head in agreement. "I think it's also helped to unify our families. I came from a different background, and I was terrified to marry into this family," she said, laughing in remembrance. "But cooking and canning together helped me understand the family dynamics better."

"Your lasagna and tortellini sure helped," said Aunt Clara slyly with a wink in Nell's direction.

"There is that. No one can resist the Sabatelli family lasagna recipe," said Aunt Sarah, snapping Aunt Clara's arm with a towel and laughing as she did so.

"Who can resist anything Italian?" asked Nell.

"Apparently teens can't these days," said Aunt Sarah. "They seem to be able to eat pizza any time of the day or night. I've given up making it from scratch. I keep telling Craig we need to buy stock in the pizza joint around the corner from us."

"It looks like we'll be learning Mexican dishes next," observed Aunt Galeah.

"Wasn't that corn casserole at the fiesta delicious?" asked Aunt Grace. "I got the recipe and have made it several times since the party. Garrett and Justin can't seem to get enough of it, and Geoffrey, away at college, just groans with envy whenever Justin tells him I've fixed it again."

"Speaking of college, how is Kielah doing?" asked Aunt Clara.

The talk drifted to the cousins in college, including Preston, Nell's youngest son who was taking several college courses his last year of high school.

Meanwhile, Lawton had finished showing Aunt Galeah the information he had discovered, and he had joined the uncles and Corey on the back porch.

"Do we know what day Jeremy Saxon is coming?" asked Uncle Garrett.

"No. He can come any day this next week," answered Uncle Davey.

"Have all the new 'No Trespassing' signs been put up?" asked Uncle Galen.

"Yes. I did that yesterday. Excellent job, by the way, of finding that sign online, Galen!"

"Apparently, some people in California are having problems with county officials trespassing on their property as well," said Uncle Galen. "I especially like the $7,500 per day land use fee. That might help us in court if the County doesn't follow protocol."

"Have any property rights cases been heard in California?" asked Uncle Craig.

"No," answered Corey. "I checked. They have done such a good job of 'educating' people in California that most Californians buy into Agenda 21 hook, line, and sinker."

Well," he amended, "at least those in the southern part of the state do. Some northern Californians understand that the United Nations is trying to supersede the Constitution as the basis for law and authority. A group of them even wants to divide southern California and northern California into two separate states."

"The 'No Trespassing' sign will probably help us in the future, but what are we going to do about trying to be here when Jeremy Saxon comes?" asked Uncle Phil. "We can't take the entire week off from work. I have a football team to prep for Friday's game."

"Maybe we can each be here a different day if we can get the time off," said Uncle Davey.

"I have Wednesday off already," said Uncle Garrett.

"The only day I'll be able to be absent is possibly on Tuesday. Football is every day until the season is over," said Uncle Phil.

"Thursday is my light day at the college," said Uncle Galen.

"I'm sure Scotch will cover me for any day except tomorrow," said Uncle Craig. "We have an in-service training tomorrow."

"I can come any day," said Uncle Davey who was the president of his own company.

And so they made arrangements.

Jeremy Saxon came on Tuesday. Uncle Phil had not been able to get any days off, so Uncle Davey was there.

Corey was also present. His mother had wanted to meet the two Mexican families that had been rescued. Tallie and Blake agreed to take Nell to visit the Garcias and the Floreses.

Then Bob Worthington had wanted to view the property so he knew exactly why the County seemed to make the Merrills an example. In addition it would give him more insight in exactly what he needed to say before a judge.

Uncle Craig made arrangements to pick him up in Summerville and drive him to the farm since Corey and Uncle Davey were already there, helping Grandpa Merrill and Grandpa Galbraith prep the garden for fall produce.

They were standing beside the tiller. Grandpa Merrill had tilled about a third of the garden, and Corey was getting ready to take over.

Grandpa Galbraith and Uncle Davey had set up a makeshift table with two sawhorses and a piece of plywood. They were arranging the plants Grams had bought Saturday and deciding where each crop should go.

"Well, look who's here," said Uncle Davey softly as Jeremy Saxon pulled into the driveway.

Uncle Craig and the attorney pulled in immediately behind him.

Again, two armed men, law enforcement guessed Grandpa Galbraith, were with Jeremy Saxon.

"A waste of tax payer money," snorted Grandpa Merrill who had come to stand beside Uncle Davey with Corey behind him.

"What do they think we're going to do to poor Mr. Saxon?" asked Uncle Davey, still speaking softly as Mr. Saxon was now out of the car, looking around as if to scent out the enemy.

"String him up to one of the trees and tickle him until he tells the truth and shames the Devil," said Grandpa Merrill with a twinkle in his eye.

"Most people would have a very different method of punishment in mind," said Corey as Grandpa walked forward to shake Mr. Saxon's hand.

"Oh, that's what he meant," said Uncle Davey, "but he won't put voice to such words. He's too much of a gentleman for that." He sounded somewhat regretful.

Introductions were made. Corey saw that Jeremy Saxon still believed him to be one of the grandsons and passed over him without more than a casual glance.

But when Mr. Worthington was introduced as the Merrill's attorney, he stiffened immediately, glanced meaningfully at the two men with him, and rearranged the papers on the clipboard he carried.

He obviously wanted to begin his inspection and leave as quickly as possible, but Uncle Davey asked him if he had seen the signs posted at the front of the property and on either side of the driveway.

"No."

"Then I think you should read them before you begin your inspection."

Mr. Saxon looked like he wanted to decline, but Mr. Worthington spoke.

"Surely the County is not so busy that it can't find time to read and record in its records what is on the signs."

Mr. Saxon pressed his lips together in a firm line. He strode to the front of the driveway, the officers behind him. They had hesitated, wanting to keep an eye on the rest of the men. But Grandpa Merrill and Grandpa Galbraith refused to budge. They would not be herded forward by men with guns. This was not a police state.

Instead, Uncle Davey, Uncle Craig, and Mr. Worthington accompanied Mr. Saxon to the front of the driveway.

As Mr. Saxon read the sign, his face twisted in a sour expression.

Uncle Davey slipped his hand in his pocket and, pulling out a camera, he captured the moment on film.

Jeremy Saxon finished reading the sign without comment and began walking rapidly without talking, checking only what was on his list. Uncle Davey, Uncle Phil, and Mr. Worthington followed him. Uncle Davey snapped a few more pictures.

As they moved back toward the vehicles, Uncle Davey finally broke the silence. "We haven't finished removing piles of brush. The grandkids break those up and put them in boxes for Dad and Mom to use as kindling during the winter. But we did re-roof the shed, and we have a buyer coming next week to look at the old cars which we've moved and cleaned a bit."

"You're still in violation until everything is clean," said Jeremy Saxon in a clipped voice.

"We've been held up by rain and the need to harvest, but I wouldn't expect a city boy like you to understand such things," said Grandpa Merrill, scathing ire in his voice. He handed Mr. Saxon a paper.

"Here's a copy of the 'No Trespassing' sign for your records."

Mr. Saxon slipped it under the papers on his clipboard. "Don't start with me," he said, looking meaningfully at the two law enforcement men behind him.

He strode to his vehicle. "You'll receive a copy of my report before the end of the week." He slammed the door of his car as the two men with him jumped into the back seat.

"That went well?" said Corey.

They all laughed, a release of tension rather than true humor. Then they went to the kitchen for some iced tea and discussion with Mr. Worthington.

Chapter Twenty-Six

At the end of September, Harry arrived in Summerville for a short visit.

Gina's first indication he was in town was a commotion in the hall as she was returning from recess with her third graders. Her students were lined up against the wall by the bathrooms; those not in the restrooms were taking turns by threes at the nearby drinking fountain.

Gina, Renee and her students were startled to hear a fourth grader yell, "Ouch! You stepped on my foot!" The fourth grader glared at the man in the yellow collared shirt, who stood with a bouquet of brightly colored daisies, looking perplexedly down at the outraged child.

Squatting down, the man looked her in the eyes and apologized profusely. Then pulling several daisies from the cellophane wrapping, he handed her the brightly-hued orange, blue and yellow flowers.

The girl grinned at the man and scampered back to her teacher who was holding the door and looking apologetically at the man.

As he turned to face her, Gina's breath caught in her throat. Oh heavens. It was Harry!

Her first thought was that now her day, which had been flowing so smoothly, would be interrupted and changed. But she quickly banished that thought, reproaching herself for not being more loving and supportive.

She turned quickly to Renee. "Can you take over? When the students get back to the classroom, have them work on their science projects. I won't be too long."

Smoothing her hair quickly with her hand, she hurried forward, quickly lest another unfortunate event occur.

Harry saw her at last, and his face lit up with a thousand-watt grin.

Gina ran the last few yards and into his arms. Here was safety if nothing else.

"Harry, it's so good to see you! But you should have let me know you were coming."

"Then it wouldn't have been a surprise now would it? I just couldn't wait to see you. Don't worry; I've already been lectured by the secretary." He frowned in remembrance.

"I'm not to waste more than fifteen minutes of your time. But I did get the dragon-lady to let me see you and give you my flowers personally," he said, grinning unrepentantly, and bowing ceremoniously as he handed her the flowers.

"They're beautiful, Harry. How long will you be here?"

"I get at least five days this time. We've been on some dangerous assignments, and the boss thinks a total break from such activities will make us sharper for the next go around. Working out and playing extreme basketball can only relieve so much tension."

Gina looked at her watch. "I have to go, Harry. But I'll be finished in two and a half hours."

"I was thinking I could go sleep at your place while I wait," said Harry.

Gina shook her head. "My keys are in my purse in my classroom. When I get back there, I need to teach. Your parents are just around the corner. Do they know you are here?"

Harry shook his head. "You are more important, Gina."

"That's sweet of you Harry. I've got to go."

He bent down, and regardless of any onlookers, kissed her hard on the mouth, leaving her breathless before he exited through the double doors.

Gina shook her head and let out a sigh. She remembered now that he had been hinting at having her apartment key.

She had strong reservations about such a move. She had carefully rebuilt her life after the debacle with Jack, and she just wasn't ready to hand her key over to someone else who could appear, basically out of nowhere at unexpected times, disrupting her life. She was beginning to like her life the way it was, and she wasn't about to make any sudden changes.

Smoothing her hair again, she readied herself to enter the classroom where twenty-nine pairs of eyes would be on her and the flowers in her hand. She had two new students who were every bit as inquisitive as the rest, including Renee.

Three hours later, Gina and Harry were walking in Azalea Park in downtown Summerville.

The afternoon sun slanted through the trees giving a golden edge to leaves on trees and shrubs. Only a few trees had begun to turn yellow. Most were still green. Bees buzzed busily, and birds called to each other across the crepe myrtle trees blooming in white, red, and fuchsia.

As they walked by the pond, turtles poked their inquisitive little heads through the surface, looking for bread, and a white egret, standing next to the bronze sculpture of a blue heron, took startled flight.

Harry held Gina's hand, and she leaned in against his shoulder, content for the moment with his solidness, his masculinity, the familiarity that was part of her experience with him.

"Have you thought about setting a date for our wedding, Gina?" he asked.

"Yes, I have. Would April work for you? I looked at the calendar, and spring break occurs the second week of April. We could get married at the beginning of spring break and have the rest of the week for our honeymoon."

"That sounds good. My boss will have to let me off for my wedding!"

"Well he'd better," responded Gina. "Have you thought any more about what we will do after the wedding, where we will live and what our lives will be like?" She really didn't want to ask lest it create tension for his entire visit, but it was a question that needed answering for her peace of mind and probably also for his clarity of thought.

"I've thought about it some," Harry said. "I really like my job, Gina. It makes me feel as if I'm saving lives every time my team removes a live bomb. The money is good, too; very good."

"I don't want to make this all about me, but I need a husband who is going to be at home at night. I like the regularity of nine to five and weekends free, especially after working all those weekends at Wal-Mart."

"I make plenty of money, enough for both of us, Gina. Why can't you just quit your teaching job and travel with me?"

"Because I've worked really hard to get where I am, and I don't want to throw it all away," answered Gina, starting to get angry and defensive.

"If you really loved me, you would do it," said Harry stubbornly.

"I don't see how you can say that. It's not a matter of whether I love you or not. And besides, how many other wives travel with your team?"

"None of them," Harry admitted.

"See? And maybe I should use emotional blackmail, too, and say that if <u>you</u> really loved <u>me</u>, you would be willing to get a regular job with much less travel."

"That's not fair, Gina."

"Your expectations aren't fair, either, Harry."

"Do you really expect me to quit my job, Gina?"

"Have you even looked at doing anything else?"

"No."

"I'm sure you could find another job that makes you feel like you're making a difference, something that keeps you closer to home."

"Maybe."

"Well, let's say we did marry, and we both kept the jobs we currently have."

Harry, who had his head down, looked up hopefully. But Gina continued.

"You would come home for what? Five days every other month or so. For all practical purposes, I would still be a single mom most of the time. I would have no one with whom I could live my day to day life except my son. That kind of life benefits you but definitely not me."

"That's not true."

Yes it is. It seems to me you would have all the benefits of being single <u>and</u> married at the same time: guiltless sex whenever you came home but no one to whom you had to answer on a daily basis."

Harry spluttered, but Gina continued. "Just tell me, what are the benefits to me in being married to you?" She crossed her arms and waited for his answer.

Harry thought for a few minutes. "You wouldn't have scum of the earth like Jack trying to compromise you. You would be very well provided for. We could even buy our own house, close to your parents or mine."

The idea seemed inspired. "You could do whatever you want with the house because it would be yours....ours," he amended when he saw the expression on her face.

"I don't want to be married to a house, Harry. I want to be married to you. Though for what reasons, I can't seem to remember at the moment."

They had come full circle to where her car was parked. Gina found she was trembling, and all she wanted was to get away by herself for a while.

"I'm going to pick up Caden."

She moved toward her car, but Harry caught her arm.

"Gina, don't leave like this. Let's talk this over."

"We have been talking, Harry." She pulled away and opened her car door. "I suggest we think for a while before we talk again and decide what we're willing to compromise on."

"Okay, okay. Let me pick you up for dinner. At seven, okay?"

"I'll be there. Faithful Gina, waiting patiently," she said sarcastically and slammed the door.

Five minutes later she was filled with remorse. What had gotten into her? She had never talked like that to anyone in her life.

But she was right, wasn't she? Her head was beginning to pound, and she suddenly realized she was crying.

Heavens! She couldn't let Caden or even her parents see her like this. She pulled into a store parking lot and tried to stop crying, but the more she tried, the harder she cried.

She finally regained her composure. When she arrived at her parent's home, she saw her mother's car was already parked in the garage.

Darn! Her mother would know immediately something was wrong. Maybe she would still be upstairs changing. But no. She was in the kitchen, peeling potatoes.

"Hi, Sweetie. How was your day?" asked her mother cheerfully.

"Fine," said Gina, trying to avoid looking at her mother.

But Grace swung around sharply and reached with a damp hand to turn Gina's face toward her.

"You've been crying! What's happened?" She dropped the potato into the sink, turned off the faucet, and grabbed a towel in one motion. Then her arms went around her daughter to give her a hug.

"Harry surprised me at school today, but when we went for a walk in the park, we had a fight." Gina began crying all over again as her mother held her tightly. She never saw the look of satisfaction that came over her mother's face at her words.

"Do you want to tell me about it?"

"It's silly, I suppose. But he wants to keep working his job after we're married, and I don't want that. I want someone I can live life with. My day to day life. Is that wrong, Mom? I don't want to get married just as an excuse for consensual sex." Some of the anger she felt returned, tingeing her voice with scorn at that idea.

"No, I don't think that's wrong at all, Sweetie. I'm glad you are thinking through these things before you get married. You both need to have a realistic picture of what your lives will be like. And if you don't like what you see, you need to do something to change it."

"For so long, I've just been letting things happen," said Gina. "Well, not as far as getting a teaching degree is concerned I guess. Just in our relationship."

"So what made you ask questions?" asked Grace although she was pretty sure she knew the answer was contact with another young man.

"I don't know," said Gina. "But I'm not going to just go with what life hands me. I can't believe I've never seen it this way before, but I want to shape my life and make it the life I want, not the life I'm settling for."

Grace patted her hand. "I'm so glad you're starting to see that. You're on the right track, Gina. Go for the best in life and accept that sometimes change and pain accompanies real living."

She hugged her daughter. "Now let's go find your very best reason to hold out for the best."

Chapter Twenty-Seven

Dinner with Harry was pleasant. He didn't like the small town atmosphere of Summerville like Gina did and wanted to go to downtown Charleston, but Gina begged for something closer. She had to teach the next day.

They went to Gilligan's Seafood and sat in a booth. Although the restaurant was full, the tall backs of the benches in each booth effectively blocked the noisy clink of silver and china and muted the conversations of the other diners around them.

Harry was a good conversationalist. He kept Gina's attention riveted on the stories he told about his perilous adventures and close escapes from terrorists on land and from bombs under the sea.

He was in the middle of a story when the waitress brought the check. His story was about a rigged checkpoint and how he and his team had discovered who the bomber was and had shot her before she could detonate her bombs, killing, not only his team, but also a large group of Bedouins who were leaving town with three or four months of supplies.

Gina shivered slightly and realized they had not discussed any of the real issues troubling her. But then she also realized she wouldn't want to discuss their personal, private issues in a public place anyway.

On the way back to her apartment, Harry brought up one of the issues.

"I've been thinking about what you said this afternoon, Gina. I'm sorry that I haven't taken the time to see things from your point of view. I just want you to know I'll be looking around for another job while I'm here, and if I don't find one right away, I'll keep looking online while I'm overseas."

"Thank you, Harry," said Gina softly. "It really means a lot to me."

Harry escorted her to her door. Gina was very conscious that on the other side of the door Gwen would be finishing her homework or watching a show on TV.

"Are you going to invite me in tonight?" asked Harry. The expression on his face let Gina know he would not leave easily once he was inside. He was asking for much more than she was willing to give.

"Not tonight if you don't mind, Harry. I'm really tired, and I have a busy day tomorrow at school. Besides Gwen is inside, and she needs to get home, too."

Harry pulled her possessively to him. Gina felt the hunger in his body, in his mouth as he kissed her passionately. His intensity, while it thrilled her, also frightened her somewhat.

Compared to the fire in his kiss, her response was mediocre. It worried her some. What if she just couldn't love again as she once had? Could Harry's passion be enough for both of them?

But probably she couldn't respond more because she was so tired. Their fight had exhausted her both emotionally and physically.

Harry rested his forehead against hers, breathing heavily. "I'm talking about after she leaves, Babe."

"I know, Harry, and I'm not ready for that yet." She pulled away and studied his face with a mixture of frustration and remorse visible on hers.

"I wish I could," she said softly, "if that's any consolation."

He took his turn, studying her face. Her eyes were large in her pale face. She really was tired, he thought, feeling guilty once again for not thinking of her needs before his own.

"I'd better go," he said. He gave her one more quick kiss and then headed down the short hall of the apartment building to the outside door.

Gina let herself inside quickly and sighed. It was going to be a long week with Harry here.

Gwen looked up from the TV show she was watching. Hearing Gina's sigh, she asked, "Everything okay?"

"No. We had a fight this afternoon."

Gwen turned off the TV. "Really? You and calm, easy-going Harry? What about?"

"Tell me if I'm wrong," started Gina, sitting on the sofa, kicking off her shoes, and tucking her feet under her.

"I told him I didn't want to still be a single mother after we married. Because if he goes back overseas, that's what I'll be. I want someone who will marry me and live with me and share the trials and joys of life on a daily basis. So I told him he needed to look for another job. Is that too much to ask?"

"No. Not when you put it like that. What did he say?"

"At first he said he enjoys his job, feels like he makes a difference, and if I really loved him, I wouldn't ask him to give it up."

"But if he really loves you, wouldn't he want to be closer to you, not five thousand miles away?"

Gina's eyes flew to Gwen's. "You understand? I thought it was just me." She felt so relieved.

"Of course I understand. Not to be all mushy, but you need someone to cherish you. Jack the Jerk never did that."

Gina thought of what Corey had said about Jack not appreciating her and how she'd thought that the girl fortunate to have his love would never doubt it. Did Harry love her like that?

It wasn't fair to compare Harry to Corey, she told herself sharply. They were two different people entirely. But she was starting to doubt that Harry truly loved her.

Oh, he was passionate alright, but passion was only one aspect of love and didn't necessarily guarantee love as she had already bitterly experienced.

"Earth to Gina. Was it something I said?"

"Sorry, Gwennie. I was lost in thought."

"I've got to get home." Gwen stood and began gathering her things.

"Thanks for listening. It really helped," said Gina.

"Of course. What are sisters for besides a good cat fight now and then?!" She gave Gina a big hug.

"We haven't had one of those for a long time now."

"No. We're more mature," said Gwen with a toss of her head. "Now get some sleep. It will give you a better perspective on everything. Love you," she said as she opened the door.

"Love you, too," said Gina and closed the door behind her.

She watched through the front window as Gwen started her car and blinked her lights on and off to signal all was well.

Caden was sound asleep. She brushed back his hair and kissed his forehead. If she was going to give him a daddy, she'd better make sure it was the right man. She'd never want to put her little boy through the emotionally wrenching devastation of a divorce.

They went on a carriage ride for two in downtown Charleston and ate dinner at the Fish Market afterwards, they visited Charleston Tea Plantation and bought peach tea, they sipped wine and nibbled on cheese and fruit at the new wine bar, Accent on Wine, in downtown Summerville. But Gina and Harry never revisited their points of disagreement.

Harry continued to hint at sleeping with Gina, and she steadily refused him. The flags raised in her mind were not quite red but more of a fuchsia. Yet she couldn't bring herself to sleep with someone until she had absolutely no reservations.

In addition to that, she had been raised "old school" to believe she should save sex for marriage, and she greatly admired Chelsea and Jasper who made no secret of the fact that they were saving that special intimacy for the honeymoon.

They were both too phlegmatic, Gina decided. Neither of them liked change or confrontation. Harry, however, must be more phlegmatic than she was. She was not so laid back that she would just drift, failing to plan for the future.

The same day Harry left, October first, Corey arrived. He walked into her grandparent's house as cocky as ever, giving high fives and knuckle bumps to Lawton and her other male cousins, lifting Grams off her feet and swinging her around as he hugged her, and then holding his arms out for Gina.

She sniffed and ignored his arms as she continued nibbling her oatmeal raisin cookie.

"Hi, Corey," she said sweetly, batting her eyes at him.

"She's in a rare mood since her boyfriend left," Lawton informed him.

Corey raised his eyebrows questioningly. "Good time or bad time?" he asked.

Gina gave a thumb up. What else could she do? She wasn't going to tell him all the details. He was way too intuitive about her life already.

But, usually sensitive about such things, Lawton wouldn't let it alone. "She and Harry had a fight, but I guess they made it up."

Corey raised an eyebrow. "Really?" He looked at Gina for a response.

"I refuse to dignify your gossip, gentlemen, with a response," she said with a toss of her head.

"Touchy, that one," said Lawton. "But tell me more about Mr. Worthington, the attorney. Did you bring him?"

"Yes, I did. We spent the morning going over possible scenarios. He was right behind me, but I think he spotted your father outside and stopped to talk to him."

Gina remembered that Corey had spent two years at Harvard Law School. This situation was right up his alley although to her mind, he was taking it much more personally than he had a right to do.

After all, he really wasn't a part of her family. But then she'd heard various comments about his real estate dealings in Charleston and Summerville. That must be why he was always around. And he seemed to enjoy hanging with Lawton as well as Gordon and Paul when they weren't in school.

Uncle Davey, her father, and the attorney entered.

"Yes, we just received the bill for the last inspection in the mail today," Uncle Davey was saying. "Let me go get it for you."

"We have some more news," said her father, Galen. "One of Grandpa Merrill's cronies at the breakfast club today told him that Neal & Webster, that huge company that develops 'sustainable cities,'" he said, using his fingers to supply the quotes, "is buying the land behind the farm."

"Really?" asked Lawton and Aunt Galeah who had entered with Uncle Davey. Uncle Davey handed the billing to Mr. Worthington.

"Old Gouvenor North's land?" asked Aunt Galeah.

"Yes. In my mind, that provides more of a motive for harassing us with these inspections. What do you think?" he asked, directing his question to Mr. Worthington.

"We'll have to investigate that possibility," said Mr. Worthington, looking at Corey and Lawton.

"Already on it, Sir," said Lawton. "I've been digging into Neal & Webster's background on the internet, not because I knew about them buying old Gouvenor North's land, but because I've been hearing about their possible involvement with Agenda 21.

Things look pretty squeaky clean. But I still suspect some connection with the United Nations and Agenda 21. They both use the same wording in much of their materials. I'll keep digging."

"You do that, Lawton. Drop into my office some time next week, and let me know what you've discovered." Mr. Worthington handed Lawton one of his business cards.

"Will do," said Lawton. He and Corey disappeared into Gram's living room.

"Bob!" said Grandpa Merrill as he entered the kitchen door. "Give me a minute to wash up," he said, disappearing into the laundry room to use the sink and soap.

"We've been mucking out the chicken coop and laying new straw," said Uncle Davey. "I had the cleaner job."

"Did he get the papers?" asked Grandpa Merrill, reappearing and wiping his hands and arms on a towel. He had hastily changed his pants and shirt, and he winked at his wife who had, early in their marriage, laid down the law about cleanliness in her house and especially her kitchen where they all seemed to congregate.

"Yes. Let's go in the dining room and discuss this with Bob. Gina, can you help Galeah bring us some tea and cookies?" asked Uncle Davey.

"Sure," said Gina, jumping from her stool. Caden was "helping" her mother in the garden with the fall and winter crops, so she was free.

"Hey, Gina," Lawton called just as she finished. "Come here."

She stood in the doorway to the living room. As usual, Lawton had his computer going, and she saw his mother's pink laptop on the coffee table as well.

"Lanie, Corey, and a group of us are going to listen to Kirby tonight at Single Smile Café. Do you want to come?"

Gina thought about what she needed to get done for school on Monday. Renee had finished all the grading before they even left school on Friday. She had worksheets and activities to prep for next week, but her lesson plans were nearly ready.

Caden was spending the night at Grandpa and Grandma's house at her Mom's request.

"Sure," she said. "I'll meet you up there. I want to go home first and shower and change. Is it open mike night?"

"No. This is a special called 'Kirby Easler and Friends.' I thought Corey might enjoy the show."

"He probably will. Kirby does this really cool effect on her guitar called chiming," she said, addressing Corey directly for the first time.

"She has some pretty amazing musician friends, too," said Lawton. "It should be a memorable evening."

And it was as Gina remembered forever after.

Chapter Twenty-Eight

Gina had been given a golden brown velour jacket that had quickly become a favorite. She paired it with dark brown slacks and a pretty topaz colored set of beaded earrings and a necklace for the evening.

As Gina entered the café, without even thinking about it being the ingrained result of his mother's insistence on manners, Corey stood courteously and seated her at a table in the windowed alcove. There they could listen to the music yet still hear to talk.

Lanie and Lawton were already seated. They had also already ordered at the counter, and their food was being prepared.

"What would you like, Gina? I haven't ordered yet; I can order for both of us," said Corey.

Gina studied the menu on the wall. "I'll get a chicken croissant plate and a hot vanilla chai."

"I got the same thing!" said Lanie. "It's a little nippy outside tonight, and I wanted something to warm up my insides. Our chai always hits the spot."

She spoke proprietarily although she wasn't working tonight, happy to have a job there at the cafe that was flexible enough to accommodate her study schedule as she obtained her nursing degree.

Corey went to the counter to order, and Gina unwound the simple cream cashmere neck scarf she had worn, then sat back and took a deep breath of the richly coffee-scented air.

A wave of nostalgia and homesickness hit her. She had so loved the scent of the aromatic coffee her mother brewed every morning. Gina didn't drink coffee on a regular basis, but she loved the smell of it, and once again, she realized how much she missed it.

She looked around, noting the changes Dawn, the owner, and her manager, Ed, had made. A small stage had been added against the inside wall. The piano was uncovered, and here the guitarists were tuning their instruments and bantering back and forth with each other.

The shelves past the counter still held more than ninety-three varieties of both loose leaf and bagged teas, a Mecca for the serious tea drinker. Aunt Clara loved the raspberry cream tea sold loose leaf while Aunt Sarah, the Italian in their family, couldn't live without her Irish Breakfast tea. Idly Gina wondered if the Italians and the Irish were somehow related.

In addition, an eclectic assortment of flavorings, local honeys, biscuits, biscotti, teapots, teacups, and various other accoutrements of tea drinking were displayed for sale.

In the bay window near where they were seated, Gina saw an "Alice in Wonderland" teapot and cups beside her in the window. In the other part of the bay was a bright, red teapot that was square.

Muted clinks of silver and glass punctuated the conversations at the ten or so tables around them. Not quite seven o'clock, the tables were nearly full, and the expectancy that shimmered in the air promised an evening of incredible musical talent.

Corey returned and asked, "Did you see all the bottles of root beer in that cooler? There must be at least twenty-five different varieties! I've got to bring my mother here! She would love this place!"

Lawton and Lanie's food arrived. When Gina saw the cubes of melon, grapes, strawberries, and thinly sliced apples that accompanied Lanie's chicken salad croissant, she was glad she hadn't eaten dinner yet.

Just then Kirby stepped to the microphone. "Good evening everyone. Thank you for coming to our concert tonight. I'm going to start with a Beatles Medley."

She sat on a stool and began playing her guitar.

Just then their food arrived. As she ate and listened to the beautiful music, Gina felt herself relax by degrees. Corey helped by lightly resting his hand on the back of her chair and occasionally rubbing her left shoulder with his thumb.

The first time he did it, she thought it was an accident since he lifted his hand often to gesture as he talked. But by the third time, Gina was sure it was intentional, and she didn't quite know how to react.

She couldn't make a scene, and, truth to tell, it felt nice, like Corey cared, as a friend she added hastily to herself. She decided to just relax and enjoy the evening without analyzing anything. Besides, Kirby was playing "Somewhere over the Rainbow," one of Gina's favorite songs.

Lanie leaned forward. "She's doing that chiming effect everyone's been discussing," she said, referring to Kirby's playing technique. "Can you hear it? It sounds like all those beautiful notes on a harp.

They listened more closely, and Gina did hear it. How incredible to be able to play a guitar like that, she thought. No wonder Kirby was receiving notice in the music world.

When Kirby finished, everyone applauded. Then she introduced her friend, Joshua Jarman. He sang a gutsy song with almost a rap feel to it Gina thought. It was about the possibility of changing the world through love. She could tell Corey was enjoying the more primeval beat and driving rhythm of the song.

While Joshua played and sang, Kirby chatted with some friends and drank some water. Lanie motioned her over to their table and introduced them to Kirby.

"We really liked that chiming technique you use," said Lanie.

"I started taking lessons from Tommy Emmanuel. He's teaching me how to do that technique. It's also called artificial harmonics."

She sat and played a riff to give them an example.

"It's like playing an arpeggio on the piano," said Corey after a moment. "Only you go back and continue to repeat the notes in whatever chord you're playing for as long as you need in the song, right?"

"Right," said Kirby.

"What was the name of the song Joshua Jarman sang," asked Corey.

"I think it's called *Love Someone* by this amazing artist in Australia called Dub FX. I'll tell him you liked it."

"Very cool," said Lawton. "Thanks for showing us that chiming technique. I want to go home and try it."

"I'll show you more at the end of the evening," Kirby volunteered. "We always have several extra guitars around here. I'll get you started."

"Awesome," said Lawton.

"Nice to meet you," Kirby said politely before she moved away.

"She's really nice," said Gina. "Very down to earth and excited about her music."

"That makes me want to pull out my guitar," said Lawton with a dreamy look in his eyes.

"We have open mike night here on Tuesdays," said Lanie. "You should come, Lawton."

"Now you've done it," said Gina to Lanie.

"I'm not that good," said Lawton. "But I do think I'm going to start practicing my guitar again."

Kirby was back onstage announcing the next performer, the man who had first invited her to perform, Mr. Keith Miller. Keith played an old Eagle's song.

The song once again made Gina felt so conflicted. Although she and Harry had their differences, major ones right now, she was still engaged to him. So why was she enjoying the attentions of someone else? Was she that fickle? Apparently.

And here she was analyzing things again. Enjoying the company of someone was not grounds for denouncing herself or declaring herself an unfit fiancée. For the second time that evening, she commanded herself to relax. She was just here with a few friends, enjoying the music.

Keith played another song, *Take Me Home, Country Roads*, and asked everyone to join him in singing. Everyone did, and the light-hearted chatter following the song showed it was a hit.

Lanie excused herself to use the restroom and asked Gina to go with her. Gina was glad to escape. They made their way around chairs and the queue ordering at the counter.

"Are you okay?" asked Lanie. "You seem a little jumpy tonight."

"I'm okay. Does Corey seem, oh, I don't know."

"Friendly? I'm glad to see you two are getting along, especially with the wedding only a month and a half away. It would be awkward if you two hated each other."

"Yes, I guess that's it. He's just being friendly."

"You two didn't exactly hit it off, but Lawton and I agree he's a super guy. Lawton thinks the world of him, and they way he's helping your grandparents, well, I'm sure he has his reasons, but still it's very kind of him."

Well, thought Gina a trifle sourly. Another conquest by the incomparable Corey. But then she had to accede that he was being excessively generous and kind.

As they exited, Lanie exclaimed, "Oh great! We didn't miss David Metts. I really like the words to some of the songs he has written."

Gina found she preferred Kirby's playing, and Corey liked Joshua Jarman's songs.

"So which artist do you like best?" Lanie asked of Lawton.

"I think I like Keith Miller best. He seems the most polished. He's been around longer to perfect his craft, I guess."

As the hour grew later and more patrons left, the manager obligingly pushed a few tables together to create a small space for dancing. Lawton and Lanie joined the older couple for whom the space had been created.

Gina sipped the last of her hot chai and watched them idly. Corey was buying another coffee, so she had a chance to watch him covertly.

He really was fine looking with his slightly curly, mahogany hair, his clear brown eyes and engaging manner. Add to that the elegance of his clothing: the bomber-style leather jacket over a steel blue sweater, the khaki Dockers, and the worn and comfortable leather loafers.

Gina sighed. She was not unaware of the attention he attracted from all the females in the room. He really was being a great friend to her as well as to the rest of her family from the older generation down to her son.

Corey turned just then and caught her look. Joshua Jarman was singing a song called *You and Me*. When he came to the line, about not taking my eyes from you, Gina thought her heart would lodge permanently in her throat.

His eyes never wavering from hers, Corey came to the table with his coffee.

"Dance with me, Gina."

It wasn't a request; it was a command stated very quietly and dangerously low.

Gina stood as if on autopilot and went without a word into Corey's arms. She couldn't have said a word if she'd had to do so. He held her close, but not too closely, acting the gentleman as they circled slowly.

She couldn't look into his eyes. It would be too intimate, especially with the words to the song reverberating in her ears. Not quite laying her head on his shoulder, she breathed in the cleanly sensual scent of his cologne, felt the strength of his arms.

When the song ended, they broke apart. Her eyes fell on Lanie and Lawton who were ending the dance with a kiss.

"Let me take you home, Gina," she heard Corey say.

"I brought my car," said Gina breathlessly.

"That was a nice way to end the evening," said Lanie brightly, ignoring the undercurrents at the table as Gina put on her scarf and gathered her things.

Gina was never more grateful for the intrusive chatter of a friend. It brought her back to earth and reminded her of her duties. She had school to teach the next day and a little boy for whom she was responsible.

"I really enjoyed this. Thank you for inviting me," she said to Lanie. "I'll have a hard time staying awake to teach tomorrow, but just to relax totally with friends has been worth it." She hoped Corey caught the emphasis on the word "friends," for that's all she could be.

Kirby placed a guitar in Lawton's hands. "Let me show you how to do the chiming technique," she said.

"Look's like I'll be here for a while," said Lanie with a laugh. "Might as well help clean up." She gave Gina a hug. "Good night."

Corey held the door for her and opened her car door.

"Sweet dreams," he said, bending down and looking deep into her eyes. Then he closed her door and backed up as she pulled out.

She tumbled into bed exhausted after checking on Caden, paying Gwennie, and making sure her sister left safely. She dreamed of strong arms and hazel eyes and a dance that never ended.

Chapter Twenty-Nine

Blake was smiling a lot these days. Right now he was smiling at the picture Tallie made, her hair in pigtails, teaching Francesca, Susanna, and Susanna's little sister, Cissy, how to jump rope.

He sat at the kitchen table with Mrs. Garcia and Mrs. Flores, sipping the latter's very delicious version of Southern sweet tea. It had some spices in it and the sweet tang of orange, if he wasn't mistaken.

They watched Tallie and the children at play in the back yard. It was one of those rare October days when the sun shines warmly, but the little breeze has a bite to it, to let everyone know colder weather is coming.

The ten or so trees in the backyard were turning brilliant shades of vermillion and gold while three tall pines stood sentinel, their needles as green as ever. Squirrels chattered and hunted busily for nuts, and dragonfly wings gleamed silver in the sun's golden beams.

While Tallie worked with Francesca, Susanna, and Cissy on the patio slab, Emilio, Eduardo, and the three Garcia boys zoomed around with the toy airplanes Tallie had brought for them.

"She is muy bonita, both inside and outside," said Mrs. Flores, referring to Tallie. She still held Blake in high regard, but she had finally lost her fear of talking to him although she still averted her eyes many times when she first saw him.

"Si," said Mrs. Garcia. She looked sideways at Blake, and seeing the smitten look on his face, she poked him in the ribs to get his attention.

"You dating her?" she asked.

"Si," responded Blake. Since the fiesta, they had spent every day together except for the two trips to Tampico and another day when he had to testify in a Florida court for a previous case.

Galeah and Davey Merrill had invited Tallie to stay with them whenever she was in town, and Chelsea had insisted that Tallie stay in her old room. Blake had found himself drawn more and more into their family, eating breakfast there many mornings and attending church services with them on the weekend.

He had even been to the farm on several occasions. His grandfather had been a farmer, and Blake enjoyed stripping to the waist and working with the sun hot on his tired but happy muscles.

Making sure Tallie was fully engaged with the girls and holding a finger to his lips, Blake pulled a small, square case from his pocket. He lifted the lid from the box and a single diamond in an antique setting with small pearls clustered around it, gleamed brilliantly.

The women oohed and ahed softly.

"Silencio," warned Amelia Flores, and Blake quickly recapped the box and slid it into his pocket.

Tallie and the girls trooped through the sliding glass door. Simone Garcia rose and retrieved cups from the cabinet so the thirsty girls could get some water.

"Do you think you can do it by yourselves now?" asked Tallie when they were finished.

Francesca and Susanna nodded exuberantly.

"Gracias, Senorita Tallie," said Francesca, giving her a big hug. Susanna also hugged her, murmuring her thanks as well. Cissy, however, had to climb into Tallie's lap and whisper something in her ear.

"I think you are just dear," she said. She jumped down and ran outside where the other girls were already practicing with their jump ropes.

"And she is so sweet and dear herself," said Tallie. "How is she adjusting in school?" she asked Simone Garcia.

"She like school," said Simone. "She have, no has all As."

"Good. And how about the boys?"

"As and Bs. Not bad. Little Horacio, he like to read. All the time he bring home books to read, and he reads them to me, so I get education, too," said Simone with a laugh.

"Your English is improving," said Tallie admiringly. "Bueno."

They all laughed.

"How about the nightmares? Do the boys and Cissy still have nightmares?"

"Just when they hear loud motorcycles now."

For a while, the three boys, Horacio, Hector, and Gustavo, had awakened most nights whimpering and then screaming about bullets and men on motorcycles. After a month of this, Simone and Stephan were at their wits end. The nightmares had gradually diminished, however, when the boys started attending school.

Turning to Amelia, Tallie asked after Emilio and Eduardo and baby April, who was sleeping in a carrier in the living room.

"They are fine. We don't go to any place that has alligators, but I think only Francesca knew what those evil men were planning. The boys, they just remember the car ride."

"And the airplane ride," commented Blake with a grin as Eduardo, Emilio and Gustavo ran by the sliding glass door, left partially open by the girls, making zooming noises.

He stood, loathe to leave the homey atmosphere and the simple pleasure of watching children play.

Tallie stood also, briefly stopping to kiss little April on her head as she made her way to the door with Blake. She turned and gave Simone and Amelia a hug each.

Tallie noticed with satisfaction that as Blake hugged each one of the women, he was less stiff and formal than he used to be.

They stopped at a sandwich shop in downtown Summerville, and then headed to Azalea Park. Blake parked by the tennis courts, and, holding hands, they walked to Tallie's favorite bronze sculptures of children playing in the park.

Their delicious lunch finished, Tallie snuggled next to Blake who sat propped up against the trunk of a tall pine tree.

"How long have I known you now?" he asked.

"We met the beginning of August at dinner. Then we evacuated the families from Tampico, and I've been here or in Georgia ever since."

"It's only been three months, but I feel like I've known you all my life," commented Blake.

"You are an easy man to be around, Blake," said Tallie. "Although I will say you keep the best parts of your personality hidden from most people."

"Not with you," said Blake, pulling away slightly so he could look her in the face.

"No, not with me. I get to see your humorous side and your vulnerable side sometimes. And there's your romantic side, too," she added softly.

"My romantic side has a question for you." He drew the small, square box from his pocket, and flipping off the lid asked, "Will you marry me Tallie? I can't imagine spending the rest of my life without you."

"Oh my, Blake! I'm so surprised! I didn't see this coming!" she stammered, and Blake finally had the pleasure of a complete surprise.

"Yes, of course, I'll marry you."

Taking the ring from the box, he slipped it on her third finger, left hand and sealed the action by kissing each finger and the palm of her hand.

"I love you, Tallie, more than life. It frightens me how much I love you sometimes."

"Blake, why does it frighten you? Help me understand." Then her mood changed from serious to mischievous. I don't want to get offended right now. You propose and then tell me you're frightened."

"No, don't get offended." He looked at her a trifle anxiously. He was still learning about her quirky sense of humor and how to read it. Yet he really wanted her to understand.

"I think it's because everyone I've ever loved has passed away. My mother, my grandfather."

"That's very intuitive of you," said Tallie. "You're finally getting in touch with your inner self." She was half complimentary, half teasing.

"We both have dangerous jobs, and it would kill me if you lost your life on one of your assignments."

Tallie became very serious. "Yes we do have dangerous jobs. Either one of us could lose our lives. But don't you think it's better to love and lose a love than to never love at all, to paraphrase the immortal poet? Besides, I think your job is way more dangerous than mine."

"Right now you're pretty safe, and I'm the one flying into danger. But you've been in dangerous situations before, and I'm sure you'll be in dangerous situations in the future. I won't ask you to give that up."

"Thank you for that. I really do enjoy my job. But I have been thinking more about asking my bosses if I can work state side, helping families transition into their new lives here. We'll see."

She held her hand up to the light so the diamond sparkled. "It's beautiful, Blake, but it looks like an antique. Does it have a story?"

"It was the ring my father gave to my mother. She would want you to have it."

"Then it is even dearer to me because it's a part of you, your heritage."

She flung her arms around him and thanked him in a very satisfactory way.

Several minutes later Blake came up for air. Tallie was not shy about showing her feelings, and he couldn't help but respond hungrily.

He was, however, always conscious of people and situations around him, and unless he was in a secure place such as his own home, he felt extremely vulnerable and unable to explore their passions as he would like.

Which was a good thing. After spending time with the Merrills and looking up Tallie's family on the internet, he had a feeling that her father would not appreciate any hint of scandal regarding his only daughter.

He also knew that as soon as her family learned of their engagement, he would be subject to an even closer scrutiny. And that was only fair although he felt certain he could hold his own.

He had not informed Tallie, but he planned to visit her parents in the next few days. They could take his measure then.

By mutual consent, they disposed of their trash, linked hands and walked toward the back of the park where a quaint bridge arched over the little creek that meandered through the park, and leaves still created a canopy through which the sun shone and pooled in golden glens of light.

They were nearing the trail by Main Street when Blake's phone rang.

It was Jose in Tampico, and Tallie immediately sensed the young man, Blake, fading away to be replaced by Blake, the bounty hunter, who spoke in clipped, cold tones and was focused solely on getting his man. Only this job was on his own time, and he was hunting the kingpin of the human trafficking business in Tampico.

"I'll be there by nightfall. Did you get the equipment I ordered?"

Tallie could hear Jose's cheerful, "Yes, Boss" in response.

"We'll need a beat up, unidentifiable taxicab for this job."

"Ricardo already has that, Boss, and a boat in the harbor if we need it."

"Bueno, bueno," responded Blake. "Hasta luego."

When Blake snapped shut his phone, he looked at Tallie apologetically, but she was already talking.

"You need to go right away. I think one of our pilots is in town. Let me call him and see if he'll fly you out right away."

Blake drove to the two rooms he rented from a Mrs. Carter and picked up his already packed duffel bags, one with guns and other paraphernalia for his job and the other with clothing and sundries.

He invited Tallie in for the first time, apologetically telling her it wasn't much. And it wasn't. He clearly spent more time away from the place than in it. Everything was immaculately neat, but since he had very little furniture— just a bed, desk, dresser, and sofa—it was easy to keep his things neatly.

When they pulled into the airport, Blake gave Tallie his car keys, and they headed into the small building to meet the pilot.

And the first person they saw was Corey.

"Well, hello, cousin," he said. "I didn't know you knew my itinerary."

"I don't. Blake is here to catch a flight. Where is that pilot?"

Just then the manager hurried to them with a message. Tallie's pilot had received an emergency job shortly after their conversation. He hadn't even had time to call her since it involved organ donor transport.

"Well, it looks like you'll be flying with me then," said Corey. "Where are we going?"

"But what about your business here?" asked Blake. "I don't want to impose."

"It can wait." Corey finally caught sight of Tallie's ring. He caught hold of Tallie's hand and looked questioningly from Tallie to Blake.

"Yes, Blake and I just became engaged, but no one else knows. You're the first, so you'd better keep your mouth closed."

"My lips are sealed as they say in the movies," said Corey. "But congratulations you two. He hugged Tallie.

"Well done, Man!" he said as he shook Blake's hand.

"So now, one more time, where are we headed? I have to file a flight plan, and I need you two to go get some food for me and Jonathan."

"I'm headed to Tampico, Mexico."

"Any special reason?"

"I'll fill you in on the details when we get in the air."

Chapter Thirty

After arranging for Blake and Tallie to pick up some subs with plenty of chips and drinks, Corey turned to go back into the small building that housed the facilities for small, non-commercial aircraft.

He decided to file a flight plan using his Droid since he didn't exactly know the nature of Blake's business in Tampico. He could guess it would be related to the human trafficking ring Blake was determined to uncover.

If anyone was tracking flights in and out of Charleston, it would add another layer of obscurity. So he bypassed the computers in the main room and strode to the back where Jonathan was still at the airplane, tidying their equipment. They had been investigating properties in Costa Rica for Corey's dad.

A huge group of expatriates lived there, and Mr. Peters-Templeton was considering several properties. He had wanted Corey to do some simple surveying and mapping, especially of a rather large tract of land perfect for a slow development project.

"We have another flight to make," Corey told Jonathan. "I'll be the pilot this time. Blake is coming with us; he can be the co-pilot while you catch some sleep in the back. Hop in while we get some gas at the FBO."

Used to Corey's quick change of plans, Jonathan hopped smartly into the co-pilot's seat. "Where are we headed?"

"Tampico, Mexico."

"Does this have anything to do with the girls kidnapped by the human trafficking ring?"

"Probably. But since Blake needs to get there as soon as possible, instead of getting all the info, I sent him and Tallie to get food for us. I hope subs work for you!"

"You told them to get banana peppers and olives for me, right?"

"Of course. I should know by now how you like your sandwiches."

Corey filed his flight plan while the attendant gassed up the big C-47 Corey had bought and retrofitted for trips to more undeveloped parts of the world where his dad wanted to expand.

Normally he flew a Gulfstream IV to various points in Europe, most often Stuttgart, Germany, but for trips to South or Central America, he preferred the C-47.

Not only did the section in back of the cockpit contain an office, sleeping quarters and restroom facilities, but Corey had stripped the twin radial engines and replaced them with turbo prop engines. He could transport an all-terrain Hummer in the very back, plus he'd had a Garmin G 1000 instrument panel installed with GPS approach and onboard weather radar. And he had some fire power stowed in the back for 'unfriendlies' just in case.

Thirty minutes later, Tallie kissed Blake good-bye and Blake donned his headphones. Jonathan shook hands with Blake and disappeared into the back to get some much-needed sleep.

Corey radioed the tower for clearance to Tampico. Minutes later the tower responded that they were holding runway twenty-one ready for takeoff, and then they were in the air.

Once he achieved his desired altitude, Corey turned to Blake. "So, I take it this trip is about the families you evacuated?"

"Yes. Jose thinks he's discovered the kingpin of the entire human trafficking ring. Last time I was down there, I put him and Ricardo on that task while Carlos and Pietro are guarding the Monterrey family although the family has no idea."

"So what are your plans for tonight?"

"I'll check into headquarters and then go on surveillance with Jose and Ricardo. You are welcome to come if you want."

"Wouldn't miss it!" said Corey with relish. "We can leave Jonathan to guard this ship although it should be perfectly safe at the airport. Where is headquarters?"

"I bought some property on the outskirts of town. It's surrounded by swamp on three sides. Built a small house there and a large warehouse, camouflaged, of course."

"Sounds like my kind of operation," said Corey, "especially when going up against the bad guys."

"Jose is bunking there right now and keeping an eye on the two armored vehicles I ordered. Those vehicles won't stop for anyone or anything toting a gun."

"I've heard about all the Americans carjacked and murdered in that area. In your estimation, is it a real problem?"

"It is. That's why I ordered the cars."

"So if you find the big, bad hombre tonight, what's your plan?"

"I'm going to go in tomorrow night and bug his place, put a few small cameras on the walls to give us live video feed of transactions. Then I'll equip an old, beaten up van or some other vehicle with the screens to show us what he's doing and how his operation works. Once we know his MO, and we have plenty of evidence for the international police, we'll go in and take him down."

"Do you think he suspects anything?"

"I'm sure he's somewhat suspicious. Two big armored vehicles suddenly appear immediately after most of the families are airlifted to safety? He's not stupid. He's got to be questioning whether or not anyone suspects. That is unless he's totally arrogant and thinks he's invincible."

"Do you think Tallie and the rescued families are safe?"

"They'd better be," said Blake darkly. "I've been doing surveillance around the Merrill home where she's staying, and I've seen nothing."

Corey relaxed a fraction in his seat, confident now that Blake had a workable plan.

"I've got some toys in the back. My dad has tangled with some pretty crooked people. I went through some of the same training he did, and so I, uh, borrowed, some of his hardware. Go check it out. Everything's under control up here."

He didn't tell Blake that his parents were members of an elite force of freedom fighters who worked privately around the world, quietly rescuing people and securing locations from dissidents. He, too, was a junior member of this unnamed, unobtrusive group.

Thirty minutes later Blake returned. Corey couldn't say he was grinning from ear to ear; Blake's face was too impassive for that. But the gleam in his eyes and the smug set of his jaw told Corey he'd found the small arsenal of guns, missiles, and other miscellaneous but lethal items stowed securely on board.

"A surface to air missile?" questioned Blake with a chuckle.

"Sure. Never know when you can use one of those!" responded Corey with a chuckle.

"You never got to eat, did you?" asked Blake when Corey's stomach suddenly growled.

"No, and actually, I could use some chow. Breakfast is a dim memory."

"Would you like me to take the controls?" asked Blake.

"You know how to fly one of these?"

"Sure thing. When my grandfather realized I was serious about becoming a bounty hunter, not only did he have me trained in the Native American skills of tracking, but I took flying lessons as well. I'm certainly not the pilot you are, but I can do a decent job."

"Good. It's all yours, my friend."

"I put the food in the galley in back. Stowed my stuff in a closet back there, too. Hope you don't mind."

"Not at all." Corey stood and stretched. "You want some coffee when I come back?"

"Sounds great. Two teaspoons of sugar, one of cream."

Corey disappeared, and Blake sat up straight, enjoying the feel of flying such a large plane although with their course preset, he really didn't have much to do.

When Corey returned some thirty minutes later with coffee for both him and Blake, they were over the gulf. They had about an hour and half of flying time left.

Corey settled in his seat. "So, tell me about your engagement to my cousin. Does her family know anything about it?"

"No. We just became engaged today. I had planned to visit her parents in the next few days, but then Jose called, and here I am."

"Can I give you some advice?"

"Sure."

"Don't expect them to understand your job. Heck, they don't even understand Tallie and her propensity for escaping certain death."

"What are they like? They are your aunt and uncle, so give me their personalities."

"Uncle Thomas is sharp enough to have started his own banks, and he is fabulous with numbers, but he's really

246

rather laid back. In three words I would describe him as genial, hard-working, and smart."

"What about Tallie's mother?"

"Aunt Paige?" Corey chuckled. "Well to start, she has red hair, so now you know where Tallie gets that. She's very smart and loves a good joke, but when she gets angry, watch out! She will rant and rave and throw things, but if she's wrong, she's very generous with her apologies. She is also very smart and hard-working, but she's much more exuberant and out-going than Uncle Thomas."

"How are they related to your family?"

"Uncle Thomas and my dad are brothers."

"Do you have any advice on how I should approach them?"

It was the first time Corey had ever seen the calm, unflappable Blake even remotely nervous. Women will change us all, he thought.

"I know you want to talk to them first, but I would let Tallie tell them first instead. Then go talk to Uncle Thomas at his main bank. I'll give you the address."

"I already have it."

"Good. He'll probably invite you to lunch and call his wife and Tallie to join you all. As long as Aunt Paige can see that Tallie's happy, and heck, even I can see that, you will be accepted."

A few muscles in Blake's face seemed to relax. He turned to Corey.

"So how did you get so smart about women?"

"Practice," said Corey dryly.

"Do you have someone?" asked Blake.

"Yes. Well, kind of. I've met someone, but she's engaged to another man. I only have a few months to convince her she should be marrying me."

Blake didn't want to ask the girl's name. This was only the fourth time he had been around Corey, and he didn't want to pry.

Wait. At the fiesta. Who was that tall, leggy blonde Corey had escorted? If he wasn't mistaken, it was Chelsea and Lawton's cousin, Gina. Well, I'll be, he thought to himself.

Corey, watching him, saw that he had made the connection. So the "butt-boy," to quote Shakespeare, had not turned his brain to mush. That was good because they were on a mission here.

"After I land this ship, how do we get to your 'headquarters'?" he asked so they could refocus on the matters at hand.

"Jose is meeting us with one of the armored cars. One of the airport officials is his cousin, so he is going to drive right out on the tarmac to pick us up."

"We're thirty minutes out. Can you go back and wake up Jonathan? But before you do, two duffel bags are with the arsenal I brought. Pack up whatever small stuff you think we can use. I'd rather be prepared than not."

"Are you packing some hardware?"

"Oh, yeah!" Corey grinned and pointed to his jacket, the back of his waist, and both boots.

"Good!" said Blake simply, and he exited the cockpit.

Twenty-five minutes later, their plane was approaching the runway. Blake had resumed his position in the co-pilot's seat, and Jonathan was sitting in a small, pull-down emergency seat right outside of the cockpit behind Corey.

The plane taxied smoothly to a stop. The shiny black of the armored vehicle had been replaced by a dull camouflage finish. Blake grinned to himself. Jose had certainly been hard at work.

Blake jumped out at first opportunity with his bags and greeted Jose, automatically pulling on his sunglasses, while Jonathan helped Corey with some others. Jose had brought Juan with him, and they made short work, transferring the rest of the bags.

As an airport worker told Jonathan where to park the plane, Blake caught a glint from one of the upstairs windows of the aeropuerto's tower.

"Everyone in," he yelled suddenly. They all dived for the car except Jonathan who hurried to the plane.

Corey pushed up his glasses and asked, "What was that about?"

"Since we've not been turned into a vaporous mass, I can only guess that our arrival has been noted. I saw a glint, probably on binoculars from a tower window."

"We'll have to be doubly on guard. I just hope the sunglasses we're all wearing will hinder them in identifying us," said Corey.

Blake had his doubts, but he didn't voice them. He would concentrate instead on making sure they found this bastard and on getting enough evidence to put him away for a very long time so he couldn't hurt any more children.

Chapter Thirty-One

The speed boat Pietro had borrowed from one of his friends was a beauty and a "sweet goer," as Blake liked to say. Sleek and black, the motor had been adjusted to accommodate the owner's need for speed.

Jose had discovered that a new "shipment" of victims had been kidnapped in and around a small impoverished area south of Tampico.

Now they were patrolling up and down the coast and the river, watching for the transfer to a ship. The slap of the waves against the hull created a hypnotic sound as they waited and watched. Stars twinkled in the inky sky while wisps of fog eddied here and there. The fog wasn't dense, but it could create illusions of movement.

Blake had two cameras. The one with a wide angle telephoto lens he would use, and the other, waterproof, would be used by Corey. Corey had packed a lightweight diving suit and could swim like an eel. He would try to get close enough to snap pictures of the victims.

"Right there," said Corey suddenly. Through their binoculars, he and Blake had both seen a white van that was approaching a ship moored near the mouth of the river.

Pietro brought the speedboat as close as he dared. Ricardo, piloting a small fishing boat, provided the cover they needed to conceal their activities. Corey slipped over the side and was gone before they were aware of it.

Blake waited tensely, holding his camera up and adjusting the focus. He watched as three men exited the van and looked warily around them.

Appearing satisfied, one man opened the side door and hauled a small figure from inside. Its head was covered with a gunny sack, and it stumbled and nearly fell.

To hold the unproductive emotion of anger at bay, Blake began snapping picture after picture.

Not all of the children had their heads covered. Blake realized from their blank stares and lack of muscle coordination that most of them were drugged.

One child, apparently unconscious, was carried up the gangplank to the ship. Blake guessed her age was about four or five.

Pietro held the boat steady, but using his binoculars, he was watching, too. "Madre de Dios," he exclaimed when he saw the pequena being carried aboard.

Jose, his face glued to his camera as well, was filming the event and quietly recording a scathing dialogue to go with it.

Blake counted twelve victims, ranging in age from about four to about fourteen. Two were boys; the rest were girls as near as he could tell. Only two men were on deck to greet the new arrivals.

When the last victim had been boarded, the three hombres hastily retreated to their van and left in a cloud of dust. The squeal of their tires created an exclamation point of sound on the otherwise quiet waterfront. All of the bustle was further down the river at the docks.

Corey appeared. "We need to get out of here pronto," he said. "The captain is eyeing our boats suspiciously. I think he's radioing for backup."

"And here it comes," said Jose, spying another boat in the distance.

"Go below everyone, and hide all of your equipment," ordered Pietro. "And call Ricardo. Tell him to stay where he is. I'll lead these hombres on the chase of their lives. Then he can move to safety and join us at the rendezvous point. Here we go!"

Pietro thrust the throttle forward, and the modified 1350 engines screamed to life. He headed upriver, the area he knew most intimately. He would lose these bastards, but not before he led them on a merry chase.

Blake slipped up beside him. "Can you get close enough that I can get pictures of their boat and possibly the men on board?"

"I try. Depends what kind of guns they have. Have to turn around and go out to sea again."

"Okay. I'll just start snapping pictures. Do whatever you have to do."

Corey, too, had appeared beside Blake, but then he disappeared below.

Pietro made a sharp turn to the left and headed back out to sea. At first he turned slightly right as if to tack south down the coast. But then he swung back and raced on a collision course with the boat tailing him.

Corey reappeared. He was holding something in his hand.

As they neared the other boat, Pietro could hear bullets hitting the boat, the water.

"Get your pictures!" he yelled to Blake. As they zoomed perilously close.

He laughed gleefully as they passed the other boat, moving the boat in a zigzag course designed to counteract the accuracy of the enemy fire. He was especially delighted to see two of the three men aboard scrambling for cover from the imminent collision.

At the last minute Pietro swerved to avoid the oncoming boat, but still, a loud boom reverberated over the water.

Blake and Corey high-fived as Pietro turned in disbelief to look at the burning, sinking enemy boat.

"Grenade," Corey said simply at Pietro's questioning look. "A lucky shot, but it was worth a try, especially since we were going to be so close."

They continued to talk elatedly until Blake realized Juan had not come up to join them. He ducked below board and then yelled for Corey.

Juan had taken a bullet to the chest. Blake was pretty sure it had missed his heart, but he was bleeding heavily. Quickly, he ripped Juan's shirt open and found the wound. Above the heart. Okay.

"Hold this on his wound while I check for an exit."

Blake tilted Juan on his side, lifted his shirt, and looked for an exit wound. None. Gently laying Juan on his back again, Blake pulled his phone from his pocket and hit a button.

The next hour was a blur as Corey continued to apply pressure, and Blake got Ricardo on the phone. Ricardo simply knew everyone worth knowing in Tampico.

Ricardo met them down river past the hulking gray metal hull of the ship incarcerating the kidnapped children. No one seemed to be watching their movements. Blake guessed the explosion had satisfied the captain, especially if he hadn't been able to distinguish any differences between the two boats as they were both black.

Ricardo led them to a small dock nearly obscured by overhanging trees. They tied up and, as gently as possible, carried Juan to the house. Juan had regained consciousness, but the pain of being moved caused him to pass out again.

Not waiting for their knock to be answered, Ricardo helped them carry Juan onto the unlocked porch. A man came to the door. He was short and looked extremely weary, but his eyes and his manner were kind.

Ricardo explained urgently in Spanish Juan's situation. The doctor indicated that they should carry Juan inside. The doctor's housekeeper led them to a downstairs examining room where Juan was laid on an examination table.

She must be a nurse, Blake thought as she deftly removed Juan's shirt, placed a thermometer in his armpit and placed a blood pressure cuff around his other arm.

Juan was running a fever, and his blood pressure was low but stable.

The doctor shooed them out, and the nurse prepared Juan for surgery. Blake left a large fistful of pesos with Pietro who would stay with Juan. Blake and the rest still had work to accomplish this night.

"Donde esta, Boss?" asked Jose as Ricardo piloted the black speed boat back down the river toward the Gulf.

"When that boat appeared, which direction did it come from?" asked Blake thoughtfully.

"We were going to head up river past the ship with the children. But when Corey warned us about the captain calling for backup, I turned the boat around facing the open sea. They came from down south," said Pietro, retracing their movements in his mind's eye and then pointing dramatically down the coast away from Tampico.

"It makes sense that the captain would radio the person who would have the power and authority to help him the most. Any ideas, Ricardo?"

"It makes sense. A few calls I overheard I traced to south of the river."

"I wonder," said Blake thoughtfully. He didn't enlighten anyone else about his thoughts, but a nasty suspicion was growing in his mind. Could the man they were seeking be the new owner of the place his stepfather had owned?

He had kept an eye on the place, but it had changed ownership last year. Could the new owner be the one who was making money selling children for a huge profit to debauched, immoral people in the United States? He would only need a crooked ship's captain and a couple of thugs willing to kidnap children.

On a hunch he asked Ricardo to let him steer the boat. He knew this coast and this area like he knew Tallie's face. If the head of this nefarious operation was indeed the new owner of his stepfather's estate, he had the advantage of knowing it better than the new owner did.

Hadn't he been the shadow who knew every nook and cranny, every hiding place to disappear into? He had even discovered a paneled closet in the library accessible only by a button on the side of the door jamb.

By now, the temperature had dropped, and sky and sea were an indigo black. He was looking for that one thread of current from a creek that ran by the property out to the sea.

How he found it, he never really knew. Instinct and determination surely played their part. He killed the motors and started the trolling motor off the back of the boat. It would reduce noise announcing their presence, make the boat more maneuverable, and also help to prevent them getting stuck in the shallower waters of the creek.

Everyone was quiet. Noche diablo, the devil's night was upon them. Who knew what or who was in the woods on either side of them?

Both Jose and Ricardo came to stand beside and behind him to hold a whispered conversation. Blake could sense Corey behind him listening as well.

"You know where this hombre live, Boss?" asked Jose.

"I'm not sure. Just going on a hunch here. Most of the people in this area very poor, right? So who has the biggest casa, the most money?"

"Oh," said Ricardo who knew some of Blake's past. "Whoever owns your stepfather's old place, right?"

"Right," said Blake, still whispering. "Do you think you can try to intercept some phone calls, listen to radio frequencies, and pick up something, anything below deck where you can keep it quiet, Ricardo?"

"Sure."

Ricardo and Jose went below to tinker with the radio, and Corey took Jose's place beside Blake.

"What's your plan once we find this place? Are you just going to tie up at the dock?

"No. He has a neighbor. House looks like a shack, on purpose. He has a hidden pool and all the conveniences, but everything's hidden. My stepfather never even knew this man existed. He let me use his pool house when things got tough at my house. He goes by the name of Algier or Big Al."

"Okay, so we tie up there. Then what?"

"Depends on if this guy still has the same alarm system my stepfather had. If he does, piece of cake. If he doesn't, well, I'll at least figure out his alarm system tonight."

"So who's going with you?"

"You volunteering for the job?"

"Yes, if you'll let me. You don't know me very well, but I've done some jobs like this with my father."

"I did hear about the attempted heist at the Midsummer's Eve Ball your mom organized," said Blake, humor in his voice, "and how a group of marksmen took the bad guys out from the ceiling."

"Really? That was supposed to be kept quiet."

"I make it my business to be in the know about such things and the people associated with my friends. Nice work, by the way."

"How did you?....never mind."

A faint light in the distance had gradually been growing brighter. As they rounded a bend in the creek, the villa where Blake had quietly spent his formative years glowed yellow in the security lighting that also accented the best features of the place. It was still far enough away that their motor would not be heard, but Blake was taking no chances.

The boat, already at a crawl, idled while Blake looked around. At last, he backed the boat up about fifty yards and shone a flashlight at a small dock nearly hidden by bushes. Fortunately, no alligators or crocodiles were using it. Blake tied up the boat and the group huddled below deck to discuss their plans and the chatter on the radio.

Chapter Thirty-Two

Gina closed her phone and sighed. Harry wasn't making her life any easier right now. He had told her that his boss wasn't too happy about him looking for another job.

What Gina suspected was that his boss had told him to ditch her. She was being too demanding, too high maintenance.

And now she had a meeting with Mrs. Weston, the principal, after school tomorrow. She had been informed of the meeting by the secretary, and the way she had said it didn't sound very good.

Gina's stomach was in knots. She didn't want to borrow trouble, but at the same time, she wanted to be prepared. The problem was that she couldn't think of anything she had done wrong.

And why was she borrowing trouble and imagining it would be about something bad? Maybe it would be about something good. She was tracking well with her lesson plans, the students seemed to be learning, and she had no heinous discipline problems, a result of the students' second grade teacher last year, she was sure.

She sighed again, and went to the kitchen to pack lunches for the next day. Later, in bed, the thoughts swirled around in her head, keeping her from sleep. As a result, she woke late with a headache. Fortunately, she made it to work on time. She didn't need to add tardiness to any list of transgressions.

Renee noticed something was wrong immediately. "Don't borrow trouble," she advised Gina.

"I think I already have," Gina confessed.

"You've done nothing wrong that I can think of," said Renee staunchly. "Keep your chin up, Girl, and march into her office with your head high. You know whatever she has to say, it can't be that bad."

The day dragged. The final bell rang, and Gina nervously packed her bags and put them in her car before heading to Mrs. Weston's office.

When Gina entered, not only was Mrs. Weston present, but so was the secretary, Deb Lawrence, and two men Gina had never seen. Their badges announced they were from the district office.

If Gina had been nervous before, she was doubly nervous now. Why in the world would people from the district office be present in this meeting?

Deb patted the only empty chair in the room which was beside hers, but she didn't look very happy.

"Have a seat, Gina," said Mrs. Weston pleasantly enough.

"Let me get straight to the point. I've called this meeting today because someone brought to my attention a terrible incident that occurred in our school, and both of you were involved in it."

Gina's mind raced. Terrible incident? She involved? Deb Lawrence too? She could think of nothing.

Mrs. Weston continued. "Deb, you allowed a man in the building without adequately checking his identification. We have it all on the security video. Not only am I concerned about this, but so is the district office" she said, indicating the men who were seated next to her.

She turned to Gina. "Once this young man was in here, you left your class unattended and spent five minutes in the hall with this young man, engaging in inappropriate displays of affection. We have this on security video as well."

Gina's mind raced. The one thing that rankled the most was saying she had left her class unattended.

"May I speak?" she asked.

With a look at the men, Mrs. Weston nodded. "Yes," she said.

"I did not leave my class unattended. My assistant took them to the class room for me. I would never leave my class without an **adult** to watch them. And I'm sure you've timed it on the video, but they were with my assistant for slightly less than five minutes. When I returned to class, they were all working on their science projects."

Gina took a deep breath and continued. "The visitor was my fiancé who has been overseas, and I did not know he was coming. Of course I would hug him since I haven't seen him for a while and he has a very dangerous job. I never know when he leaves if I'll ever see him again."

"And in Deb's defense, he can be very persuasive. She knows I have a fiancé since she has delivered flowers to my class frequently enough." Gina didn't add that the flowers were from others.

But Mrs. Weston didn't like her own assessment of the situation criticized.

"What you say may be true. Nevertheless," she said, "I feel disciplinary action is necessary and appropriate at this point. With your approval," she looked at the two men from the district, "I am recommending that Deb Lawrence be required to take a three day absence without pay."

Gina and Deb gasped in disbelief, but Mrs. Weston continued. "Allowing people in the building without amply checking their background could put the lives of our students in jeopardy as well as the rest of the staff."

"And as of now, Miss Galbraith, you will be placed on probation for the rest of the semester. If you perform your duties well enough between now and then, the probation will be lifted. However, this will be noted in your file."

"Any questions? No? Then you are dismissed."

Numbly, Gina walked to the door. Once in the hall, Deb rounded on her.

"I didn't need you to defend me," she said hotly. "I am perfectly capable of defending myself and would have done a better job. Next time leave me out of your comments." With one last withering glance at Gina, she went down the hall to the office to pack her things.

Now Gina felt doubly wretched. Hot tears scalded down her face as she made her way to the parking lot. She was so glad she had already put her bags in her car. She could never have spoken coherently to Renee.

Gina drove straight to her parents' home. A walk could not assuage the turmoil troubling her brain nor the tears rending her heart.

Her mother met her at the door, concerned that she was late. Gina flew straight into her mother's arms and cried until she had nothing left but hiccups. By now her dad was in the room.

As she told them the story, her anger began to churn. Gina so rarely got truly angry. The black bile boiled up inside of her until she was in a rage.

Once again, the tears welled up and she cried and cried. Her mother took her to her bedroom where there was a large chair. She sat Gina on her lap, stroking her hair and letting her cry.

When Gina was calmer at last, she said, "It's just so unfair. I didn't ask Harry to come to the school."

"I think you defended yourself very well," said her mother. "When everything fell apart with Jack, you were so numb, I didn't think you'd ever feel again. I have to confess, although this situation is rotten to the core, I'm glad to see your emotion in response."

"Why do you think the school district is so upset by it, Mom?"

"This is only a guess, but I would bet that Mrs. Weston has been pressured by the school district about something. She's using this situation to prove a point to them. You and Deb are really only pawns in a bigger situation."

"So what do I do now?"

"You walk into school tomorrow, holding your head high because, really, you've done nothing wrong. You gut it out just like you gutted it out to get your degree even though it was so difficult for you. You are a good teacher, Gina. Cream always rises to the top. Who knows? Maybe you will be in Mrs. Weston's place someday."

"I don't even know if I'd want her position. But thanks, Mom. I don't know what I'd do without your support. And Dad's, too," she added as she remembered he was still watching Caden for her.

"Why don't you stay and eat dinner with us? That will be one less thing for you to do tonight."

"That would be awesome, Mom. Thanks."

"Now go find Caden and give him a hug."

Gina did and was dismayed to discover that Caden had heard her crying and was very anxious.

"Mommy cry?" he asked, patting her face with his hand.

"Yes, Mommy cry. Someone was mean to Mommy, but I'm okay now. How about you?" she asked, hugging him and then tickling him.

"I'm okay."

"How was school today? What did you do?"

"We colored pictures."

"Pictures of what?"

"Trains! Big brown and red and blue and green trains." Clearly, Caden was excited about both trains and colors.

Dinner was nearly over when Uncle Phil called. Jeremy Saxon had just made another inspection of the property that afternoon, and not only would they be billed for the inspection, they would also be fined for noncompliance.

"How close are we to finishing the clean up?"

"Nearly there. We just have a few more piles of wood and those tires to take to the dump. Dad was trying to find a place to recycle them. I don't think he's had time what with the fall planting and hay from the back forty to harvest and get into the barn. But we have a bigger problem."

"What's that?"

"Mr. Saxon has added some more things to clean up."

"Really? What more does he want done now?"

"He thinks that because the bee hives at the back of the hay field are uninhabited, they need to be destroyed."

"We'll have more bees come spring."

"I know that, and you know that, but apparently Jeremy Saxon is too much of a city boy to know that," said Uncle Phil sarcastically.

"I wonder if this has to do with the sale of Old Gouvenor North's land in the back of the farm? Do you think Jeremy has been ordered to get those bee hives removed so they can begin working on their development?" asked Uncle Galen.

"That wouldn't surprise me."

"I guess we'll all be at the farm this weekend."

"The silver lining in a losing football season is that I get to be there with you all. By the way, what is our total bill with the county now?"

"I'm not sure. I think it's around three thousand," said Uncle Galen.

"Corey will want to know about this latest development. Where is he, by the way?"

"He flew Blake back down to Tampico. Apparently, he received a hot tip about the head honcho for the trafficking ring."

"Those boys are going to find more than a peck of trouble is my guess," said Uncle Phil. "You and Dad are the praying men in the family. Better send some up for those boys."

"I'm already on it," said Uncle Galen. "So is Dad, if I don't miss my guess."

*****

In a lonely office across town, Bob Worthington had turned down a hot meal and a warm bed to work on the Merrill land rights case. He rubbed his face wearily.

The case was going to be a bear. His clients were going to have to sue the federal government. He couldn't find any way around it. The best course seemed to be a 1357 Action to recover damages.

This really shouldn't even be a case. The property had been purchased in fee simple in 1959 or so. Therefore, technically, Mr. Saxon should have produced a search warrant the first time he had inspected the land. He would have his paralegal research that tomorrow.

Chapter Thirty-Three

Everyone had their earpieces in place. Ricardo and Jose were staying on the boat, ready to pick up Blake and Corey at the dock if they needed immediate rescue.

Blake would rather have taken Ricardo in with him, but Ricardo knew the waters of the creek almost as well as Blake did. Furthermore, he could come into the compound if Blake needed rescuing.

Before disembarking, Blake drew a map of the place as he remembered it.

"This window is probably going to be our point of entry. I broke the fastener so I could get in and out as needed. Here's the main staircase to the second floor, but over here is the back staircase, and over here by the kitchen is the service staircase."

"Which one will you use?" asked Ricardo.

"We'll use the main staircase if we get stuck by the library where we'll first search for incriminating evidence and plant the bugs. But we only go upstairs if we can't find evidence of illegal activities downstairs. My stepfather had an upstairs office when he lived there where he conducted his private business."

"In what instances will we use the other staircases?" asked Corey.

"I prefer to use the service staircase by the kitchen. Most people rarely use it although I used to sneak down quite often for a midnight snack." Blake smiled in remembrance.

"So where are the hiding places on the second floor?" asked Corey.

"First let me tell you about the hiding places on the first floor. Underneath the grand staircase is one of the best places to hide. It's dark, and very few people think to look there. Plus you can get a great deal of information just by listening."

He took a sip from the canned energy drinks he seemed to crave when he was on assignment, and then he continued.

"Two other places to hide are in the kitchen pantry and in the library itself in that hidden closet I was telling you about. The button for that is on the right hand side of the door jamb, halfway up. The door automatically closes ten seconds after it opens. Once inside, you can open the door by feeling for the knob in the same position."

"And the upstairs?" asked Corey.

"You said you'd done some climbing with a grappling hook?" asked Blake.

"Affirmative. Very rigorous course, first in mountain climbing, then on buildings, and then at night for a spec ops program in which I was involved."

"Do you have your equipment with you?"

"Yes. I have a retractable folding hook, my ropes, carabiners, and a folding crossbow plus an outfit that makes me virtually invisible. Lots of fun at Halloween!" Corey added with a wink.

"Okay. The reason I ask is because the back of the house has black steel grilled balconies for every window and door. Those make great hiding places, but the hook and rope will be helpful if you're discovered."

"The upstairs office had a large cabinet used for hanging coats of visitors," continued Blake, "although I don't know if the present owner uses it for that. I garnered a great deal of information in that hiding spot, but I'd have to go on an empty bladder. My stepfather would often spend several hours at a time on the phone in that room." Blake's remembrances were, obviously, grim.

"The earpieces will help," said Ricardo. "I set them on low, so picking up sound will be more difficult, but since we're going in at a quiet time, I don't want to speak and alert someone of your location. Some people have extremely keen hearing."

"You will be ready to leave and to provide cover fire for us if necessary, right, Ricardo?"

Ricardo nodded.

Blake continued. "Hopefully this will be an in and out operation, clean and quick. I just want to get information and plant the bugs. No arrests tonight. No shooting if we can help it. No noise."

"I know I'm backup, but is there anything else you want me to do?" asked Pietro.

"Make sure those bugs start recording information as soon as I have them in place. If any of them don't work, let me know. We may get lucky tonight. I've got a feeling."

They bumped knuckles and then each of them donned their nighttime surveillance outfits. Ricardo and Pietro stayed bare-headed, but Blake and Corey donned the black hoods that would make them nearly invisible in the night.

Ricardo steered the boat to the compound's dock. Waves lapped gently at the hull of the speedboat moored there alongside two jet skis. Even in October, the air was muggy this far inland, and mosquitoes swarmed around their heads.

Corey brushed at them impatiently, but Blake ignored them, his mind already focused on the job ahead. Quietly, the two men followed the faint trail to the edge of the lawn.

The ornate lamps that lit the place were encircled with halos caused by the humidity of the night.

Blake followed the edge of the lawn as it curved toward the back of the villa. He motioned for Corey to stand with him behind a tall but thin bush where they could easily view the back and near side of the house.

As they waited and watched, Blake could see that the lights were on in the downstairs library. And now as they waited quietly, patiently, he could hear the faint clink of glasses from the direction of the kitchen, the low rhythmic pulse of Latin music, and once the amused, indulgent laughter of a woman's voice.

The scent of tropical plants blended with the faint odors left over from dinner, some kind of chicken dish if his nose was accurate. Nearly a half hour later, the rich scent of a Cuban cigar made his nose twitch and then the unmistakable smell of a cigarette.

Corey, impatient at the delay, nearly choked when he realized that a guard had been standing, looking out toward the sea some forty feet away from them. He had never seen the man.

A cell phone vibrated, and the guard answered it. He lounged against the stucco wall as he talked, and from the few phrases Blake could decipher, he was apparently talking to his girlfriend.

And still they waited. Beside him, Blake could sense Corey's impatience. But Blake knew from bitter experience that if he did not take the time to get all of the information and documentation for the courts, the perpetrator could walk away free if he wasn't killed in the final showdown.

No. They would wait. Blake noted with satisfaction that the light in the library had blinked out. After five more minutes, a clock chimed the hour of eleven. The guard stubbed out his cigar, and sauntered in the direction of the kitchen.

Blake took a deep breath. "Here we go," he said softly.

Corey nodded and they stole from the cover of the bush to the side porch and one of the long, low windows. While Blake worked with the window, Corey covered his back, looking from side to side for any other guards.

"Wait here while I take care of the alarm," muttered Blake. He was gone a mere sixty seconds before reappearing by the window.

He held the heavy drapes back for Corey, and Corey stepped into the drawing room. It was a large room with plush carpeting and groupings of antique furniture, and it spanned the entire width of the house. It smelled somewhat musty, and obviously did not get much use.

"Two more security systems to go," murmured Blake.

They moved quietly to the doorway at the back of the room and entered a small room that seemed to be used by servants as a preparation room for food when guests were being served in the drawing room. At the other side of that room was a wide corridor that spanned the back of the entry and the courtyard.

Blake slowed down as they neared the doorway at the end of the corridor. He motioned Corey to wait, and he took a few minutes to disarm the security system for this side of the house.

The room they entered was similar in size to the preparation room by the drawing room, but was obviously used more by the occupants. The television was off, but the music, muted outside, was louder and came from a stereo system in the far corner.

Blake gently pushed at the door to the library. Nothing happened. Blake slipped inside. "Disarming alarm," Corey heard in his earpiece.

But then Corey heard footsteps on the tile floor in the next room. "Company coming," he said urgently.

"Got it. Come in here," commanded Blake.

Corey entered. The footsteps continued. The person approaching the library was on the phone. Her low, husky voice was reproachful.

"Of course I sent help. I lost two security guards. And what for? Just because you were suspicious? Did you actually <u>see</u> anything?....Now where did I leave that paper?"

Corey and Blake had mere seconds to decide where to hide. Blake slipped quickly into the cabinet he had spoken of earlier. Not wanting to be cornered, Corey opted for standing behind the heavy curtains.

A light snapped on.

"Getting audio and video on camera one," Corey heard Pietro whisper. He was amazed that Blake had taken the time to plant a bug in his haste to find hiding.

"Of course, Darling. But just think. If the occupants of those boats were spying on you, you just cemented their suspicions. If they were not spying on you, you just gave them plenty to report to authorities." She snapped her phone shut with a click of outrage.

Corey's mind reeled as the implications of what he was hearing donned on him. A woman was mixed up in this? A woman? It made his blood boil and his stomach clench.

Blake was actually able to see the woman though a hole he had created years ago. She was a stunning beauty with long, black hair and flawless skin. The red dress she wore clung to her body, displaying delicious curves.

She opened drawers on the desk and rummaged through the tray on top. At last she found the paper she wanted and, snapping off the light, left the room through the door to the kitchen and the back staircase. Blake and Corey listened to the tap of stiletto heels across a section of the kitchen floor and then her light tread on the stairs.

Blake snapped on the light again and handed Corey a small camera. "Take a picture of every paper in this tray," he said.

Corey began taking pictures of the papers in the tray on the desk, working as fast and efficiently as possible. Meanwhile, Blake began placing the bugs where he wanted them. He held a whispered conversation with Pietro to get the best angles and views of the room.

Corey finished the papers in the tray and moved to the desk drawers. The brains behind the desk must be ruthlessly organized he thought. Everything was meticulously labeled and filed.

He didn't see anything that seemed to be linked to the kidnappings or the ship. Blake joined him, pulling another camera out of his pocket. He began perusing papers and taking pictures. They were nearly finished when they both heard the curvaceous woman's voice through a cell phone in the next room.

Corey moved noiselessly to the nearest window again while Blake quietly closed the drawer and disappeared into the nearby cabinet.

"Everything looks in order," said the guard, carelessly looking around. Corey breathed a sigh of relief. He couldn't remember if he had closed the drawer or not.

"No, I didn't see anything suspicious from the outside. I've been patrolling the front and the dock like you asked. Si, Senora, I'll turn off the light. Perhaps you left it on."

The guard winced at the string of abusive words he heard through the phone. Even Corey and Blake could hear her angry voice from their places of hiding.

"As you say, Senora," the guard said politely enough. Clearly, he did not agree with his employer, but he was not going to say so.

He turned the light off with a definite snap and left the room, closing the door as he did so. This was a definite help.

Blake and Corey held a whispered conversation, still in their respective hiding places. Blake, who knew more about the case would finish photocopying papers and files. Corey would guard the doors.

Corey took his position, watching the one open door to the kitchen area as well as the closed door back to the den.

Blake, not wanting his light to give any indication of their presence, carefully removed the contents of the last drawer to be examined and took them with him into the cabinet where he could shine his light without it showing, especially since he could just fit his mini flashlight in the peep hole he had created.

An hour later as he was returning the contents to the drawer, he decided to plant one more bug under the desk. As he did, he hit a small protrusion, and part of the top section of the desk opened, revealing a recessed rectangle right under the leather inlaid padding of the desktop large enough to hold several file folders!

Blake took them to his hiding place and nearly gasped in delight. Here were records of kidnapped children going back four years, some from Nicaragua, Guatemala, Honduras, and most recently, Mexico. The most recent records noted dates, ships, and even some of the names of the kidnapped.

Snapping picture after picture, Blake finally had what he needed. He returned the folders to the desk and closed it.

"Let's get out of here," he said softly. He and Corey made their way through the now quiet house, taking care to not bump into furniture. Blake had to, once again, turn off the alarm systems. Let that mess with their minds in the morning, he thought with grim satisfaction.

He left Corey twice to place bugs in the grand entry, under the stairwell, in the kitchen, and even in the bathroom. Including the two in the den, Pietro would have ten cameras to monitor although the one under the desk and the one under the stairwell were for audio only.

They were about to exit the window when the guard walked past. Apparently he was patrolling this side and the back of the house. They had to wait another fifteen minutes, but once again, watchfulness was rewarded, and Blake and Corey finally returned to the dock.

Their mission had taken three hours and forty minutes, but Blake was very well satisfied with this night's work.

Pietro was already busy monitoring the cameras on his laptop. He turned to Blake enthusiastically as he and Corey descended below deck.

"Guess what? Ten minutes after you leave, beautiful lady go back to library to check on everything! She suspicious alright. She even open the top of the desk and check her papers. Then she talk to guard about releasing the dogs. You get out of there just in time!"

Chapter Thirty-Four

Thirty-six hours later, Blake was in Virginia, sitting across a desk from Tallie's father.

Tallie had already called her parents to tell them the news of their engagement when Blake had arrived back in South Carolina. They had suspected as much, especially when Tallie's Aunt Nell had apprised them of the situation following her visit to South Carolina.

Corey and Jonathan had accepted the Merrills invitation to stay in their bunk house because, as Jonathan had said, he just wasn't up to sleeping on the floor at Blake's apartment.

Blake had looked ruefully around his place, realizing he would need to get a better place for him and Tallie to live if they were going to stay in South Carolina instead of at the farm he owned in North Carolina.

Corey corroborated his thoughts. "Man, you need a place of your own. I have something to show you later. It's somewhat small, but Tallie will like it, and so will you. It's very private."

Blake snapped his mind back to the present and the lush bank office on the outskirts of Fredericksburg where Mrs. Peters-Templeton had done the decorating for her husband.

The rich green rug had an inlaid border of gold done in pineapples and fleur-de-lis. The old walnut desk was heavy with carving, and the forest green leather and maple chairs were placed between accent tables with bowls of fresh, golden chrysanthemums and crystal and gold based lamps.

A large window framed by heavy tapestry curtains in green and gold looked over a beautiful park that contained huge maple trees, their leaves not quite bare of large crimson and gold leaves and a small pond with goldfish and koi.

"And where do you plan to live with my daughter once you are married?" Mr. Peters-Templeton was asking.

"Summerville, South Carolina, Sir, at least for now. Tallie needs to stay close to the families she's helping, and I have plenty saved to buy a house and care for your daughter," said Blake, then added, "although I wouldn't dare say it quite that way to her."

"I know all about your financial status, young man. I want to know how you will deal with my daughter although it sounds as if you know her quite well already if you will allow her the freedom to think she's perfectly capable of making her own way," he said heartily. "And please call me Dad like my sons do. We may as well start out right," he added.

"Okay, Dad," said Blake, trying out the new title. He nearly choked because he could not imagine calling anyone "Dad" except for the man he had enshrined in his memory from his early boyhood. On the other hand, he was not against calling this man "Dad." It would just take time to accustom himself to it.

He was sure Tallie would tease him and tell him he was becoming more tuned to his emotions.

"So tell me what you think about Tallie's job."

"She has a dangerous job, I know that, but she is very good at working with people and helping them through difficult situations. I could never ask her to give it up although I know I won't like knowing she's facing danger, especially when I can't be with her."

"What about your job? You face extreme danger in your job. She will be feeling the same way when you are on assignment."

"True. And I'd like to say it's different because it's my job, but I know that argument won't fly with her. So we've agreed that we both have dangerous jobs, and we need to be supportive of each other no matter how difficult that will be."

"Good answer, good answer," said Mr. Peters-Templeton. "Let me call those women and see if they can join us for lunch." He punched a button on the machine on his desk. His secretary answered immediately.

He asked her to call his wife, but she answered that his wife and daughter were already on their way up to his office.

The door opened, and there they were. Blake stood, ready to shake hands with Mrs. Peters-Templeton. Instead, she nearly bowled him over when she threw her arms around him and impetuously gave him a huge hug.

He looked over her shoulder at Tallie who just smiled, understanding his discomfiture all too well.

"Welcome to our family," said Mrs. Peters-Templeton warmly. "I hope my husband hasn't been grilling you too mercilessly."

"He hasn't grilled me at all. Well, maybe a little," amended Blake.

Just then a young man entered the room. Blake knew immediately that he was Tallie's brother. Tyler Clay had the same fine-boned facial features as Tallie who was a younger image of her mother, but instead of the red hair, he had his father's dark hair. He also had his father's mannerisms which kept him from coming across as effeminate.

He crossed the room, clapped Blake on the back, and then shook his hand. "Welcome to the family, Blake.

Anyone who can keep up with my sister and her activities has our deepest respect."

Turning to the others, he said, "I've made reservations for us at Gino's Italian Bistro, but he will weep if we are late. He is 'most anxious to meet Tallie's intended.' Tyler Clay used his fingers to demonstrate the quotations around what Gino had said.

"Well, then, let's go," said Mrs. Peters-Templeton. "I must admit I'm famished."

As that was her usual state, her family laughed.

"Mom can eat more than anyone else I know and still keep her great figure," said Tallie, linking her arm in Blake's. "I hope I become just like her."

"Oh, you already are, Sis," said Tyler Clay. "I'm the one who has to watch his figure." He snapped his fingers in the air whirled his mother across the carpeted floor to the door in a tango. Mr. Peters-Templeton watched them fondly then gathered his things.

"We are a crazy family," said Tallie. "Are you sure you want to marry into this?"

Blake was marveling at the exuberant joyfulness displayed by this family. Now he knew how Tallie could see such painful sights, endure such deprived conditions, and still retain her optimism. She had a family who knew how to enjoy life and each other.

Instead of being intimidated by their outlook on life or put off by it, Blake found himself wanting to be part of it. He wanted to learn this freedom from the eternal cautious restraint he imposed on himself as an adult, a cautious restraint he had learned following his mother's second marriage. What would it be like to have moments of such uninhibited joy?

Blake never did answer Tallie's question verbally. The look on his face was enough of an answer. It was the first time she had seen his face so unguarded. She pulled him into a quick foxtrot and was gratified when he responded by following her lead.

Blake leaned his forehead against hers and smiled. "I think I'm going to love your family," he said simply.

"Okay, that's enough, you two," said Tyler Clay. "Gino is waiting, and his meals are not to be missed."

Gino had a table reserved for them in a back corner. He had just placed glasses of iced water at each seat and two pitchers of the sweet tea they liked. Just as they were about to be seated, Corey entered.

"Well, hello, Cuz," said Tyler Clay breezily. "You're just in time to eat lunch with us. Impeccable timing as always."

"You know it," said Corey with a wink in Tallie and Blake's direction.

Gino's niece, Bella, came to the table with a loaf of freshly baked bread just from the oven. The olive oil accompanying it was light and loaded with fresh herbs. She was followed by her mother who brought the antipasto plate the family always ordered. Then Bella began to take their orders.

"I'll have the roasted shrimp and garlic with fettuccine alfredo," said Mrs. Peters-Templeton. Her husband ordered his favorite lasagna.

Corey, who loved seafood, ordered the parmesan encrusted salmon served with a side of green beans marinara.

Blake also favored seafood. He decided to try the prosciutto-wrapped tuna with linguine while Tallie wanted the chicken parmesan.

"So tell us what you've been doing, Corey," demanded his aunt. She had learned that even when Corey appeared to be idle, he was usually involved in some sort of interesting scheme.

Corey looked sideways at Blake. "I think Blake should tell you what we've been doing as it's his story and his news. I just went along for the ride. Well, actually I was his ride."

"I'm sure you did much more, Corey, you always do, but tell us what you are doing these days, Son," said Mr. Peters-Templeton to Blake.

Blake considered. Did they know much about what their daughter had been doing lately?

Sensing his discomfiture, Tallie said, "Do you remember the families from Mexico I told you I was helping?"

Her parents and brother nodded.

"Blake," she looked up at him with shining eyes, unconscious that she had just revealed her love for him in that one glance, "thinks he knows who is perpetrating all of the kidnappings in the Tampico area."

Corey took up the tale. "He needed a quick flight there, and I just happened to have flown into Charleston on the way back from Costa Rica. His pilot had an emergency call, so I volunteered to take him."

"My men in Tampico have been scouring the area for clues. They had discovered that more kidnappings were taking place and that the victims would be loaded on a ship that night, so I wanted to get there right away," said Blake.

Blake and Corey wisely kept their mouths shut about the grenade, the blown up boat, and Juan's injuries.

"We saw the victims being loaded, and then my man, Blake here got a hunch about who the kingpin is after talking to his men. We followed a little creek to a villa, and did a little scouting around. It was fun. I got to practice my undercover sleuthing abilities." Corey finished, making them laugh and drawing their attention away from the case and onto his seemingly amateurish actions.

His uncle, realizing this was still an open case, wisely changed the conversation into other channels.

He asked if Blake and Tallie had set a date for their wedding yet.

"Not yet," responded Tallie. "Mom, Dad, do you mind if I don't have a very big wedding? I really, really only want to have my family present when we get married."

Her mother looked at her daughter, her eyes bright with unshed tears. "I've always dreamed of a big wedding for you. You are, after all, our only daughter."

Tallie's face took on a patient look that Blake was beginning to recognize. She was very adept at getting people to see her point of view. Her parents would be no exception.

But her mother was continuing. "I can see, though, that it doesn't fit you personality, does it? Okay, very well. I just have one request. Please let me be part of the planning. I don't think I could bear not to have some small part."

Tallie rose from her chair, nearly tipping it over. Blake caught it before it fell. She flew to her mother on the other side of the table and gave her a hug.

"Of course, Mom. I wouldn't dream of excluding you. I love you, Mom!"

"I love you, too, Sweetie!" This time the tears did overflow.

The reaction of the men was mixed. Mr. Peters-Templeton looked on with amused affection.

Tyler Clay whipped out a handkerchief for his mother, saying, "Here you go, Mom."

"Oh, thank you, Tyler Clay. You are always prepared," she said taking it and dabbing her eyes.

Corey looked at Blake who was at a loss and somewhat embarrassed by the scene.

"You'll get used to it," he said. "Aunt Paige is very emotional when it comes to her family, but so very businesslike about her hotels. Quite a conundrum and never boring."

"I don't think any of you are boring," said Blake looking around the table.

They all laughed.

"I will be the boring one, I'm afraid," he said.

"Oh no," said Tallie reseating herself beside him. "You may be quieter than the rest of us, but you could never be boring."

"To never being boring," said Paige Peters-Templeton, raising her glass of sweet tea.

They could all toast that.

Chapter Thirty-Five

The action had been filed, and Bob Worthington and his paralegal were eyeball deep in research. Corey was in their conference room or "war room" as he called it. They were piecing together arguments and writing them on the huge white board.

Underneath the white board was a low, four-shelf bookcase that extended two feet on each side of the board. On it, in neat piles according to dates, were all the documents the Merrills had received from the county and that the attorney had filed on their behalf.

"But how can the possessions on the Merrill property be construed a 'public' nuisance when it is clearly 'private' property?" asked Corey.

"None of the items they were asked to fix or remove can even be seen from the road," said Barbara, the paralegal. "So none of it can accurately be called 'visual blight.'"

"Correct. There was no 'public nuisance.' The property and what was on it was not affecting the rights, general welfare, safety, health and/or well-being of others, or the public. However, Collcton County believes it has that right because of the passage of the Rebeautification Ordinance," said Bob Worthington.

"So you have to show that the Rebeautification Ordinance is unconstitutional, right?"

"No. Actually, the Ordinance itself is not unconstitutional. The bylaws created as a result of the

Ordinance and the ways they are implementing them are unconstitutional, however."

"What do you mean?" asked Corey.

"The Constitution of the State of South Carolina states that a city, town, or county may create and enforce laws, ordinances, and regulations not in conflict with 'general laws.' General laws would be laws already on the books of the state and of the United States government."

"So the bylaws of the Rebeautification Ordinance are regulations or ordinances that are in conflict with the Fourth Amendment?"

"That's what we have to prove. According to *Marbury v. Madison*, 'all Laws which are repugnant to the Constitution are null and void,'" Bob Worthington said.

He continued. "In addition, in *Miranda v. Arizona*, the court clearly stated that 'where rights secured by the Constitution are involved, there can be no rulemaking or legislation which can abrogate them.' And *Bouvier's Law Dictionary* makes clear it is a 'universal rule with NO Exceptions: A right protected by the Constitution can NEVER be curtailed by an Act of Congress or by the State Legislature.'"

Barbara thumped the pages of the book from which she had been reading. "The Constitution itself states in Article Six, 'This Constitution, and the laws of the United States which shall be made in pursuance thereof,....shall be the supreme law of the land; and the judges in every State shall be bound thereby...the Senators and Representatives and members of the State Legislatures, and all executive and judicial officers of the United States and the several States, shall be bound thereby, anything in the Constitution or laws of any State to the contrary notwithstanding.'"

"That seems pretty clear," said Corey.

"But we have a problem," said Bob.

"What's that?" asked Corey.

"Since the Merrills are the party bringing the 1357 Action, we also have to prove that they have sustained real damages."

"Those would be the fines imposed, wouldn't they? What about the stress and duress on Gram Merrill?"

"I don't know if I can prove it. That woman's faith is so strong, and she has so much peace even in these difficult circumstances, I don't think trying to prove undue stress would be worth the time."

"I understand," said Corey. "So your game plan is to address the public nuisance issue, then the unconstitutionality of the bylaws in Colleton County, and then the damages?" He wrote "public nuisance," "unconstitutionality," and "damages" on the white board.

"Yes, and it will be a fight, I can tell you. You've been reviewing older cases for me, but the new cases going before the Supreme Court seem to favor property owners, which is encouraging. I think the Court is finally realizing that property owners are fed up with having to satisfy petty requirements of municipalities and their unwillingness to cut a fair deal with the property owners."

"That's interesting," said Corey. "What are some of the latest cases?"

"In a Florida case, the Supreme Court ruled the extortionate demands of the county a 'taking' under the fifth amendment. And in the last election, the people of Virginia voted overwhelmingly in favor of an amendment to their state constitution to protect landowners from overreach of state and local governments. But you should know about that one as you are from that state," Bob added somewhat wryly.

"Of course," said Corey. I debated it with several people from the law class with which I would have graduated. We still keep in touch."

"So tell me what you found in your research."

"It seems there are two very divergent schools of thought on property ownership," said Corey. "Harrington, Blackstone, and Locke, for instance, believed strongly in an individual's property rights. On the other hand, those with more of a socialistic leaning believed that all property should be held in common, owned together by members of a community."

"The only problem with the latter," he continued, "is that while all may 'own' property collectively, not all will be willing to work on that property equally hard. So some would end up doing all the work while the rest would be slackers. It seems that mankind is no more 'evolved' or different than they were in the Dark Ages, at least in that respect."

"Go back to 'unconstitutionality,'" said Barbara. "I think the searches Jeremy Saxon made were especially egregious and aggressive. Bringing two armed men with him? That seems to be an 'unreasonable search,' as the Constitution calls it."

"Maybe," said Corey, writing "unreasonable searches" and underneath the words "two armed men." "What else about the searches would be unconstitutional?"

"Who determines what is trash or junk on another person's property? Jeremy Saxon? Or has the County drawn up a list of exactly what is considered trash and what is considered treasure? That kind of micromanagement is really ridiculous. Jeremy Saxon is a city boy. He doesn't understand what equipment is necessary to work a farm or to make a farm work."

"You're absolutely right, Barbara. In fact, I'll bet their grandfather's tractor could be considered an antique by some of the artsy-fartsy people my parents know," said Corey. He wrote "trash/treasure" on the board with the words "micromanagement," "necessary equipment," and "tractor" underneath.

Bob Worthington had been listening to the exchange between his paralegal and Corey. Now he spoke.

"I think we also need to bring before the court the lack of due process in this case. The Merrills have the right to have a court determine if the searches by Jeremy Saxon were legal or illegal. Since he did not obtain warrants for any searches until after the 'No Trespassing' signs were posted, he didn't follow due process; therefore, no fines should be imposed."

"Do you think the judge will buy that line of reasoning?" asked Barbara.

"I don't know," said Bob Worthington, rubbing his face wearily. Jeremy Saxon's position may entitle him to immunity; furthermore, the two men with him were police officers."

"In addition to all of that, the 'public nuisance' part of the case may be seen in the cars that were parked at the back of their property," said Corey. "If the court deems that after fifty years the cars could still be an environmental hazard, they may rule against us."

"That's why I told the Merrills at the very beginning that they only had a fifty percent chance of winning this case. It's very complex with overlapping constitutional and civic laws that apply," said Bob.

"And while this may be a ploy to incrementally destroy private property ownership in America as outlined by the United Nation's Agenda 21 as most of the Merrills seem to believe" he continued, "that result won't occur for another ten years here in South Carolina, maybe a few years less, maybe a few years more."

Corey crossed the room restlessly. "While we may believe Agenda 21 is a very real threat to our personal liberties in the United States, many people just don't believe it. They think it's another of 'those conspiracy theories.'"

"Although it may be an underlying issue, it definitely has no place in the court room," Bob said rather sternly.

"Oh, I know," said Corey. "It was just a response to your comment."

"Well team, I think we need to do more digging. I think we have a good shot with the lack of due process argument, but I'd like to see if we can find any more cases that are very recent that address this issue."

"I'll work on that," volunteered Barbara.

"I think we should also work on proving the unconstitutionality of the bylaws that have been created since the Rebeautification Ordinance was passed," Bob said to Corey.

"Are the bylaws too specific? They were just formulated and implemented recently; they are less than a year old. If we can attack these bylaws, we may be able to get some relief for the Merrills," Bob added.

"What about the 'public nuisance' argument?" asked Corey.

"I will certainly mention the reasons why I don't believe the items described by Mr. Saxon can be considered a public nuisance, but that is not the crux of our argument. Unconstitutionality and lack of due process is."

"Okay. To work we go!" said Corey. "But first I have a young lady I want to surprise. I think she'll be walking in the park soon, and some flowers seem to be needed."

Barbara smile at him, her eyes misty. "If I was ten years younger, I'd give that girl a run for your affections. My Bill brought me flowers for no reason at all. You go court your girl. I'm betting on you."

Barbara knew all about Gina and her fiancé, Harry. She was also friends with Gloria, so she knew the family was happier with Corey for their Gina.

She sighed. She still missed Bill even though he had been gone for nearly ten years now, killed in a motorcycle accident. They had only been married for eight months.

Corey found a flower shop where he found a beautiful bouquet of asters and chrysanthemums. Then he headed to Azalea Park.

He saw Gina long before she saw him. She was walking slowly with her head down. Her posture showed dejection, and as he drew near, he saw that she was quietly crying.

Gina's day had been rough. She could feel the stares of the other teachers who knew she had been placed on probation but not why. Renee was the only one who knew the whole story instead of the vicious rumors the secretary was telling.

For the second time in her life, Gina found herself the object of lies and innuendos, and it was, once again, breaking her heart.

She knew someone was coming, but she didn't look up. She didn't want to talk to anyone, not even a simple "hello."

Two booted feet placed themselves directly in front of her. A bouquet of flowers was pushed into her hands. She finally raised her head and saw Corey.

"Corey!" she managed to say before she burst into tears and began sobbing in earnest.

Corey didn't say a word. He just encircled her in his arms and let her cry. When the tears slowed, he pulled a handkerchief from his pocket and led her to a nearby bench.

"Now tell me what's wrong, Gina," he said tenderly.

Gina told him the whole story, her fingers fidgeting with the flowers he had brought.

"I will take care of it."

Her eyes flew to his, and she began to object, but Corey hushed her.

"Just listen. I won't make it obvious, but I know ways to drop strategic hints that will kill the gossip. Trust me?"

"Yes." Gina was surprised to find that she did trust him. "Yes, I do," she affirmed.

Corey leaned in and kissed her on the cheek, much as he'd done the first time they'd met. He stood and offered her his hand to help her up and escort her to her car.

"Thank you, Corey. I feel so much better," she said. She felt rather shy because of the kiss, but she told herself that was his style. He was just being kind, a good friend.

Chapter Thirty-Six

Gina watched as Harry's plane taxied down the runway. Beside her, little Caden was hopping up and down in his excitement. Once school was finished for the day, her father had met her there to drop off Caden, and Gina and her little boy had left immediately for the airport.

Gina gazed at the plane with unseeing eyes. She was filled with such conflicting feelings. The phone calls from Harry had become briefer and briefer and spaced out over several days instead of every other day.

She thought maybe Harry would want to break their engagement, and while she dreaded the ensuing confrontation that would bring, she discovered the idea was not as unbearable as she had thought it would be.

The gate from the plane to the terminal wasn't working properly. This was going to take forever, Gina thought. Bored, she leaned against a pillar and glanced around the waiting area.

Two men who sat at a small table looked vaguely familiar, especially the one with the dark hair and the mustache. A woman carrying a poodle with a red, diamond-studded collar walked past. She was talking angrily on a cell phone, the poodle cringing at the tone of her voice.

Just then Gina saw Blake. He was with Tallie and a young Mexican man. They were headed for the Java House in a corner of the waiting area, and when Blake saw her, he steered the group in her direction.

She turned to grab Caden's hand, but he wasn't there. She looked wildly around the waiting area but couldn't see Caden anywhere.

The panicked look that crossed her face resonated immediately with Blake. Tallie was chatting happily with the young man and didn't see Gina's expression at first.

"What's wrong, Gina?" asked Blake.

"Caden, my son, he was right here, I don't know where he is," she stuttered.

"How long ago did you last see him?" asked Blake.

"Three minutes? Five minutes? He was looking out the window at Harry's plane, but I was bored, so I looked around, saw you and when I went to grab his hand, he wasn't there."

Blake reacted immediately. He strode to the nearest policeman, showed him his badge, and the man began talking into his radio.

"What is he wearing?" asked Blake.

"Blue jeans and a blue and red striped, long-sleeved shirt."

"Blonde hair, blue eyes, right?"

"Right," said Gina. She looked frantically around. Where could he be?

Blake began speaking in Spanish to the young man and Tallie. Tallie headed for the front of the airport. The young man went to check the bathroom. Gina saw several security guards scurry by.

"Let's check these gift shops here," said Blake.

Gina looked frantically but thoroughly in each of the five shops, but she couldn't find Caden. Overwhelmed, she sank to the floor of the airport and began sobbing.

Harry was upset that Gina hadn't met him as she had promised to do. When he saw her on the airport floor, he was annoyed that she was making a spectacle of herself, especially when he saw a cameraman from a local news station taking pictures of her.

He strode over to her. "Come, Gina," he said, pulling her to her feet.

"Harry, I'm so sorry; I forgot."

"What's wrong? You need to pull yourself together now. You're in a public place." He did his best to shield her from the cameraman.

He waited for an answer, but she had begun to cry again. Tallie returned just as Blake, who had been talking to law enforcement, appeared also.

Tallie motioned urgently for Blake. Out of Gina's earshot she said, "I think I saw him in the back seat of a car. It was a white Camry and the first two letters of the license plate were three two. One of the letters was either a "D" or an "O.""

"Go help Gina. Her fiancé...." Blake made a face, and Tallie understood at once.

Blake signaled to the police man to whom he had been talking. He relayed the message Tallie had given him.

The police officer began speaking on his radio.

Meanwhile, Tallie led Gina to a table in an alcove and sent Harry to get her a coffee.

"You've got to stop crying right now and talk to me," said Tallie sternly to Gina. "You can't help Caden by crying."

When she had Gina's attention, she said quietly but intensely, "Now, tell me exactly what happened."

Gina described waiting for the plane and becoming bored when they'd had problems with the gate. "I turned just slightly. I thought he was standing right beside me watching the plane."

"When you looked around, who did you see?"

Gina told Tallie about the lady with the poodle and the two men.

"Describe the men."

"One had dark hair and a mustache." Gina stopped and frowned. "He looked familiar like I had seen him somewhere before. But that's silly."

"What did the other one look like?"

"He had light brown hair and a very young face. Oh, and a scar above his right eye."

Tallie motioned for Blake as Harry returned with two coffees, one for him and one for Gina.

"Those two men I saw in the car? They were here before Caden went missing."

"Why did you think it was Caden in the car with those men?" Blake asked Tallie.

Gina listened, intent and wide-eyed.

"Because he was crying, and a man was trying to push him into a car seat."

"What was he wearing?"

"I didn't see his pants, but his shirt was blue and red striped." She indicated stripes that were about an inch in width.

"Describe the men again," said Blake.

Tallie described them with Gina concurring.

"That sounds familiar." Blake frowned, concentrating intensely on some elusive memory. He shook his head in defeat. "It will come to me."

Just then Corey appeared. Tallie stood and let him take her place. He took her cold hands in his, and looking intently into her eyes, he said, "I came as soon as I could. We're going to find him, Gina. You have my word on that."

"Thank you, Corey." She tried to smile. Once again, she knew she could trust him unquestioningly.

Where he sat over to the side, Harry glowered, but no one paid him the slightest attention.

A police officer approached the group. The entire airport had been searched. They had found no sign of

Caden. "I need to talk to his mother and to the one who first called us."

Mercifully, the officer was brief with his questions of Gina. Corey turned and looked up at Tallie. "She needs to get home and get a hot shower, eat some hot soup. Can you make that happen?"

Tallie nodded.

Harry glowered again, but, again, no one noticed. Was he invisible to these people?

Corey stood and looked at Blake. "I heard an amber alert on the radio as I came over here from court. Do you think this has anything to do with the court case?"

"I don't want to assume anything right now," said Blake.

"You did hear that the attorney's home was blown up yesterday, right?"

"No! I hadn't heard that. Tallie and I just got back from Virginia." The news startled the usually calm-faced Blake. He frowned. "I still don't think we should assume it is connected with the Merrills property rights case. We'll get down to the bottom of this."

Tallie shepherded Gina and Harry to Gina's car. When Gina saw Caden's backpack in the back seat of the car, she began crying softly again.

Tallie looked from the weeping Gina to the sulking Harry and took charge.

"Gina, you sit up here with me. I'll drive. Harry, how was your flight?" She listened to his answer and kept him talking about himself most of the way to his house. Once she had dropped him off there, she took the numb and now silent Gina to her apartment.

"I'm going to fix my favorite comfort food while you take a hot shower. Don't worry; I'll find everything. Off with you now." She directed Gina toward the hall, giving her a little push to get her started.

Gina ran the water as hot as she could stand. It did help. She was so tired, and how in the world would she teach tomorrow? She wouldn't be able to concentrate at all. She already had a sub coming for Friday; could she possibly cover Wednesday and Thursday as well?

And the wedding. How in the world could she help Chelsea if she was worried sick about Caden?

And Harry. Well, Harry was an adult. He needed to act like one. She could see clearly now that he was still so immature in so many ways. Every time she was with him, everything had to revolve around him. He could tell amazing and funny stories, but stories would not provide the emotional stability needed for a marriage, a life lived together.

She felt as if a gauzy veil had been ripped from her eyes, and now she could see everything clearly. But why did she have to lose her son to be able to see?

Where was Caden right now? Had he had anything to eat for dinner? She remembered that Grandpa always put mini packages of Skittles or M & Ms in his pocket. "For later," he would say with a wink at his grandson.

She took comfort in the little things. And she began to pray earnestly for the quick return of her sweet son.

She dressed in warm sweats and an old gray and blue sweatshirt. Her body felt warm enough, but her soul was still so cold.

Tallie had heated some tomato basil soup and made grilled cheese sandwiches.

"Blake just called," she said cheerfully. "He and Corey are following leads, and the police are trying to match the partial license plate numbers I managed to see with what's in the Department of Motor Vehicle's database."

Gina nodded. "They're doing their best. I just hope it's good enough." Her voice broke, but she had determined to stop crying.

She and Tallie sat down at the table. Tallie said a brief blessing and added a prayer for Caden's safe return. Gina bravely did her best to eat everything. She was nearly finished when her mother and her sister arrived.

"Oh, Honey." her mother said, embracing her. It was Gina's undoing. All three of them ended up hugging and crying together.

"Where is Dad?" asked Gina.

"He's at the church. They've organized round the clock prayer in the chapel until Caden's return.

How Gina made it through the night she didn't know. She had the presence of mind to call the assistant principal for a sub for Wednesday and Thursday.

Gwennie finally sacked out in Caden's bed. Her mother slept in the recliner, and Tallie curled up on the end of the sofa while Gina, when she wasn't pacing, slept at the other end.

Morning brought no relief and a slew of reporters to her door.

"May I?" Tallie asked.

"Go right ahead," said Gina.

Tallie made short work of dispatching them. Her phone rang just as she had closed and locked the door.

It was Blake. He reported that they had finally traced the license plate to one of the men they believed had kidnapped Caden. Police had stormed his residence, but clearly he had not lived there for several months at the very least.

He wanted to know if Gina had received any demands for ransom.

"No. We've had a quiet night," Tallie said looking at Gwen, Gina, and Gloria huddled together on the couch.

Another knock sounded at the door. Gina looked at Tallie who nodded. She would make short work of nosy reporters. But when she opened the door, she saw Mrs. Flores looking shyly up at her. Beside her was Francesca.

Tallie invited them inside. Francesca seemed very relieved. As she passed her, Tallie could feel that she was trembling.

"Francesca, she have, no has something to tell you. Go on, you are safe here," Mrs. Flores encouraged her daughter.

"We saw on TV about the little boy. I think I saw him last night," Francesca said.

Chapter Thirty-Seven

"Wait. How did you know where to come?" asked Tallie.

"We have a friend, a neighbor who drive a taxi. I told him we need to talk to lady who have missing little boy," said Mrs. Flores in her halting English. "He know right where to come."

Tallie looked at Francesca who was still trembling. "Can you tell me what you saw?" she asked gently.

"I saw the little boy. He was crying and looking out the window."

"Where?"

"In a house by Zoe's house. She's my new friend from school."

"Does she live by your house?"

"No. She lives two blocks over, but since the nightmares are almost gone, Mama let me walk there by myself. That's when I saw him."

"Did you go back home and tell your mama?"

Mrs. Flores took up the story. "No. She saw the TV. I try to turn off the news, but she saw about the little boy, and she know it is him right away."

"Were you afraid to say anything?" asked Tallie as Gina, Gloria and Gwen listened intently.

Francesca hung her head. "Yes," she said in a low voice. "But then I had a nightmare, so I told Mama about seeing the little boy. I also" she swallowed convulsively, "saw one of the men. I think he was one of the kidnappers."

"One of the little boy's kidnappers?"

"No. One of my kidnappers!" Francesca began sobbing. "I only saw his shoes because they put a sack over my head. But I remember the shoes," she said between sobs.

Tallie knelt in front of the weeping child. "If he is one of your kidnappers then you are a very, very brave girl. Did he see you?"

"I don't know. I ran all the way home. Then I see the little boy on TV, and I <u>know</u> it's him."

"How did you know I would be here?" asked Tallie.

Mrs. Flores spoke. "We don't. We come to see the momma," she said, pointing to Gina. "But I so glad you are here. We must catch those bad hombres."

"Now I know why Francesca is so brave. She has a very brave mother," said Tallie. She held up a finger and, pulling her phone from her pocket, speed dialed Blake.

"We have a break in the case," she said, and then she told him breathlessly about the news from Francesca.

Blake was astounded. "Don't go anywhere," he said. "We're on our way."

"Wait. Do you think the rest of the family is in danger? And what about the Garcias? They live two doors down from the Floreses."

"Call the schools. Make sure they are doubly alert. And tell them to keep the Garcia and Flores children there until further notice. The school officials know you since you helped register the children at the schools, right?"

"Right. We also need to make sure Mr. and Mrs. Garcia are alerted as well as Mr. Flores."

"I'll take care of that."

"Wait a minute," said Tallie. "Mrs. Flores says they already know. Mr. Flores is at the Garcia's home right now. Both men took off from work today, and Mr. Flores made sure all the children got on the school bus."

"Great! We'll go there first and pick up Mr. Flores and the Garcias." He hung up his phone.

Gina was crying again, this time in hope and relief. Tallie just hoped it wasn't a false lead, but Francesca was usually a pretty reliable and truthful girl.

"Have you had breakfast yet?" asked Tallie.

Francesca and Mrs. Flores nodded.

"We haven't. How about if you help me make breakfast?"

Tallie found the pancake mix and some eggs. Mrs. Flores volunteered to make Mexican hash browns. She began scrubbing and peeling potatoes at the sink. Tallie put Francesca to work mixing the batter for the pancakes as she added in the ingredients.

Blake and Corey walked in with Mr. Flores and Mr. and Mrs. Garcia just as Tallie and Francesca were handing plates of food to Gina, her mom, and her sister.

Behind them was Harry. Ignoring the others, he made his way to the sofa, and urging her to scoot over, sat down right beside Gina.

He put his right arm possessively around her. "Did you get any sleep at all last night?" he asked her.

"A little," said Gina weakly.

"When this is all over, we need to get away."

Ten responses reeled through Gina's mind, none of them kind. "I need to eat right now," she said instead. "Can you get me some apple juice out of the refrigerator? We'll talk later."

Reluctantly, Harry stood and headed for the kitchen.

Blake caught Corey's arm. "Let's go out in the hall and plan our strategy. Now," he added as Corey sent a murderous look in Harry's direction.

They exited. Harry returned with the apple juice, but Gina had traded places with her mother to sit in the recliner.

Gloria patted the sofa cushion beside her. "Come sit by me, Harry, and tell me about your flight back to the states."

Harry's scowl left, and he sat beside Gina's mom and had a pleasant talk with her about his return trip. Listening, Gina realized he really was a fascinating story teller. He made even a routine flight home sound like an adventure.

She was going to have to break off their engagement. She cared for him and hoped he would never lose that ability to tell an interesting story. She would let another girl have the privilege of listening.

Because he had stood by her when, after Jack, she had felt like damaged goods, she would be as kind as possible as she talked to him. But he had needs, too. He needed a girl who would idolize him and hold onto his every word. She was no longer that girl.

On the other hand, at this time when her entire focus should rightfully be on her son, she was glad her mother was willing to listen to him.

And where was her son? She missed him so much it was an ache deep inside of her. Had they fed him breakfast? Were they hurting him in any way? If they sodomized her son, ... Her mind went black with fury.

Corey and Blake had disappeared. She wanted to find out what was happening. She stood and crossed to the window. The vehicle Corey had rented for the wedding with all the bells and whistles was still parked in front of her apartment. Where was he?

She slipped out the front door and saw him and Blake deep in conversation. They stopped talking and looked up when they saw her.

"Can you ask Tallie to come out here, Gina?" asked Blake.

"Sure," said Gina.

She went back inside to find Tallie. "Blake wants to talk to you in the hall," she said.

She followed Tallie. Whatever was being discussed was about her son, and she was going to be a part of it.

"We need to identify the house where Francesca saw this little boy," said Blake. "Corey's car has tinted windows. Do you think the Floreses will let her come with us and show us the house? Then we can bring her right back."

"I don't think it will be a problem. But why don't you let Mr. and Mrs. Flores come, too. You have the room, and I'm sure they'd like to be a part of it."

"I'm going too," said Gina flatly. She didn't ask. If they didn't let her ride with them, she was going to follow in her car. She didn't care what they thought about it. Her son's life was in danger.

Corey looked at her consideringly. He could almost see the thoughts going through her mind.

"You can come. But I want you and Francesca to sit between Mr. and Mrs. Flores in the car," said Blake.

He, too, realized Gina would probably follow them, and once there, just might try to enter the house herself, endangering both herself and her son. No, it was best to have her in the car.

She was about to argue with him over the seating arrangement, but Blake held up his hand.

"I don't want you or Francesca by the window just in case it is your son and his kidnappers. If it is him and he even thinks he sees you, he may raise an alarm in the minds of the kidnappers, and they may go to another location with him. Then we may not be able to find him in time." He looked very grim at this last statement.

"Let's go back inside and talk to the Floreses," suggested Tallie.

Five minutes later, they were on the road. As they approached the street where the Floreses and the Garcias lived. Francesca leaned forward, directing Corey on where to go.

The blinds in all the windows of the house were closed. A car in the driveway matched the description that

Tallie had given. Corey turned at the stop sign at the end of the street and doubled back on the next street over. He pulled to the side of the road where he and Blake could just barely see the front of the house.

They discussed several scenarios and how best to achieve their goal: nab both kidnappers without endangering Caden any further if, indeed, Caden was really in the house.

Listening to them talk in low tones, Gina was impressed with their caution and thoroughness.

"Drive around to the back of their house," instructed Blake.

"I don't think we can. I think the property backs up to woods."

They approached the house again from a different direction.

"You're right," said Blake in disappointment. "Let's head back."

When they returned to Gina's apartment, Uncle Craig and Aunt Clara had arrived. Aunt Clara had messages from everyone.

The entire family felt torn. Most of them were assembling at the court house to support Gram and Gramps Merrill although they really wanted to be with Gina. Aunt Galeah was very stressed since the wedding was only four days away. This was a difficult time for everyone.

Uncle Galen arrived. Gina ran to her dad, and he enveloped her in a huge hug. "It's going to be okay, Sweetie," he said over and over.

Corey and Blake chose that time to slip out of the crowded apartment with Uncle Craig.

Quickly they apprised him of the situation. Some more news media appeared in the hall with their cameras ready to roll. The men ducked out of sight and made their way down to the stairs at the other end of the hall.

After a quick question of Corey, Blake placed a phone call to Tallie.

"After you get rid of the media, Darling, why don't you take everyone over to Flowertown Bed and Breakfast. Corey has rented the whole place, and he's calling Veronique right now."

"Great idea," said Tallie gratefully. "It's getting very crowded in here."

"Just make sure the media are all gone before you head over. Either way, this should be over in about two hours," he said.

"I just hope it's really Caden," said Tallie softly. "Here they are," she said, referring to the media. "Be safe."

By this time, they were in Corey's vehicle.

"I have a plan," said Blake. "Can you get us a truck and i.d. from the electric company?" he asked Uncle Craig.

Craig nodded.

"Good. Let's make Corey the electrical repairman. While he goes to the front door, I can circle around the back. When the one guy answers the doorbell, signal us, and I'll go in the back."

"But before that," he continued, "let's try to get the location of Caden."

"I wonder if we can send a helicopter overhead with infrared."

"I can get that, too," said Uncle Craig.

Corey drove to the electric company around the corner where they obtained the work truck they needed. Blake drove Corey's vehicle, and they parked at either end of the street after making sure the kidnappers' car was still in place.

A helicopter flew overhead, and Uncle Craig began relaying information to Corey and Blake through their earpieces.

Corey pulled up in the driveway of the house right in back of the car. He got out of the car as Blake left his car and circled around the back of the house.

"Small figure in bedroom on the east side of the house. One subject approaching the front door. The other one appears to be in the kitchen at the stove. Stay away from kitchen windows, Blake."

But Blake was already at the back door to the garage. He worked feverishly to unlock it. If he could walk into the kitchen from the garage, he might be able to take down his man without a shower of glass.

"Subject at stove moving toward front. Go, Blake, go!"

The door gave at last. Yes! The door from the garage to the house was unlocked. He opened the door just as a startled man turned from the kitchen doorway to look at him as he entered from the garage.

The man didn't stand a chance. Blake had him pinned on the floor with his hands behind his back before he could even reach for the gun he had carelessly left on the kitchen table.

Blake could hear Corey still talking to the man at the front door. He handcuffed the man who was starting to yell to his companion.

"Get the kid, and run," the kidnapper shouted.

But it was too late. Uncle Craig was there, snapping handcuffs on the man at the front door.

Corey went immediately to the bedroom where he found a very sad Caden. As soon as he saw Corey, his whole face lit up. Corey scooped him up into his arms and Caden clung to him as if he would never let go.

Corey held Caden just as tightly. Now that Caden was safe, he was overcome with love for this little boy whom he hoped to one day call "Son."

"Let's go get your momma," Corey said.

Chapter Thirty-Eight

Gina rode with Harry to the bed and breakfast.

"Why don't we stop at the park?" she asked, needing to end their relationship. She could see no point in delaying. Some might criticize her timing, especially with her son missing, but she found that she trusted Corey and Blake with the welfare of her son as she had never been able to trust Harry.

To come to this point of being willing to let go of this relationship had taken forever, but once her mind was made up about something, she rarely put off what was necessary to do.

Harry was pleased. Finally, he would get some one-on-one time with Gina. When he was apart from her, he just wanted to end their relationship, but when he was with her, he didn't think he could do it.

And now her mind was focused solely on her son. He couldn't very well break their engagement at a time like this. He wasn't that callous. He wanted to be available for her, but she was always so calm and composed, at least on the outside.

They walked side by side without touching, past the tennis courts and toward the little ponds with the fanciful sculptures and marsh rushes which neither saw nor enjoyed.

Gina spoke first. "Harry, I just want to tell you that I'm grateful for the time we've had together. I will never regret it or think ill of you."

"Uh-oh. This sounds like a breakup speech."

"It is." Gina stopped and grabbed both of Harry's hands. Tears came to her eyes as she realized that she still considered and would continue to consider him a friend.

"I have to break our engagement. I don't love you the way you deserve to be loved, and I take all the blame for that."

He started to speak, but she shook her head and rushed into speech. "I think I've used you. Yes, I have. I was so surprised when you first asked me out on a date. It was so nice to feel hope once again after all that Jack did to me. And I thought I loved you, but I think it's more of sisterly love than a "lover-ly" love. And now we are growing apart. We have different needs and desires. I'm so sorry, Harry."

By now the tears, always near, were coursing down her cheeks.

"I will never, ever think poorly of you, Gina. I've always enjoyed making you laugh, making your eyes light up when I tell stories." He rubbed the heel of his palm and his thumb on her cheek.

She twisted off the engagement ring from her left hand and placed it in his palm, curling his fingers over it. "You will make some girl very happy one day. I'm going to walk the rest of the way to the bed and breakfast."

She turned to go.

"Wait," said Harry. "Can I still come to the wedding Saturday?"

"Yes, Harry. I don't want to lose your friendship. I hope you will come around as much as you can as long as it won't hurt you if I ever date someone else."

"Is there anyone else, Gina?"

"No, Harry. There isn't."

She turned and left, walking fast, blinded from the tears until she knew she was out of his sight. She could never appear at Veronique's like this. So she slowed down. She decided to walk past Aunt Galeah and Uncle Davey's house and circle around to the church where she could wander through the cemetery, certain she would be alone there.

As she walked, her mind quieted, and she prayed for the safety of her son and the three men who were risking their lives to save him. And then, all of a sudden, she knew she needed to get to the bed and breakfast immediately.

She cut through several yards, knowing the owners wouldn't mind. As she made her way through Veronique's garden and followed the path to the gravel parking area, she heard the crunch of tires.

Could it be? It was Corey's rented vehicle. She waited, practically holding her breath. He hadn't seen her yet. He got out, but his shades hid the expression in his eyes. He opened the back door and pulled her son out!

Gina ran to the two of them, sobbing yet with a face wreathed in smiles.

"Momma!" yelled Caden when he saw her. Without a word, Corey handed her son into her waiting arms. He and Blake stood watching the scene. Uncle Craig was still at the police station, deriving much satisfaction in booking the kidnappers.

Blake's phone vibrated, and he excused himself to take a call.

Corey led Gina to the back of the house and the veranda where the families waited. He had called ahead, and they knew Caden was safe. When they heard the tires, they waited patiently so Gina could have her own private reunion with her son.

Blake and Tallie went to the school and picked up the Flores and Garcia children. They walked into a most joyous reunion. Gina was seated in a wicker chair with Caden on her lap. But that ended when Caden saw the other children.

"Momma, can I play now?" he asked, wriggling to get down.

"Sure, Sweetie. Just stay in the garden area with your friends, okay?"

He looked at her with solemn eyes. "Yes, Momma."

"Let's get some lunch together for everyone," said Aunt Clara to Gloria and Veronique.

"It's all taken care of," said Veronique with a look at Corey.

When Caden had complained of being hungry, Corey had given him half of a candy bar from his emergency rations. But having been a boy himself, he knew the candy bar would not last long. He'd placed a call during the short ride home to a barbeque place they had passed.

In less than thirty minutes, the barbequed chicken and pulled pork had arrived along with cole slaw, potato salad, baked beans, green beans, gallons of sweet tea, and banana pudding—the kind with vanilla wafers, bananas, and whipped cream—for dessert.

"It's one of those Southern favorites over which the rest of the calorie conscious country shudders," said Tallie, who had tried to surreptitiously clean her plate of the banana pudding with a few swipes of her finger.

Blake, watching, was amused. "Should I look the other way for a few minutes so you can lick your plate clean?" he asked virtuously.

Corey laughed a deep belly laugh that was good to hear after the recent events. Blake's comment and his laugh were a tonic to Gina's soul.

Gloria sat with Mrs. Flores, Mrs. Garcia, and Aunt Clara on the deep piazza as they ate lunch. They had shared recipes and comments on the children. All four rejoiced to see Gina's wan smile.

"I see this is missing," said Aunt Clara, pointing significantly to the ring on her left hand.

"The young man is missing too, her intended," said Mrs. Garcia.

"I don't think he's her intended any longer," said Gloria.

"Es good," said Mrs. Flores. "He doesn't love her the way the other young man," she indicated Corey, "love her."

"Does she know how he feels about her?" asked Aunt Clara.

"I don't think she does, not really," said Gloria. "She was able to use her engagement to another as an excuse. It will be fun to watch what happens next," she said with a twinkle in her eye.

"You'll keep us all posted, won't you?" asked Aunt Clara.

"Oh yes," said Gloria drolly, and they all laughed.

Blake needed to have a private word with Corey. The call he had received was the information for which he had been waiting. If everything went well, they would have their man, the kingpin of the human trafficking organization by Thursday at nightfall.

However, his understanding was that Corey was scheduled to fly Chelsea, Jasper, and the rest of his family down for the wedding tomorrow. Would it be too much for him to leave immediately after and fly with him to Tampico?

Corey thought it would be possible. "Let me call my mom and dad and explain the situation to them. I think they would be willing to leave sooner rather than later. If Jonathan will fly with us to Tampico, we'll get the sleep we need."

Blake had already told Tallie the news. "You'd better bring Corey back alive," she said, "and you'd better be back on time. If you mess up Chelsea's wedding plans, she'll never let you forget about it."

Corey returned from his phone call. "Chelsea has been threatening to drive down here by herself, so Dad was getting ready to call me. Jonathan is going to fly everyone down in the C-47 this afternoon since you already have the Gulfstream down there."

314

"Good. That means we can leave at the crack of dawn tomorrow after a good night's rest tonight."

"I told Dad what we are going to do. He's, uh, adding to the arsenal in our cache at the back of the plane. He wanted to know if we needed the Hummer. I told him to bring it just in case."

"Sweet. We probably won't need it, but to have just about anything we can possibly need will make our job easier."

They were standing in the graveled parking area and were surprised when the attorney pulled in with his car followed by the rest of the Merrills who weren't at work or school.

"What happened?" asked Corey when Bob Worthington stepped from his car. "I thought you would be in court most of the day."

"So did I. But a rat decided to run across the courtroom floor, and the solicitor/ district attorney has a phobia of rats from his childhood when he was bitten by a pet rat."

"A rat for a pet. Even I find that disgusting."

"The judge knew about Caden's kidnapping, so when someone in the courtroom received a message that he had been found, the information circulated like wildfire. Then the rat thing occurred, and the judge decided to dismiss court for the rest of the day."

"Do you think Caden's kidnapping might work to our advantage?" asked Corey.

Mr. Worthington looked at him sternly. "Don't repeat that. Next thing you know, they'll be accusing your family of staging it." He relaxed a little. "But possibly. I think the judge was very eager to get information on the kidnapping from his own sources if only to determine that it was not related to the case."

Blake spoke. "Actually, I think it's related to the case I'm working with the human traffickers in Tampico.

One of the men looks familiar to me. I think I've seen him before."

"I don't know about the rest of the family, but I'm famished. Dare I hope food is available?"

"It is. Southern barbeque."

"Banana pudding?"

"Of course."

"Lead the way, men."

They made their way to the porch where Gina still sat, watching her son play with her heart in her eyes, eyes that were ready to close from fatigue. She was talking to Gram Merrill and Great-Grandma Laura.

Just then Lindy arrived with her friend, Mandy. "I wish you all had let me know you were going to be here," she said somewhat petulantly, helping herself to a plate of food. "I couldn't even get to your apartment, Gina. Reporters and cameramen, some really cute ones, too, are all camped out there."

Gina's dad held up his phone. "The neighbor just called. They're on our doorstep, too," he reported.

Gloria stood and called Caden. "Nap time," she said firmly to both him and her daughter. "I'm sure Veronique will let you use a bed upstairs."

Gina didn't need any persuading. She let her mother fuss over them both. Her sleeplessness and tears of the previous night as well as the emotional upheaval of her breakup with Harry left her exhausted. She just wanted to sleep, with her son curled up beside her, for a week.

While she slipped into a sound sleep upstairs, down below Blake and Corey were telling the uncles and Mr. Worthington about their upcoming trip to Tampico.

"You'd better be back in plenty of time for the wedding," was the advice given over and over to the two young men.

Corey looked apologetically at Mr. Worthington. "I'm sorry to desert you in the courtroom, Sir."

"I have a feeling you're going to be needed down there, Son. Just come back in one piece."

Chapter Thirty-Nine

This time, Blake drove one of the armored vehicles while Pietro and Ricardo piloted the speed boat down the river to the compound where they had uncovered so much evidence on Blake's last trip. The other armored vehicle ahead of them was driven by Jose.

Pietro and Ricardo, by now, had traveled up the same creek more than ten times on their own. Ricardo had made friends with Big Al, Blake's former neighbor.

"So, the little boy make good," he had said jovially. "He was so quiet and so intense, but I see the potential."

Big Al had become an invaluable informer about the movements of the occupants of the "big house," as he called the compound where Senor and Senora De Luna lived.

Senor De Luna was absent much of the time. Senora De Luna entertained frequently in spite of living off the beaten path, so to speak. She flew a small plane that was parked on the south side of the house. She had a pilot on call but usually piloted the plane herself.

Not only did she keep rather active socially, she was also carrying on a clandestine affair with a businessman who lived several houses from the house of the doctor who had treated Juan.

The captain of the ship that carried victims to the United States had arranged to meet someone in the big house at six that evening.

What Ricardo and Pietro couldn't discern from the planted cameras and intercepted phone calls was whether the captain was meeting Senor or Senora De Luna as both were home. Some kind of device scrambled the voices on all phone calls, making identification nearly impossible.

Could the brains behind the organization be a woman? Or was it her husband? She knew where all the incriminating papers were located. Did she understand what those papers contained—the lives of children, especially girls, stolen in their innocence and condemned to a life of slavery and all kinds of sexual debauchery?

Today's expedition would be even more risky than the one they had embarked on during the dead of night. But this time, Jose had seven other trustworthy friends with them, three who were on the police force.

If things went right, those three would become the heroes for bringing down the kidnappers terrorizing Tampico.

Jose had found or created hiding places all around the compound. He had brought his seven friends with him in the past few weeks, one at a time, to help them familiarize themselves with the terrain.

In addition, they had met in the back room of a bar several days ago to discuss strategies. Jose and Blake both knew the owner of the bar. Esmeralda knew how to keep her mouth shut and offer privacy for those who were fighting evil in her little world.

The plan was to drug the guard dogs and enter the house at the same point of entry as last time. Ricardo, Jose, Corey, and Blake would be stationed at various places in the house. They would converge on the meeting place once they had enough video to determine who the Captain was meeting and to implicate both parties.

Pietro would be relating information from the video and audio feeds to the other eleven. After securing the perpetrators and the premises, Jose and two of the three police officers would escort the criminals to town while the rest stood guard.

Once the police had come to search the residence, Blake and his men would melt away into the landscape and disappear.

At first the plan worked. The dogs snored in a drug-induced slumber. The perimeter was established. Ricardo was stationed under the stairs, Jose was on the balcony outside the family room, and Corey and Blake were stationed in the library.

And then three of Senora De Luna's friends arrived.

"What do we do, Boss?" asked Jose in his ear.

"We wait," Blake whispered. "The meeting is not until six. We still have three hours. But let's eavesdrop on the women's conversation. We may glean some kind of information that will be helpful."

The women convened in the little sitting room at the front of the house, located between the grand foyer and the kitchen. Ricardo, under the stairs was closest although if Jose moved into the family room and the dining room beyond it and found hiding near the doorway, he might be able to hear the women better than Ricardo.

In addition, Pietro was hearing most of the conversation over the camera Blake had placed in the foyer.

Senora De Luna was serving tea to her friends. They made appreciative comments about the choices of food.

"I didn't think I would get anyone in this little town to cook properly after Joaquin left, but Maria is finally learning. To think I had to show her how to cut these little sandwiches into pretty little shapes myself," she said disdainfully.

She sat in an expensive emerald silk outfit consisting of pants and a kimono-styled top. It contrasted beautifully with the whites and golds of the draperies and furnishings in the room. Her glorious cloud of black hair was swept up on top of her head, but tendrils had been allowed to fall in graceful curls to her shoulders.

The sharpness of her eyes contrasted with her languid, bored manner. Her friends here in Tampico were not quite so interesting as the ones she'd had in previous locations. She wished she could have moved to Lake Chapala or San Miguel de Allende, but they were landlocked areas.

The ladies were chatting, telling funny stories about their neighbors. They liked to talk and laugh about the family carrying on about their daughter who had been killed and half eaten by a crocodile, the teens who tried to look so grownup as they flirted with a member of the opposite sex, the grown man who had cried about losing his taxicab, his only means of making a living.

Senora De Luna's eyes narrowed at that story. Blake and Jose, listening, had varying reactions. Blake deliberately cleared his mind and took deep, cleansing breaths. Jose became so angry, he nearly choked and revealed his position at the dining room door.

He turned to see Maria regarding him quizzically from the kitchen door. He moved quickly to her and introduced himself.

"Hola. Me llamo Jose, Senora De Luna's new guard." He flexed his muscle and made a comical face.

Maria relaxed and giggled. "Me llamo Maria," she said with a brief curtsy.

She returned to the kitchen.

"What was that about?" asked Blake. I introduced myself to Maria the kitchen maid."

"Senora's new guard?"

"It was all I could think of spur of the moment."

"Did she buy it?" Blake was clearly worried.

"She seemed to. She laughed when I flexed and went back to the kitchen." By this time, Jose had moved to the family room so his low voice could not possibly be overheard by the women in the salon.

"Okay. One more hour men." The women's talk was nauseating to Blake, and even more so since he had met Tallie and her extended family. What was that saying sometimes attributed to Eleanor Roosevelt, "Great minds discuss ideas, average minds discuss events, but small minds discuss people'? He would rather be around the first group of people.

At last Senora De Luna's friends left. Moments later, one of the police officers announced that the Captain's jeep had been spotted on the dirt road leading to the compound.

"Everyone in place?" questioned Blake softly.

The Captain was early. Interesting. Senora De Luna met the Captain at her front door and led him to her library at the back of the house.

Jose, stationed in the family room, noticed that he was pale, seemed very ill at ease, and continually twisted his hat in his hands. He wore worn and somewhat dirty and unkempt clothing, making him a stark contrast to the beauty and refinement of his surroundings.

Blake had taken the time to create another small hole in the cabinet where he was hiding so he could stand and view the proceedings at eye level.

"What do you want, Captain?" Senora De Luna asked coldly. "I thought I made it clear to you not to contact me or try to see me in person."

"But I want to get out. I don't want to keep doing this. What will happen to all those little children?"

"Haven't I paid you well enough? I pay you for their passage, not to think or ask questions."

"I don't need any more money. I tell my wife about the children. She say stop immediately. She doesn't want the money. Not that way."

Senora de Luna's eyes narrowed. To his horror, Blake saw her draw a very small pistol from a concealed crevice in the right hand side of the desk. She sat with it palmed in her hand. Quickly he signaled his men. They had enough evidence.

"I'm sorry, Captain, but you have overstepped your bounds."

She lifted her right hand with the pistol pointing at the Captain's heart and didn't even flinch as Blake pushed open the doors of his hiding place.

By this time, Ricardo was at the doorway. He dove for the Captain, pushing him down. As he did, the bullet grazed his left ear and carved a furrow in the back of his head.

Senora De Luna had been trained in martial arts. She turned to shoot Blake in one sweeping motion, but he dodged her right hand and tried to put her in a choke hold. She extricated herself with practiced ease and again brought her hand up to shoot him.

Blake blocked her arm before she could raise it, and a bullet slammed into the carpet one inch from his left big toe. At the same time, he reached around her waist, lifted her and slammed her against the floor.

She brought up her right hand again from her position lying on the floor. Blake dodged, but the bullet slammed into right arm. He could feel it just nick the bone as it flew out the back of his arm and hit a chandelier hanging above the desk.

Meanwhile, the Captain had been handcuffed and he and Ricardo had backed to the door to watch the fight between Senora De Luna and Blake and stay clear of the bullets.

Senora De Luna sprang to her feet, and Blake realized he was going to have to break her arm to be able to pry the gun from her hand where it was clamped.

Deftly he wheeled and took his stance, then attacked, bringing his left hand down with lightning speed on her wrist. She pulled the trigger while his hand was on the gun, and only his quick reflex of twisting to the side saved him from taking a bullet in his abdomen. He clamped his hand on the gun and refused to let go.

By this time, Corey had come up behind Senora De Luna. He put her in a choke hold and held her firmly while

Blake wrested the gun from her grip. She swung her free hand to hit Corey on the side of the head, and when that didn't faze him, she pulled a small sword from the pile of curls on top of her head.

Blake pulled that from her hand as well, receiving a slashed palm for his effort.

Jose joined the fray just as the men stationed outside sprang to life. Four of them took down the extra security guards stationed outside, while two found the inside guard.

Senora De Luna screamed, cussed, and wiggled, trying to throw off her captors, but Corey pulled out his hand cuffs and firmly cuffed her wrists. As a precaution, Blake hobbled her as well.

The three policemen entered and took over. The two armored vehicles were brought to the front door, and the guards, the Captain, and Senora de Luna were loaded.

The men who were not making the trip to town wanted to relax, but Blake was not satisfied. Where was Senor De Luna?

He, Corey, and Jose went upstairs to search while Ricardo went to the kitchen to calm the terrified Maria and get his head bandaged. He could use a stiff drink as well; he was beginning to feel a little woozy from the loss of blood.

They found Senor De Luna cuffed to the bed and shot through the heart. He had been dead nearly six hours.

Chapter Forty

Gina woke from her nap four hours later refreshed and so very thankful for Caden's rescue.

Caden, too, was stirring. She watched him wake up slowly. Children were so innocent in their sleep. She hoped she could keep him innocent forever, and God help those kidnappers if they had taken more than she already knew about.

She saw him open his eyes and stare at the ceiling and walls, his face showing his bewilderment. She saw remembrance of his recent terror snap into his eyes, and she wanted to reach out to him, but something held her back.

His face suddenly smoothed out. Was he remembering Corey and Blake's rescue of him?

"What did you just remember?" she asked softly.

He turned and saw his mother's sweet face. He reached for her, and she sat up and gathered him into her arms.

"I was membering when Corey and Mr. Blake came for me. I knew they would."

"How did you know that?"

"Jesus told me. He came at night when it was dark outside and sat beside my bed. He told me not to be afraid. He said after I woke up, Corey and Mr. Blake would come, and they did. He stayed beside me until I fell asleep."

Gina was amazed. How in the world? She considered just what to say but found she needn't say anything. She would believe it had happened just as her little boy had said.

She squeezed him close. The faith of a child was also an awesome thing.

"Let's go find Mr. Corey and Mr. Blake and thank them," she said.

Gina found her purse and pulled a brush and comb from it. She combed Caden's hair in spite of his protest and had him wash his face at the little basin in the room while she brushed her own hair.

Refreshed, they went downstairs to find Corey and Blake, but both of them were gone. Corey had gone to meet his family at the airport, and Blake was with Tallie and the Mexican families.

"Don't go back to your apartment, Sweetie," said her mother. "I took the liberty of going there with Gwen and getting some clothes and essentials for you and Caden. Just come stay with us for a few days. Those reporters are still trying to find you."

Gina agreed. She would see Corey and Blake later. But she didn't. Later stretched into evening, and the next morning the men were gone to Tampico.

Thursday dragged for everyone. Court was still in recess. More rats had been discovered in the building, so many that it was called an infestation, and the building was closed down.

They made short work of decorating the church and fellowship hall. Then someone suggested they all go out to the farm to help Gram for the Thanksgiving dinner the next week, and to help keep her and Gramps informed of all that was happening.

Gina found she was desperate to go. The reporters had stopped trying to get her to talk. Now they were popping up at unexpected times and snapping pictures of her and Caden.

She was even more vexed to find herself thinking about Corey. Was she more concerned about his safety than she had a right to be? Now that she was no longer engaged to Harry, she suspected she might care for Corey. But she didn't want to even think about it.

The cozy atmosphere of the old farmhouse kitchen enveloped Gina as soon as she stepped inside. Here was peace, here was belonging, here was family.

She gave Gram a big hug. Gram caught her left hand and looked questioningly at Gina.

"Did he hurt you, my sweet girl?"

Gina shook her head no.

"Well, something is troubling you. Let me get this crowd settled, and we'll go talk about it in my bedroom."

Gram's bedroom had been the scene of many confessions in Gina's life. Gram talked strongly, but she was never hurtful. And Gina knew that whatever was said in that bedroom never made it to another's ears, not even her mother's, unless she gave permission for Gram to say something.

Thirty minutes later, Gina sat on the side of Gram's bed with Gram beside her. She told Gram about breaking up with Harry and why.

Gram listened without comment. When Gina was finished, she said, "That's not what's troubling you, is it?"

Gina's eyes flew to hers. "How did you know?"

"I know you, and even more, I love you. What else is troubling you, Gina?"

"I think I may love Corey." There. She'd said it. "But I don't really want to love him. He's too brash and bold and crazy for adventure, and I'm just not like that. I don't think I could ever fit into his family, and I don't think he loves me," she finished in a rush.

Gram stood, took hold of her hand, and drew her to stand in front of the dresser mirror.

"Tell me what you see, Gina, when you look at yourself," she commanded.

"I see a girl who let herself get knocked up because she had stars in her eyes and dreams in her head," she began. "I see a girl who is shy and just wants to stay quietly in the background." She took a deep breath.

"What else?" prodded Gram.

"I see a girl who has a young son that she loves deeply, but who will not fit in with what most guys want for a date," she finished sadly.

"Okay," said Gram. "Now let me tell you what I see. I see a young lady who bravely had a son conceived out of wedlock and made that son an integral part of her life instead of getting an abortion or giving him up for adoption. I see a young lady who courageously went to school to get her teaching degree, refusing very little help from others. I see a young lady who exudes a sense of quietude and peace because she knows what is important in life. I see a young lady who conversed pleasantly with the President of the United States and his wife and can hold her own with anyone from any stratum of society. And, finally, I see a young lady who is loved so deeply by a young man that he has helped her grandparents pay for an attorney to represent them in court."

Gina looked shocked at this last statement.

"It's true." Gram nodded her head in confirmation to the girl in the mirror. Gram turned her around and took her hands.

"Gina, Corey loves you more deeply and has waited more patiently for you than many young men would. He wants you to find out for yourself just who and what you are for yourself so that you will come to him without reservations and without any false ideas or pretensions about how you will fit into his family."

She took a deep breath and continued. "You bring peace and calm to his life, two qualities for which he admires you greatly. Your caution will keep him from rushing impetuously into situations, and his daring will bring excitement and joy to your life. His family already loves you. When Nell was here, she could see immediately why he was so over the moon about you, and she can't wait for you to accept her."

"Me accept her?"

"Yes. Sometimes people who have much are prideful and arrogant. But sometimes people who don't have as much are prideful in the opposite way. Both are wrong. Corey's family is not like that, and you will disappoint me if you act that way toward them."

"I would never. I think they're so kind and so generous and so sweet."

"But you didn't always feel that way," Gram said shrewdly.

"No. I guess I didn't," Gina said slowly, thinking back over her initial impression of Corey. She was suddenly aware of the tears slipping quietly down her cheeks and wiped them away impatiently. This was no time for tears. Corey loved her? She just wanted to hug that thought to herself for awhile.

She threw her arms around her grandmother. "Thanks so much, Grams, for helping me to see all of this."

Her soul began to fill with joy. Corey loved her. Gram wouldn't say it if it wasn't true.

Gram patted her hand. "Wash your face and compose yourself, then go for a long walk around the farm. Think through what I've said, and when you see Corey again, give him the chance he so deserves, yourself as well."

"Oh Gram, I feel so much better."

"I can see that," said Gram dryly. "Do what I say now. Your parents are watching your son like two fierce eagles."

Gina went for the walk Gram had suggested. She returned with a lovely light on her face that everyone in the family could plainly see but about which they were afraid to comment.

*****

Blake and Corey returned Friday morning. The same doctor who had treated Juan had dressed the gunshot wound in Blake's arm and the slash on his hand. He had warned Blake that he needed to have his wounds re-examined state side.

Ricardo, too, had been treated. He had lost a lot of blood. Before they left, they had taken him to his mother's house. Plenty of rest and good food would heal him.

Blake had no choice once Tallie saw him. He went immediately to see a doctor. The doctor was impressed that the doctor in Tampico had taken so much time to cleanse the wound. That was critical if he didn't want the bone to get infected. He prescribed more heavy antibiotics.

Gina didn't get a chance to see Corey before the rehearsal. She had spent Thursday night at Gram and Gramps' house. Once she left Caden with her parents, she spent most of the day Friday running errands with Chelsea.

They picked up Uncle Davey's tux and the miniature tux Caden would be wearing as ring bearer; helped Aunt Galeah choose some strappy, sexy sandals to go with her dress; made sure they had extra panty hose in various sizes in case anyone needed them as well as bobby pins, hairspray, and gel; went to look at the cake that had just been delivered to the church and placed in one of the refrigerators; and then stopped by Gina's apartment to check mail and make sure everything was alright.

Tallie and Blake were with them by then, and as Chelsea took the shortcuts she knew to Gina's apartment, they passed the park where Gina had taken Caden so many months ago.

"Wait. Stop for a minute," said Gina.

Obediently Chelsea stopped. Gina sat for a moment. She turned in her seat to talk to Blake in the back seat with Tallie.

"This is where I first saw them. Right after I had taken Caden to the park way back in, was it July or

August? I don't remember, but I noticed them in my rearview mirror."

"Noticed who?" asked Chelsea a bit impatiently. They needed to get to the church for the rehearsal.

"The kidnappers. Oh my. They must have been watching us for a long time."

Blake snapped his fingers. "That's where I saw them!" he exclaimed. "They were parked in front of your apartment building at least twice that I noticed. I just thought they were tenants. Wait. I wonder...." He thought for a moment.

"Tell us," urged Tallie.

"I just received pictures of the captains and first mates that Senora de Luna was using for transportation of the slaves, including the ones Uncle Craig shot and killed. That's why the dark haired man with the mustache has looked so familiar."

Chapter Forty-One

Corey couldn't take his eyes off of Gina during the rehearsal. She seemed different somehow since he had returned from Tampico. She looked weary, but the peace in her eyes seemed to radiate from deep inside.

As he walked her down the aisle in time to the music, he placed his right hand over her left one when she nearly tripped.

"Sorry," Gina said apologetically.

"Don't be sorry. I'm not. I rather like coming to your rescue."

"Why? So you can be the big, brave hero?" she asked teasingly.

"No, so I can make your eyes change color. I always thought they were blue, but they change to green when you're irritated or surprised. Like now."

"Is that a compliment?"

"Are you irritated or surprised?"

"Surprised."

"Then it's a compliment."

"Why, thank you, kind sir!"

Just before they split to go their separate ways on either side of the minister, he said, "I'm glad to see your left hand ringless, by the way."

She was glad that they were at the end of the aisle. She was spared having to answer him.

Gina's eyes kept straying to Corey, but she was also conscious of many other details. Her mother took care of Caden for her so she didn't have to do so. He was so cute walking down the aisle, somewhat intimidated by all the big people and happy when his duty was over and he could stand by Corey and watch everything.

The first run through took the longest. Once Gina knew what she needed to do, she could enjoy the second run through much more. Preston and Lindy went down the aisle first, then Blake and Tallie, Kielah and Jonathan,

Gwen and Tyler Clay, Lawton and Lanie. Finally came her turn with Corey.

Corey's stomach growled, and Gina giggled.

"Sorry," he said with a lopsided smile. "I didn't have much time for lunch today. I can't wait until this is over and we can eat."

"We may as well get the practice," said Gina philosophically.

"Why do you say that?" asked Corey.

"Look at who preceded us down the aisle. Who do you think will get married next? Blake and Tallie or Lawton and Lanie?" She wanted to say "or us?" but she kept that delicious thought to herself.

"If I was betting, I'd bet on Blake and Tallie. They want a very small wedding with only family in attendance."

Gina made a small moue of disappointment.

"Oh, don't worry," Corey said with a laugh. "Her mother will make up for it with a large reception. They will both get their way! See you later," he added as they parted to take their positions on either side of the bride and groom.

The rehearsal dinner took place at the Flowertown Bed & Breakfast with Veronique and her husband presenting Chelsea and Jasper with a wedding armoire with some beautiful table linens inside handed down to Veronique from her grandmere.

When Corey had eaten his fill, he and Gina took a walk in the garden. Corey led her past the guest cottage to a bench under an arbor in the back corner. They stood facing each other.

"Do you want to tell me about Harry?" he asked.

"Yes. I broke off our engagement the day you brought Caden back to me."

"Why, Gina?" he asked tenderly, needing to hear her say why.

"Harry's not ready to be a husband, let alone a father. I finally realized that. And I was wrong, too."

"Why do you say that?" asked Corey, somewhat surprised.

"I was wrong to date him just to be able to date. And then I thought if I got engaged to him, the passion, the spark I wanted in the relationship would come. When it didn't, I thought it was just me. I was afraid I would never find it, and I was willing to just settle for less."

Her head was down, and Corey could barely hear her. But then she raised her head to meet his eyes courageously.

"Until I met you. When I met you, I didn't want to be attracted to you. You approach life so differently than I do, but Gram helped me realize that different is good. Our strengths and weaknesses compliment each other."

"Yes, they do, Gina." Corey caressed her cheek tenderly. "We compliment each other. I knew it almost from the first time I met you. You have so much strength in you, and grace and beauty, but you don't know it."

Gina was shocked. No one had ever said that to her before except for Gram.

Corey saw her expression. "Yes, you do. And my goal is to tell you every day how beautiful you are to me, how much I admire and love you."

He bent to kiss her, tenderly at first, but then with the passion he had so long denied himself.

As he deepened the kiss, joy exploded in Gina. She had never felt this way with Harry. Here was the promise of an intimacy she had never dreamed of, never dared hope for before.

Finally, Corey rested his forehead against hers, holding her until the passion subsided.

From an upstairs bedroom window, Nell watched her eldest son with satisfaction. Her husband's arms came around her.

"Spying on our children again, are we?" he asked, teasingly.

Nell rested against her husband. "I've been so concerned for him. He had built such a wall around his heart where girls were concerned. They all chased him for his money and his good looks except for this one. She is one special girl, and I'm so happy."

Nell turned, her eyes misting with unshed tears. "Kiss me, Carter," she commanded.

Very willingly, he obliged.

*****

A warm front from the tropics brought rain that Friday night, but dawn tinged the clouds with pink and gold, a bright omen for the wedding day.

By eleven, all of the bridesmaids were at the church, the flowers had arrived, and the groomsmen were being rounded up by a diligent Pammy and her husband Jonathan. By now everyone knew why she had declined the honor of being in the wedding party: she and Jonathan were expecting their first child in March.

Family pictures were taken at twelve thirty, and at one fifteen, the first strains of soft wedding music from the string quartet resonated in the candle-lit sanctuary. The stained glass windows added their beauteous hues, and the sweet odor of roses and gardenias fastened to the end of each pew mingled with the scent of the candle wax.

At two o'clock Grandma Laura, Gregory and Aleah Galbraith, Will and Mary Merrill, and Charles and Caroline Peters-Templeton took their seats in the grandparents' section.

Nell and Galeah were escorted by their husbands to the front of the church. The two men waited, standing tall, as their wives lit the two candles on either side of the unity candle. Nell's eyes met Galeah's as they turned, and their spontaneous hug brought tears to a few eyes.

The music changed, and the bridesmaids in their shell-pink dresses glided beside their respective groomsmen, taking their places in a staggered vee-shape on the stairs.

Corey and Gina, their steps and hearts in perfect unison, smiled at each other as they parted to take their positions. Francesca came next with her basket of rose petals, and then came Caden, his little face creased with anxiousness. His audible sigh when he finally reached his place by Corey brought smiles to the crowded assembly.

Once again the music changed, the groom and the pastor entered, the mother of the bride stood, and the audience caught their first glimpse of Chelsea in her bridal glory.

If Gina had been asked to describe the ceremony, she would have used two words: solemn and joyous. As Jasper and Chelsea exchanged vows, her eyes met Corey's. His eyes were filled with promise and hers were filled with love.

Gloria, the aunts, and Mrs. Flores and Mrs. Garcia watched the unspoken communication with satisfaction. And Gloria's heart overflowed when Caden reached up to take Corey's hand. Corey was going to be such a splendid father for her grandson.

Bob and Belinda Worthington held hands, too. They would be separated again soon when the court hearing resumed. But they were pleased to share this special occasion with a very special family.

Much later, when Chelsea and Jasper were opening just a few gifts before their departure, Corey entered the room carrying a basket with a cover. He whispered in Jasper's ear.

Standing, Jasper announced that Corey had a special presentation to make.

Everyone expected him to have a gift for the new couple. Instead, he announced that he had something to return to the Worthington children, something they had recently lost in a tragic accident.

Taking the basket to their table, Brian was the first to peek inside the basket.

He turned excitedly to his mother.

"Look!" he exclaimed as first one whiskered furry face and then another popped out of the basket. "It's Bianca and Butterball! Butterball didn't die, Mom! Butterball's alive!"

THE END

As you've noticed, Gina and the rest of the family really like Gram's cookies. Here are a few cookie recipes from their kitchen to yours!

Gina's Favorite Oatmeal Raisin Cookies

1 c. raisins
1 c. water
¾ c. shortening or butter
1½ c. sugar
2 eggs
1 t. vanilla
2½ c. flour
½ c. chopped nuts, if desired

1 t. baking soda
1 t. salt
1 t. cinnamon
½ t. baking powder
¼ t. cloves
¼ t. nutmeg
2 c. oats

Simmer raisins in water over medium heat until raisins plump (about 15 minutes). Drain raisins, reserving liquid. Add water to make ½ cup.
Heat oven to 400°. Mix shortening, sugar, eggs, and vanilla thoroughly. Stir in liquid. Blend in remaining ingredients. Drop dough by rounded teaspoonfuls about 2 inches apart onto ungreased baking sheet. Bake 8-10 minutes or until golden brown. Makes about 6 dozen cookies.

Aunt Clara's Pineapple Coconut Cookies

1 c. shortening
1½ c. sugar
1 egg
1 c. crushed pineapple
  (with juice)
3 ½ c. sifted flour

1 t. baking soda
½ t. salt
¼ t. nutmeg
½ c. coconut
½ c. chopped nuts
  (macadamia nuts are great
  in this recipe, but Aunt
  Clara likes to use cashews
  as well!)

Mix shortening, sugar and egg thoroughly. Stir in pineapple and coconut. Sift dry ingredients together and stir into batter. Add nuts last, if desired.

Chill at least 1 hour. Heat oven to 400°. Drop by rounded teaspoonfuls about 2 inches apart on lightly greased baking sheet. Bake 8-10 minutes until no imprint remains when touched lightly. Makes about 5 dozen cookies.

This is Gina's favorite cookie recipe if she needs to bring something. They are always a hit, and they take very little time to make.

Gina's Missouri (No-Bake) Cookies

In saucepan, combine 2 c. sugar
3 T. cocoa
½ c. milk
¼ lb. butter or margarine

Boil 1 minute.

Add   pinch of salt
2 T. vanilla
½ c. peanut butter
3 c. quick oats.

Drop by teaspoonfuls on wax paper and let set.

Pumpkin Cookies

½ c. butter
1½ c. sugar
1 egg
1 c. pumpkin
1 t. vanilla
2½ c. flour

1 t. baking powder
1 t. baking soda
½ t. salt
1 t. nutmeg
1 t. cinnamon
½ c. nuts (walnuts or pecans)

Cream together butter, sugar and egg. Add pumpkin and vanilla. Stir together dry ingredients in separate bowl and blend well. Add to wet mixture. Add in nuts.

Heat oven to 400°. Drop by teaspoonfuls on greased cookie sheet and bake 8-10 minutes.

C = cup
t = teaspoon
T = Tablespoon

A Word about Property Rights and Agenda 21

My family has faced a property rights case in California similar to the one the Merrills are facing in South Carolina. While many Californians believe government officials have the right to come and go unannounced on their land and tell property owners what they can and cannot have on their property, my friends in high places say that such cases would never occur in South Carolina. I hope they are right.

I have done an intense 300+ hours study of documents left by our founding fathers, using sources dated no later than the 1860s. I am continually amazed at the arguments, sometimes bitter ones, that occurred. Yet these men collectively created one of the most profound and lasting documents ever created in the history of mankind.

I am saddened to see our rights being stripped from us, especially when our forebears worked so hard to spare us from these same indignities they faced at the hands of the British.

Join me in the fall as Lawton finds his true calling and the Merrill property rights case is finally resolved in *A Secret Place*.

Meantime, enjoy a sneak peak of the prequel to *Secrets of the Enemy* and *Secret Agendas* coming soon!

This is the story that begins *The Secret Series* two generations earlier in the late 1950s and early 1960s! Enjoy a sneak peak at the prequel, coming soon, *Secrets of Two Sisters*.

Chapter One

As I waited impatiently for Davey, I thought about how this culminating moment had begun in a convent with a news clipping, a body, and a box containing the brief shining moments of a young mother's life. Well, actually, it had begun earlier than that, but this was a secret I hoped would never have to be revealed.

Rosalie came through the office door and into the great room with its magnificent view of the lake and great ceiling timbers of oak and gave me a thumbs-up sign. "He's really coming! They just called, and they are on their way."

She came to the chair where I sat and gave me a quick hug. "Now don't you get too uptight. You want to look your best for your young man." She gave me a roguish wink that contrasted with the angelic look of her delicate face and shining cloud of blond hair.

Rosalie had become a great friend during my treatments at the Hope Cancer Treatment Center. Her tireless energy had unearthed the whereabouts of my Davey after several years of fruitless wondering.

And now he was on his way.

"Would you like anything before he gets here, Mary?"

"No, I'll just sit here and reminisce a bit," I said patting her hand. "I know you'd like to look around more."

She gave me another hug and strolled to the terrace and the gardens beyond.

I gazed out the window overlooking the lake. I didn't mind being left alone with such a view. It rested me, yet the pageantry of the changing seasons was like a kaleidoscope of color. The far hills were a dusky blue today and the pale willow green of the leaves by the little stream . . . reminded me of the green in the basement of this place when I had taken the records of Robyn Montaigne.

Although I outwardly looked composed, my heart pounded in cut time as I walked from the end stairwell of the convent in Lucerne, California where I had cloistered myself.

What I hoped to accomplish, while not rank disobedience, would certainly not be approved of if discovered. Last night the remains of a young woman from France had arrived overnight air to be held in the holding room located in the basement until family could be found to grant her spirit eternal rest.

We called it the holding room. It was really a morgue, but that word sounded so final and lifeless. In spite of the debilitating disappointments I had experienced the last several years of my life, I still believed in the goodness of God and that the spirit lives after death.

Why I still believed that at that time in my life I don't know. I still hadn't worked through the guilt, anger, and bitterness of my experiences. Instead I had submerged my feelings beneath a mask of calm acceptance.

Normally I avoided this area of the basement; I couldn't abide being around the lifeless bodies awaiting burial. But Allee de Lamente Paris, France? There couldn't possibly be a connection.

Just as I was about to open the door to the holding room, a group of noisy twelve-year old girls burst into the hallway. They had been practicing a play and were thirsty. Unfortunately, a small kitchen was next door to the holding room.

"What are you doing?" asked Nancy, a blonde, with protruding blue eyes and a keen perception of anything out of the ordinary.

"Taking care of some business," I replied noncommittally. Then before she could ask me what business, I asked her some questions. Perhaps if I took the empathy approach, I could avoid her curiosity.

"I'll bet you girls are thirsty after all your hard work. Will the play be ready in time?"

"We have two more weeks until our first performance, and if Margaret here would learn her lines..." suggested Nancy in a needling tone.

Margaret, a petite child with long, dark, lustrous hair hung her head. She was a little slow, but once she learned something, she never forgot. Although I gave music lessons to the girls who showed a proclivity, it was Sister Anne who was helping them produce dramatic plays. And here she is, I thought with relief.

"Come along, girls," she called as she bustled down the long hall that ran the entire length of the basement. Her round face was red and her body rocked back and forth as she marched swiftly to keep up with her charges.

Nancy and her friends disappeared into the kitchen. Anne winked at me and asked, "Was Nancy insulting Margaret again? That child has got to learn the grace of kindness or she will never realize her potential." She winked again and followed the girls through the doorway.

Anne optimistically found the good in every person, young and old, and in spite of her flyaway appearance, she was universally liked for her cheerful acceptance of situations and people.

Now was my chance. I slipped into the mausoleum and shut the door softly behind me. My eyes adjusted to the muted light playing through the four small square windows placed three inches down from the ceiling on the opposite wall.

It was a large, rectangular room with a huge table in the middle, and a sink area filled with dissecting equipment along the wall closest to the door on my immediate left. The block wall with the windows was bare except for four large anatomy charts showing nerves, muscles, and organs of the body.

The long wall opposite the wall with windows was lined with caskets and interment equipment, but it was to the far wall on my right lined with vaults holding dead bodies that my mind was riveted. I knew the body from France was in one of those vaults.

The undertaker who serviced our convent would arrive in two hours. How would one go about finding the right vault? I didn't want to have to examine every vault, not to mention my distaste at looking into lifeless faces of the deceased. Although not large, our convent acreage contained the burial grounds of the entire area and was used frequently by others in this community located in the California mountains. I swallowed down the lump in my throat, told my stomach to behave, and walked softly across the tiled floor.

I decided to begin on the left and work across the eight rows of three. Gingerly I pulled on the cold metal handle of the first vault. It slid out soundlessly, but heavily.

Oh no! I'd have to pull back the sheet to look at the face. Steeling my taut nerves, I pulled it back and saw the face of old Mr. Peters. I pulled the sheet up quickly and crossed myself. The next one was empty. The third one gave a little groan as I opened it.

I jumped and looked toward the door. Anyone passing by in the hall might hear the noise and investigate. And then there was the group of girls. Hopefully, they were being too noisy. I slowly pulled back the sheet and then sucked in my breath!

It was true! I knew this woman whose body had been shipped back from France. Robyn had passed away and in the prime of her life at the age of thirty-one. I caught sight of cardboard then and pulled the drawer out further to investigate. The vault groaned again.

A rustling noise on the other side of the door caught my attention. I pushed lightly on the drawer—fortunately it did not groan going back in—and dashed quickly but quietly to the nearest empty casket.

"Miss Anne! Do you believe in ghosts?! We heard someone groaning in there," announced Nancy. The other girls giggled nervously.

"Nonsense!" said Anne. "Anyone who has the misfortune of being placed in that room is well and truly dead. Come along girls. We need to walk through the second act again." I heard her voice cadence lower as she walked down the hall.

"I'll bet it's that nosy nun, Miss Mary," said Nancy.

"She's not nosy, she's nice," said Margaret. "You're just jealous 'cause you can't take music lessons."

"Am not!"

"Are too!"

With relief I heard their voices fade. At least Margaret knew how to stand up to Nancy sometimes, I thought wryly. And it was nice to have someone, even a child, stand up for me.

Five minutes later I ventured from behind the casket and pulled open the drawer again. It was easier this time. I knew what to expect. The cardboard was really three small boxes piled on top of the torso and legs of the deceased. I wanted to examine them, but what if someone came?

I decided to pull them all out and take them up to my room. The undertaker likely wouldn't know of them anyway and would not miss them. I pulled them out, covered Robyn's face, and shut the drawer. Carefully I opened the top of each to see if they were worth the effort it would take to conceal them on the way to my room.

The first box contained a six-inch stack of papers and files. I could easily conceal the stack with my habit if I discarded the box. The second and third boxes contained what looked like family memorabilia. My heart stopped, then beat painfully when I saw a small box with Christmas paper on it.

It couldn't be! I opened it and with shaking fingers pulled out tissue paper surrounding four glass-blown ornaments. The sound of my sob shattered the silence and shocked me.

Hastily I shoved every thing back into the boxes. I placed all the boxes beside the door and carefully opened it. No one was in sight. Quickly I gathered the files and papers from the first box and began the journey to my room on the third floor. I saw no one.

When I returned to the holding room, I decided to dispose of the box in the kitchen. Quickly I took it next door and put it in the capacious trash can. It sank nearly to the bottom. Good! More trash would cover it before it was emptied. I looked at the cups in the sink and longed for some water myself, but I had work to do.

"What are you doing?" a young voice demanded.

I swung around to see Nancy glaring at me, curiosity etched on her face.

"I was looking at the mess you all left for me to clean up," I retorted.

"Are you going to wash dishes? I'll help."

"Aren't you supposed to be practicing?"

"We're all done for the day, so I guess you're stuck with me," she announced gleefully.

Frantically my mind returned to the two boxes. I at least had to get the one with the ornaments up to my room. But I didn't need Miss Nosy suspecting anything.

"All right," I muttered.

We ran water and began washing. Nancy kept up a lively chatter about the play and her starring role in it while she dried the glasses and put them away. We were nearly done when Anne heaved through the doorway.

"There you are, Nancy. You shouldn't wander around, dear, and keep your aunt waiting for you," she scolded gently.

"But I've been helping Miss Mary clean up," she protested righteously. When Miss Anne said nothing, she added, "What's she doing down here, anyway? I bet she knows something about the ghost next door."

I flushed and glanced nervously at Anne, but she was already out the door. Her "Come along, dear," floated back to us.

Nancy looked at me triumphantly, then ran after her. That little brat! Had she seen anything after all? Or was she just suspicious?

My nerves tautened, but I turned resolutely from watching them to the stairwell and once again opened the door to the holding room. I clasped the box with the ornaments firmly in my arms with the black sleeves billowing around it. Again, I encountered no one.

Only ten minutes until the undertaker arrived. I ran down the three flights of stairs, hoping I would run into no one who would question my lack of sedateness. I quickly scooped up the third small box, closed the door gently but firmly and climbed the stairs one last time.

As I began on the flight to the third floor, I heard a door clang open beneath me. Cautiously I peered over the railing. It was Miss Sebastiani and the undertaker! I heard low murmurs of their conversation, and then another door clanged. I was home free! I made it to my room and closed the door.

I fished a small box from the closet in my room for the papers and then placed it on the bed. The three small boxes of various shapes stood on my bed like the three gifts of the magi. Though far less ornate, they were infinitely precious to me.

*****

Chapter Five

Will was the golden boy, tall with blonde curly hair, brown eyes and a long Roman nose set in his narrow face. He smiled easily, and loved to tease. He had been my boyfriend since tenth grade, and the semester away at college had not changed our relationship.

The Merrill family had moved down from the Portland, Oregon area in August, so Will was one of the few new faces in high school my tenth grade year. All the girls were crazy about him. Even the senior girls, more subtle than the freshmen in initiating conversation and sending coy glances, were entranced.

When it was discovered that Will was an exceptional basketball player, there was even more of a fuss. I watched the adulation from afar. How would I, plain Mary Johnson, ever attract the attention of such a superstar? I refused to throw myself at him in such an obvious way as the other girls were doing.

Once he caught me watching him when Ashley Lynn, the tenth grade beauty queen, was talking to him animatedly. He pretended to be listening to what she was saying, but when the bell rang, he looked absently around. When he caught my glance, he smiled ruefully in a self-mocking way and took his seat.

It was that weekend I discovered Will's second love, and we became friends. I wasn't allowed to have a job yet. My dad was very strict, and ruled our household with a somewhat draconian harshness. To escape, I often went hiking in the hills that surrounded Santa Rosa.

One of my favorite places was called Bald Eagle Knob. The crag of rocks protruded out over a small valley with a meandering stream. Because of its isolation, I could spend many undisturbed hours sitting in the lap of the rocks. It was my thinking place where I could be alone, and yet not alone, for there was always nature and her beauty to contemplate.

But the way there was usually treacherous and overgrown, with the danger of rattlers always present. The first part of the way was easy. I just followed some old logging roads. On this early Saturday afternoon, the sun shone warmly, and the air held just a tinge of early October chill in the mountains. I breathed in the purifying pine scent, and knew that whatever was wrong in my family, somehow it would work its way out.

It was too bad that Mom had to stay at home when I could tell that she, too, longed to get out and away for awhile. She had been red-eyed this morning, and had given my sister too-ready consent to spend the night at a friend's house, although with strict instructions to be in church, and on time, too, so that Dad wouldn't be mad again the next day.

Putting away thoughts of guilt, I took the faint path that cut off to the right of the logging road where I was walking. It led into a dell that, after the rains in the spring, became a vernal pool with exquisite and short-lived ferns and delicate flowers. I jumped over a small stream in the middle of the dell. It was fed by a spring halfway up the mountain on my right. I turned slightly to the left and looked up the path.

Right before it grew steep and disappeared into the manzanita scrub, a huge pine tree, scarred and twisted by a bold streak of lightning down one side, stood sentinel. Around its base a small copse of young pines was growing.

About twenty feet tall, the tips gleamed in the sun with the fluorescent greenness as of new growth. Slowly and silently I stepped into the copse and entered my own enchanted fairy cathedral.

The sunlight filtered through the lacy pine boughs, and the air was a mite cooler. The ground was nearly six inches deep with pine straw from many ages. I always felt safe and cherished within this copse, as if God's hands totally surrounded me and provided protection from all evils.

During the summer when it was hot and I needed to think, I would come here and lie on the cushion of pine needles, cooling off in this quiet place. But today, with the wine of autumn in the air, I wanted to sit in the warm sun.

Backing out of the copse, I headed up the steep path that angled to the left and wound around the mountain to Bald Eagle Knob. The silver-green leaves on the manzanita lay nearly flat, a good indication that there would be no rain in the near future. Underneath the smooth, but twisted red branches, the danger of rattlesnakes was always present, especially on sunshiny afternoons. With only a few scratches from the low-growing scrub, I made it to the Knob.

The Knob was really an outcropping of rock close to the top of the mountain, but was located on the opposite side of where the spring-fed brook meandered and where the pine copse cathedral grew. The path approached from the top and then wound across and down the mountainside into thick woods.

Carefully climbing down so I wouldn't pitch into the valley below, I seated myself into a scooped out piece of the rock, perfect for sitting in, and let my legs dangle down against the rocky face. Leaning back against the rocks I had just scrambled over, I watched an eagle gliding on the wind currents in the cerulean sky.

My mind relaxed and drifted, and I wondered what it must be like to be a bird. What would I see in the valley far below? Its perspective must be so much keener than the perspective that we as human peons must have on life; that is, if a bird could have the kind of brain people have. Did a bird just enjoy the feel of the wind rushing along its wings, or was everything cut and dried, only the instinct of survival, of searching out and finding the next meal, the most important thing in its brain?

The sound of a snapping twig on the path above interrupted my reverie. I twisted quickly around, and on the path, coming the opposite direction from which I had come, was Will Merrill.

Between the glare of the sun and his golden hair, I was nearly blinded, but I could barely discern a green T-shirt, camouflage pants and boots. He was holding a gun; I deduced that he must like to hunt.

His face wore a happy grin as he made his way carefully down to the outcropping of rock where I was sitting. My stomach fluttered, and my hands became clammy. What would I say to him?

"What's your name?" he asked. "I've seen you in my Math and English classes, but I don't know your name."

"Mary. Mary Johnson. And you are Will Merrill. Everyone knows that."

"Yeah, that's part of being the new kid in town, I guess."

"So what are you doing up here? I mean, I didn't think anyone knew how to get up here to Bald Eagle Knob."

"Is that what this place is called?" he asked. Then he leaned over the protrusion of rocks. I gasped in alarm. It looked like he was going to pitch right over on his head into the valley and the trees below us.

"See that house way down there with the white fence by the road? That's the house we moved into. We live out in the sticks, I guess, compared to most of the kids in school, but I like it 'cause I like to hunt. There's plenty of hunting around here."

"Anyway, when I was mowing out back with the tractor this morning, I saw what I thought might be a trail. It sure winds around a lot, and there are several interesting looking forks, but one of them comes here." He stopped for a moment and looked at me consideringly. "How did you get way up here?"

I was tempted to tease him and say "I hiked," but I didn't know him very well. "You must come past my house on the way home from school every day. We live in the yellow house, the second to the last one on Timmons Road before you come up all those hairpins and into this little valley here."

"That's a pretty steep road to hike." He looked at me admiringly.

"I'm in pretty good shape," I said with asperity. "Besides, I know a few shortcuts. I came in from the opposite direction you came," I said, indicating the trail behind me to the right. "I didn't know there was a trail down behind your house. I've never gone that far."

He had been leaning against the rock, carefully balancing his gun across his knees. Moving restlessly, he squatted and rubbed his backside.

"This is a mite uncomfortable. You want to see something I discovered a ways back there?" He pointed down the trail from where he had come.

"Sure." I moved to scramble up, but Will held his hand out to me. I took it, pretending nonchalance, but inside I felt trembly again. He released my hand and took the lead.

"I'd better go ahead," he said, "since I know the way."

I followed him silently, wondering where he was leading me, but too entranced with the awe of walking with the wonder boy of our high school to question his motives too deeply. As the trail wound down from Bald Eagle, we entered the shade of tall pines. The sound of the birds calling to each other was muted under the quiet canopy of old pines, and the sound of our footsteps was merely a faint 'pad-pad' due to the pine needles and soft dirt.

Will soon stopped at the base of a small platform about twenty feet high with a short and shaky ladder leading up to it. I looked at it dubiously. Will interpreted my glance.

"You go up first. I'll catch you if you fall."

I looked at him questioningly again, but with a wither-thou-goest-I-will-go attitude, I began the ascent. Will came up directly behind me. We situated ourselves side by side on the small platform with our legs dangling down over the front. I took a breath and looked around.

It was breathtaking! The stand was situated ten yards from an intersection of three different paths. Though trees still towered above us, the view was commanding; surely no one could come along without us noticing them first.

Will asked me about my family. I answered hesitantly; my tongue seemed to get tangled up with the words I wanted to say, so he began to tell me about his family. He had four brothers, two who were in their early thirties, living in Charleston, South Carolina, and two who were younger and still lived at home.

Caleb was twelve and took life seriously. He loved building electrically- and battery-powered toys and was experimenting with his friend Andrew on a small robot they had developed together. Will spoke with admiration of his brother's brains, and I could tell he admired Caleb tremendously.

The youngest brother, Eric, was a whirlwind of energy, enthusiasm, and inquisitiveness. At seven, he could get into more trouble in twenty-four hours than any other child in the elementary school. His reputation had begun when he had climbed a tall pine tree on the playground to "see what a squirrel was doing." When he had fallen down, still holding onto the tree, he had skinned his stomach up royally and had also broken his ankle.

A cast had not stopped the irrepressible child. He simply became the Master of Ceremonies on the playground and had turned the place into his own three-ring circus.

By this time I was laughing, and the nervousness I felt had disappeared. I was even bold enough to ask him about his accent. Not only did he have a slight accent, but his word choice was often peculiar and sounded different to me.

He grinned when I asked. "Mary, you have finally met a real southern gentleman," he teased. "I was born in Charleston, South Carolina and we lived there until, when I was ten, we moved to Portland, Oregon. Portland was nice, but there's nothing like the Old South with the Spanish moss hanging from gnarled oak trees and alligator eyes watching you from the water." He broke off and turned his head slightly to see my reaction.

I was watching him admiringly. I could tell he knew, too, but I refused to feel embarrassed. Still watching my face, he reached for my hand, turned it over and kissed it. Faraway, a bell sounded.

Will reached for his gun. "That's my Mom's dinner bell," he said. "It's time we were going."

I snapped from calm bemusement to sudden fear. "Oh, no! My dad. If I'm late for dinner, I'll be in so much trouble."

"Don't worry. We'll stop by the house, and I'll tell Mom I'm walking you home."

My alarm increased. "No! I mean, if my Dad sees you, I'll really get in trouble."

"Well, how about if I walk you just to the end of the hairpins?"

"I know a faster way. I don't mind walking by myself."

"Tell you what. I'll give my Mom a signal, and then I'll walk part way with you. You can show me your shortcuts."

"All right," I assented.

He shot his gun into the air twice to signal his Mom. We walked for the most part in silence. After helping me over a log, Will held my hand the rest of the way. I was filled with elation and apprehension all at the same time. He liked me! I could tell he liked me!

When we got to the last hairpin, Will asked, "Why don't we meet here next Saturday, too? It will be fun to talk to someone about what's going on at school and get the inside scoop about everything."

"Sure," I said. "But I don't know what time I'll be able to come."

"I'll just wait around the outside of the house until you come. Then you can meet my Mom. She's the best."

Human Trafficking Facts

Did you know.......

- Of the reported cases of human trafficking in the United States, about 83% are U.S. citizens?

- More than 40,000 people are enslaved in the United States right now?

Human trafficking is a blight on our society, not just here in America, but all over the world. It's time for all of us who love freedom and hate enslavement to DO something about it.

And we, you and me, CAN do something about it. For every copy of *Secret Agendas* that sells, I will donate $3 to two ministries that work against human trafficking.

"The A21 Campaign" is an international organization that works to stop human trafficking.

"Doors to Freedom" is a local ministry that provides help for victims of human trafficking.

Both ministries are making a difference, and I'm proud to contribute to their work. By purchasing this book and encouraging others to purchase this book, YOU are making a difference, too! Thank You!

HUMAN TRAFFICKING HOTLINE (Use to report suspicions or to be rescued): 888.3737.888

www.ingramcontent.com/pod-product-compliance
Lightning Source LLC
Chambersburg PA
CBHW071155020726
47502CB00002B/422